T0078224

BOOKS by JEAN M. PONTE

Slipping the Fold

Gathering Sara

Member of the Show

A Season to Remember

Jean M. Ponte

Wisdom is the daughter of experience
Leonardo da Vinci

iUniverse LLC
Bloomington

Member of the Show
A Season to Remember

*This is a work of fiction. All of the characters, names, incidents,
organizations, and dialogue in this novel are either the products
of the author's imagination or are used fictitiously.*

iUniverse books may be ordered through booksellers or by contacting:

iUniverse LLC
1663 Liberty Drive
Bloomington, IN 47403
www.iuniverse.com
1-800-Authors (1-800-288-4677)

ISBN: 978-1-4759-2935-5 (sc)
ISBN: 978-1-4759-2936-2 (e)

Printed in the United States of America

iUniverse rev. date: 10/31/2013

ONE

1949-1950

*T*he October sun flashes in and out of the car windows as we pass wooded glades and streams along the country road in Massachusetts. It's a lovely fall scene, I think, as I watch out the windows from the back seat of the car.

I hear Denny, sitting next to the driver, ask in his fake British accent, "George old boy, are you sure this is a shortcut?" He relishes casting doubts to lower George's self esteem whenever he gets a chance. "God knows where we'll end up," he mutters half under his breath.

Not far in front of our car an old Dodge truck, driven by Tom, slows up on the hill and I wonder why, but considering the age of the truck, I'm not too surprised. The truck is heavy with our scenery and props for the <u>The Lost Princess</u> production.

Now, the truck slows even further. In exasperation, George tap-taps irritably against the steering wheel as he closely watches the truck ahead. "What's Tom think he's doing?" Denny answers him with an indifferent shrug.

I wonder what has upset George so much. The truck changes gears and begins crawling up the hill once more. It's so painfully slow and tedious in its climb that Carl, who has been riding next to Tom in the truck, steps down and limps along by the side of the road to break the monotony of his hour of jouncing on the seat that has a broken-spring.

The truck is freshly painted red except for the huge letters on the back of the double doors. If one looks closely, they can see a faint but visible outline still to be filled-in with fresh paint identifying the truck as belonging to the Lu-Travis Children's Theatre. The guys in the troupe are supposed to fill-in those letters with white paint, but it becomes increasingly clear to me as time goes by, that the job will never get done. Now the truck pulls completely off the road onto the gravel shoulder and jolts to a stop half way up the hill.

I glance at the two girls sitting in the back seat next to me. Fay is engrossed in her book, and Jessica has her head and body wrapped tightly in her plaid stadium blanket. Both girls seem completely oblivious to the fact that the car has even slowed down.

George shifts gears and adjusts the car's speed to keep pace with Carl's limping gait, then shouts across to him through the right hand window. "What's the matter with the truck this time?"

"Running hot," Carl puffs, not breaking his stride as he continues to limp up the hill to the spot where the truck has finally pulled off the road.

"Not again! From these little New England mole hills?" George's voice is disdainful. "What's going to happen when we get to some real mountains?" Impatiently, George guns the car engine, passes the truck and pulls the car off the road to wait. As the car bumps onto the gravel shoulder, he jams on the brakes and we three girls in the back seat slide forward and I barely avoid landing on the floor. "We waste too much time waiting for that lousy truck," George grumbles.

Our slow travel progress gives me time to look at the bright red and yellow October leaves. Maybe, I think, I should be keeping a journal to record our trip and the beauty of the fall colors on the distant hills. I muse over my first entry as though I'm writing it here and now. After the date, October 11, 1949, I'll add the poem that's been tumbling around in my head all day…something like "colors fun-falling to earth…caught up in a web by the…"

"Who's got the map?" Abruptly, George turns around to face the back seat. "Might as well check the route while we're sitting here wasting time. Ann?"

Quickly I hand the map across to him, and in return George sends me a look of utter disgust. "You might try to fold it properly next time."

By now I have lost the thread of my poem and give up trying to retrieve the rhythmic words in my head.

Fay, finally realizing that the car has stopped, looks up from her paperback novel, "What are we stopping for?" She tucks her thin legs into a cross-legged yoga position, then leans forward and allows mild interest to peek through an otherwise placid expression. Anything closer than the first row in the theatre reveals a thin, bony nose and frugal lips. But the overall impression, if one is sitting further back in the audience, is that of childlike prettiness.

Actually, Fay is twenty-one but her underdeveloped chest and blonde hair, worn long, allow her to portray the part of a young princess in the children's play we are taking to schools and theaters around the country. Denny plays the part of her father, the king, and Jessica, being barely five feet tall, performs as the princess's little brother. George and Carl are attendants in the king's court, Tom exudes fear as the villain, and I play two small parts: the queen and, using a fake name on the program, a servant girl.

"Why did you say we've stopped?" Fay repeats her question in her vague, preoccupied manner as she props her open book against her flat chest.

"I didn't say." George impatiently tosses the words back to Fay like a volley from a shotgun. "You'd know why...if you...ever paid attention to what...is going on."

In the middle of the back seat, Jessica, a human lump wrapped in her colorful wool blanket, slowly unfurls and pushes Fay and me even further into our respective corners of the back seat. Jessica eases the blanket away from her face and blinks in the sharp sunlight. Her first words are a sleepy request, "George, will you please close that window?"

George answers grumpily, not even bothering to turn around, "It's warm outside."

"I can feel the breeze, and I've already caught a cold."

Denny laughs and turns half way around from the front seat to face Jessica. "Then wind your long gypsy hair around your neck."

"Look, you two," Jessica begins to argue, "just because it's warm up there in the front seat doesn't mean it's warm back here."

"Fay and Ann aren't complaining," counters Denny.

"Actually the wind does blow back here when the car is moving." For once I have to agree with Jessica though I'm tired of her whiney behavior. Fay says nothing. She has gone back to reading <u>Opus 21</u>.

Ignoring all of us, George spreads the large road map across the steering wheel and begins to trace our route with his finger. Jessica leans forward and rests both arms heavily on the front seat just behind George's head.

"Listen, George Krucos, can't you be a gentleman? I told you I have a cold. C-O-L-D, and I asked you to *please* close the window."

Without turning around, George's elbow shoves Jessica's arms off the back of the seat. "We get too warm up here in front; I'm not going to close the ventilator."

"Yes, you are!" Jessica flings herself across George's left shoulder to grab at the handle of the vent, forcing the whole upper half of her body past George's head as though it isn't directly in her way. As Jessica stretches and her hand nears the vent handle, her ample breasts mess up George's neat dark hair and her right arm sends the map, which George is carefully studying, flying to the floor.

"Sit down, Jess old girl," Denny releases a gleeful laugh.

I suddenly realize how much Denny enjoys this diversion. No need for an actual stage. A drama is unfolding right here before his eyes; he even promotes it.

Denny's next words, spoken jovially in a loud stage whisper, whip George into retaliation. "Don't let her push you around."

As Jessica actually makes contact with the window vent, George pulls back his elbow like the arrow on a taut bow, and lets it loose, viciously jamming it into Jessica's chest.

"Who the hell do you think you are? No gentleman hits a woman in the boobs!" Jessica pulls herself part way back to her own seat before beginning a low whine. "That's dangerous, hitting a woman in the breasts."

Self-induced tears begin to pool in Jessica's huge brown eyes, almost pony-like, I think, noticing the thick fringe of coarse lashes. Cuddling her chest with her own loving arms, Jessica moans and groans, then settles herself back in the seat between Fay and me.

The curtain has just rung down on a big theatrical production over nothing more serious than a window vent. The peevish quarrels are sometimes laughable, yet they make me feel uneasy. Maybe I'll turn out to be like the guy in the movies who gets slammed by a fist that is actually meant for the bad character in the bar.

I assure myself that no one is going to quarrel directly with me. Why should they? I consider myself reasonable and more mature than to get involved in childish behavior like the scene that just took place. Still, I feel the precariousness of walking on an icy sidewalk, as though the shouting and the meanness have also been aimed at me.

Denny, George, Jessica, and even Tom seem to have grown up in a world different from mine—one that I'm unaccustomed to and haven't even been aware of until just recently—a world where it's all right to flood the air with screams and vitriolic language one minute and false endearments the next.

I had never heard my parents scream at each other, though they argued a bit about politics and constantly disagreed on the directions of the compass when out for their Sunday afternoon drive. Even those disagreements were unemotional, flat sounding, the tone of voice as off-hand as the one used for "pass me the salt, please."

Perhaps my parents had been brought up to smother their emotions under a blanket and put a good face on everything...to dutifully accept the situation, any situation. "Duty" was an oft-used word in our family. Aunt Julia had "dutifully" brought up two nieces, and Uncle Dudley had "dutifully" stayed home to care for his ill mother all those years of his youth, lives that were entirely wasted in my opinion.

So now I ask myself, is it my background...all that focus on duty and common sense instilled by my elderly parents that causes my feelings of separateness from the others in the troupe, or is it just a difference in ages? I'm a couple of years older than everyone except Carl, and three years older than Denny. Whatever the reason for my incompatibility, it makes me feel like an observer looking down from far overhead instead of a joiner. Maybe it's best to keep it that way, to stay aloof, put a safe distance between me and the others to avoid getting caught up in their crude squabbles…to avoid getting hit on the jaw, figuratively speaking. Certainly there is no way to stay physically apart. I can barely twitch a leg without bumping Fay or Jessica as we jounce down the road in the car each day.

We had begun the theatre tour in Missiac, a little town just north of New York City where the Lu-Travis Theatre had its headquarters in a converted warehouse. Lu was short for Lucy and Lucy was synonymous with old, crotchety, and tough. She had been in the business of sending out theatre tours for forty years. The plays were kiddy fare like Hansel and Gretel, Cinderella, Peter Pan and of course this play, The Lost Princess.

I sighed to myself and wondered in retrospect if it had been wise for me to sign up for six months of touring with a third rate traveling troupe. But my other choice was to go back to my hometown where life would most likely continue in its prosaic, lack-luster way. There were no interesting jobs back there for someone like me. Even here in the East, creative type jobs were scarce, especially in the theatre. The exception being a few third-rate traveling troupes exactly like this one. With just one summer of professional acting and my hometown civic theatre experience, I was lucky to get a job at all, and I wouldn't have gotten this one either except for Silvia and Josh Wilson whom I had met during the past summer at Seaplace Barn Theatre.

Josh had telephoned Lu-Travis on my behalf, and I had overheard him refer to me as "reliable," someone who could be depended upon to stick out the whole tour. I felt the weight of his expectations, and I had no intention of letting him down. So now, as I rode along in the car, I spoke firmly to myself: *you'll just have to ignore the quarrels and bad tempers for the next six months.*

I recalled the letter my mother had written recently, "It's a hard life," she had said, referring to the tour. "I hope you won't be disappointed." Mother always said things like that to dampen my enthusiasm. She was so disgustingly practical. All her thoughts were on the *here and now*; they were pragmatic thoughts that brought my own flights of fancy crashing to the ground. If my mind had been in a state of dreamily creating a poem, hers were more likely on the high price of meat. Already it seemed as though the dream-smashers far outnumbered the dreamers in my world.

Immediately after thinking about my mother's letter, my mood suddenly swung back upwards because I recalled something interesting...something I had forgotten.

Josh and Silvia had met each other for the first time on a Lu-Travis tour. It was Peter Pan. She was Wendy and he took the part of Peter. Not long afterwards they had gotten married. How romantic it seemed...just like a storybook ending. Even now in 1949 the movies were full of those happy endings where everything worked out to the advantage of the ingénue. She always got her man or achieved her career goal, usually both, with a grand finale of soaring music, an embrace, and a prolonged kiss. Just fantasizing over those movie endings gave a lift to my spirits. Wasn't it possible that my own future could be just as intriguing as any of those movie heroines? Upbeat dreams like those made me impatient for the tour to move along more rapidly. Let the more interesting phases begin, I thought, almost hearing the orchestra tuning up for the overture.

Indeed, what I actually hear is the sound of the truck resuming its slow climb up the hill and George turning the ignition key to start the car. I just have time to adjust my gray skirt, a quick shift from front to back, so that the seat section won't bulge out like an oversized rump after sitting all day in the car. George steers the car roughly, as though he's still full of anger over the window incident. Denny turns around to face the front again and begins to sing a Judy Garland song. Apparently the emotional incident of five minutes ago has been erased from Denny's mind, a form of purposeful amnesia. I'm beginning to see that Denny has a personality as flexible as a rubber band. To me the quarrel is still a cloud hanging there waiting. Eventually it might flood down on all of us.

Jessica rewraps the plaid blanket around and over her head, becoming once more a lump in the middle of the back seat. Fay continues to read her paperback novel, having missed only a sentence or two during the quarrel. Now that the car is moving along smoothly again, I allow my thoughts to wander back to the days before the tour began, back when we had all rehearsed—except Jessica—in the converted warehouse in Missiac.

✳

Soon after I had arrived in Missiac to rehearse, a commute of sixty miles or so from New York City by train, we were informed that our first salary wouldn't be paid until a few days before leaving town on tour. I had counted heavily on being paid at the end of the first week of rehearsals because only five dollars remained in my purse. Immediately I cut back to one meal a day, and finally spent my last coins on a box of cereal at the grocery store. I had resorted to this same survival tactic back in college a year ago. Living on cereal had kept me alive all right, but every time I had tried to study, I grew terribly heady and usually fell asleep. My professors gave me a lot of bad grades that term, yet I had proudly gone on living without begging for money from my parents. Now I planned to survive in the same way.

In Missiac I had rented a room from a Mrs. Vines, tall and aloof. Why did she behave so distantly towards me, I wondered? It was as though someone had harnessed her with my presence against her better judgment. Perhaps she felt ashamed of having to rent out the room, or was there another reason? Maybe she had an innate suspicion of all theater people, chameleons not to be trusted and prone to capriciousness...an unnatural breed of people totally unlike responsible citizens such as herself. If so, she and my father would have understood each other perfectly

To my "Good evening, Mrs. Vines," I'd received a slight inclination of her head as I passed through her front hall and directly up the stairs to my room. My growing hunger made me more vulnerable to her cool attitude, just as a virus is more successful on an already weak constitution. In my mind her snubs became exaggerated; her disdain I interpreted as a belief in her own superiority. As I became hungrier and more depressed, I also felt less friendly towards everyone else, not just Mrs. Vines. I made less and less effort to be amiable, or to converse with the others in the cast. Usually I sat quietly in my folding chair at rehearsals and waited for my cues.

The hours from six in the evening until bedtime were particularly difficult…hard to get through with the smell of Mrs. Vine's cooking; twice I recognized the whiff of stew full of beef, potatoes, carrots and onions. It wafted up the stairs and slipped under the door of my room. Sometimes to avoid the cooking smells, I'd take an evening walk, but dark fell earlier and earlier as fall approached. Then the rains began keeping me indoors. Anyway, my legs felt too unreliable from lack of food to walk very far. Walking several blocks to rehearsals in the mornings and back again in the afternoons was all I could manage.

The round of miserable rains fell, four days of dampness following one after another. Though most of the colorful leaves still clung to the branches, some were nothing but dirty brown puree under my feet. I'd hurry through the streets of the little village feeling the wet ooze into my toeless high-heeled shoes and all the way up to my armpits, or at least that's what it felt like. I spent more and more of my evenings reclining on the bed and thinking about my friends from last summer.

My reminiscences filled up an hour or more of my empty evening. Propped against the mirror in my room was a colored photo of my friends at Seaplace Theatre. Looking at the picture once again, I realized that there had been seven of us last summer just as there are seven of us in the cast of The Lost Princess, but as far as I could tell, the seven were utterly dissimilar.

There was dear Peter clowning around as the picture was snapped. He had taken the part, among others, of Grumio in Taming of the

Shrew. I felt my own lips curl into a smile as I remembered how bright and happy we all were. I could actually see the flecks of light in Dorothy's nearly black eyes, and my own, hazel, were scrunched up against the flash from the camera. The warmth of our companionship spreads over me as I try to ignore the rain outside and fight the desire to crawl back into bed, close my eyes, and fall into an endless sleep.

Dorothy's parents ran a vacation home for guests out on Long Island. It was called Seaplace. Usually the same families returned there each summer to the big estate with its tenant cottage, barns, greenhouse, pool, and formal gardens. Last summer for the first time, the largest of the barns had been converted into a theatre. The old cow and horse stalls became our dressing rooms.

Seaplace didn't have a star system like most summer theatres. Dorothy, myself and the other five members were unknowns. We were brought together because we were each a friend or relative of Dorothy's. There was Peter, Joe, Thomas, Dorothy's brother, Robert, her high school sister, Nancy, and myself. Thomas's mother was Lady Trussey, and she came to one of our performances in her English touring car. I'd never seen a car like that except in the movies. I was so impressed with its elegance. Peter's father was in banking in Ohio. Joe and I came from families boasting no titles, no bankers, and no spare money.

Each of us at Seaplace took turns directing the plays and getting our picture in the local newspaper. I still carried mine around in my wallet. The photographer had lighted my face to accentuate my cheekbones, and I looked extremely serious, knowledgeable, the way I assumed any experienced director ought to look.

One afternoon during the second week of rehearsals in Missiac, I was handed a letter addressed to me in care of the Lu-Travis Children's Theatre. While Fay as princess rehearsed her simple little dance number for the play, I sat in a folding chair nearby and read my letter. It was from Peter, a wacky account of the guys and gals in the repertory company he had joined in Virginia. His humorous letter made me feel a part of the Seaplace family once again, a person who belonged somewhere and with someone. At the moment, in spite of my empty stomach, I felt buoyantly happy, as though I'd received a letter from a long lost lover. Only Peter was just a dear friend. He had signed the letter: Love, Grumio.

Fay finished her dance and sat down near me to put on her rain boots. "Must be a great letter to make you giggle out loud."

"Did I?" I smiled eagerly at Fay. "It's from a friend who was with me at Seaplace Barn Theatre last summer. How I miss that place; it was lovely...an eighteenth century estate out on Long Island." Now that I had grabbed a listener, I was ready to spill out everything about my whole wonderful summer, but Fay interrupted me as she hurried into her raincoat.

"I've got to catch the four-fifteen back to the city."

I'd forgotten that she still commuted back and forth to New York City each day. No wonder she dashed away from rehearsals before I could really get to know her.

Tom, who was sitting on the other side of Fay, must have been listening to our conversation. "Sure doesn't sound like a typical summer theatre."

"More like a damn country club than a theatre," Denny's flippant voice joined Tom's. His disdainful words were followed with a smile that drew horizontal wrinkles across his brow like those of an innocent little puppy dog with too much loose fore-skin. I remembered thinking how innocuous he really seemed, an affable, harmless sort of fellow.

During those last few days of rehearsal before we were paid, my arms and legs began to feel like celery left out of the refrigerator too long; the limpness even came across in my voice. At rehearsals, everyone kept urging me to "speak up; we can't hear you." At night, with the aid of my hand firmly on the stair banister, I pulled my wilted body up the steps to my rented room wondering if I could hold out any longer.

TWO

Now, as I ride along in the car and think back on those first rehearsals days, I wonder if I've given everyone the wrong impression. Did I appear snobbish because I never joined them for lunch? But at the time I was truly anxious to make new friends...to alleviate my lonely, displaced feelings now that my summer family had split-up and each of us had gone our separate way.

Just a few weeks later, I'm far less eager to be buddy-buddies with my new companions. Since the bickering has begun between George, Jessica, and Denny, I feel nothing but dismay. They are untamed as animals in a zoo. The bad manners and raw language are synonymous with flexing of claws and big cat snarls. No one I have ever known before has used the word "boobs" or spoken about Jesus in a vulgar way.

At this moment the car is passing through a leafy New England bower, and I catch the glint of a stream far below in a ravine. I can hear Denny telling Fay, "That's not the way Lisa would have behaved." Behaved how? Done what, I wonder? And who is Lisa? Fay is asking the same question.

"Who is the girl you keep talking about all the time?" Fay leans forward from the back seat so she can hear Denny's voice above the plip-plip noise made by the car tires on the pitted road.

With a heave Denny shifts his overweight body half way around in the front seat and runs his right hand in a dramatic gesture through his dark hair before answering. "Lisa played the part of the witch in Hansel and Gretel, the play I toured with last year." An old-wise, sad expression permeates Denny's face as though he carries an immense burden around, not for himself but for someone else. "Only Lisa didn't have to act very much. The dear girl really was a witch spelled with a 'B'."

It seems to me that Denny is always exaggerating. Why should I believe what he says about Lisa or anyone else?

"Oh?" Fay is half believing. "Which play is she touring in this year?"

"Are you kidding? She got sacked last year." Denny adds, almost smugly, "I remember the exact date: January 14, 1948."

"She sounds interesting." I am openly curious to hear more about Lisa.

"Interesting? That's an understatement; she was a personality-kid...not exactly beautiful, but she could charm the pants off anyone if she wanted to...and she usually did...off the men." Sourly he adds, "And she didn't care if she stole someone else's lover or not." Denny lets out a long sigh, and I think to myself, he sounds like a jealous woman.

"Somehow Lu-Travis found out about her fraternizing with men."

"But how could she?" Fay asks. "Weren't you touring around to different towns all the time just the same as we're going to do...unless Travis has spies everywhere?"

"I'll bet someone inside the troupe tattled on her," I suggest, then watch Denny's face closely to catch his reaction. His face reveals nothing.

"How should I know? But this I can tell you: Travis doesn't like boy-girl relationships interfering with the performances. Besides, she's Baptist or something strict. So watch out."

To myself I consider it a ridiculous warning unless Fay is right about the spying. "We won't be staying in one place long enough to get acquainted with any men at all."

"Oh we'll probably have a one-week layover somewhere," Denny is quick to add. "Just hope it isn't in some little jerky town with nothing to do."

Jessica pulls the blanket away from her mouth long enough to interject, "It's none of Lu-Travis' business if we want to make friends while we're on tour."

"She makes everything her business." After that dire warning, Denny turns around to face the front of the car again and we each revert to our own thoughts.

Looking back again on those last days before we left Missiac, I remember wondering how I was going to get through them without begging for a handout or phoning home for money. I didn't want to be forced to call home; pride had something to do with it, but there was another reason as well. If I had phoned my folks, they would have said, "For goodness sake, Ann, don't starve yourself. We'll send you the money, but you should use some of it to come right home."

Going home was the last thing I wanted to do. I had already cracked the shell, struggled out, and wobbled forth. Why would I want to go back to the nest? There was nothing for me to do in my small hometown except office work or clerking in a store.

Once when I was eighteen and had quit an office job in a local factory because it was so monotonous and unfulfilling, I had tried to explain my feelings to my father. I had actually expected him to understand and give me sympathy.

"You can't always like a job." He was astounded by my attitude and added in an angry tone, "That's not a good excuse for quitting."

I couldn't make him understand that for me a job had to have other rewards besides money. Later, I realized how irrational that must have sounded to someone who had seen people suffer from joblessness in the 1930's. Back then he must have had those same fears for himself even though he hadn't lost his job.

In the past I had worked at filing, bookkeeping, typing, and waiting on customers in gift shops. I soon discovered that there was no feeling of reward in typing a perfect letter or never misfiling one either. Where was the applause? Didn't everyone need the clapping hands, the curtain calls, symbolically if not literally? Wasn't it a sort of hunger like the need for food? Certainly approbation must be as basic a need. Empty stomach: put in food. Empty ego: put in applause. Awfully simplified, I conceded to myself, for how did my father fit into that grand theory? His paycheck seemed to be all the reward he ever aspired to. I didn't understand him and he certainly wasn't able to fathom me at all. I didn't fit into his mold, or he into mine.

✫

The car is climbing more hills again, slowly, because the truck is dragging along at less than thirty miles per hour. I feel cramped and make an effort to squeeze an inch or more of seat space away from Jessica; she, however, is as firmly settled as a beanbag and weighs a lot more. My attempt fails.

Anyway, I decide, reverting to my former thoughts, I'm not going to go back home in spite of the crudeness and quarrels in the troupe, and since I'm not man crazy, I have little fear of being kicked out of the troupe like that poor girl, Lisa. Again I wonder, who was the one who did the tattling on her? There must be more to the incident of her firing than Denny is letting on to. Otherwise, why would he remember the exact date of her leaving the troupe? Unless he was the one who did the tattling.

THREE

O ur first out-of-town performance in Poughkeepsie is ragged, partly because Lu-Travis is in the audience and she makes us feel nervous, but also because we have a new member in the cast...Jessica. Since she's never been with us before to rehearse, this performance is nothing more than a dress rehearsal for her.

"Spoiled eighteen year-old with no acting experience," Denny whispers in my ear after the performance, and I, so confident of my own acting ability, whisper back, "Not that she needs to be much of an actress; she doesn't have many lines."

Like Fay, Jessica has been chosen because she is short enough in height to play the character of a child. Unlike Fay, Jessica's body is not all straight up and down. Her voluptuousness has to be trapped inside a corset to flatten out her ample breasts and curves and squeeze her into the little prince's purple velvet costume.

As if we aren't burdened enough with the problem of packing the truck and the trunk of the Plymouth each time we finish a performance, we now have to bother with a guitar, Jessica's. Because of it fragility and need for protection, it takes up one-third of the car trunk. We all exchange glances of skepticism as Jessica gushes childishly, "Oh, I'll soon learn to play it. I've even brought along my instruction book and extra strings."

Mrs. Travis, gray-haired and portentous, is standing near the rear of the car talking to Jessica's mother when I attempt to fit the guitar into the trunk next to the huge paper mache jug and the phonograph. Surely, I think, Travis can see what a nuisance it's going to be to load and unload a guitar at each stop. But strangely enough, she says nothing. Jessica's mother gives Jessica a kiss and turns to those of us nearby. "Now be sure to take good care of Jessica," she smiles, as though we all exist for the sole purpose of being Jessica's nursemaids.

"And who's going to take care of us?" snorts Denny, again in my ear.

✷

During that first performance when the villain pretends to beat the little prince, the children in our audience *Oh, ohhh'ed* in a chorus of worry, and their warning shouts later in the play beg the king to save the princess. At the end of the third act when we all appear on stage to make our final bows, the children stand up and clap even louder and longer. Their applause feels so immensely rewarding, as if I'd just received a noted prize of some sort…or voted most likely to succeed at graduation.

To think that such a simple thing as applause could make me feel so fulfilled. Who else placed such value on me as those anonymous children? Not anyone in the offices or shops where I had once worked, though I had to admit that a teacher or two had bolstered my self-esteem. One had written on a page in my autograph book: Ann, I expect you'll become a famous poet someday. What a tremendous boost to my ego…instant belief in myself that lasted two whole days. Still, nothing that I had ever done thus far in my life, felt quite so satisfying as performing on the stage. I was totally free to be someone else, someone other than my mundane self. That my performance would be entirely forgotten as soon as the curtain dropped never, ever, occurred to me at all.

✷

Now, just one week later after that particular performance, we are in the car heading north and west towards Chatham, Massachusetts.

"The itinerary says we're to stay at a place called Fairview House." I lean far forward in the seat so that George and Denny can hear me better. "Doesn't that sound more like a tourist home than a hotel?"

Denny turns half way around to face me. "I don't know, but it's definitely not the place where we roomed last year."

"So you did perform in this same town last year, Denny?" Fay has put her book aside as we approach the town.

"Yeah, it's just a little place with one main street and one movie house. Boring! Nothing to do. Give me New York any day."

Jessica clears her throat and begins to uncoil from her red and blue stadium blanket. "Then we can go to a movie," she says, clearing her throat again.

"If anything decent is playing," Denny sighs his doubt. "We get PC you know, in most of the towns we visit."

"What's PC?" Jessica sneezes, and I quickly turn my head away hoping to avoid her germs. Maybe she really does have a cold. She could at least cover her mouth.

"PC stands for professional courtesy. They let us into movies free of charge because we're in a related profession, sort-of."

"Wonderful!" Jessica's eyes sparkle in anticipation.

"Just wait till you get near the end of the tour; you'll be searching every town for a movie you haven't already seen. Why, last year..."

Rising to the surface between my own thoughts, I hear Denny going on and on about his tour last year and how he had said this and someone else had said that. Most of his stories center hugely around himself, and this fact becomes even more apparent just a few weeks further into the tour.

✳

Denny's ample girth was well suited to the character of the king in the play. He also had the dark good looks one invariably associated with young Italians. He could make his eyes roll around in their sockets to emit exaggerated emotions that must have been perceived by the children in the audience as far back as the last row in the theatre. The children were enamored with King Denny, and so was Lu-Travis. The only time I had ever seen Mrs. Travis's face soften markedly and the lines between her eyes smooth out occurred when she spoke to Denny. Was it his rich theatrical voice and broad smiling manner that erased her sour expression or was it the "helpless, little boy with big brown eyes" persona he exuded around her? Maybe it was a motherly instinct that fostered her interest in Denny since she knew that both of his parents were dead. Later in the tour I perceived that it definitely was not a maternal instinct at all. More likely Lu-Travis identified with Denny by recognizing herself and her own selfish drive to get ahead. Seeing the same tendency in Denny must have amused her greatly.

I had suspected even during the rehearsals back in Missiac that Denny was performing off-stage as well as on. For him there was no hard, clear-cut line between the two situations. On stage or off, he projected his voice in the guise of one character or another. Perhaps he had never learned the difference between reality and make-believe. Even more likely, he didn't particularly care to.

The town of Chatham was down in a deep leafy valley. Enclosed by its hills, it seemed like an entirely separate country from the commuter towns closer to New York City. One could almost believe that it existed on no highway map at all. Somewhere in that valley there must have been a town dump or a similarly disgusting spot, but if so, it was well hidden. In every direction I turned, the view offered the prettiness of a framed watercolor painting.

Fairview House where we were to stay was up on a hill above the village and the scenery from there all the way to the bluish horizon was splendid. The house itself was large and old fashioned with a bay window, the kind of house I pictured in my mind as the typical white farmhouse because it looked much like those I was familiar with back in Michigan. To one side of this house stood a separate two-story structure, which quickly dispelled the initial impression of charm and beauty. It was built crudely, like a kid's summer camp building, and it was called the Annex. As it turned out, it really had been a summer camp, and that's where we were to stay for several nights.

The lower floor of the structure contained a ping-pong table, two sagging cots or sofas, tables and chairs of thickly varnished knotty pine and an old wind-up record player, which Jessica pounced on immediately to see if it worked. It did. But it always slowed down to a blurred, agonizing "gerowww" before the end of each record and needed instant winding up again or the music died. The second floor was divided into twelve tiny bedrooms, all very plain with bare unpainted, unvarnished wood floors, and raw knotty pine partitions that didn't extend all the way to the ceiling. Each cubicle had a single bed and a dresser, but no rug. There were two bathrooms, one at each end of the building.

*

After we check-in at the big white house and pay our rent in advance, Tom unlocks the rear doors of the truck and hands down the luggage. "Do you want that box, too?" he asks me.

"No. Leave it in the truck. Thanks, Tom." I have just one suitcase. All the rest of my belongings fit into that one carton which is about the size of a case of canned peaches.

"I want both suitcases," Fay calls up to Tom, "and I need something from the costume wardrobe, too."

"Jesus Christ!" Tom heaves at the cumbersome reflector light, which is used to backlight the entrance flats, and moves the heavy prop chest to one side in order to have room to open the wardrobe doors. "If I have to move everything to get into this wardrobe at each stop, it's going to take twice as long to load back up again. Can't you girls get all your stuff into your suitcases? This wardrobe is supposed to be just for costumes and nothing else."

Fay doesn't bother to answer Tom. I can't understand why she and Jessica have brought so many clothes. They wear pants most of the time even though few women in 1950 do so except perhaps for really dirty work like gardening or painting scenery. Not many women wear slacks on the street, and I seldom see them in a restaurant.

Denny lifts his heavy black suitcase from the rear of the truck. "I'll bet we'll think of this place for a long time to come," he says.

"Yeah," George agrees. "Probably the last time we'll have rooms all to ourselves."

Tom nods and yawns, "Right now I could sleep with ten to a room. That truck has no springs left in it; I'm tired just from bouncing around." He slams the doors on the truck and moves with the rest of us towards the Annex toting his own suitcase. "We get a free breakfast along with our room, I guess. Is that right?"

"Sure," Denny laughs. "Served at eight o'clock in the morning! I'm going to sleep instead."

"Free breakfast? Are you sure? Then I'm getting up," I see George's usually glum face break into a smile.

"Yeah, you would." Denny lets out another laugh as George walks away carrying his suitcase. "He'd do anything to save money."

Carl cautions, "You'd better too. You've already borrowed ahead on your salary, haven't you?"

"You're so right, dear boy. How much is there in the company fund?"

"No borrowing from the company fund," I hear Carl tell Denny as I also follow the others and head for the Annex.

"We all did it last year and old tightwad Travis never found out."

It's the first time I've heard about a company fund. But naturally there would have to be one for emergencies such as the car or truck breaking down.

Our breakfast in the big white house is family style with long oval platters of bacon and eggs, pitchers of juice and milk, and bowls of hot oatmeal. The coffee is strong and rich tasting and the homemade jams are passed around in heavy glass dishes. As soon as everyone in the cast discovers the quantities of food being served, they turn up for breakfast regardless of the early hour. Plate after plate of toast circles the walnut table; the coffee pot goes around three or four times. It embarrasses me to hear George and Denny asking for second helpings of bacon and eggs when the first helpings have been so generous.

After breakfast, Fay discovers a piano in the parlor and there she camps, playing for over an hour. I long to play the piano, but I'm too self-conscious to play in a strange house and be heard by strangers. Whenever I have to play for an audience, my fingers behave like wet noodles slapping at the keys. Still, I want to play music, and I envy Fay for her nerve. Inwardly I rant over the fact that she has taken advantage of an opportunity that I have missed. I tell myself that it will be poor manners to impose another hour of piano practicing on the house after Fay quits. Her piano playing, I am pleased to note because of my jealousy, is like her personality. It reaches no emotional heights.

I learn very little about Fay's background. Neither of us has ever gotten around to unveiling anything of a personal nature when we talk, though at first I make an effort to find out all I can about her. That occurs soon after my uprooting from Seaplace when I have an aching void left by Dorothy and all of my friends from last summer.

There is one interesting fact I do know about Fay. She has vacillated between accepting this part of the princess in the play and going back to college. She actually stops coming to rehearsals for nearly a week. During that interval I temporarily fulfill her role as the princess, along with my own two small parts, until someone else can be found. I covet the part of the princess, but I'm told that I'm too tall, five feet three, and though I once was told that my brown hair has nice golden glints, it cannot pass for blonde. Blond seems so appropriate for a princess. Fay returns a few days later and never changes her mind again as far as I know. Yesterday in the car I overhear Fay explain in an undertone to Jessica how her mother tried to persuade her to go back to college.

"But this is going to be a far more exciting experience than college," Jessica protests breathlessly.

"Anyway, for a while I wonder which to do: take this job or go back home to Jacksonville. The last thing Mother said was, 'You'll be home in six weeks from that sleazy road tour.' After she said that,

I decided to make myself stick out this tour no matter how awful...
just to prove she's wrong."

"It's not going to be that terrible. Stop worrying. You'll do fine...
we all will," Jessica lowers her voice, "especially if we can get rid of
George."

"At least we know where we stand with George. Some of the
other guys aren't exactly..." Fay leans over closer to Jessica's ear and
whispers something that I can't hear. Whatever it is makes Jessica let
out a loud *guffaw* followed by, "Do you really think so?"

Fay nods in answer. What can she mean, I wonder? But I empathize
with Fay over her feelings towards her mother. I too want to prove
to my mother that I'm self-reliant. What amazes me at the time is to
discover that Fay, with her seemingly flat, monochrome personality,
actually possesses something as colorful as stubbornness. She is just
as determined to finish out this tour as I am.

On the same morning when Fay discovers the piano in the parlor,
we are subjected to additional music over in the Annex.

"I'll piss blood if I have to listen to George sawing away on that
violin a minute longer! Can't someone stop him?" Jessica gripes in a
voice intentionally loud enough for George to hear, though apparently
he doesn't hear as he draws the bow across the strings in a grating
shriek.

"It's better than I can do," I say and wonder why I am sticking
up for George. "After all, he hasn't had a single lesson." It's too bad.
They all seem to be down on George, but I understand why. We are
never quite sure if George is merely going to flash his white teeth at
us or take a bite with his sharp words. In <u>Princess,</u> George has to play
a violin, though it's merely pretend because the music actually comes
from a record played on a Webster phonograph behind the scenery.

Just now George accidentally drops his bow on the floor,
momentarily stopping the shrieks that pierce our ears. As he picks
up the bow from the floor, he glances around at us proudly. "Doesn't
sound so bad for a secondhand, five dollar violin." No one answers
him. He seems entirely inured to the pained expressions on our faces.
As George raises his bow again, Carl quickly interrupts, "You'll

accomplish more if you learn to synchronize your playing with the palace music on the record."

"Can't do it…without the record. The record…is locked in the truck." George begins to screech through another tune, which very faintly resembles, *I'll Get by as Long as I have You.* I decide to escape the noise. From my cubical I quickly snatch some paper and a pen and escape outdoors.

✷

Already I have found out how relaxing it is to get away from this raucous bunch of kids, as I have begun to label them, in spite of my previous vow to focus on their better qualities. I don't include Carl in my evaluation of "raucous" or "kids". Carl is more refined. I realize that it's only an exterior quality, but "refined" is far more comfortable to be around and a lot less embarrassing in public than the crude attention-getting behavior of Denny and Jessica.

Carl is the only male member of the cast who maintains some dignity by dressing neatly in a sport jacket and trousers instead of loud plaid shirts and jeans. Tom never bothers to tuck in his flannel shirt at all, not even when we go out to dinner in the evenings. Carl, with his quiet demeanor and modulated voice, lends polish to our group.

Things like external appearances are important to me. I always notice someone's elegant nose, a firm jaw line, and the clothes that fit well because I crave such things for myself. Oh, I have been told and retold by my mother—like double under linings—that genuine beauty is an inner quality of a person and doesn't depend upon good looks in any way. It isn't that I disagreed with her; I don't. But who am I, a yearner after beauty, to fail to respond to that which is so easy to spot without looking under the surface? The nice manners, a soft melodious voice, and a smile with perfect teeth—incidentally, another thing I crave very much—may be superficial, but none-the-less I want them. So naturally they are the first things I notice about other people such as Carl.

Lu-Travis had designated Carl as the manager of the Princess Troupe on the day we left Missiac. Carl, like Denny, had been with the Lu-Travis Children's Theatre before. That's how he had gotten his bad leg with its resultant limp. He had been injured in a car accident on the New Jersey Turnpike when touring with a different road company a few years back. During the present tour, the payroll was to be sent in Carl's name each week to the hotel where we would stay on Friday or Saturday. He was also responsible for reporting to Lu-Travis any problems the troupe might encounter such as a mechanical breakdown of the car or truck.

So, it was to Carl I looked up to during those first weeks of the tour. But as my mother never failed to remind me as I was growing up, *good looks and nice clothes do not make a person.*

FOUR

*A*fter leaving the Annex to escape George's violin screeching, I spot a picnic table across the lawn under an oak tree where a few brown-winged leaves still cling. I kick at the leaves on the ground as I wade through them and recall the fun I once had in jumping in the raked up piles each fall at home. I have a terrible urge to plunge into them right now; probably would have, but I'm afraid of being seen. Since my dignity no longer allows me to throw myself bodily into the leaves, I determinedly shuffle my feet to stir up the pleasant scent, dry and aromatic, and to hear the familiar brittle crunch.

My irritation towards George and everyone begins to evaporate as I turn my face to the warm sun and close my eyes. From this tranquil hilltop my mind easily slips off to another place. It's the shore in front of the family cottage back home. The breeze moving through the branches of the old tree, which fans out over my head, translates into the sound of water gently fingering the rocks and reeds. Thinking of that familiar, peaceful place brings on a bit of homesickness. The craving draws me almost as strongly as the urge to be in the theatre. They both satiated some need in me that I'm unable to pin down. But the water, the shore, and the cottage are tranquil and private. Already I begin to realize that there isn't going to be much of either on this theatre tour.

I snap my eyes open. How have I allowed such wishy-washy musings to take over my mind? Much as I might want to, I can't spend my life passively dreaming on a hilltop or on a beach listening to the lapping of water. Just then a falling leaf with stiletto points, dried and sharp, smacks me on the forehead. Exactly what I deserve, I admit peevishly to myself and begin to write the letter to my parents.

I write a cheerful letter describing the New England countryside and never mention anything about the outrageous quarrels going on among the members of the troupe. With the letter completed, I fold it, and take the extra sheet of paper to begin a drawing. It's a rough sketch of a red barn far away in the valley below, but the drawing is never completed.

Suddenly, Jessica comes dashing out of the Annex with George close behind her. She is laughing so hard that she can barely gain a lead on George. I notice immediately that she is hugging something tightly to her chest. It's the violin, the source of all the squealing discordance. Jessica runs straight towards me and drops the violin like a football into my lap, a diversion to keep George away from herself. It's a wise move for apparently George is not taking the incident in the spirit of frolic...more like murder. He wrenches the violin from me and shouts after Jessica, "You damn bitch!"

The word "bitch" grates on me like an unshelled walnut down one's backside. I have never heard the word used at home. It repels me. How can one feel secure around people who spew out their emotions like flying shrapnel? The ugly word and the incident shatter all the serenity I have achieved just moments ago.

As I watch, George disappears back into the Annex. I sooth myself with the notion that George and the others never actually mean all the hate words strewn like rat droppings throughout their conversations anymore than they mean the "lovey" ones they toss around indiscriminately. They constantly address each other as "darling" or "sweetie," the meanings having no relationship whatsoever to their actual feelings.

*

I knew how my friend, Dorothy from Seaplace would handle these kids. "It's just a matter of right thinking," she would say. "Ignore their faults. Go for the 'good' in them. Everyone has some good in them."

How simple Dorothy had always made it sound. I had to admit that her philosophy seemed to work like a miracle for her. Last summer I had witnessed the changes in some difficult people, at least in the way they reacted towards her. But I wasn't Dorothy. To me the flaws in people stood out like tomato sauce on a white blouse, whereas their good characteristics were deeply hidden.

As I gather my writing materials, the aborted sketch, and take my time shuffling through the pungent leaves back to the Annex, I promise to renew my efforts to discover something "good" about each person in the troupe. Jessica, for instance, has a sense of humor. George is honest. Denny? He is certainly outgoing, jovial. Fay is never raucous. I can get no further with my attempt at a Christian view of everyone, not in the positive way my friend Dorothy does so ably. In my head I keep hearing Denny dominate all our conversations and Jessica asking the same childish questions over and over again. I shiver at George's abrupt, knife-like manner of speaking. Fay was almost furtive in her lack of warmth.

My negative thinking about each person in the troupe wasn't going to make living with them easy, but I assured myself, six months would go by quickly. Somehow I would manage. Besides, it was too late to leave the troupe. I didn't have enough money to take a bus back to New York. And even if I did? What would Josh and Sylvia think of me? That I was a "quitter" of course. Ah, there was that foolish pride of mine again, creeping insidiously into everything, though not quite the false pride my mother had so often warned me against.

*

As I open the door to the lower floor of the Annex, I catch the sound of Jessica's voice. "…and who knows, some Hollywood director might see one of our performances. At least," she adds after seeing the disbelieving expressions on each of our faces, "there will be lots of interesting scenery. Don't you agree?"

"Sure," Tom agrees affably. "Niagara, the Ozarks, and New Orleans are on my list of places to see."

"I wonder how far West we'll go?" George lowers his fiddle into its case.

Carl answers dryly, "Travis will deign to let us know exactly one week in advance. Don't set your heart on anything."

"All the same," Jessica persists in her enthusiasm, "just think, each town will be a surprise...like opening one of those dated boxes. Well, you know...the kind they place in cornerstones."

"Yeah," Denny laughs sarcastically, "you mean each dinky little town will be like a box in a cemetery...deadly."

"Dope! You know what I mean. There must be lots of kids in those small towns who are hungry for a live theatre performance."

"That's what you think. People in those little hick towns don't give a shit about genuine theatre."

"Denny, you're such a jerk." Jessica flounces out of the room and Fay follows.

Why does Denny have to be so cynical, I wonder. Carl echoes my feelings out loud.

"What makes you such a killjoy?"

Denny gestures grandly, "Life, my dear boy, life."

"Probably just constipation," quips Tom, and all the guys roar with laughter.

Why do they have to be so vulgar, I wonder in disgust? Yet, when the others laugh at Tom's retort, I find myself also smiling. One gets caught up in a mood without intentionally meaning to. Besides, I don't want the guys to think of me as some kind of old maid prude.

FIVE

"*I*'m going down into town. Anyone want to come with me and take in a movie? Carl looks around the threadbare Annex room at each one of us. Denny is displaying his newspaper plaudits to Fay and shakes his head. Tom is reading a pocket edition with a lurid cover showing a girl being ravished and George is fussing with the strap on his violin.

"I might go," I answer, wondering who else will and hope there isn't going to be a packed car so that I'll have to sit on someone's lap. As it turns out, Carl and I are the only two interested in going into town and that suits me fine. A quiet evening free from the embarrassment of appearing with the whole troupe is almost too much to hope for.

"I've seen that movie. It's not the greatest," Denny calls from across the long room where he now closes his album and stretches out on one of the lumpy sofas. I discover later that he almost never turns down a movie.

"We're not suppose to use...the car...for pleasure," George repeats Lu-Travis's rule in his usual blunt, stop-and-go speaking manner.

"I have to buy a prescription at the drugstore," Carl points to his leg, "for my leg...it aches. So I'd be using the car for medical reasons as well."

"A convenient defense." George sounds disgusted over Carl's flimsy excuse for using the car.

Carl ignores George's crack and we leave. While Carl is occupied with driving, I steal glances at him from the side. His white skin appears stretched tightly across his sharp cheekbones and then abruptly collapses around his mouth into deep parentheses. Carl is not much more than an inch or two taller than myself with a head proportioned for a larger, more robust man. Even after two years of recuperating from the automobile accident that damaged the muscles and nerves in his leg, his thinness is still that of an emaciated girl. The leg continues to break the rhythm of his life just as it does his walking. It takes very little imagination on my part to feel a pain shooting up through my own leg. Then I stretch my leg out to its full length and break the circuit of my sympathy. What an immense relief, knowing that Carl's leg isn't mine after all.

"If I had my own car, we could explore the town a bit," Carl remarks before we arrive at the movie theatre, "but rules are rules."

"It's really getting too dark to see much anyway," I reply. We exchange few other words either going down into the valley of the town or returning up the hill to Fairview House and the Annex.

"Have a good time?" Denny smiles in a manner implying that Carl and I have gone off to the movie to be alone with each other.

I ignore Denny's insinuation. "As you warned us, it wasn't the greatest movie."

"What took you so long?" George eyes us suspiciously. "It's past nine-thirty."

I let Carl answer. "We stopped at the drugstore after the movie."

Jessica winds up the old record player and drops a 78 rpm record on the turntable. "Come-on, Carl, I'll teach you to rumba."

Carl manages the dance steps remarkably well on his stiff leg. I feel proud of him, as though I am responsible for his welfare. He isn't afraid to try difficult twists and turns with his crippled leg. Perhaps the medicine is already working. Carl responds to Jessica's exuberance with a relaxed smile and an easiness that I haven't noticed in him before. Certainly he isn't that informal around me. Is it possible that Carl likes Jessica? So what's wrong with that, I ask myself. One movie doesn't mean you own the guy. Still, I wonder what Carl can possibly see in Jessica? She is wiggling and swaying suggestively in a very lascivious way. How forward of her. I hang around and watch longer than I intend. The dress Jessica wears tonight has smoothed down some of her bumptious looking curves, making her shapely and feminine...but still terribly short-waisted and plump, I assure myself.

Jessica is never without earrings, except on stage; the earrings are a glittery part of her personality. Usually she wears odd dangles, coins, or as now, spiders in a silver web. Too bad, I think, that her feminine appeal is so often lost in her child-like insistence upon having her own way. But maybe a guy like Carl wouldn't be aware of her spoiled nature. Maybe he only notices how voluptuously she appears tonight under the forty-watt bulbs of the Annex.

✳

I close the door to the small cubicle, my room, but it fails to shut out the music from downstairs and the voices from over the partition. Over the wall on my left I can hear Denny telling Tom, "I couldn't live without my theatre scrapbook. Take a look at these newspaper write-ups...that one for instance. It's the first one I show to agents when I'm making theatre rounds."

Tom's voice is quieter, as Tom himself is most of the time, except for his swearing during the loading and unloading of the truck. He spends a lot of time reading fantasy paperbacks when he isn't driving the truck and doesn't seem to be affected by George and Jessica's fights. He simply ignores them. Tom tells us that he is going to be inducted into the army soon, but evidently he hasn't told that same story to Lu-Travis. Tom, in a fake beard, plays the scoundrel in the play and, as a true villain should, riles the children in the audience to the point of yelling out warnings against his vile deeds to the innocent princess. "Watch out, watch out!" they warn the princess. Off stage, Tom resumes his benign appearance, heightened by the fact that he wears thick-rimmed glasses.

Now over the pine wall, which doesn't extend all the way to the ceiling, I hear Tom say, "Here's a good review."

"Yeah, my best one." Denny happily expands upon his career. "We presented <u>The Man Who Came to Dinner</u> at the Baltimore Civic Theatre."

"Hey, I see you underline the compliments about yourself in red...same as I do."

That figures, I smirk to myself. Denny's like a kid who never stops boasting. Kid...that's the way I tag all of them...just kids... except for Carl and myself. The six-month tour will be a lot more interesting if Carl and I can be friends, just friends. I'm not thinking in terms of anything more, for I honestly feel no great spark of a physical nature between us, unless it's something that might develop as time goes on.

"So that's what Lisa looks like," I hear Tom's admiring tone coming over the wall. "A bit like Garbo...even the straight hair. A real picture grabber."

"That's not all she grabbed."

"She actually stole things?"

"No, no. Not *things*. I don't mean that. Forget her. Did you see this other clipping?"

From the other side of the knotty pine partition I again pick up the name, Lisa. She piques my interest, and I'm hoping to learn more about her, but Tom says he's turning in, and I hear the door shut as he goes off to his own cubical.

As I lie in bed listening to the music coming from the old wind-up player from the floor below, I try to imagine what it will be like from now on as we perform in all those strange places without ever seeing the stages ahead of time. I'm a little apprehensive about it, and I wonder if the others feel as anxious and uncertain as I do, probably not Denny, though. He's done it all so many times before.

Yesterday morning at breakfast, I remember Jessica asking Denny, "Do the sponsors send back reports about our performance to old Mrs. Travis?"

"Oh sure, but it doesn't matter. Most of them don't know good acting when they see it anyway." Denny flips his hand expressively. "Who cares."

*

The next day we arrive at the high school in Chatham two hours ahead of the scheduled curtain time. The boys unload the truck, lash together the canvas flats for the first act, and I arrange the props where they are needed. The stage is so shallow that a cross-over behind the scenery will be impossible unless we eliminate four flats. That leaves far less space for Fay to perform her little dances and no time left before the curtain rises for any of us to rehearse in the new smaller space. Later, after Fay is in costume, I see her out there on the stage pirouetting, trying to plan her dance steps to fit the small space so that she won't accidentally bump into the big throne platform, which takes up at least half the depth of the small stage.

A classroom down a hallway is designated for our dressing room with several other classrooms between it and the stage. Screens have been placed in the middle of the room to divide the girls' from the boys' dressing areas. Actually it makes very little difference to us. We are used to seeing each other in shorts and panties, but the school probably thinks it's up to them to keep everything looking proper.

I wonder if all the school stages are going to be as inconveniently designed as this one. For makeup and costume changes between scenes, the dressing room is too far away; yet there is no space immediately behind the set on stage to make quick changes. We solve that problem by leaving the stage door open to the hallway. My quick change from servant's shabby clothing to queen's costume is done in full view of anyone who might happen to be walking down the hall. Whoever isn't performing on stage at the time holds the mirror for me as I hastily pin back my hair and don the elaborate queen's crown.

It's a good thing my mother didn't know all about this immodesty. I could almost see her lips firming-up in disapproval. She would certainly make me feel guilty once again just like that night at home when one of our roomers, a college man, came downstairs late at night. I had just opened up the sofa bed in the sunroom where I slept, and was about to pull the long monks cloth drapes across the arch to shut the living room off from my sofa bed when Jeff appeared in the opening at the bottom of the stairs. I grabbed my bathrobe and slipped it on.

Jeff said he had heard me typing earlier in the evening and wondered if I'd type his term paper for him sometime that same week. "I can pay you," he offered, and I accepted since I needed the money for my next term at the college. Then Jeff tiptoed back to his room upstairs. Perhaps if he hadn't acted so furtive…anyway, immediately afterwards my mother came down from her bedroom and slept on the living room sofa nearby for the remainder of the night. She claimed, "I couldn't get to sleep," but her firmed-up lips spoke of distrust… of me or Jeff? She had a way of making me feel guilty even when I hadn't done anything out of line.

During one of Fay's dances on the small stage in Chatham, she finished a sedate little twirl to the music of a Mozart Sonata and accidentally stepped on George's toes. His response was a nasty grimace, which I presumed the children in the first row or two of seats could easily see. Fay also missed some of her lines in the second act. Denny covered up for her by converting her dialogue into lines of his own, making the later cues sound unfamiliar to Fay and that threw her even further off the track.

"The performance stank!" Denny bellowed as he lifted up the last piece of the palace scenery to Tom who was standing just inside the tailgate of the truck. "Whew," Denny wiped the perspiration from his forehead, smudging the fake age lines with his hand.

"It sure did," Tom agreed. "Aren't you going to get rid of all that makeup?"

"I'll take it off after we get started." Denny had his own theatre makeup kit with a mirror in the lid. The rest of us share the motley supply of makeup in squashed leaky tubes provided by Lu-Travis.

"There's no excuse for Fay to flub so many lines," grumbled Tom. "She had three weeks of rehearsal back in Missiac. Damn it! What makes this prop box so heavy?"

"Shhhh." Denny signaled to Tom. A few children have suddenly gathered in the parking lot to watch us load up the truck and car. Just then, Fay also arrived at the rear of the truck carrying her costume to be hung back inside the wardrobe. Denny whispered in her ear, "Missed a few lines, didn't you, kid."

"When?"

"In the second act. You missed the line where you say, 'Don't cry, little brother...'" Denny knew most of the script by heart.

"Oh, did I? Give me a script." Fay turned to Carl who also appeared at the rear of the truck with his costume. He handed Fay his script.

"Ann?" George came over to me carrying the paper mache' jug that was used in the second act. "Where do you want this packed?"

"In the car trunk again, I guess. It's still not thoroughly dry inside."

"Actually it stinks." George wrinkled up his nose in distaste.

"Roll it up in that old blanket." Without asking for the job, I had become the organizer and packer of the car trunk. Now I'm reminded that Jessica's bulky guitar hadn't been out of the trunk since the beginning of the tour.

"Is that everything?" Tom made ready to close the wide doors on the truck and padlock them.

"Everything except the phonograph," I call up to Tom.

"Put that in the car trunk, too," said Carl. "Fay can practice her dance tonight. She keeps bumping into everything." The monotone level of his voice removed the sting of his criticism.

"Yeah," George grumbled, "step on someone else's toes next time."

Tom slammed the doors on the truck. "Who's riding with me?"

"I will," Denny volunteers, "but only for a short distance. That seat's too hard on my ass. Come on, let's get the hell out of here...I hate this circus." In complete reversal of his comment, Denny laughs, baring his teeth in a gracious, luminous smile intended for the kids who are still hanging around the truck watching.

One boy wearing a baseball cap rode his bicycle along beside our car for a whole block yelling and waving, "Good-by...good-by!" He made us feel important, like legitimate big-time Broadway stars, admired and adored by our fans even though we all knew that the performance had been barely mediocre.

As we drove along to the next town the wind began to rise and dried leaves dropped making sharp, staccato noises against the metal of the car, a windy prelude to the rain that soon began to fall in giant drops. Maybe the rain would wash the dust off the car, I thought. It looked so trampy, especially inside. Jessica was careless with her cigarette; often she reached for the metal tray set in the back of the front seat just as the gray ashes began to fall...usually too late. "This car is a mess!" I looked at the floor in disgust.

"Oh, don't be so fussy," Jessica retorted. "Look, we're coming into town already." Rain spatters the car windows as a few houses appeared.

"It sure didn't take us long to reach Hudson." George spoke with a touch of longing in his voice, "We could have enjoyed Fairview House one more night..."

"...and all that good food," Jessica interrupted.

"Hudson was just fourteen miles or so from Chatham, but the itinerary orders us to travel this afternoon, not tomorrow. Doesn't make sense." Carl looks again at the sheet of paper in his hand.

"Where are we?" Fay looked up from her book.

"Hudson," I answered.

"One...two...only two movie houses," George sighed, plainly disappointed as we drove down the main street looking for the hotel listed on the itinerary.

"How long do we stay here?" Fay asks.

"One night," snapped George. "Try reading the itinerary instead of your book for a change. There...that must be the hotel. The truck's here already." George toots the car horn to let Tom know we have arrived. "This hotel looks too nice, too expensive. Let's find something cheaper."

"We can decide that after we find out how much it's going to cost," advises Carl. "There's Denny now, just coming out of the lobby."

"Honk your horn again, George; he doesn't see us," Jessica shrilled and tapped George on the shoulder at the same time.

George turned in his seat to glare at Jessica. "Will you stop telling me what to do?" For once Jessica didn't sass back. Instead, she waited until George turned to face the dashboard again and thumbed her nose at his back.

"Rooms cost three-fifty," Denny reports to Carl through the rolled-down window of the car.

"Let's find a cheaper place," chimed Jessica and George in unison. I sighed. For once they agreed with each other.

"All right," Carl nodded. "We can leave the truck parked right here until we find something else." Tom squeezes into the back seat with us and takes Fay on his knees. Denny shoved his way into the front, pressing Carl under George's shifting arm. George squirmed irritably, his face registering disgust; his private space had been encroached upon.

A half hour later, we found a rooming house that would take all seven of us for just one dollar per person if we three girls consented to sleep in one room and the four boys in another. I didn't care for the arrangement, but the other two girls would have to pay more rent if I left them and got a separate room. Anyway, I was beginning to realize that I couldn't afford a private room every night.

One nice thing about the rooming house, besides being very clean, is its location. It's just a half block away from a church that holds a Wednesday evening service. It seemed like a good omen, being so nearby, a nudge for me to attend. The rest of the kids were going to a movie…planning to ask for the professional courtesy that Denny had told us about.

"I'll join you later," I told the others, feeling very noble over my decision to continue attending church even in a strange town.

SIX

Later that same evening as I leave the church, a soft rain begins to fall again, and I decide against joining the others at the movie. Asking for professional courtesy with a group is one thing, but alone? I feel a little shy. Do people really do things like that...ask for something absolutely free? Anyway, this might be an opportunity to have the bathroom at the rooming house all to myself while everyone else is at the movie. A shrewd move; I compliment myself. I'll have a leisurely soak in the tub before everyone returns to the house.

To my disappointment, I discover after climbing the stairs to our room, that neither Fay nor Jessica has gone to the movie after all. They are ensconced in the bathroom which means I'll have to forget all about that relaxing bath. I can hear their voices quite clearly and deduce by the smell emanating from under the door that one of the two is peroxiding her hair. I stand beside the door wondering how long I will have to wait.

"This is such a bother, especially on the road like this. I don't know..." It's Fay's voice I hear. "...should I let it go back to its natural color?"

"I sure couldn't stand that peroxide smell. Whew!" breathes Jessica. "What is the natural color?"

"Brown. It looks awful while it's growing out. I suppose Travis wouldn't like it. She wants the princess in the play to have blond hair."

Through the door I hear a crash and a shrill, childish scream. "What happened?" I knock on the bathroom door. "Is anyone hurt?"

"Shhhh!" Fay hisses through the door, "you'll raise the landlady. I just spilled the bottle of peroxide."

Next, I hear Jessica's excited voice, "Wipe it up quick before it runs under the door and soaks into the hall carpet!"

"With what?"

"Use the towel. Hurry up!"

Animals, I think, and go back to the room where I gather my pajamas and sit down again to await my turn in the bathroom. Fay and Jessica soon come back to the room giggling. They stop when they see the impatient, disgusted look on my face.

"You ought to color your hair," Jessica stops to study my hair, then advises me, "It needs something to bring out the highlights. In theatre you need to enhance all your assets to attract attention."

One week on tour has made Jessica an authority on the subject of theatre as though she has been born in a theatre trunk. But I don't express either of those thoughts out loud. "I prefer the natural color," I say testily. In actual fact I long for red hair, but I'm never going to confess that little secret to the girls.

As I step into the hall on my way to the bathroom once again, I hear Carl's uneven gait followed by the sound of the shower being turned on. Too late. Once more, I trudge back to the room and sit down to wait.

*

After Hudson, we gave performances in Troy, New York, South Deerfield, and Springfield, Massachusetts. Before heading on the long trek West, we drop down to Meridan, Connecticut for an afternoon performance.

The hotel in Meridan isn't bad...not first class, but I quickly discovered that we were never going to stay in hotels that were rated first class or even second class. It had become perfectly clear in just the first week of touring that we barely had enough money to stay in the cheapest places and still afford two meals a day.

Though the hotel in Meridan was very old with holes in the carpet big enough to trip an agile mountain goat, it obviously had been several cuts above cheap at one time. Yes, long ago, I judged by the elaborately carved, heavy furniture, this hotel must have been considered quite grand.

At the registration desk, Carl was handed a telephone message from Mrs. Travis. "What now?" he muttered. He unfolded the message and read it as we stood around waiting. "I'm to choose one of the guys to drive the Plymouth back to Missiac and exchange it for another car...one that's in better mechanical condition to take the long trip West. And I choose you." Carl pointed his finger at George.

"Why me?"

"You drive the car, don't you? You can ask someone to go along with you if you want to." Carl smiles enigmatically, knowing it was unlikely that anyone would volunteer. Not too many in the troupe liked George well enough to trap themselves in the car with him for an extra day unless they gained some personal benefit as well.

"I'll go if Travis is paying," offered Tom. Carl answered with a shake of his head.

"Don't look at me," Fay turned away as George silently checked each one of our faces.

"I'm sleeping in all day," says Denny, and Carl simply dismissed the idea of his going with a gesture which meant, *no thanks*. Naturally, George wouldn't want Jessica to ride with him even if she had offered. They simply didn't get along.

"Ann?"

I didn't answer immediately. I was considering: there was nothing to do at the hotel and though the main street of the town was nearby, I had no money to spend. In a magazine article, I had read about the beautiful Connecticut countryside with its lovely homes owned by stage stars and famous people like Enzio Pinza. Also, I felt a bit sorry for George, probably for the simple reason that everyone else was so down on him. Underdogs frequently gained my sympathy, at least temporarily. George was still looking at me and I heard myself say, "I wouldn't mind seeing more of the area."

I noted a faint sign of pleasure on George's dour face, but all he said was, "Good. We leave at eight o'clock. I'll knock on your door when I'm ready to leave."

"Oh no you won't!" Jessica almost spat the words at George. Once again, we girls were sharing a room and naturally the other two didn't want to be awakened so early.

"I'll let you know later whether I'm going for sure or not. If I decide to go with you, I'll meet you downstairs in the lobby. There's no need to wake up Jessica and Fay so early."

"Well, don't be late." George's curt manner was not reassuring.

When I returned to the hotel room after lunch, Fay and Jessica were busy washing each other's hair in the bathroom. Evidently, they didn't hear me unlock the door and enter the room. They were talking so loudly over the noise of the running water that it was easy for me to overhear everything they said without deliberately eavesdropping.

"Did you see the way George brightened up when Ann told him she might go along with him tomorrow?"

Fay laughs. "Yeah. His face sure changed fast. I'll bet he's had fantasies about her right from the beginning of the tour."

"Could be. I hope she knows what she's getting herself into. It's a bit like *Red Riding Hood and the Wolf*."

That's utter nonsense, I thought defensively. The image of me as a meek little gray person not smart enough to foresee trouble was an insulting one.

"Oh, I'd hardly call George a wolf. Cold fish is more like it. He's got a lot of suppressed anger. That's even more dangerous."

"Yeah, and no respect for women. You saw how he punched me in the boobs. He's a threat to all women. Don't you think so?"

"Who knows?"

I could almost hear the shrug in Fay's voice. Neither Fay nor Jessica knew anything about character, not mine and not George's. It was true that George had become over wrought with Jessica more than once, but that alone didn't mean he was necessarily dangerous, did it? The incident over the car window was still fresh in my memory, and I also recalled with a shudder the vicious way he had yelled at Jessica when she ran off with his violin. Nothing was a joke to him.

Anyway, I assured myself, George wasn't going to treat me the way he treated Jessica. She was childish and I'm not. It's as simple as that. A mature person could get along with all kinds of people...the Georges and the Dennys in the world.

Where before I vacillated over traveling with George to take the car back to Missiac, now I felt a perverse urge to prove how wrong Jessica and Fay were. The unworldly character they presumed of me rankled. I felt as though they had smeared me with chalky, shameful meekness. They'd discover that I could look out for myself quite well. George was no ogre and would certainly treat me with respect.

Quite unexpectedly, the trip with George had turned into a challenge. The conversation I had just overheard between Fay and Jessica edged me towards making up my mind, or rather my perverse nature had done it for me. I would definitely go. I even began to look forward to the trip. It gave the whole next day an aura of adventure that it previously lacked.

SEVEN

*B*efore Fay and Jessica awake the following morning, I creep out of bed and close the window. Neither one of the two girls likes to have the window left open at night, but I quietly inch it open after they fall asleep. If I don't, the room will smell of stale bodies and bedding by morning.

Through the window and above the line of trees bordering the street, I can see no sign of clouds, so I assume the day will be nice. I hurry to dress. Though I have made it clear to George that I'll meet him in the lobby of the hotel, I know that if I show up the least bit late he'll come blundering up to our room and begin pounding on the door. That will certainly wake up Fay and Jessica with catastrophic results.

I have little choice in what to wear, but at least since the day appears fine, I can leave my old wrinkled coat behind. Should I wear a skirt and sweater or the Chinese print dress with its mandarin collar? I am thoroughly tired of both. A suit would be the proper attire for this fall season. Yes, a suit with a fur casually flung across my shoulder and gloves, naturally with a hat to match. I have seen just such an elegant outfit in a Bergdorf advertisement in the newspaper that someone left lying on the sofa in the lobby. I finally decide upon the skirt and sweater and hasten down to the lobby.

I look for some hidden sign of treachery in George's usually somber face when he greets me, but his smile plus the white shirt and dark tie, all look well behaved and proper. "Let's go," he says, and stalks out the double doors.

George doesn't talk much during the first part of the trip and that suits me fine. There's enough interesting scenery to keep me occupied as we follow route six-A west and south through Waterbury and old route six through Danbury, Connecticut. The occasional glimpses of houses surrounded by acres of tall trees and lichen encrusted stonewalls awes me...weighs me down with envy. I may never be able to live in one of those charming country homes. If only George would slow the car down so that I could have more time to take in the details, or better still, if he could swing the car through one of those stone pillared gates and slowly wander up the long driveway. It teases me to whiz past, catching only the fan light above a door, a stone chimney or a cedar shingle roof and nothing more. I must have sighed audibly for I feel George's eyes glance my way.

How I envy people who can afford to live in privacy among acres of beautiful woods like those we are passing. Through all of these thoughts I can hear threads of my mother's voice warning, "material things don't buy happiness," and my own quick rebuttal, "lots of people have both." Of course, she would counter that idea by quoting: "It's easier for a camel to pass through the eye of a needle than a rich man to enter heaven."

I never can win an argument with my mother. It isn't that she's always right, but her seniority and her oh-so-reasonable tone of voice carry greater weight, and mostly seal our disagreements in her favor, especially if she begins to quote the bible to back up her statements. My mother's opinions curtail my life just like those governors that were put on cars during the war allowing them to go only so fast and thus conserve gas. Even now, a thousand miles away from my mother, I irritably press each finger of my brown cloth gloves attempting to smooth away my frustrations and loosen the restraints. I don't want my mother's voice, real or imaginary, following me around the country reasoning with me.

"You seem to know the route quite well; I guess you've driven this way before?"

"Most of it," George answers affably. "We'll zigzag down until we hit the Saw Mill Parkway. But first I want you to meet someone, a friend who lives in Mt. Kisco.

"But aren't we expected to drive straight to Missiac?"

"Oh, we've got lots of time."

So, I surmise, that's exactly why George opts for such an early start. In his mind he has this little side trip planned all along. I didn't like the idea of deviating from our route, but obviously it's out of my hands since I'm not the driver.

As George turns the car and follows a narrow dirt road, he stiffly proclaims, "I'm glad you came along with me. You're different...from the others."

"Oh?"

"You've got...more class."

It's a nice compliment but one can't come right out and agree with a snobbish sounding statement like that without projecting a self-satisfied image. Actually, I'm at a loss to respond. "They're just kids," I finally say. "Maybe they'll change as they grow up."

"I doubt it," is George's negative retort. After a long pause, he continues, "I wouldn't think...of introducing anyone else in the troupe to my mother and father. You're different. I'd really like you to meet my family."

Whoa, slow down, I think, and begin to feel uneasy. Maybe I shouldn't have come on this outing after all. George's ideas are developing in directions I haven't anticipated. Perhaps Fay and Jessica are more nearly right in their assessment of George than I am.

"George, that's a nice compliment. Thank you." I state this as formally and as impersonally as I can without making it sound like a complete rejection. I have absolutely no interest in promoting George as a buddy-buddy or meeting his family. Yet, neither do I think it very prudent to get on the wrong side of him as Jessica has already done. I hug myself to stop a shiver creeping up my spine; the chill is not from the air streaming through the open window vent, which George doesn't offer to close, but from the sudden turn of events.

"Cold? You should have worn your coat." Just then George swings the car into a long dirt driveway, overgrown on both sides. In the middle a high hump of dirt slows the car to a crawl. Further on and around a curve, there appears a stonewall with great gaps in it, the stones tumbling in gray heaps and partially covered by mosses or obscured by goldenrod. Beyond, I catch a glimpse of a rambling two-story house. The whole place looks neglected, forsaken; at one time it must have been quite handsome.

"Come with me. I want you...to meet someone." George hurries around and opens my door for me. At the front entrance of the house George rings the doorbell beside the glass door. I can see all the way straight through a wide hall and out the back entrance. To my disappointment no one answers the door. I am so close to seeing the inside of this once marvelous old house. I think of all the interesting homes that earlier flash past the car windows and now I may miss this opportunity as well.

"Follow me." George steps back. "She's probably afraid to answer the door or she's in the garden in back and doesn't hear the bell at all."

"Why should she be so afraid?" I ask, but George has already gone on ahead of me and doesn't answer. I follow him around the length of the sprawling stone and shingle house. There seems to be no one on the back terrace either, but George spots a figure in the sunken garden below. We walk down a slate path and around a fountain, no longer splashing water, and pass some overgrown rose bushes, which reach out to grab at our legs.

A middle-aged woman, perhaps in her forties, rises from a stone bench, but she doesn't come forward to meet us. Her expression is anxious; yes, I decide, clearly she is worried about something. Finally, she recognizes George and seems to relax.

George rushes forward with an outstretched hand and greets the woman in a language unfamiliar to me, but I assume that it is the language of Greece since I already know George is Greek. His voice—I can't help but notice the sudden switch from the stone coldness I am accustomed to hearing—becomes soft and gentle. I hear a quality of obeisance. The way he bends his head is almost reverential, as though he might be a vassal and wants to kneel in homage like a knight of old or even kiss the woman's hand.

"May I present Ann Gulbrith." Then George's voice switches into that other language again. But I get the impression that he's explaining about me to the countess. She keeps nodding and smiling, and is quite attractive when her brow isn't working itself up into deeper lines.

While George sits down on the stone bench beside the countess to talk, I wander around the sunken garden identifying what is left of a once cared-for, beautiful estate. Besides the scrawny roses there are also rust colored mums still blooming against the deep green of the rhododendron leaves, and beyond those I recognize the hosta plants and late blooming day lilies.

I'm truly baffled by the whole visit. Why is the woman all alone and frightened...definitely frightened? George and I stay only a short time, and I feel relief because I don't know quite how to behave as George speaks secretively in his foreign language. I look at the massive house from the rear and note again how it desperately needs care. Soon we are back in the car and on our way. George begins his explanation before I have time to form the questions.

"The countess is a refugee from Greece. The estate is being loaned to her as a refuge...a place to hide. Titled people are no longer tolerated in her country...just their money, unless people like the countess are first able to get it switched to another country. It's a political thing...that's all I know about it. She's a wonderful person and I wanted her to meet you. Her approval is important."

Approval for what? But I'm afraid to ask. If I ask, it might draw an even more personal explanation from George. Sometimes, if one ignores things, they go away. Does George need the countess's approval before dating me? Those old world customs are quite different from ours. He has also implied that he would like to introduce me to his parents. What if meeting-the-parents is synonymous with getting engaged? Oh dear, I literally squirm in the car seat. What have I gotten myself into? How can George assume so much, so soon, without any encouragement from me?

When we arrive in Missiac, George hurries around the car and opens the door for me. He helps me from the front seat and holds my arm as though I am in a sickly way or already betrothed to him. Perhaps I actually do look sick from my recent thoughts. I glance up at the window of the building, hoping no one from the Lu-Travis staff is watching. How have I gotten myself into this uncomfortable situation, and how, I wonder, am I going to extricate myself without hurting George's feelings and making an enemy of him for the whole tour?

George is going to be one of my six constant companions for the next half year and if I bluntly reject him, he can make those months very uncomfortable. On the other hand, I can make those six months quite smooth for myself if I use some of my acting ability to stay on the good side of George. But it isn't honest. Anyway, I'm not adept at keeping up pretenses for long. . .only the length of a stage show. People who say one thing and think another leave an aroma around that can eventually be sniffed out. All these unsettling thoughts snarl up my thinking, and leave me apprehensive.

✫

The car, which we drove back to Meridan, was identical in appearance to the Plymouth we had exchanged, except that this one was pale green and dirtier. With Lu-Travis's permission, George stopped at a filling station to have the outside of the car washed.

"You girls will have to clean the inside," said George, the implication being that since we were women, it would be in our field of expertise. "Fay and Jessica will probably be too lazy to do it," he added.

We arrived back at the hotel about five-thirty in the afternoon and soon located the other members of the cast in the hotel coffee shop where they had just ordered their evening meal.

"What took you so long?" Carl asked, glancing casually up at George and me. How I wished his voice had held less placidity, more interest. . .even a little worry.

George's answer was an enigmatic grin, and I felt, rather than actually saw, five sets of eyes raising quirky eyebrows at me, as though they were now able to confirm some aberrant behavior between George and me that they had all along suspected.

"We stopped to eat on the way back," I explained. Maybe George wanted everyone to think we had been engrossed in a love affair, but I wanted no such ideas clouding my reputation.

"There's some mail for you at the front desk," Jessica said.

"Thanks." I slipped away from the booth and headed for the lobby. There was a letter and a small package, both from my mother. I returned to the coffee shop where I opened the package first. It contained a pair of hosiery, a belated birthday present. Not too exciting a gift, but my folks seldom surprised me with anything unusual, just practical, and never anything expensive. My disappointment was nothing new. I sighed and wished they would surprise me just once. Then I opened the birthday card and began to read the letter inside.

As soon as I had read her first words, "I just came back from the hospital and...," I felt the ominous chill that precedes bad news. And it was bad. My face quickly drained, my lips began to feel numb, and I had to take a deep breath before rereading the letter. I must have hoped, because of the poor lighting in the booth, that I had misinterpreted in some way...that things at home weren't really as upsetting as Mother said they were.

Well?" someone asked; I don't remember who, "You look pretty shook-up...bad news?"

I nodded. It was almost too much effort to speak with my numb, frozen-lipped mouth. "My father had a stroke."

"Then you'll be going home, I suppose." Fay made it sound so definite, so matter-of-fact, that I felt immediate resentment. I'm sure I gave her a nasty look or at least one of surprise. Then I began to feel very sad...a bit weepy. But the sadness was for myself, not my father.

My poor father was lying ill in the hospital, yet all my thoughts were only about myself....about being trapped into going home...

about working nine to five in some dull office adding up accounts or filing...taking my mother grocery shopping every Friday and taking both her and Dad, if he were able, for their usual Sunday afternoon ride in the country. Trapped. So there it was...out in the open at last. SELFISH.

I didn't like the truth about myself: I wanted to stay away from home because I was selfish.

Feeling guilty was very uncomfortable but not uncomfortable enough to make me rush straight out to buy a bus ticket for home. I would drag my feet and put it off as long as possible.

"Sorry you've gotten bad news," George said. "I hope you can stay," he added, and his eyes were trying to send a message, though I think he was quite unpracticed at conveying sympathy.

"Yeah, too bad," Denny said mechanically.

"I'll have to let Lu-Travis know if you're going to leave." Carl didn't include any words of condolence.

"I won't know definitely until I make a call to my mother later tonight when the phone rates are lower," I told Carl, wishing he and the others would show much more reluctance over my leaving the tour.

That evening we all gathered in the hotel room occupied by the boys. Someone brought beer. How I hated the smell of beer. Under normal circumstances I would have left the room to be off on my own. But not tonight. Tonight I needed companionship, even if those companions had beery breath. They talked a lot and I, still feeling numb, listened. As usual, Denny out-talked everyone about what he'd done in theatre, whom he'd met, and what he was going to do next year.

After awhile we began to sing. We whipped through *Pistol Packin Ma Ma,* but none of us could remember all the words to the Betty Hutton song...something about an "orange colored sky." We were quite noisy and half expected the hotel management to knock on the door at any minute and evict us. It grew later and later and I kept delaying the phone call to my mother.

Finally at ten-thirty, which was nine-thirty in the Midwest, I knew that I could not put off the phone call, not even a minute longer. Even under normal circumstances, my folks went to bed before ten o'clock, and now with Dad in the hospital, Mother might be emotionally drained and go to bed even earlier.

From the hotel receptionist I got a handful of change and went to the phone booth across the lobby. There were few phones in hotel rooms at that time, and anyway what hotel management, after taking a look at our rag-tag gang, would have let any of us make a long distance call and charge it to the room?

Just one day ago I had questioned my ability to stomach the six long months of touring with guys and gals who constantly bickered and quarreled, taking nips and bites out of each other, a slow undermining and a chipping away of egos. Suddenly faced with the fact that I might have to hasten home because of my father's stroke—a perfectly good excuse to quit the troupe and escape—my ambiguity had vanished. No longer was I uncertain...there were no more "should I or shouldn't I's?" Discord was forgotten. I knew without a doubt that I wanted to stick with the tour. Even George's unwelcome attentions, which triggered ominous body chills, didn't affect my decision. I wanted to stay; only now perhaps I couldn't. Maybe I no longer had a choice.

"Families should stick together." I wished I could stop my mother's voice from floating to the surface of my conscious mind. I really didn't want her opinions constantly weaving in and out of my thoughts...swaying me emotionally in just one direction...familial.

The phone booth was small and warm. Somehow that was a comfort to me, like a warm blanket for a nearly drowned victim, for that's the way I thought of myself. I was shivering like one. I took a deep breath and gave the long distance operator the phone number in a quivery, uncertain voice. Putting the phone call off even this long made me feel guilty, a self-centered daughter. That's what my mother thought of me anyway. I'd heard her say it one time... "self-centered." If she wanted me to come home, I'd have to go without a whimper. Slowly, I dropped the proper coins into the slot.

EIGHT

I stood in the phone booth listening to the ringing far away in the small house where I had grown up in Michigan. The house was white with brown shingles on the upper half, a bungalow, and people always said it "looks friendly". To me it just looks squat and insignificant.

The phone goes on ringing for a long time. Mother must have gone to bed, I decide. Why hadn't I called her just a half hour earlier? Maybe, if she doesn't answer, I'll have an excuse to wait until tomorrow evening to phone. Then, I can pretend for one more day that everything is the same as *before* the letter arrived. Just as I am about to hang up the receiver, a faint voice answers, "Hello?"

Mother sounds tired, so the first thing I do is apologize for calling so late. She says it's all right. My phone call has caught her in the bathroom getting ready for bed.

"I'm so relieved that the call isn't from the hospital," she says. I can visualize her taking out the gray hairpins, untwisting the bun she has worn as long as I can remember, and letting it drop. From behind it will appear coarse, ropey.

Back when I was in grade school, I remembered wishing that she would wear her hair like the other mothers of my schoolmates, short or permed. To me the other mothers looked soft and lighthearted, as if their lives were pleasant, but my mother with her hair parted severely in the middle with just a wave or two on each side, looked older, more serious. She didn't smile much either.

Tonight when I ask Mother about the condition of my father, she says he is getting along reasonably well, but I notice that her voice isn't ringing any bells of joy. Of course, she never expresses excessive joy or sorrow or bitterness in her speech. No extremes. Her calm "reasonableness" is in sharp contrast to the high voltage, overly emotional behavior of my tour companions.

"Can he talk?" I ask.

"Oh yes, he can even stand-up for a few minutes…and swear." I hear a light chuckle from her. I can almost hear the *Jehoshaphat*, my father's favorite expression. "Today they started therapy on his left leg and the hospital will release him when he can use a walker. It's going to be difficult to get him through that narrow bathroom door using a walker…but I'll manage somehow."

Poor Mom, I think, but don't express myself out loud.

"I don't know what to do about the car. I'll have to learn to drive I guess." Is she hinting that I should come home and do the driving?

"How do you get your groceries right now?"

"Oh, the neighbor, Mrs. Allison, takes me. I hate to intrude upon other people though."

Yes, how well I know. Mother is very independent. Now, right now, I tell myself, you've got to ask. You cannot put it off even one minute longer. I take a deep breath. Dear Lord, I am scared out of my wits that she'll give me a definite "yes" to my question.

"Shall I come home?" I ask weakly.

"Only if you want to," she answers. I swallow with relief.

"But can you get along?" I leave no pause for her answer but go right on talking, "Perhaps I should stick to the troupe at least until we travel closer to the Midwest. I'm sure to get home for Christmas… maybe Thanksgiving too," I add, as though throwing out a wonderful, juicy bone of hope.

The operator interrupts to tell me that my three minutes are up. In my family we never talk over the three-minute warning. I tell Mom that I'll write. I quickly hang up the phone and plunk down hard on the wooden seat in the booth. I am breathless…from my close encounter with family duty. I am miraculously alive after suffering a near catastrophe. I won't need to go home, at least not immediately, and my escape from duty leaves me feeling guilty...so guilty. That night I write a letter, longer than usual, to my parents.

Dear Mom and Dad,

As usual when talking to you on the phone, I forgot to say all the important things. I meant to thank you for the birthday stockings and the card. Listed below are the towns where we'll be performing, but I've listed only the names of the Saturday hotels because that's where you should send your letters.

Buffalo, N.Y., Oct. 18 and 19
Albion, N.Y., Oct. 21 and 22...Hotel Orleans
Oil City, Penn., Oct. 23 and 24
Warren, Penn., Oct. 27 and 28...Hotel Carver

Yesterday we gave a performance here in Meriden and tomorrow morning we move on towards Buffalo, about 450 miles away. We'll probably stay all night in Cazenovia, N.Y. on route 20.

We exchanged cars here (drove back to Missiac today) as the other car needed repairs. Our truck has broken down twice already. Some fun.

The Mass. and Connecticut countryside's are very beautiful. Did you know that they grow tobacco in both states? We saw it hanging up in the open barns as we passed.

Coming into Meriden the other day we stopped to buy jugs of cider. We must have looked silly carrying three jugs of cider into the Hotel Winthrop along with ten battered suitcases.

Well, Dad…I know why you got sick…you didn't have me around to argue with. I'll be thinking about you, so get up and around as soon as you can. And write.

Love, Ann

✻

Buffalo seemed like a long tedious haul, because the truck was so very slow. I doubted if it ever went over forty miles per hour on the whole trip Those of us in the car were supposed to follow behind the truck at all times. I presume it was because the truck, being older, was more inclined to break down than the car. Anyway, it was one of the rules. Later on in the tour, after viewing the mud-caked backside of the truck for thousands of miles—first slowing down and then catching up when too many cars came between our car and the truck—we broke the rule constantly. Sometimes we didn't even know where the truck was. Once when it didn't show up in the town listed on the itinerary, Carl began to get edgy. We waited another hour and had just decided to retrace our route to look for the truck when it drove up.

Somehow, Tom had taken a wrong turn and gotten lost.

In the car, Denny kept us entertained with his singing of Judy Garland songs.

Judy was one of his favorite singing stars, and he never grew tired of raving about her. More often though, he raved about his own exploits in the acting world and how he made the theatre rounds. We all knew more about Denny with his dark, over-active eyes, or thought we did, than anyone else in the cast except Lisa, and she wasn't even in our troupe. She had been with Denny on a tour from the previous year. Lisa sounded like the epitome of the "get ahead" me, me, me actress, selfish and slightly vulgar as well. Yet in retelling the stories about her, Denny often presented her as the heroine of the troupe; she was someone gutsy; she was someone to be admired, that is, until he came to the part where she got fired. Denny never explained that incident satisfactorily. As Denny rambled on, I only half listened.

"Once, Lisa and I had a fight on a street car in Indianapolis. She slapped me and I slapped her back, then, just as some strange guy tried to intervene in the name of chivalry, Lisa and I threw our arms around each other and kissed. We forgave each other right then and there. What a performance! She was like that all the time. Travis hated her guts. I've got a picture of Lisa in my scrapbook somewhere. Remind me to show it to you."

✻

While staying overnight in Cazenovia, great fluffs of snow silently touch our faces and make our colonial rooming house with its old lantern-type streetlight look like a beautiful Christmas card.

We arrived in Buffalo the following day where it was much colder and the roads were icy. Jessica and Fay began to talk about nothing else but Niagara Falls. Unfortunately, our hotel was located at least ten or eleven miles from the famous place.

"Can't we use the company car just this once? Awww, come-on, Carl," teased Jessica. "Who's going to know if we use the car or not as long as we pay for the gas ourselves?"

"Sorry. Travis says the car isn't to be used for sightseeing. Besides, it's not just a matter of paying for the gas. I also have to write down the mileage, and if it doesn't agree closely with the mileage of previous tours, Travis starts asking questions and ends up yelling at me over the phone."

Jessica pouted and said, "Then we'll just have to hitchhike."

"Isn't that a bit dangerous?" I asked.

"Not if the boys go with us. Come on, let's all go before it gets any later."

"As it turned out, the boys have enough money to pay for their bus fare to the Falls, and that left Fay and Jessica to hitchhike all by themselves.

"You're coming too, aren't you?" Jessica had taken it for granted that I'd join her and Fay.

"No thanks, hitchhiking isn't exactly safe for women."

"Scared, huh?"

I believe it was exactly on that very day, that Jessica began to label me, "an old maid." She could only admire someone with a more adventurous, gutsy behavior, whereas I had yet to break free of my cautionary, good-girls-don't-do-that, type of upbringing. My parents never let me wear those really short shorts either. When I'd balk against their attitude and began to argue, "but other girls wear them," Mother countered with, "But you don't want to be just like all the other girls, do you?"

Well, I do and I don't. I want to be different, yes, but not to the point of standing out like a nun. I looked funny in those knee length shorts when everyone else wore shorter ones. But I had already learned that arguing with my mother was futile. Experience told me that she couldn't be worn down. Once she made up her mind, she stuck to it firmly. Yes, *firm was* an appropriate adjective to describe my mother.

What Jessica didn't suspect is that there are other reasons involved in my decision not to hitchhike to the falls, snobbery and pride. How would it look for me to be standing beside the road with a gypsy-type character like Jessica? Most hikers I recall seeing were unkempt and ragged, except for the male college students thumbing rides back to the university. I had never, ever, seen a girl do such an undignified thing.

"I'd rather stay here and catch up on my laundry." That's my lame excuse. I came close to envying Jessica and Fay. They didn't have the strict boundaries of behavior that I had always taken for granted. I consider them rather juvenile. They do madcap things without thinking of the consequences. Sometime, maybe even this very day, they would have to suffer for their impetuosity, whereas I.... The phone rang and cut short such thoughts.

"It's for you, Ann. Sounds like George," Fay said.. The overtone in her voice implies, it's your boyfriend calling."

As she guesses, it is George. He asks me to go with him to the falls. I quickly deduce that George has been shunned by the other guys in the troupe. They have probably already left without him. I'm tempted to say "yes" to his offer because I really do want to see the famous place; this might be my only opportunity. But I know if I go with George today, as I did with him on the trip to Missiac, the whole troupe will then pair us off permanently for the rest of the tour. I must not let that happen.

"Thanks, George, but I've already begun to wash my hair and it takes over a hour for it to dry because it's so long and thick."

"Oh. Just thought I'd ask." George hung up abruptly, leaving me with the clear impression that he had seen through my poor excuse. Too bad that I had to hurt his feelings, I told myself, but it's all for the best...my best.

"Do you think he meant to pay your bus fare to the falls?" Jessica asked, and Fay answers before I even open my mouth, "Are you kidding? He's tight with his money."

"Probably not," I agreed.

After Fay and Jessica left, the day passed quietly, mundanely. It was peaceful to have the hotel room all to myself and to leisurely wash my hair, launder my underpants and bra, and write letters. Later, I took a walk but there was nothing much to see except tall apartment buildings. This particular area of the city was flat and uninteresting. I couldn't even find a grocery store where I hoped to buy a candy bar to appease myself for not visiting the falls.

Just about dusk which now comes as early as five, Fay and Jessica reappear, tired, but elated, and completely unscathed from their hitchhiking experience.

"We're back. Don't look so surprised," Fay said after I unlock the door of our room and let them inside.

"...and we weren't abducted either," Jessica laughed, "You look disappointed."

Perhaps I am. None of the dire things I had predicted actually happened to Fay and Jessica. They are obviously quite pleased with themselves for having managed to reach Niagara, see the Falls, and return all on their own without spending money for bus fare. Their confidence in themselves has blossomed from the adventure, and as they got ready to go out to dinner, they chatter on and on about their remarkable day.

Jean M. Ponte

The boys have also seen the falls as well. I am the only one who hasn't. I have no adventure to exchange with the others in the troupe. As they each relate their day, I feel left out. Too bad I don't have more guts like that awful girl Denny is always calling Lisa-the-witch.

"Anything doing tonight?" Denny looks around the table at each of us for ideas on how to fill up his evening.

"I'm for reading in bed," answered Tom. He holds out his hand. It's full of nickels and dimes. "Anyway, I'm broke."

Carl rises from the table. "I've got to get last week's report done and mailed off to Travis."

"Want some help?" I asked. I had worked with Carl on the report just the week before. Sometimes the mileage and the gas consumption don't tally, though they are supposed to come close to agreeing. That's how Lu-Travis checks up on the car usage.

"Oh, I guess so," Carl answers with vague interest. "Room 302."

"Should I come up about eight?" I ask. At least working on the report with Carl will give me something to do this evening. Helping with the report is how I first learn that the guys in the troupe get ten dollars more in salary per week than the girls. At the time, I fail to think very seriously about the unfairness in the salary difference between the girls and the men. I remember back in Missiac signing a small typewritten contract that stated:

I understand that my salary for the time I am playing on tour for Lu-Travis, Inc., Missiac, N.Y., will be $20.00 per week. That I shall also have a road allowance of $15.00 per week.

I also understand that should I apply for unemployment benefits, I must report my salary only, but that for my income tax I must report both my salary and my road allowance. My remuneration is so fixed at my request.

Signature_____
Social Security Number_____

An hour later when I knock on the hotel door of Carl and Denny's room, Denny lets me inside. "Well, if it isn't Mrs. Manager." He emphasizes the "Mrs. Manager" in a resonant voice that sounds far from jovial. As I enter the room, I immediately notice Carl's strained face, as though he and Denny have been caught in the midst of an argument...one which I'm interrupting.

"Well," mutters Denny, I'll leave you two all alone to work things out." He gives me a sly glance as he verbally underlines the word "alone," then quickly leaves the room.

"What a strange thing to say. What does he mean?"

Carl shrugs in answer, but I notice that he's particularly quiet this evening, more formal than usual towards me while we work on the report. We exchange not a single sentence that isn't related to the report except when I ask, "Why do the guys get paid more money than the girls?"

"They work harder. They lift the scenery and do the driving."

"Oh," is my only response. Somehow that doesn't seem like a good enough reason for some of the guys to get paid more. For example, I know that Denny sneaks out of helping with the scenery at least half of the time and he does absolutely no driving or packing of the props or loading the truck. He rarely rides in the truck except for a mile or two. He claims that it shakes him up too much. Well, I suppose, he has a lot more than the other guys to shake up. Suddenly, thinking this about him, I smile.

Denny might be earning more money than I, but he has been borrowing from the company fund right from the beginning of the tour. Carl isn't letting on to that fact in his report. I wonder if others in the troupe know about the money Denny owes, or if I am the only one. I conclude that Denny isn't comfortable with my knowing that fact, or about some other private things I learn about him later in the tour. At the time I barely give it more than a second thought.

"We're finished with the report for now," Carl tells me.

It sounds unmistakably like a hint for me to leave. "See you tomorrow." I close the room door and take the elevator down to the third floor and back to the room where Fay and Jessica are busily spreading their wet laundry all over the bathroom and even on the backs of the varnished chairs.

I have begun to cream my face in front of the steamy bathroom mirror when the phone rings.

"It's for you, Ann." Fay covers the mouthpiece. "Whoever it is, called once before."

"But I don't know anyone in Buffalo. Hello?"

"Having yourself a good time?" The voice is pleasant but not familiar to me.

"Who is this?" I ask.

"Oh, you don't know me, not yet, but I saw you down in the lobby." The voice becomes a little less distinct, a little more seductive. "I can give you a good time. Why don't you come down?"

"Who are you?" Right away I know it's a mistake to ask. I should have hung up immediately without saying another word.

"Just a lonely guy who'd like to be your friend. I *could* come up there since I know the number of your room, but I'd rather have you meet me someplace where we can talk alone."

It occurs to me that the guy really is mistaking me for someone else. "You must have the wrong room and the wrong girl."

"Oh, no," You're about five foot three with shoulder length brown hair, a nice figure in that dress with the mandarin collar. Now how about it? My name is Phil and I'll be standing by the foot of the stairs. You're very pretty, you know. You be sure to come...or I don't know what I'll do."

I hang up the phone abruptly and wrap my arms around myself, a hugging gesture to stop the body shivers. I keep hearing the silky voice saying, "...or I don't know what I'll do."

"Something wrong?" Jessica asks with more than her usual interest.

"Some kook on the phone. Someone who claims he saw me in the lobby and wants me to come downstairs to meet him."

"Well, why not?" Jessica smirks. Fay says nothing.

I'm trying to stop shivering, but the shaking still comes across in my quivering voice. "What if he comes up here?" I look to see if there is a chain on the hotel door. No chain. I hurry to the door to make sure it is definitely locked.

"She should go and have a good time, shouldn't she." Jessica seems to be urging Fay to agree.

"Leave me out of this," Fay shrugs. She is sitting cross-legged on the bed putting fat metal curlers on her blond hair. Something about her answer seems unusual. Am I missing something? I quickly glance at Fay hoping to intercept some give-away expression on her face or knowing glances being passed between her and Jessica. None. Fay's expression is its usual bland one. It occurs to me that the phone call could be nothing but a hoax cooked up to tease me. Perhaps the person on the telephone is someone from our own troupe trying to play a trick on me. If it is, I'll surely hear more about it later. Yes, I even hope it *is* someone from the troupe playing a rotten joke, but at least a harmless one.

Is it a joke or isn't it? What if it's a complete stranger on the phone and I don't show up downstairs? Will he come and pound on the door? I sit down on the edge of a chair to wait…half expecting the pounding to begin at any moment. The caller, in spite of the flattery, sounds threatening, especially his last breathy words: "I don't know what I'll do."

Every now and then Fay glances over at me, and so does Jessica. Are they wondering how the phone call has affected me? Perhaps they know something about the phone caller that I don't. What if they are supposed to report my reactions to the person who made the phone call? It seems wiser for me to put on a show of unconcern.

Just suppose the caller really *is* someone from the troupe…not a stranger at all…and I act too upset and nervous; my behavior will be reported by Jessica, and the whole cast will never stop teasing and laughing at me. I resume creaming my face, my trembling hand accidentally slipping cream up my nostrils. Fifteen or twenty minutes pass with no knock on the door, so I take my bath and finish preparing for bed.

How I wish we weren't staying in this hotel a second night! I don't have prescience, but I believe the ominous feeling injected into me by the phone call is close to that. It might be a warning, like the wind before a storm. This I do know: tomorrow morning I'm not going to step outside of this hotel room without being surrounded by two bodies...Jessica's and Fay's.

After I think Fay and Jessica are asleep, I creep out of bed and wedge a chair under the doorknob. On the angled chair I place some of Fay's surplus metal curlers precariously balanced so that they will fall and wake me up if anyone tries to enter the room, at least I hope it will wake me. In bed again, I lie there conjuring up all kinds of scary scenarios in which some stranger accosts me. It could happen in the elevator, an empty one except for the unknown man and myself. Or a wild-eyed stranger might bludgeon me from behind because he mistakes me for someone else. That's how I spend a restless night... mentally inventing horror movies in which I am the victim and always seem to be frozen to the spot unable to make my legs move to escape the danger.

NINE

*D*aylight returns and with it a feeling of uneasiness...of something left unresolved from the night before. What it is will surely seep back into my consciousness after I become fully awake. My restless night leaves me spacey. Once again the window has been closed, keeping the stale smell of bedclothes and damp laundry inside the room. That certainly accounts for some of my disagreeable feelings. Then the "why" returns to me in a swoosh as I see the chair wedged under the doorknob and recall the insinuating voice on the telephone from the evening before. I sit up on the edge of the bed and wait for the weakness in my legs to disappear. Next, I quickly remove the chair with the hair curlers away from the door before Fay and Jessica see them.

I dress slowly this morning trying to adjust my timing so that I can go down to breakfast with Fay and Jessica. Generally I'm first out of bed and go down to breakfast alone. Not this morning. Now, when I'm most anxious for their company, Fay and Jessica seem as slow as cattle ambling down a country lane, and I yearn to prod them with a switch. Fay languidly takes the curlers out of her hair while Jessica stands in the shower letting water splash over her body for a full ten minutes. As I impatiently wait, I do my best to fill my time by repacking my suitcase and filing my nails.

As we three leave the elevator, I'm careful to stay close to Fay and Jessica. I glance here and there wishing my eyes could periscopically proceed ahead of me around the corners in the hallway and behind the posts in the lobby to give me a warning. No one seems to be watching us. Actually, I'm only a couple of inches taller than Fay, but now I visualize myself soaring well above her head. Surely I am a target, as luminous as a blinking radio tower, for some psychotic killer to home-in on. For the first and only time, I wish I were shorter and could better blend in with Fay and Jessica's heights to escape attention.

Back upstairs once again after breakfast and safely behind the locked door of our hotel room on the third floor, I draw a deep breath and almost relax. Since I know that I'll feel less threatened away from the hotel, I look forward to the time when we'll all gather for the two o'clock performance at the school. In the meantime, I jump every time the phone rings, but not one of the calls is for me.

As we wait just inside the glass doors of the lobby for George to bring the car around from the parking lot behind the hotel, Denny sidles up to me. "I hear you had an interesting phone call last night."

"Where did you hear that?" I have prepared myself well ahead of time to behave casually over the incident of the phone call last evening, just in case it had been a prank perpetrated by someone in the troupe.

"Oh, I guess it was Jess who mentioned it. Are you sure you didn't give some poor slob the come hither sign?" Denny barrels this out in a voice easily heard across the small lobby. How embarrassing! He knows perfectly well that I'm not that sort of person. But isn't that exactly why Denny enjoys making the insinuation?

"Maybe it's someone from our troupe playing a joke." I smile suggestively. "It could even be you." I emphasize my words by poking my finger lightly into Denny's chest.

"Huh? Not me," is all Denny says as he hastens out the door and drops heavily into his usual place in the front seat of the car. Naturally, I don't expect Denny to admit to being the mystery phone caller even if he were, nor can I figure out exactly what he gains by pulling such a stunt, unless it's just another ploy to win attention for himself and spice up his own mundane life.

All the way to the school in the car, my mind works on the puzzle. I know already that Denny likes excitement, controversy. Look at the way he keeps repeating the colorful tales about the girl, Lisa, from the tour last year. Now, so far, on this tour things aren't too exciting, Jessica and George's little spats being the exception. Maybe Denny likes to stage a bit of drama to liven things up...or is there a more serious reason? Of course, if I had agreed to meet the man with the slippery sounding voice, Denny could claim that I picked up strange men in hotels just like Lisa, the girl with the questionable reputation, and maybe like her get myself fired. But no, it's hard for me to believe that Denny is that calculating. He's just a jovial loudmouth with an appetite for drama. Besides, what have I ever done to him to earn his dislike?

I feel George's questioning eyes on me all during the afternoon's performance when we are both off stage. Generally, I am one of the few people in the cast he speaks to with reasonable politeness. But now, as we stand side by side packing the props, George remains silent, though out of the corner of my eyes, I still catch him occasionally watching me. Is suspicion now cast like an evil shadow upon my reputation by the incident of the phone call? Has the untouched, pristine female image of me in George's eyes become contaminated, tarnished beyond redemption because Denny has implied that I have invited the anonymous phone call by my wanton, come hither glances? George's reaction is almost funny.

Now I begin to see an advantage to the incident of the mystery phone caller. Perhaps I no longer need to worry about George getting too serious and inviting me to meet his parents. This humorous angle brings relief even in my tense state of constantly looking over my shoulder for a sick-in-the-head attacker.

As soon as we leave Buffalo, I convince myself, I can relax again. Behaving paranoiac is wearing me down and so are the half teasing, half serious innuendos from members of the troupe, except George of course. He continues to remain glum and silent. I am convinced that everyone will forget the incident after we leave town. If anyone does bring up the subject of the phone call again, I decide to shrug and behave as though it's nothing but a huge joke.

✵

No amorous male phoned again nor knocked on the door of the room or accosted me in the elevator. And so, the next morning when we finally did drive away from Buffalo, I put my fears behind me and sighed with relief. Though I couldn't prove it, I suspected that the voice on the telephone was a disguised one...probably someone from the troupe. Denny remained my prime suspect.

I was making it a point to write more often to my parents, probably because it helped to ease my guilty conscience over not going home to help care for my father. Naturally I never mentioned such a thing in my letters as the questionable phone call in Buffalo. Anyhow, now that I was away from that city, the incident had lost its power to upset me.

Dear Mom and Dad,

Received your letter in Albion, N.Y. where we stayed only one night (last Friday) because of the horrible hotel. The whole place was permeated with the odor of beer and crowded with drunken hunters. The performance at the school Saturday morning went pretty well.

We give an evening performance here in Oil City, Penn. tonight at 7:00. Instead of staying in the Arlington Hotel, we are in tourist rooms, which cost only one dollar per person, and are so much cleaner than most hotels. Tomorrow we travel on to Orlean, N.Y.

Oil City is a gray little town wedged partly on the side of a hill and partly in the valley with a river cutting through the city. Streets are narrow.

Any chance of having that black lamb coat you offered me once before, cut down into a short jacket? I certainly need something warm to wear in the car that won't show wrinkles.

Your last letter was very newsy and interesting, Mother. Well, Dad, can you scrawl a few words to me?

Love,
Ann

All during the following days, Denny referred to me as Mrs. Manager. At first I considered it his usual lighthearted banter. But by the end of the week his teasing had achieved results.

After a spaghetti dinner near the Milner Hotel in Akron where we were staying, I asked Carl my usual Friday question. "Want some help with the weekly report to Lu-Travis?"

"No. I'm quite capable of doing it myself," Carl answered firmly.

His sharp tone was unexpected. I didn't know how to take it. I decided, either his pride is hurt by a woman catching his math errors in the report, though it certainly hadn't bothered him previously, or Denny's teasing had finally hit its target.

"Just thought I'd ask," I responded, trying not to let my hurt feelings show. Helping Carl with the weekly report had been a time-filler more than anything else, though at the beginning of the tour there had seemed a possibility of being Carl's particular friend. Later, I found that I wasn't drawn to him in any way except perhaps by an admiration for his good manners and neat dressing. Like the flat-chested Fay, he seemed almost sexless, a reasonably good looking piece of fruit void of vital juices. He really didn't need to worry about my chasing after him if that was his reason for turning down my help with the report.

"So, Mrs. Manager," Denny interrupted, "what are you going to do with your evenings now that your expertise is no longer required?"

I squeezed out a smile and bantered, "Oh, something exciting is bound to turn up. Who knows...maybe even another anonymous phone call." Denny quickly turned away from me before I could read the truth I expected to capture on his face.

Carl never asked me again to help him with the report during the remainder of the tour and I never again offered. Could Denny have mistakenly suspected a growing interest between Carl and myself? Even if it were true, why should Denny mind? At the time I had no inkling of why he wanted to drive a wedge between Carl and me, but I did notice that Carl spent more and more of his free time with Denny when we weren't going places as a group.

During the following week, we gave performances in Dayton, Columbus, Portsmouth, and Toledo, Ohio. It was in Toledo that George persuaded all of us to eat in a Greek restaurant. Denny made several disparaging remarks in a joking manner about George and his Greek heritage, behind George's back of course, and tried to talk everyone into eating someplace else. But George was so pleasant to all of us for a change, and begged us with such childlike eagerness in his black pitted eyes to give his food a "try, just this once," that even Fay and Jessica were reluctant to hurt his feelings. So, in spite of Denny's attempt to dissuade us with his ethnic jokes, we all went with George to the Greek restaurant of his choice.

"This wine tastes funny," Jessica muttered to Fay who answered her with a nod. I also noticed the strange taste but didn't say anything. None of us wanted to openly hurt George's feelings that evening. Anyway, the food turned out to be good. This was my first Greek dinner. See, I told myself, not realizing what a prediction I was about to forecast, this tour is going to be a great learning experience.

That evening was one of the few times when we all made an effort to let George be the center of attention. Of course, the fact that he was the only one who could read the Greek menu had something to do with his sudden popularity. He ordered all the food for us. For the first time he must have felt completely accepted, even important. I had never seen him so jovial and pleasant to everyone. Possibly the wine also had something to do with stimulating his good nature. Certainly, George was the only one who drank more than a sip or two of the wine.

Later, back in the hotel lobby after George had gone up to his room, we discussed the awful wine. It had tasted like resin and cork combined. Denny soon regained his star status by rolling his eyes and relating a humorous mime of George eating rolled grape leaves, exaggerated of course. Even when Denny's criticisms were bitingly unfair, he could make us all laugh.

After Toledo, Ohio, we traveled on to Michigan and gave a performance in Monroe on November the seventeenth. Then we played in Ann Arbor, Detroit, Sarnia in Canada, and returned to the United States to stay in Flint, Michigan.

On our way into Sarnia from the United States, we ran into our second snow of the season. As we crossed the Blue Water Bridge, huge flakes of wet snow plunked and melted against the car's windshield and prompted a serious discussion on who possessed boots and who did not.

"I came prepared," said George, emphasizing the 'I' as though the very act of remembering to pack his boots was a sign of superior intelligence. "They're in the truck, though."

I heard Jessica whisper to Fay, "Wouldn't you know a fuddy-duddy like George would remember his boots."

Denny turned around from the front seat to inform us that he couldn't afford new boots though his old ones leaked, and we already knew that Carl possessed rubbers. Later, I heard Tom explain to Carl that he didn't give a shit if his shoes fell apart from wet snow or not. "I'm not going to spend good money on boots when any day now I'll be called into the army."

"If we could talk old meany George into stopping the car," whispered Jessica, "we might have just enough time to look in one shoe store to price boots before they close. It's nearly five o'clock now."

"I'm not going to ask him to stop," whispered Fay. "He hates taking orders from girls."

"Ann," Jessica begged, "he's more likely to listen to you…you ask."

I whispered back, "I'm out of favor with him right now, so I doubt he'll listen to me either, but I'll try. George?" I called softly. There was no answer from the front seat so I leaned forward to get closer to George's ear and tried again. "George? Could we please stop at a store to buy boots...but only, of course, if you can signal the truck to stop."

George nodded, but didn't directly answer me.

In the back seat we girls exchanged eye signals of success. For once George was cooperating.

George passed some cars and caught up with the truck in the next block. Then he was able to pull right up beside the truck at the following stoplight.

Denny lowered his window and shouted directions to Tom. "Pull the truck over as soon as you can find a parking space."

George finds an empty space in the next block to park in, and Fay, Jessica, and I tumble out of the car and begin a hurried search for a shoe store. The walks are deep with puddles from the new wet snow, which is still coming down heavily but melting instantaneously on the warm cement. I didn't want to ruin my shoes, so I took them off and ran down the sidewalk in just my stockings. Jessica does the same. People turn to stare at us. I know it looks childish, but I can't afford to ruin my only pair of high-heeled shoes. The wet sloppy sidewalks still feel quite warm to my feet. In a block further ahead, we spot a shoe store that displays a variety of boots in the window. Our race against the dizzily falling snow is exhilarating, and all three of us arrive inside the shoe store breathless and laughing. A salesman eyes our wet feet and doesn't share our merriment. He doubtless thinks we are going to put our wet, dirty feet into his new shoes.

"Sorry, we're about to close." The salesman pulls a ring of keys from his pocket as he speaks.

"Oh," I exclaim, "but we need boots right now because it's snowing outside."

"And we can't come back tomorrow," adds Jessica.

"I need some boots that will fit over these shoes." I wave the nearly dry shoes that I've been carrying. The salesman's expression relaxes after discovering that I have no intention of putting my soaking feet into anything in his store.

The boots he shows me have a strip of soft gray fur down each side that hides the laces. How elegant, I think. I know that I shouldn't buy such an expensive pair of boots, but I am as starved for a piece of luxury as I have often been for a meal. Even though I can barely manage to buy myself two meals a day, I want those boots. "I'll take them," I say and add, "I'll wear them."

For the remainder of the winter those boots never fail to make me feel as though I have acquired a piece of the world's precious wealth. They give me a well-dressed feeling wherever I go...warm feet are of secondary importance, though the boots do keep me warm. "False pride," I hear my mother claim again. She doesn't seem to yearn for anything material in either clothes or furniture, but I'm not so altruistic. How can she understand that those particular boots fill a void...lift my spirits after going without nice things almost forever.

Oh, I admit that at home I never suffer from lack, at least not essentials like food and shelter, but there is another vast unfulfilled hunger...a desire for the lace on a slip, a velvet robe or a satiny nightgown instead of the flannel ones my mother stitches on her Singer Sewing Machine. Whenever I become dissatisfied with my lot, my mother never fails to remind me how, when she was growing up on a farm, she possessed just two school dresses and one pair of shoes.

I often countered my mother's conservative attitude with a pout and a protest..."but the girls in my class at school have at least five different dresses...one for each day of the week. I have only three." Then Mother would point out how lucky I was to have even three, and she would add with perfect logic, "You can wear only one dress at a time so it isn't sensible to have so many." Sensible! It was a word showing tattered edges from overuse. "Let's be sensible, Ann, and buy the shoes with laces." Sensible was always the less interesting color... never a leap into a sky blue or a flamboyant lipstick red.

In Sarnia, Canada, we all stay together in yet another rooming house. The furnishings in each room are bare bones except for beds, dressers, and a linoleum floor, cold and shiny as an ice skating rink.

The folks in that house are very frugal with the heat, but the rates are so low that I'm able to afford an evening meal in spite of the expensive boots.

*

In late afternoon after our performance at the grade school in Sarnia, we headed back into the United States. Getting back into the U.S. wasn't quite as simple as leaving. At the U.S. customs, we were pulled out of the line of cars and asked to park next to the customs building, so that an officer could check the contents of the truck and the car. Tom unlocked the doors of the truck, and a uniformed officer looked behind the flats and inside the costume wardrobe and prop box. He didn't riffle through any of the suitcases except Denny's big black one in which Denny had stuffed all his dirty laundry. We laughed as the poor officer attempted to jam the soiled, rolled-up clothes back inside the suitcase again. Finally he had to ask Tom to help him hold the lid down in order to get it closed again. The officer then inspected the trunk of our car and even felt inside the paper mache' jug that I had carefully wrapped in an old piece of cloth.

I suppose it was mainly the scruffy way we all looked that aroused the custom officers' suspicions at the border. The guys in the troupe, except for Carl, were wearing Jeans with holes in the knees, and even Jessica had worn jeans on this particular day. We must have presented a trashy image with our mud-splattered car and noisy old truck on which the lettering still remained unpainted. Nevertheless, after a half-hour's delay, we were released. The officers found nothing to confiscate among our paltry possessions.

In Flint, Michigan, we parked in front of yet another Milner hotel and sat waiting for Denny and Carl to return with a report of the room prices before checking-in at the registration desk. When they returned, Denny announced through the rolled-down window, "We got singles this time but without bath."

"How much?" Fay asked.

"Two dollars each."

"Too much," George grumbled, a look of total disgust on his face. We all enter yet another gloomy lobby, short on light bulbs under shades, once white but now yellow from dust and the heat of the bulbs. I counted fewer derelicts than usual, but it was still early afternoon, too early for the homeless to come in off the street.

"I'll register for all seven of us," Denny offered, "or do you want to make out your own cards?"

"You do it," said Fay,

"Yeah, Denny dear, you have such a flamboyant writing style. Doesn't he have lovely handwriting?" Jessica asked everyone in general.

"Shut up," Denny grinned, "you're making me mess up the registration cards."

"Tom, " I try to gain his attention, "when you open the truck, I'd like to get something from my box."

"Sure, Ann. What do you want, Denny?"

"You can guess what I want, can't you?"

"You mean the infamous black suitcase?"

"Yup, and it's all mine, but I wish it weren't."

I watched the desk clerk's face. What does he think about this loud-mouthed banter? He slapped seven keys down on the counter, but his face remained passive. Maybe, I thought, hotel clerks were trained that way...not to show their feelings. Our troupe of kids, however we appeared in his eyes, weren't run-down alcoholics off the street or magazine sales people, yet I doubted if we stood much higher up the scale in his estimation.

Carl told Tom, "When you open the wardrobe, I'd like my checked jacket,"

"Jessica? Fay?" Tom looked from one to the other.

"Nothing from the wardrobe. Just my two suitcases,"

"Ditto," said Jessica.

"Well, come-on, everybody. I can't park in this unloading zone forever," Tom started for the lobby door.

"Sure," Denny finished the last card, and we each picked up a key before trooping outside again where several curious people stood around waiting to see what would come out of the dirty red truck.

"Oh my God," Denny groaned. "This is exactly what I hate. Unloading all this ugly luggage for everyone on the street to stare at. Seven people and at least ten battered old suitcases."

"Strange," I remarked, not intending to sound critical, "how you get embarrassed at loading and unloading the truck in front of people; nothing else seems to embarrass you."

"What's that supposed to mean?"

I hadn't anticipated the need to go into details, but I tried to clarify what I meant, regretting it immediately afterwards. "Well, lots of times it seems as though you do things or say things in public for the sheer delight of drawing attention to yourself."

"Who says?" Denny challenged snidely.

I smile to soften my words, "I do." I began to wish I hadn't started this whole conversation.

"Such as?"

"Talking loud enough for everyone in a restaurant to hear you, and calling, 'Hi, honey' out the car window at girls walking along the sidewalk and..."

"You're so perfect of course, little Miss Manager!"

One couldn't win with Denny. He could criticize and make fun of us and get away with it, but it didn't work the other way around. And why, I wondered, did he always revert to calling me 'Miss or Mrs. Manager' whenever he became upset with me? It had been several weeks since I had helped Carl with the Friday report to Lu-Travis.

At the rear gate of the truck, Tom pushed my grocery box towards me. After rummaging through it for my blouse, I tied the box up again and signaled to Tom to pack it away once more. Then I picked up my small, scruffy suitcase and headed for the hotel lobby. Behind me I heard Denny grumbling to Carl in a voice loud enough for everyone to hear, "There goes another piece of ass we don't need on this tour."

I pretended not to hear Denny's remark, just hurried on ahead to join Fay and Jessica in the elevator. What if Denny started picking on me as he did on George and sometimes Jessica? I don't have the tough skin of Jessica or the passiveness of Fay to fend off Denny's venom-tipped asides. I'm like those fragile people who live in glass houses who are warned never to throw stones of criticism. My soft feelings are already crushed into shards of broken glass. Remarks like the one I had just overheard from Denny are as hurtful as a knife wound and a great deal harder to heal. Why hadn't I been wise enough to keep my mouth shut about Denny's exhibitionist, loud-mouthed ways?

TEN

*F*lint, Michigan is just one hundred and twenty-five miles from my hometown of Kalamazoo, and with a free weekend coming up, I have enough time to go home and return. But should I? Before unpacking my suitcase, I sit down on the bed facing the single window to think. What if, after reaching home, Mom and Dad ask me to quit the troupe and stay there? On the other hand, I figure by staying away, not going home, I can avoid letting myself be drawn into that situation...or allowing myself to be persuaded by going all soft after seeing their helplessness.

I debate with myself for over an hour while sitting in the narrow cell of that room where disinfectant and stale cigarette smoke vie for predominance. Finally I make a decision. It will be safer to stay completely away from home until the Christmas break. At that time, if Mom and Dad beg me to live at home, I will have gained at least two and a half months of touring experience to add to my resume. Besides, I dupe myself, isn't it fairer? Lu-Travis will then have the whole of Christmas vacation to find someone else to fill my two parts in the play. But "fairer" to whom? My conscience admits that it's certainly not fairer to my folks.

On the two bent wire hangers in the closet, I hang up a skirt and one pair of slacks, wash my face in the sink, and go downstairs to join the others in the coffee shop. On the way back to my room I'll stop at the registration desk to ask for more clothes hangers.

"I wonder where we'll be at Christmas time?" I hear Jessica ask as I slide into the curved booth with the others.

Denny shrugs, "Who knows. Last year it was St. Louis."

"Oh." Jessica sounds disappointed. "I'm hoping for Chicago."

"St. Louis wouldn't be bad," George says, unless..."

"It was bad," Denny interrupts.

"...unless the layover is too long." George has butted back in to finish his sentence.

"It's usually two weeks...same as the school vacations. Last time everyone went home except Lisa and me."

"So why didn't you go home?" Carl asks. "You've got a sister in Brooklyn, haven't you?"

"Yeah, but my best friend lives in St. Louis...well, *was* my best friend."

"Wore out your welcome?" Jessica lets out a snicker.

"What's that suppose to mean?" Denny glares at Jessica but it takes more than a glare to freeze Jessica out of a conversation.

"So what happened in St. Louis that made it so bad?" Tom asks.

"Oh, nothing much except...except a threesome doesn't usually work out very well. That bitch Lisa upstages even when she isn't on stage."

"Oh, I get it! Lisa stole your friend," Jessica says with a smug smile on her face. Denny doesn't answer her. "Come-on, Denny dear, tell us," coaxes Jessica.

"None of your damn business. Anyway, I've got better friends now. "Denny glances in Carl's direction, and I notice a quick return smile of acknowledgement. Carl must know something about Denny that we don't.

The conversation veers onto other subjects, but I'm still trying to make sense out of what Denny has unknowingly revealed. A girl like Lisa who later is fired for picking up men while on tour isn't likely to steal Denny's girlfriend. Oh no, she's likely to steal a man. So Denny's St. Louis friend must have been a man. And if Lisa had become interested in a man friend of Denny's why should he care... unless Denny isn't what most folks term "normal." That could also account for Denny's attempt to place a wedge between Carl and me, though in actuality there has never been anything to break up. All of this is sheer assumption on my part. People don't speak openly about such things as men preferring men. Not in the fifties. Males loving males is considered an aberration. Is that Denny's orientation?

*

Three days later we left Flint and headed south to Indianapolis, well over three hundred miles away. The first snow of the area had mostly melted, leaving wet grass and a few shallow puddles. Along the roadside, the ditches still carried a thin skin of bluish ice, which would disappear when the sun reached it by midmorning.

Once again, Jessica was wrapped up in her stadium blanket, probably snoozing. The blue and red blanket wound across her knees then behind her back, and over her dark hair. George had the front window ventilator wide open, directing a river of crisp morning air into the back seat. I was thankful for my warm boots, and wished my whole body could be tucked into a lovely boot of gray fur. I was freezing.

Fearful of waking up Jessica, I whispered in George's ear, "Could you please shut that ventilator part way?" He gave the vent an abrupt shove, and it moved an inch nearer to being closed. Why push my luck, I decided, and said nothing more. Obviously to George, succumbing to closing the vent was synonymous with losing his manhood.

"Close it *all* the way, George," Jessica's muffled voice came from under the blanket. She was awake after all. Immediately, feeling my nerves spring into action, I regretted having spoken to George about the window. Before Jessica could completely unwind from her blanket, I tried to think up a different approach to the problem caused by the window.

"If Jessica is cold, why don't you let her sit in the front seat for a while? It's only fair to change about every few hundred miles. In fact, we'd all like a turn at sitting in the front. How about it, Denny?"

"I'm not comfortable in the back," Denny claimed and added in his best British imitation, "Lovey, it's just too crowded. I simply cannot sit back there."

"Besides," George spat the words out and at the same time speeded up the car until he nearly rear-ended the truck, "I won't have that Jewess riding...up here with me."

"Stop this damn car!" shouted Jessica. George kept right on driving. From my corner of the back seat, I could see Denny's lips curl into the beginnings of a satisfied smile. He was hoping to enjoy a new drama.

"Stop this car!" Jessica pounded the seat in back of George's head. "You dirty Greek actor!"

"Ho," said Denny, half turning in his seat and winking at us. "I'd hesitate to add the *actor* part."

"This is none of your damn business!" snarled George at Denny.

"Stop this damn car!" Jessica grabbed Fay's paperback book out of her hand and whipped it back and forth across George's head.

The car veered onto the shoulder and then back onto the road again and finally back onto the shoulder where the wheels skidded in the loose gravel before coming to a jolting halt.

"We're still half way out in the road," Denny laughed uneasily, then forgot his own peril in genuine relish of the scene being played out before his eyes. George turned in his seat, raised himself up onto one knee, and grabbed Jessica's woolen scarf in both fists.

"Damn you, George, let go of my scarf! It's imported Scottish wool."

"You're hurting her, George." I tried to keep my voice calm.

Jessica began to scream, "Let go! Wait until old Lu-Travis hears about this...and a few other things too!" Then Jessica's voice becomes plaintive, almost begging. "Make him let go."

As George tightens his grip on her scarf, Jessica tosses out her last card: "Let go or I'll tell...I saw that other Powder Puff go into your room...ow...I saw....I...you're choking mmmmmm-me!"

"My God, George, you'll break her neck!" yelled Denny still smiling, and seemingly thrilled by the very idea.

"Stop it, George. Stop it!" I no longer cared what results my interfering caused as long as George let go of Jessica's scarf. "You really *are* choking her!"

"Dah...mn!" The tears and saliva ran down and soaked into Jessica's woolly blanket.

"Denny!" I shout. "pull George away!"

"He's just impressing her a little. He could be choking her to death and all she'd worry about is her imported Scotch scarf. Hey, keep out of this, Annie!"

To my consternation, Denny begins to sing the song from a Broadway show, "Annie get your gun, get your gun...."

"I'd like to get a gun right now!" I shout, reaching forward to loosen George's grip on the scarf.

"'Oh you can't get a man with a gu-un'," Denny sings. "'Oh, you can't get a man with a gun.'" Then, Denny adds slyly, "but you can get a man by 'doin what comes naturally.' You ought to try it, Annie, before you get any older."

"You like to watch people fight, don't you, Denny. Good free entertainment...anything for theatre...the drama of the moment!" I try again to pull the scarf out of George's grip.

"Well, I never thought you'd turn out to be just as bitchy as Jessica. My God, there isn't a person on this tour with any guts. Now last year when Lisa toured with us..."

"Let go of her, George! For heaven's sake, help me, Fay!"

"It's not my fight," Fay shrugged.

"Look at her.....she can't breath!"

"Fight on girls, fight on," chanted Denny. Then his glance caught the view out the rear window of the car. "There's a car coming. They might see what's going on. Move this thing further off the road... before we all get killed. I said *move* this car. Damn you, George!" Denny jerked George's hands away from the scarf, and Jessica plopped heavily back onto the seat.

George seemed dazed. Mistakenly he backed the car up, then finally shifted forward...accelerating in nervous spurts. Ahead of us somewhere, the truck had disappeared.

I watched George drive in the same erratic fashion, the same nervous rhythm, as his jerky speech pattern. Every few minutes his head dropped forward. Thrusting his hand against the back of his skinny neck, he snapped his head back up again with a quick motion and at the same time pressed down on the accelerator...nervously pressed and released, pressed and released.

Jessica's body was once again wedged between Fay and me on the seat, a bulky form swathed in a plaid blanket and a woolen scarf. Both now hung limply around her neck, soaked with saliva.

ELEVEN

*J*essica's body jolts along on the seat to the rhythm of the moving car for several miles before she manages with my help to rewrap the blanket around her properly. Then I busy myself by replacing the ashtray, which has fallen during the struggle, back into the indented slot in the back of the upholstered front seat.

I can hear Jessica gulping back her sobs and wonder how I can give her some kind of comfort or reassurance. All I can do is tuck the blanket around her more tightly, a motherly, useless fussing. I have never felt this protective of Jessica before. She always seems so able to care for herself, aggressively so.

"Whose turn is it to clean out the floor of the car? It's filthy," mumbles Fay. We are both looking for trivialities to focus on; anything to avoid facing up to what has nearly taken place.

My voice comes out squeezed sounding, as though I've been the one nearly choked by a scarf. "It's Denny's turn…" I stop speaking because I'm literally out of breath. "…he'll never do it." Fay nods her agreement.

My hands seem unable to remain still after the recent incident; they keep moving. I pick and pick at the trash on the car floor. Nerves, I suppose. I wish my mind was like one of those magic slates where a flap is lifted and the writing disappears. I want to lift away the picture of George tightening Jessica's scarf, her pony-like eyes getting bigger and bigger in disbelief…Denny's eager enjoyment, as though his body is feeding on the incident…actually sucking sustenance out of someone else.

Dear Lord, I think, can this sort of thing really happen? Newspaper accounts of people being choked and all types of assaults have always been sheer fiction to me. They occur someplace else as though they are nothing but incidents written on a page in a crime novel. They leave me untouched when I put the book down or turn off the radio. I'm horrified to have just witnessed such meanness... an actual attempt to choke Jessica in front of everyone. George has simply flipped out of control...gone berserk.

"She provokes me," I hear George's angry aside to Denny. Already he's found an excuse for himself...for his mean behavior. "Naturally, I would have stopped before any real damage was done." Denny doesn't answer, just grunts. I shut my eyes and wish myself back on the hilltop in Chatham again where I can look down into that quiet valley that is like a painting of Frank Church's, a picture free of everything loud and ugly. Typically, I'm trying to blank out grating reality...do the same old escape act of not looking at the dead bird on the lawn, the bloody chicken run down by a car, or watching the movie sequence showing wounded and dead soldiers...until that episode blends into a happier scene. I can't bear the violence; it's too upsetting. I always assume that I will never have to face such scenes in reality.

✷

After a few miles with no one to talk to, Denny turns around in the front seat. "Are you OK, Jessie old kid? Come on, where are the cards? I'll tell you your fortune."

Neither Jessica nor Fay nor I answer.

"So *be* a bunch of dull people," Denny huffs in a playful mood.

"Denny, is my book up there in the front seat somewhere?" Fay asks.

"Haven't you finished that book yet? " Denny gropes around on the seat. "Here it is," Denny holds the book up for Fay to see, "but it's in a semi-coma...from a very recent head bashing from which it will never recover. In fact, it has lost its cover."

"Pass it back, will you? I want to finish reading it...in peace."

"You can read it in pieces, at least," Denny answers. Fay giggles appreciatively at his pun as he hands over the torn book.

Even though Jessica's head is partially wrapped in the blanket, I can hear her sniffling; I grope in my purse, feeling around for the paper napkin I thought I'd taken from the counter at breakfast...or was that yesterday morning? All mornings are beginning to seem the same. Anyway, I couldn't find it. "Does anyone have a paper hanky?" I ask. Fay shakes her head and goes back to her reading.

"Denny? Have you got a...." My voice is drowned out by his burst into song. "*Though April showers may come your way, they bring the flowers that bloom in...*"

"What show was that from," Fay asks Denny.

"Oh, something Bing Crosby was in, I think," and Denny continues the song for his make-believe audience. "*...May, so if it's raining, have no regrets because it isn't...*"

"Denny?" I try to get his attention once more.

"Shut-up," he answers pleasantly. "You're interrupting my solo, *...upon the hills, you soon will see violets...*"

I give up. At least his singing covers some of Jessica's sniffles, and the wool scarf she holds to her runny nose muffles the rest of her noises.

We stop for lunch at a diner somewhere on the outskirts of Fort Wayne, and I expect Jessica to bolt—it's what I would have done—but maybe she doesn't have enough money to leave and return home. Maybe she has to wait until we reach the hotel in Indianapolis where she can phone her mother for help. Also, her suitcase is in the truck which is locked. Tom holds the key.

In the diner, Jessica and Fay sit in a separate booth from the rest of us and I soon wish I'd done the same.

During lunch Denny made a great dramatic production out of the fight between George and Jessica and with minimal exaggeration for once. The fight had been sensational enough without the frills he usually added. As Denny repeats each tightening of the wool scarf, George sits there at the table smiling like a celebrity, as though he's done us all a huge favor by putting Jessica in her place.

86

"She's been asking for it all along," George claims.

"Carl?" Denny asked, "shouldn't you alert Lu-Travis to find someone to fill Jessica's part in the play? She might leave today, tomorrow...who knows when she'll just take off."

"I can't very well phone Travis until it actually happens."

Denny's jovial voice has a conniving tone to it. "You could make up something about Jessica that will convince old Travis to fire her, and then she'll be forced to find a replacement."

"And good riddance!" The words burst out of George's mouth. Both he and Denny have the same fevered glint of excitement in their eyes, but George's is part of his nervousness and a desire to be exonerated. He moves restlessly in his seat, and every now and then pulls at the waistband of his trousers. Denny merely wants to witness more fireworks...more screaming and yelling...high drama to satiate his endless need for entertainment.

"We'll decide what to do after we get to Indianapolis," Carl says by way of placating Denny.

In the ladies restroom before leaving the diner, I report to Jessica and Fay what Denny and George have said during lunch, though I soften everything a bit by leaving out some of the abusive expressions used against Jessica. I see no reason to hurt her any more than she has been hurt already; I needn't have worried. Jessica has great bounce-back. She seems unscathed. Already she has regained her over-confident, brassy manner, and her own brand of insulting language remains unchanged.

"Why that pervert!" she explodes. "Someone has got to get rid of him."

"Are you going to leave the troupe?" I ask, wishing Jessica would finish applying lipstick to her full mouth in front of the only sink and mirror in the restroom so I can wash my hands. The guys hate to be kept waiting.

"Are you kidding?" exclaims Jessica. "Just wait until I get finished telling Travis what George tried to do."

My sympathy for Jessica is dwindling, my attitude rapidly reverting to my former annoyance.

"What will you do?" Fay asks.

"As soon as we reach the hotel in Indianapolis, I'm going to telephone Travis. Why would she want a strangler *and* a pervert in her troupe?"

"I really don't think George is a pervert, not the kind you mean,"

"Whose side are you on?" Jessica snaps.

"But it's your word against George's," Fay reminds her.

"Why shouldn't she believe me?"

Fay shrugs languidly, but what she says makes a lot of sense. "Money speaks with Travis. She might not want to cancel any of the performances while she looks for someone to fill George's part."

When we file out of the restroom and return to the car, the guys are already there waiting. George is nervously tapping the steering wheel.

"What took you so long?" Denny booms out in his 'reach the mezzanine' voice.

"Keep your shirt on," Jessica retorts.

Indianapolis was bare of snow. There was nothing to soften the cold concrete of the streets, and the sun, cut off by the tall buildings, was unable to penetrate. When I stepped out of the car, the wind whipped paper and dirt around my legs in a vortex. The hotel listed on our itinerary was once again a Milner Hotel, just another one in a long chain of cheaply maintained places catering to indigent males and the poorly paid like us. The lobby presented a dearth of furniture, as if the management had sold off the most comfortable pieces, leaving only the hard, uncushioned ones. Bare wooden chairs were certainly the easiest to keep free of city soot and male spit. I imagined a slow moving robot full of powerful liquid germ killer dousing the lobby, the halls, and the vacant rooms. My nose had already detected it. The whole place smelled of disinfectant worse than I remembered the ladies room in Grand Central Train Station in New York City.

It was obvious to all of us that the hotel was located on the edge of the downtown's *going seedy* section. Even so, the price was two dollars per person and we had to share rooms in order to spare enough money to eat. To make up for the extra expense, we would all have to find cheaper lodging in the next town. Even so, some of us would go hungry before reaching St. Louis where our next pay envelope had been promised.

We girls collected the key to our room and started towards the elevator. Suddenly Jessica stopped. "I'm going to phone Travis right this minute. Will you wait for me?" We nodded, and she headed for the phone booth just across the lobby. Fay and I stood waiting near the elevator, our four suitcases stacked beside us.

Denny must have spotted Jessica entering the phone booth because he paused beside us and said slyly to Fay, "Calling her mama for help, huh?"

"I don't know," Fay answered vaguely.

Denny turned to me, "And I suppose you're not talking either?"

"Depends. What do you want to talk about?"

"Hurry up," George called to Denny as he held open the wrought iron gate of the elevator.

I wasn't too keen about riding that Victorian elevator contraption. It appeared so flimsy. As I watched, the old cage-type elevator rose upwards in a series of jerky movements until it passed from sight through the ceiling to the next floor.

TWELVE

*J*essica came slowly out of the phone booth, her disappointment obvious. "Well?" Fay and I spoke in unison.

"Travis is out of town for a week. Her secretary said I was to write the whole incident down in a letter." Jessica almost snorted when she added, "It'll take weeks to get George fired that way, and besides, I'm a lousy letter writer."

"We can help you write it," I offered.

Jessica shook her head, setting her dangling earrings clicking.

"Did you call your mother, too?"

"She's not home either. I'll try tonight. Where do you think we'll be next week after St. Louis?"

"Milwaukee, I think. Carl hasn't handed out next week's itinerary yet, so that's not definite. Why?" I asked.

"Well, just suppose it's no further away from Chicago than we are right now. That's where I want to go after I leave….Chicago. I could wait until we reach Milwaukee, take off for Chicago, and not come back. Anyway, it's going to take at least another day or two to get money from home and by then who knows where we'll be? Not here, right?"

"But how will you avoid George in the meantime?" I asked. How would the two combatants manage to keep from killing each other for even one more day? But I didn't express the latter part of my thinking out loud.

"George is going to gloat over forcing you to leave." Fay's remark brought about a complete change of expression on Jessica's face.

"That sorehead! Maybe I won't leave after all, but I *will* report him."

Finally, the bird-cage type elevator returned, and we entered the shaky structure. We rose in jerks and bounces to the fourth floor.

✻

What a quick switch in Jessica's plans, I think to myself. But isn't that typical behavior of Jessica with her child-like disposition? Like George and Denny, too. They all burst into dramatic flames one minute and douse them in the next. No fire hose needed. It leaves my head spinning like one of those animated cartoon figures. Nothing seems predictable. One can't even count on quarrels running true to form. Not that I want George and Jessica to stay angry at each other, but the mercurial changes leave me feeling insecure, at risk. Again, I remember the movies in which the wrong guy often gets the fist in the barroom brawl. For the moment I concentrate on grabbing for a wire hanger in the closet before Jessica or Fay can confiscate all of them.

In my present state of uneasiness some of my past friends, even those I have considered rather dull, begin to look awfully good to me. They are predictable, stalwart, reliable characters. It's exactly this reaching out to, someone dependable as a life preserver, that prompts me to write a former friend, Michael, even before the recent scene between George and Jessica. Mike works in a suburb of Indianapolis or did the last time I had heard from him. My note to him mailed in Flint, Michigan, was to let him know when I'd be passing through Indianapolis.

How refreshing it will be, I think, to associate with a mature person again, to have someone outside the troupe to converse with, someone normal, for that's how I think of Mike in comparison to George and Denny. Is Mike as nice as I remember him, or have I endowed him with fine qualities supplied by my imagination and the passage of time? Time does have a way of putting a softer edge on experiences. Time smoothes over weaknesses, blurs disagreements of which Mike and I have chocked up a few.

Ever since posting the letter and traveling to Indianapolis, my anticipation over seeing Mike once again has been building. I even write and rewrite the scene of our reuniting in my mind. Mike will be so delighted to see me that he will fling his arms around me and tell me how much he misses me. Naturally, I envision this happening right in front of all six members of the troupe so that they can see that I have friends in the male department. Denny's recent hint about my being an old maid has had its effect on me—this I admit—otherwise I would feel less inclined for Mike to make a public display of our reuniting.

After unpacking, I phone the reception clerk. "Are you quite sure there's no message for me?" He answers, "No."

"And no phone calls either?" Again he asks my name.

"Ann B. Gulbrith." Once more I hear him flipping through his small pile of messages.

"No, nothing. Sorry, Miss." The splendid scene of my "flying into Mike's arms" will have to be rewritten; maybe even written out of the script in my head. I try not to show my disappointment in front of Fay and Jessica, but I feel very let down...jilted. If I had kept quiet about my supposed reunion, there would be less to feel embarrassed over.

When the desk clerk calls our room a half hour later and asks for me, I am hopeful that the message is from Michael to explain why he can't meet me, but the desk clerk says, "There's a package for you, Miss, and we don't deliver to the rooms."

Flowers from Mike, I imagine; surely an apology for not being able to meet me. Flowers will prove to Fay, Jessica, and Denny that I really do have an old boyfriend here...that I haven't just made the whole thing up. I feel that I need to impress them for some juvenile reason. I hurry into the slow, open-cage elevator and descend in a series of bumps and jerks to the lobby floor. The clerk hands me a flat box that is far too wide for flowers.

"Oh, thanks." Because of my disappointment, I must sound to the clerk as though he has handed me a box of wasps.

On the way back upstairs, I check the address on the box. It's my home address. The box has been smashed so I peek in one of the broken corners and discover the black, curly lamb coat that Mother has previously mentioned. The gift helps to assuage some, but not all, of my hurt feelings over being stood up by Michael. Why couldn't he at least have left me a message? Perhaps he no longer works in Indianapolis? There is certainly that possibility. I cling to that idea. Still, my pride takes a fall.

Fay and Jessica look at the black, curly lamb coat with interest when I open the box to show them.

"A bit somber for a young person," Jessica remarks.

Maybe she's envious, I decide, not giving much thought to the underlying meaning of the remark. Now I will have to find someone, somewhere, to cut the coat off to the proper length for a jacket; at last, I'll have something warm to wear. At the time, even though it is winter, I am wearing my gray spring coat with a sweater underneath and still can't keep warm.

Except for attending one movie with the guys, we girls stayed in our sun-less room, which faced a brick well. It doesn't seem safe to walk the streets alone here in this section of Indianapolis, and the lobby was often full of old men and drunks who ambled in off the street and were usually booted out again.

Not a single phone call comes from Mike, so I am more than anxious to move on out of town and put my disappointment behind. Everyone seems glad to get away from the monochrome grays of the city, except Denny. He appears to thrive on the noise of traffic and sirens. He gains a certain energy from the pace of the city, which is his natural milieu. It also gives him a chance to make up jolly new jokes about old men and fallen woman. It's George who bares the brunt of Denny's more recent teasing.

"George, didn't I see you enter the lobby the other night with a woman?" A slow smile passes George's long face as a result of Denny's teasing. George doesn't mind folks thinking he's had a woman in his hotel room. It's Jessica's insult, implying that he has had a man in his room that hurt his pride.

"You must be pretty hard up," Denny hasn't finished with George, "she was at least eighty years old, wasn't she?" George clamps his jaw down tightly, cutting his recent smile to shreds. The other three guys join in laughter.

After Jessica's traumatic scene with George, all the guys expect her to turn up missing, either to run for home and Mama or head for Chicago. Ever since the tour has begun, she has talked of wanting to see the Windy City. Fay and I both know she is waiting for some money to arrive from her mother before she makes any final decision, but even we didn't know exactly what she meant to do or when.

Jessica certainly has "staying power." Would I have had the guts to continue even one more day after someone tried to throttle me?

At breakfast before Jessica and Fay came down to the coffee shop, I heard George say, "If Jessica reports me to Travis, I'll just say she started the whole thing."

"Yeah?" Denny of course knows otherwise.

"You saw her hit me with that book."

"Sure, but that was after your racial slur about Jews. Nothing's going to help you keep this job unless we all stick together and claim that Jess is lying about the choking."

George looked at Tom, then at Carl and back again to Denny, hoping to read on their faces whether they were ready to lie for him or not. He, like all of the guys, had forgotten about my presence. I was in the enemy camp and could report to Jessica exactly what I had overheard.

"Well?" George didn't get an answer.

"Maybe Jessica won't report the choking." Tom offered hope to George, though I don't believe he personally cared one way or another. "Jessica is more interested in getting to Chicago than going home, so maybe she'll stick with us a little longer until we get closer to the Windy City."

"Of course," interjected Denny with a glint of pleasure in his voice, "Jessica may try a little revenge on the way."

Jessica did keep everyone guessing, especially Carl. He couldn't report to Travis that she needed to hire someone new until Jessica actually left...and not even Fay or I knew when that might be. Perhaps Jessica wanted everyone to think she was staying, then, when we traveled to Milwaukee, she would suddenly disappear without notice and without a replacement. Until Jessica made her move, we were all left hanging in suspension with no idea when the stool might be kicked out from under our feet.

There was another mystery as well as the one concerning Jessica. Why hadn't Carl reported the whole choking incident to Lu-Travis immediately after it occurred? Surely it was part of his duty as manager to do so. Why hadn't he?

At breakfast that same morning, George made a remark that was puzzling, at least it was an enigma to me. His words, usually tumbling out sharply and packed with blame against one or another of us, seemed carefully chosen this time and they were spoken in a firm, concise manner. "There are probably some other things going on in this tour that Travis might like to know about...besides my fight with Jessica."

When did George gain this new insight? What did George know that made him behave with such confidence? I noticed how Denny and Carl exchanged quick glances while Tom simply went on gulping down his eggs and bacon. Could George's words be construed as a disguised threat of some kind...a threat that would guarantee that Carl and Denny would not report his assault on Jessica? Nothing remained a secret for long on this tour, so eventually I would discover everything. George's superior knowledge about *other things going on*, sounded very much like a threat.

THIRTEEN

We make an overnight stop in Alton, Illinois, after an afternoon performance at the grade school there. The landlady in the rooming house where we girls rented a room seemed pleased to make an extra three dollars by cutting off the black lamb coat and hemming it as well. She did it all in one evening.

Now I assume that I will lend a touch of quality to the troupe when we register at hotels and arrive at schools for performances. The awful truth becomes apparent to me much later in the tour: young girls do not wear funerary black lamb...only ladies over forty do.

Our hotel in St. Louis appears almost luxurious to us after the Milner in Indianapolis. Even so, it's rated as a third-class hotel. We aren't accustomed to vast lobbies with many squishy-soft, though old, couches and chairs. The lobby is also full of well-dressed people milling about, and there is even the novelty of seeing a courtesy desk for theatre tickets.

I sniff in surprise as we enter our hotel room. "No antiseptic smell," I announce.

"Yeah," Jessica cracks, "but the carpet has been smoking stogies for fifty years."

The hotel, though several miles from the downtown area, is on a main thoroughfare where we can ride a trolley-bus downtown for a nickel. Just a block away is a park with tall trees surrounded by older homes. With nothing better to do, I spend a lot of my time there wading through the deep snow, white in the morning but speckled with soot by late afternoon. I pretend that I live in one of the grand old Victorian homes, especially the one with two towers and a frilly white porch. The length of my walks is usually measured by the strength of the wind, which pushes the cold straight through me like drifting snow through the slats of a snow fence. Even my new boots fail to save my toes from numbness on the cold windy days in St. Louis.

The women's group that sponsors our play in the St. Louis public school, presents Carl with two free tickets to a symphony orchestra performance and several free passes to one of those old fashioned melodramas performed on a Mississippi River boat. Carl and Fay attend the concert. Jessica, Tom, and I ride the trolley bus one evening towards the Mississippi River and then walk downhill through dark, deserted streets to the boat.

"It looks like it's going to sink," I warn. We stop where the gangplank touches the wharf. The boat itself lists in the direction of the shore and appears to be held up in the black slippery water by nothing except the hawsers at the bow, mid-ship, and stern...a tipsy boat held up by suspenders. Testing the solidity of the boat's gangplank for rotten boards, we cautiously make our way aboard and on into the main cabin where the performance is to take place. The play is a simple trite thing, not something that I'd ever spend good money to attend; however, it's free, and I enjoy it in spite of its shallow plot.

"What are they doing that for?" Jessica whispers in my ear as we watch the first act.

"I don't know. Just listen and maybe you'll find out," I whisper back.

"Shhh." Tom moves a seat further away from us and pretends he isn't associated with Jessica or me. There are plenty of empty seats.

"Is he supposed to be the villain?" Jessica whispers again.

"Yes, that's why he has that funny mustache." I am beginning to get upset at Jessica's interruptions.

✳

In spite of her quarrel with George, Jessica had retained her old aggressive behavior…always asking the questions that seemed to have obvious answers or the ones most likely to annoy people. She seldom sat quietly except when asleep in the car. Her prize possession, the guitar, had been relegated to the truck long ago because she had grown tired of it just after her first two weeks on the road. At least we no longer had to bother loading and unloading it each time we wanted to get something from the trunk of the car.

Occasionally, I saw George as I passed through the lobby of the hotel in St. Louis, but because it was a large lobby, I was always able to avoid a head-on meeting with him. Then today, our last day in St. Louis, he cornered me as I waited for the elevator. As he came nearer, I shivered, wondering what it was about him that caused such a reaction. Was it some inner, wiser sense? Could it be a warning to be careful? Yet, right then, as I looked into George's face and heard his pathetic attempt to gain a companion in his loneliness, I felt sorry for him. It was impossible to believe that he might be dangerous in any way. Even so, when he drew too close to me, I took a step backwards. Above his full mouth of white teeth, his brown-black eyes pleaded along with his words: "I thought maybe you and I could do something or go somewhere together."

"Sorry, George," though I really wasn't sorry at all, just relieved that I had a legitimate excuse to avoid him, "I'm going downtown with Jessica and Fay. See you later when we load up the truck." I stepped quickly into the elevator, which had at long last opened its doors.

The snow in Milwaukee was deeper than in St. Louis, cleaner too. I spent hours walking through Macy's department store looking at the lovely things on display that I couldn't afford to buy. Christmas was just three weeks away, and the store was unusually full of tempting luxuries: diamond earrings, purses of aromatic leather that I bent down to sniff, and filmy blouses meant to be worn with long velvet skirts to festive holiday parties…parties I wouldn't be attending. I felt so deprived…one of the have-nots allowed to see and touch, but not permitted to possess. Maybe the next Christmas would be different, I told myself. But how was I to afford presents for my folks this Christmas? Of course the solution would have to be the usual one: skipping a meal here and there. I bought a pair of small gold earrings for my mother, conservative looking and inexpensive. I also bought for one dollar a pair of green glass earrings that I discovered in a tangle of other junk on sale. They were for myself.

One afternoon I watched a movie, St Joan, starring Ingrid Bergman. I knew ahead of time that the theatre manager would give me professional courtesy because he'd already given it to Carl and Denny the previous evening; otherwise, I would have been too embarrassed to ask. It would have been like asking for a handout even though no money exchanged hands. I remembered, when I was young, the free meals my mother handed out to men at our back door when times were hard. At least those men did some yard work to pay for their handout. They had kept some of their pride intact, but my pride told me never to admit how close I was to being broke. There was something terribly embarrassing in admitting that I didn't have enough money for a movie...a matinee at that. Matinees were always cheaper.

As soon as we had finished our afternoon performance in Milwaukee, Jessica and Fay went off to Chicago on the train to spend one night and part of another day. All of us, those who remained, speculated on whether Fay would come back alone without Jessica.

There we sat: Denny, Tom, George, and myself around a table in the coffee shop of the hotel where we were currently staying. We had so much extra time on our hands and nothing to do—or rather nothing that we could afford to do—because most of us were broke, except for Carl perhaps. So we sat like squatters and managed to make our coffee last for two hours. The waitress had finally stopped refilling our cups.

"The little bitch will never come back," smirked Denny, referring to Jessica. I noticed George was trying to keep his mouth from curling up into a satisfied grin. If Jessica ran off, it proved something to him

I suppose. He probably thought it made him the "victor" in their squabbles by default.

"Whom are you talking about," Carl asked as he joined us at the table.

"Who else but Jessica. I for one don't care if she does stay in Chicago. Did she say anything to anyone else about leaving the troupe?" Denny looked around at each one of us in turn and finally at Carl.

"Nothing," Tom said. I shook my head as George did also. Of course, she wouldn't have told George.

"Maybe you'd better call Travis and alert her to round up someone else for Jessica's part...just in case." By lowering his eyes, Denny failed to cover his delight at the prospect of an enormous upheaval. After gaining control, he showed us an expression full of deep concern for the well being of the Princess Company.

What a faker, I thought.

"Let's wait and see," said Carl. "There are only five or six more days until we break for the Christmas vacation. Chances are Jessica will wait until then to leave so that she can collect her pay check."

"The sooner she goes the better for all of us." That was Denny's advice.

"Why?" Tom shrugged.

"Well, *you* don't have to ride with her," George snapped back. "She's always complaining about something."

"You're no barrel of fun, either," countered Denny.

George responded with a dour expression on his face. "She's spoiled rotten. Where do you think...she got the money...to go off to Chicago?"

When George got emotional, he began to revert to what I called his "stop and go" manner of speaking.

"Oh, yeah, her mama has plenty." Denny assured us and added, "You saw how her mother delivered her to that first performance... brand new car and fashionable clothes."

"And speaking of clothes..." I don't complete the sentence. Instead, I aimed a nasty look at George who had just set his cup down with such a hard smack on the table that it slopped coffee on my skirt.

"I'm sorry," George said. He sounded contrite, as though he really was sorry. "Will it come out?"

"I doubt it." I dabbed away at the spot with my napkin after first dipping it into my water glass. "It's coffee mixed with cream so it probably won't come out." I felt exasperated. "Now if I had lots of clothes it wouldn't matter so much..." I left the sentence dangling, but there was no doubt about my disgust.

"Don't make such a big deal out of it," Denny said. There was an edge to his voice.

"George didn't mean to spill on you," added Tom.

Utterly amazed at the guys speaking up on George's behalf, I softened my tone of voice. "Of course not." What a quick switch, I thought. One minute the guys are jumping all over George, and the next they're lined up on his side. The incident was trivial, yet it made me stop and reconsider: Would the men always take a side against the women in the troupe? I now realized all too clearly that I was not immune to the nasty treatment they had dished out to Jessica. Once the guys decided to stick together against someone, it would be prudent to take cover. I glanced at Carl to see if his reaction to the incident had been the same as the other guys. He, out of all the men, had remained silent and still remained silent; apparently his mind was on something more serious.

"If Jessica doesn't come back, what will we do with her guitar and her extra suitcase?" Tom wondered.

"Smaaaassshhhh the guitar." George drew out the word "smash" to sound like the air brakes on a bus.

"Right-o," agreed Denny. "Or we could tell Lu-Travis that it got accidentally left in some town or other." He bellowed out a rousing laugh, "ho, ho, ho," exactly the same words he used as the benevolent king in the play.

"Not me," interrupted Tom. "I'd sell it and make some money."

"Any bets on Jessica coming back?"

"You're on! Fifty cents says she doesn't return." Tom held out his hand to shake Denny's.

"Loan me fifty cents, Carl." Denny turned and stretched out his other hand. I watched Carl dig in his pocket and plunk two quarters into Denny's beckoning hand. Carl didn't think twice over giving Denny his money.

George smirked, "Are you broke again?"

"I'm no damn pinch-penny like you." Denny's face displayed a smile, but his voice came out in a sneer.

"What do you spend it on?" Tom asked. "Mine mostly goes for paperback books."

"Food, my dear man, just food."

Tom shook his head in disbelief. As we sat there in the coffee shop a bit longer, Denny invented more wild jokes about Jessica. George who was usually so grim faced, nearly laughed himself off his chair in appreciation. Hearing adverse comments about Jessica, fed his ego. But when George wasn't around, Denny made just as many nasty innuendoes about George.

Denny often claimed that George wasn't able to perform in a men's room much less on a stage, and while he usually made his criticisms sound like jolly clean fun, they always left a residue, a dirty scum that I couldn't forget. It was my theory that Denny needed our laughs, our responses to his lewd, remarks as nourishment for his ego, just as he needed food for his ballooning body.

I already knew what Denny would say about me when I was not around to hear him. Just a couple of weeks into the tour, I accidentally overheard him telling Carl that I was too fussy about packing the car trunk and too fussy about keeping the car clean inside. I could easily slough off such criticisms until he added, "exactly like an old maid."

Denny's remark jarred. I'd known a girl who really was a typical example, if there was such a thing as *typical*. She was barely thirty but dressed like forty. She lived with her mother and was very neat and sedate…and fearful. My friend Teddy and I finally talked her into going canoeing with us. We tipped the canoe sideways in two feet of water to scare her. She screamed and carried on; we thought it was hilarious. Poor girl. I hoped there was no similarity between her and me. At least I didn't think it was my clothes that brought on such a label as "old maid," unless it was the black lamb jacket. But no, Denny's criticism came before my mother sent the funeral-looking coat to me.

Upon thinking it over, I decided that I wouldn't feel too badly if Jessica did leave the troupe as long as a substitute could be found. All along I'd wished we had someone on tour who was more thoughtful about taking up half of the back seat of the car with her butt and most of the chairs in the hotel rooms with her wet laundry. Wouldn't it be nice for me to have a companion in our group? One who could carry on an intelligent conversation about something besides chasing men? Someone who wouldn't constantly ask questions like: Where are we now? When do we get there? Why do we have to rehearse? If one wasted the saliva to answer Jessica's questions, she'd turn right around and ask again, "Why?" Talking to Jessica was like talking to a six-year-old child. Once George had said, "Who does she think she is...always keeping us on edge with her questions?"

✻

As I stand on the train platform that evening with the others in the troupe waiting for the girls to return from Chicago, I'm aware of Carl's prominent forehead, its usual paleness flooded by a greenish glow from the lights high above the platform; the remainder of his face is nothing but guess work, just shadows. His gloved hands are in the pockets of his belted coat, and the briefcase, which he totes everywhere, is under his left armpit. Carl doesn't really need to carry that briefcase everywhere like a woman's purse. Perhaps though, it's a status symbol, like announcing: I am *The Manager*, or an aid to his image of himself, like his trench coat, which makes him appear broad shouldered when underneath there is only a narrow, frail-chested body. Carrying that briefcase around all the time must be a burden...

like playing a character part with no beginning and no end. Now I notice that Carl is shivering from cold just as I am.

"If Jessica doesn't return," I hear Carl tell the guys standing on the snowy platform next to me, "Travis might cancel the whole tour. Ever think about that?"

"Oh God," groans Denny as he wipes his hand across his forehead, a frequent gesture, "That will put me right back where I started… behind the sandwich counter at Walgreens."

"It's the army for me anyway…doesn't matter if it's now or later," Tom says.

George just shrugs.

No one asks me how I feel about it. Tonight I am ignored, invisible. Anyway, I'm shivering badly, so I go inside the station to get warm. Once inside, I can barely make out the forms of the others through the dirty, steamed-up windows. Inside the body-packed station, the slush is almost as deep as out on the platform.

I still go on shaking. Maybe it's from the thought of the tour being cancelled more than the cold weather. What if it really happens? I'll have to go back home. This time there will be no excuse to stay away and no money to go back to New York City. I repeat to myself: Absolutely no excuse…not with my father still recovering from a stroke.

It takes very little imagination to see myself working the rest of the year, then the next, and the next, in some small dress shop or filing bills in a local dairy office. College will be out of the question until I save up some money. Oh yes, I find myself deciding, it certainly will be much better for everyone, especially me, if Jessica comes back on the train with Fay from Chicago. I glance again at the station clock above the door. If last night's new, deeper snow hasn't drifted across the tracks to delay the train, it should be pulling up to the station in just a few minutes.

FOURTEEN

The loudspeaker inside the train station announces the commuter train from Chicago coming in on track two, so I push my way through the scarred double doors along with dozens of others and step from the cold waiting room to the colder platform. At first, all I can see down the dark track is a round light growing larger. Then I can make out the black outlines of two engines seemingly floating above steam. There's a fantasy-world quality to the sight, like prehistoric animals crawling out of the darkness of a cave. Now, as they grow closer, I can see the gigantic head engine pushes a snowplow. It over-reaches the station but gradually slows. The car wheels begin to screech and complain, and like real live animals the cars appear to shake off roof-loads of heavy snow. This is followed by two reverse jolts. A release of steam from under the passenger cars clouds the platform for a few minutes. Finally it clears.

I discover that I have been standing there watching the train as if metamorphosed into a statue, not even breathing, feet frozen to the spot. I finally take a deep breath and blow it out. The warm air hits the cold and floats outward like the steam still breathing from under the train. The conductor finally opens the door of the car near me and flips up the heavy metal floor section to reveal the steps. The passengers begin to flow down onto the platform one at a time. The conductor keeps repeating, "Watch your step—watch your step—watch..."

Ten or fifteen people get off the train, then I spot Fay. Right behind her is Jessica waving and smiling and greeting us as though we were her long lost family with never a mean word exchanged between any of us.

Denny ambles over and gives Fay a hug and then kisses Jessica on one cheek. What a hypocrite, I think. George carries Fay's suitcase, a first for him, but no one offers to carry Jessica's. I step forward and join the group with a smile on my face, a genuine one. The tour will go on...at least for the time being.

☆

On December eleventh, we performed in the small town of Waterloo, Iowa, and then remained there for another three-day layover. The guys stayed at the YMCA so they at least had the gym and the pool to occupy their spare time, but there was no YWCA for us girls. We stayed in the Ellis Hotel, shabby maybe but without the big city smell of grime.

There is nothing to fill my time except window shopping and walking, neither of which I can do comfortably. It's well below zero outside, even during the daytime, and the cold wind takes cruel bites out of my face leaving it red and smarting.

Fay was peroxiding her hair again. I heard her tell Jessica that it hadn't been treated since Toledo. Disliking the stench of peroxide, I braved the outdoor cold to take a walk, but it turned out to be more of a *run*.

There weren't many people out on the streets, though the citizens of Waterloo were surely more used to this kind of weather than I. The sidewalks and streets had a thick bedding of snow in most places in spite of being well-plowed. The piles of new snow were higher than my head at each intersection. At one main street corner, the sharp wind caught me and pushed me up against the glass of a store window. I decided that I'd had quite enough of the freezing wind and stood huddled against the building waiting for the street light to turn green so that I could safely cross the snow-covered street and head back to the hotel.

As I waited for the traffic light to change, I glanced through the steamed-up window next to me and saw the vague outlines of tables covered in white cloths. How soothing it would be to eat leisurely in a place like that instead of in the metal diners where the jukebox blared and where there was likely to be food under the table, maybe even more than on the table. Not having a staunch stomach, I had long ago kept my eyes confined to the area above my knees.

Even in the bitter cold temperature, I felt my face flush as I recalled going to restaurants with the others in the troupe. They often dressed sloppily and acted brazenly, especially Jessica and Denny. Their voices, as well as their demeanor, literally screamed out their presence. Their raucous laughter brought heads swiveling in our direction. Oh, I knew I was too self-conscious, too easily embarrassed, yet I still wanted to shrink out of sight and fervently hoped people didn't think I also behaved in such a crude manner.

On an impulse, I decide to partake of the calm, luxurious atmosphere of the tearoom which I can dimly see through the window scrimmed by steam. Didn't I deserve a treat…an experience to carry along with me, something to wash away all the crummy places I'd been forced to eat in? This tearoom, for that's what the sign proclaims, will give me something nice to recall again and again, at least until the end of the week when I will most certainly come up short of cash and once again regret my extravagance. It's the story of the boot-buying weakness all over again.

The next cold blast of wind settles any further uncertainty I may have. The wind almost sweeps me inside the tearoom door where a hostess seats me at a cloth-covered table, and I order hot tea and choose a tiny wedge of pink frosted cake from a tea cart pushed silently across the carpet by a waitress in a dazzling white apron, starched and ruffled over a gray uniform. She speaks in subdued tones befitting a maid in a movie, but her Midwestern accent dispels any notion of this being an elegant English tearoom. Still, I feel quite like the main character in a play and prolong the nibbling of the cake and the sipping of tea as long as I possibly can. In this manner, I can more completely absorb the genteel atmosphere. My theory is this: Whenever I am in need of a future lift to my spirits, I can bring forth this pleasant episode to soothe me...to carry me through a rough period.

I pretend that I belong here in this muffled, carpeted softness just like the two elderly ladies I see at a table nearby. They are wearing suits and I, feeling assured and smiling inside, congratulate myself upon wearing a skirt and stockings instead of slacks in spite of the deadly cold weather. Slacks would most certainly not have been appropriate in this rarified atmosphere. The cake and tea come to an end even before my stiff fingers regain their circulation from the outside cold. Leisurely, I slip my arms back into my black lamb jacket. The waitress has left a small silver tray with the bill discretely placed upside down on it. I reach inside my purse for my billfold and my fingers come up empty. I hold my breath while I sort more carefully through the papers, cosmetics, and miscellaneous junk. No billfold.

How embarrassing! I have no way to pay the bill on the silver tray. All my elegant pretenses collapse...replaced by a hot flush sweeping across my face and spreading down my neck. Surely it must be visible to the waitress, the hostess, and even to the two women whose fur coats are flung carelessly across the backs of the frail gold chairs. Where has the billfold gone? Then, I remember removing it from my purse to show Jessica my driver's license.

There has always been the uneasiness, the fear of reaching inside my billfold and not finding quite enough money to pay a bill, but never have I experienced the bewildering feeling of hunting for a nonexistent billfold. My self-confidence crashes, a light bulb shattered on a stone floor. A few minutes ago I had felt like a princess, head high and elegant. Now, I have all the outward symptoms and the nervous head-hanging of the shamed because I can't pay for the tea and cake already devoured. Surely everyone in the tearoom must be aware of my flushed face, my shame. I feel spot-lighted and guilty as though I have stolen something or cheated at cards.

"Is everything all right?" The waitress returns, expecting to see my money on her little silver tray. The tray is empty.

"Yes, fine," I say, flushing even deeper. "But I seem to have left my billfold back at the Hotel Ellis." I open up my purse and point inside as though the waitress can see, past the lipstick, compact, hankies and all the other junk, that the money really is not there.

"That's all right, Miss."

I don't think she believes me. Does she think I've done this on purpose?

"I'll go straight back to my hotel room, get the money, and come right back."

"We'll just forget the bill," she smiles.

Her belief that I never intended to pay the bill right from the beginning upsets me even further.

I am so shocked that I stumble over my words and repeat, "I'll... get the money...and be right back."

Trying to behave as though nothing is amiss so that the others in the tearoom won't be alerted, though I am already convinced they know, I take my time carefully buttoning my jacket and smoothing on my gloves. But as soon as I am through the door, I run as though chased by a bear, all the way back to the hotel, grab my billfold, and rush straight back to the tearoom. In the heat of my anxious state, I fail to feel the biting cold wind.

Once again inside the tearoom, I spot the waitress busy at another table. She has already cleared the table where I had previously been sitting, so I stand by the door and wait for her to notice me, feeling like a prime suspect in a crime. Has the waitress told anyone that I'm culpable? Are their eyes on me? At last, the waitress comes over to me and with stiff, clumsy fingers I count out the money plus a tip.

"Thank you, Miss," she says.

Strange that I feel it is so important to pretend to the waitress that I'm really not poor and destitute. Pride of course. Actually I am terribly poor...too poor to have squandered my money on a minuscule piece of pink cake and tea at tearoom prices. After a last glance at the pristine tablecloths and the warm velvety carpeting, I hasten back to the cement-floored Ellis Hotel through the stinging air.

The next day we leave Waterloo behind, though not my acute embarrassment; it remains with me for a long time. We head southwest towards Des Moines, the terminal from which our Christmas vacations are to begin.

Just outside of Marshalltown and still ninety or so miles away from Des Moines, the car breaks down. Carl makes his first phone calls for help from a nearby farmhouse. It's still bitter cold outside, and Jessica lets us share her stadium blanket which we tuck around our legs. It's sheer good luck that a wrecker is able to come and tow us back into Marshalltown where we learn that the engine block has frozen and cracked.

While the car is being repaired, we wait four hours in a nearby coffee shop not knowing exactly when the car might be ready. Jessica, as usual, avoids sitting next to George at the table, but otherwise we all sit together. Carl returns from the phone booth and the onerous duty of phoning Lu-Travis to tell her about the expensive repairs on the car.

"What did Travis say when you broke the bad news?" Tom asks.

"She isn't there, thank heavens. Olivia is going to phone the garage here. She wants to make some deal to pay by Western Union."

"Why can't we pay the bill from the company fund, or is that gone?" Jessica leers at Denny knowing very well that he continues to borrow from the fund. Jessica never disguises her blunt questions in subtle language.

Carl stays mum on the subject, but I catch him taking a surreptitious glance at Denny.

"None of your damn business." Denny adds a grin to soften his answer. "Anyway, the company fund isn't meant to hold enough money to pay for a major repair like this one."

I deduce that Denny is still borrowing from the fund...probably far more than he can repay. Why Carl wants to stick his neck out for Denny I can't comprehend. Later, however, I do understand...that and much more.

"We don't all have a dear mummy to throw money at us whenever our little hearts desire," Denny retorts, using his baby talk voice. Surprisingly, Jessica simply ignores his accusation over her spoiled nature.

"We're lucky this breakdown didn't happen out in some cornfield even further from town." Tom sucks calmly on a toothpick and shakes his head. His toothpick sucking reminds me of one of my uncles, who embarrasses me with his lack of manners.

"This is a town?" counters Denny, the big city lover.

"It's at least got a garage, thank heavens," George says. "We'd actually freeze…sitting in the car on a day like this…just waiting to be rescued."

"Jessica whispers loudly to those of us sitting close to her, " And it would serve him right…especially if it's his thig-a-ma-jig."

"Shhhh," Fay hushes Jessica, then projects her voice to the front seat, "You guys in the front seat are lucky. You have the heater to keep you warm, but the heat never reaches us in the back seat."

"She's right," I second. "Why don't you guys switch around with us? Let some of us sit up in the front seat once in a while." Too late, I remember the other time when I'd suggested the same thing…the scene of the choking…the terrible thing George had said about Jews. The memory quite literally cuts off the air from my lungs. I wait for an explosion of oaths to rain down on my head, but there is only a shrug from Denny and glum silence from George…and no generous offers to let the girls sit in the front seat. I take a deep breath like a prayer of relief and drop the subject. So does Fay.

✻

It was four o'clock before the repairs were completed and we could leave town. Dark had long overtaken us when we finally arrived in Des Moines after six o'clock in the midst of the heavy evening traffic. We wasted a lot of time making wrong turns but finally, after stopping to ask directions at least twice, found the storage garage where the truck was to be kept during the two-week Christmas vacation. In the parking lot beside the garage, George directed the car headlights to shine on the double doors of the old truck so that we could see to remove our suitcases and take the clothes from the costume wardrobe that we would each need during the Christmas vacation. It might have looked as though we had broken into the truck to steal except we were far too noisy to be pulling off a heist. Denny was bellowing out <u>Rudolph the Red-Nosed Reindeer,</u> and we all joined in singing <u>White Christmas.</u>

George, testy as usual, finally got our luggage into the car trunk by first emptying it of the paper mache jug, the Webster phonograph, and other miscellaneous props which were transferred to the truck. We squeezed ourselves, seven of us plus one suitcase that wouldn't fit into the trunk, into a space meant for five. Husky Tom groaned dramatically, his knees bearing the weight of Jessica, as we rode to the bus station where Jessica, Fay, and I were to be dropped off first. Both Carl and George were planning to take a late train back to New York.

Denny and Tom were staying in Des Moines for the Christmas holiday, and both Jessica and Fay were heading for Chicago. Once again, I suspected that they had gotten some monetary help from Jessica's mother. Surely, I thought enviously, they would have a more interesting holiday than I. Chicago would have live theatre, the latest movies, galleries, and Saks Fifth Avenue including a host of other gorgeous shops. My hometown had little of interest except a civic theatre and a symphony orchestra, neither likely to be open during my vacation weeks.

Outside of the bus station, I said a quick "Merry Christmas" to Tom, Denny, and Carl, and received an unenthusiastic "Same to you," in return. I think we were all weary of each other's company. Jessica, I noticed, was taking her guitar with her to Chicago, a sure sign that she didn't intend to return to the troupe. She remained mum about her plans, not openly discussing them with anyone except Fay.

"Ann, I hope you can come back," George said.

"Thank you, George. It all depends upon how well my father is. Merry Christmas." I had wanted to say the same to Jessica and Fay, but they had picked up their luggage and disappeared into the bus station without saying goodbye to either George or me. Manners didn't seem of interest to anyone is this troupe. We might not ever see each other again, but why did I particularly care? I knew their foibles, and they knew mine, though to myself I didn't admit to any. Inside the bus station, I saw Jessica and Fay standing in a nearby ticket line but they made no attempt to make further contact with me, so neither did I.

I had anticipated so much more from this tour: not the cold back seat, cramped and thick with cigarette smoke, the ugly sections of large cities, the moldy or stale smoke of hotel rugs, schools with skimpy stages, or the quarreling. I groaned to myself: Oh, the constant bickering! In two and a half months, I'd met only desk clerks and waitresses and been exposed to the same six faces of people I never would, under different circumstances, have gone out of my way to meet. So why was I so anxious to go on touring after Christmas? The answer had always been obvious: going back to the tour was simply the lesser of two evils. I didn't want to stay home with my two steadfast, but elderly, parents.

The exhaust that was sucked back inside the bus at each stop invariably created a hazard for me on long trips. As usual my head began to ache within the first hundred miles. Next would come. nausea if I didn't get more fresh air. This was not an express bus, so it made lots of stops in small towns during the night; some of the stops were long enough for me to get off the bus and breathe in the fresh night air away from the idling motor. This trip, I congratulated myself on not getting sick.

The closer I got to home, the less confident I felt of being able to return to the Lost Princess Troupe. What if my father grew weaker during my Christmas vacation at home...even suffered another stroke? But what if my staying at home or returning was less definite and more a matter of ethics...of my "doing the right thing"? At home I would be exposed first-hand to the trials my mother went through every day in caring for a man who needed help to get dressed and to use the bathroom. Wouldn't I be overcome with guilt if I left my mother to face those chores all alone?

I knew I was selfish, at least I was willing to admit that, but I didn't think I was an unfeeling slab of cold marble either. If my mother wanted me to help her take care of my father, I'd have to stay at home. I'd often heard Mother tell about her dear friend Nana who cared for her elderly mother as she grew senile, and also about the bachelor cousin who never married at all because he had to support his elderly mother. There had been an engagement in his past, or so it had been hinted at, but his betrothed had finally given up waiting for him.

Just contemplating my lost freedom made me feel depressed. Did I really have no choice in my own future? Other girls my age did. Why not me? I suppose it was because their parents were younger or had more wealth. Anyway, I began to feel more and more sorry for myself, and more trapped, the closer I got to home. Why me...why me? A few tears trickled down my cheeks, so I averted my face away from the woman sitting in the seat beside me on the bus and closed my eyes. It was easier to make a pretense of being sound asleep than to have my tears noticed.

FIFTEEN

*A*fter riding all night, I arrived in my hometown the following evening.

One hip was numb from putting all my weight towards the window side of the bus, partly to avoid talking to the woman sitting next to me. Tire and motor noises had been sending humming, mantra-like sounds through my head all night. Even after getting off the bus and standing on a corner for fifteen minutes in the cold, my head continued to hum down the highway. Finally a city bus came along to take me the last two miles home.

I got off the local bus a block beyond the house. In the early winter dusk, I could see that the little white bungalow looked much the same except for the crack in the cement step of the front porch. It had widened and the edges had crumbled in upon themselves.

The same ecru lace curtains appeared at the windows. Naturally, I thought, Mom wouldn't buy new curtains or anything unnecessary now that Dad had retired from his job, and especially since there were hospital bills to pay. Anyway, my mother probably didn't care to have new curtains. She was not one for promoting surface beauty. Her flowered chair slipcovers, which fought with the flowered carpet, were proof of that. The beauty of material things had no lure for her, whereas it was always calling me, a proverbial siren. Her lack of interest in beauty did not apply to natural things like sunsets, birds, or flowers, but it did carry over to people. "Beauty is only skin deep" was one of her favorite homilies in reference to my desire to have a pretty face and straight teeth.

My folks were genuinely glad to see me but, in sharp contrast to the exaggerated emotions of the kids in the Lost Princess Troupe, they were not effusive. Mom and Dad had always been sparing in showing their feelings, as though their emotions, once spent, could never be replenished. The most I could expect from them was a quiet, "nice to have you home," but never a joyous, "it's so wonderful to have you home." I never received strong messages of either love or dislike from them. How I'd love, just once, to bask in a huge, gushy greeting, like one given a great traveler just returning from a trip around the globe, though I'd been no further from home than Iowa and New York.

✳

Mother gives me a brief hug, and I kiss my dad on the forehead. I always avoid his prickly mustache. "Well, Princess," he says, "you've certainly done a lot of traveling."

Calling me "princess" is a sign of my dad's teasing. He has called me "spooter, funny girl, and pumkin" at various times in my life, and now because of the play's title, he's beginning to call me "princess."

"Pa has kept track of all your travels by marking your routes on a map," says my mother.

Right away my dad wants to know, "Where is the troupe heading next?"

"I'm not sure. Somewhere West, I guess. We'll receive our new itinerary when we get back to St Joe, Missouri after vacation. Lu-Travis never lets us know where we're heading more than a week in advance."

"You're looking a bit thin," my mother comments. "Have you been getting enough to eat?"

"Oh, sure," I lie. I decide that it will be prudent to keep back some of the bad things about the tour…particularly the skipped meals. If I complain about conditions too strongly, my folks will feel justified in urging me to stay home in their safer, more orderly environment.

"Want some milk toast?" my mother asks. "Pa always has milk toast about this time of evening before going to bed."

"Sounds great to me." I try to hold back my enthusiasm, but my stomach is already on the way to the kitchen before the offer quite leaves my mother's mouth. I am starved after the long bus trip with nothing but coffee and a Danish for a day and a half. I have spent almost all of my money on the round trip bus ticket.

"Princess, give me a start here." My father indicates that he needs someone to pull him up from the depths of the low-slung chair that has always been suited to someone with long legs.

"Dad, you're looking much healthier than I expected," I exclaim cheerfully as I pull him up from the chair and position his walker where he can grab it. His face has a lot of pink color, but I note that he is thinner.

We sit at the kitchen table in the small kitchen. As the warm milk trickles down into my stomach, my head begins to feel less thick but a whole lot sleepier. My father's enjoyment of the food comes across in purposeful, deep swallows. Between gulps, the sounds of his poorly fitting false teeth make an annoying click, click. I tell myself that I can surely learn to tolerate the noises for the short period I'll be home or hope to be home.

"Princess, did you travel through Ft. Wayne?"

"Yes, on our way to Indianapolis."

"I worked there once, you know. Did I ever tell you?"

"Yes, you've talked about it before."

"This Lu-Travis woman, does she pay you regularly?"

"Every week."

"Well, there's nothing as important as receiving a regular paycheck," he states with emphasis.

To me, there are certainly other important considerations, but I resist pointing that out, though if he hadn't been a sick man I probably would have continued to argue as we so often did in the past. Before fifteen minutes has elapsed, we have exhausted most of the topics of conversation my parents and I have in common. My parents are at least seventy and I am in my twenties, but our problem of communication is seldom the fault of that gap in years. Our personalities are quite opposite.

"What does that woman pay you?" my father asks, and I tell him the niggardly amount of my salary.

"You should get a regular job, nine to five, one that pays a good steady income," he advises. "You don't get paid for all those extra hours you have to work in the theatre."

He's right. We never get paid for the very late night hours we drive from one town to another, but a "regular nine to five job" as he phrases it, is of no interest to me. My dad and I have been through this same discussion many times before, and I have never succeeded in convincing him of my need for a "creative" type of job, so in the interest of a peaceful first night at home, I refrain from stating my opinion all over again.

I vow that my life is not going to come to the disappointing mundane end I see right here tonight in this kitchen. Oh no, not my life! Time seems to have worn my parents down to the nub where getting through life free of debt is their only goal, their prime accomplishment. Is this all they expect from life? Haven't they ever dreamed of painting a canvas, writing a book, running for mayor, or exploring the world? Don't they need other rewards besides money? Where is the applause?

Knowing that the topic of jobs often leads to an argument between me and my dad, my mother changes the subject. "I imagine you're tired after that long bus trip. We go to bed early these days, about nine o'clock. If you stay up later, Ann, be sure to turn off all the lights."

Nothing has changed. No matter how many times I turn out the lights at night without ever forgetting, my folks still think I'll forget and remind me, . . .*don't forget to turn out the lights.* Why can't they learn to trust me?

At first it was refreshing to be home where my folks said what they meant or rather meant what they said, instead of making exaggerated statements either witty or scathing as Denny had. There were no "sweeties" or even "darlings" to add frills to embellish the conversations, but I also knew that I wouldn't be called a "little bitch" if they didn't happen to agree with me over something or other.

To wake each morning realizing that today I could eat three complete meals with juice and milk was sheer luxury. That feeling of being blessed didn't wear thin until the second week of my visit when I began to take a full stomach quite for granted once again.

One Sunday afternoon Mother said she would treat me to a movie. My hometown movie theatre was unique in my eyes. After entering and sitting down in the orchestra, one felt as if they were outdoors surrounded by high stucco walls of a Spanish villa. Small ornate balconies with wrought iron railings were attached to the walls and there were secret looking alcoves and niches for statues and gigantic vases. Lush ivy climbed the walls, and dimly lighted lanterns peeked through small arched windows. But what awed me most when I was younger was the deep blue-black sky over my head where stars sparkled and clouds drifted slowly across. Today, as Mother and I sat down to enjoy the matinee, the deep carpets and soft lighting still exuded the same tranquil fairytale appeal, but to my keen disappointment the clouds weren't being projected across the sky.

Right from the beginning of the film, I felt an empathy with the main character, a girl about my age. Now at the end of the movie when her father died, I gulped back a sob. Mother too was dabbing at her eyes with a white cloth hanky. At the conclusion of the movie, the girl was free of her father's domination and became reunited with the man she loved. Everything had turned out exactly as I thought it should. Sometime during the movie a transition had evolved, and I had become that girl, initially enveloped in sadness, but now at the denouement so blessed by good fortune. Like the heroine, I felt euphoric, a floating being.

Still cozily enveloped in the movie character, I crept slowly up the aisle. The theatre lights slowly rose, and the soft organ music took over where the film music left off. I felt light and happy, as though I were now going off with the man I loved, just as the girl in the movie had...all my hopes fulfilled.

"I wonder what I should cook for dinner," said a voice beside me, my mother's. We had barely reached the doors at the top of the aisle.

"Ummm?" I tried to close out the voice.

"The leftover beef stew will probably be enough, don't you think?"

The voice wouldn't be ignored. "Oh, how should I know!" I snap. She has broken into my lovely daydream.

"Now Ann, what's come over you?"

I didn't answer. I was busy trying to recapture the last wonderful bits of the movie, but they were as elusive as attempting to catch steam from a teakettle. By now the serene well-being that I had felt just minutes ago was gone. My lovely daydream was drifting away, usurped from me by my fall into reality. The loss left me irritated. Who but my mother would think of something so prosaic, so mundane, as food at a time like this? It wasn't the first time she had spoiled a movie for me either. I turned and took one last look at the serene sky above in the movie theatre.

I said nothing to Mother until we were in the car and on our way home. By then I had dropped my angry tone, but there was something I wanted to know, "Don't you ever lose yourself in a movie, completely?"

"What do you mean?"

"Don't you ever feel that the events in the movie are actually `happening to you?"

"Why, no. It's just a movie, not real life."

✼

While my mother is grocery shopping—she simply doesn't trust me to do a proper job of selecting the best fruits and vegetables or the right brands at the most economical prices—I sit in Holly's Grill across the street and drink coffee. I keep hoping someone interesting will turn up and sit down near me...someone my own age to talk to instead of someone elderly. But it's Christmas vacation for the two colleges in town, and most of the young people my age have either gone home or somewhere else for the holiday. Ironically, a former boyfriend attending college in another town, doesn't come home for Christmas this year. There is no one to talk to.

Even the local civic theatre, where I know quite a few people, is empty except for the girl in the office. I walk into the silent workshop and find no sawdust on the floor. Tools have been hung on hooks almost in their proper places. The pot of glue is cold; I miss the smell of the glue. I look at the buckets of paint on the shelf with dried stains slopping over their rims and down their sides and remember painting the canvas flats late into the night just before a show opening the next evening. The sight of those paint buckets also brings back a hilarious paint fight that occurred between Dorothy, Peter, and myself at Seaplace Barn Theatre. The paint had been a particularly nauseating violet color. Before any more nostalgic memories can overtake me in the empty, too clean workshop, I walk out.

Later at home, I fill a vacant hour by leafing through my scrap book from years ago in which I have glued pictures, doubtless cut from the Good Housekeeping Magazine or the Saturday Evening Post. Below each picture is a poem. The poems are not unusual... about what one could expect from a ten or eleven-year-old child. Each is a gift written just for my mother. "It's for you," I hear myself saying, hoping to see her smile and tell me how proud she is of me.

"You'll improve as you grow older," she says each time and hands the poems right back to me. This is even more hurtful to my pride... the fact that she doesn't want to keep the poems, even though I tell her specifically that they are a gift. Now, as I think about it, I can easily recapture the disappointment from way back then. Why is it so hard for Mother to let a few words of praise pass between her thin lips?

I give my mother the earrings for Christmas, the ones I bought in Macys in Milwaukee, and Mother gives Dad a sport shirt, which she says can be a present from both of us. But I'll never forget what they give me because it is one of the most expensive presents they have ever given me.

Mom and Dad aren't prone to giving lavish gifts, not ever. Both Mom and Dad come from conservative farm families, not poor ones, but very prudent families. Mom often tells me about her one pair of good school shoes per year and how her mother made paper cutouts of the feet of each of the seven children in the family and then took the cutouts to the city to buy shoes. "The shoes didn't always fit very well," Mother said, "but we children had to wear them anyway."

Now that Mom and Dad are retired, I expect even less than usual in the way of presents at Christmas. In the past when Christmas morning arrives and we are all seated near the tree, I'd allow my hopes to rise, thinking that this year they'll give me something exciting, something a bit unusual...something beautiful. This year I know better than to anticipate; I never look for surprises any longer. Besides, why should I expect any gifts at all since I have almost nothing to give in return?

This year we each open one package on Christmas day and mine turns out to be stockings. Then Mother says, "Pa and I have another gift for you, Ann, but we didn't want to waste gift wrappings on it since it's rather large. It's there in the closet under the stairs."

I open the closet door, and there on the floor I spot a brand new suitcase, maroon colored. "For me?" Imagine my face...the unexpected is happening at last...a genuine surprise on Christmas Day! The suitcase is not any larger than the shabby one I now carry, but it's sturdier and unscathed by rough handling. I certainly will never need to feel ashamed of carrying this one into any of the hotels in which we stay on tour.

My emotional "thank you" must be a surprise to Mom and Dad. "What a surprise!" I keep repeating, "thank you" and mean it. The suitcase is an extravagant purchase for them.

Knowing how fussy I am about colors, Mother says, "You can go down to the luggage store and see if they have a suitcase color you'd like better than this one, if it's the same price."

"I might go and see what they have just out of curiosity," I say casually, trying not to let on that I'm even slightly dissatisfied with her choice of color.

I don't have anything to go with the maroon color...didn't even care for that color especially. Perhaps something in gray would be more suitable. But I soon discover, after a quick perusal of the price tags in the luggage store, that the maroon bag is the only suitcase on sale. There is no way for me to switch to another color or to something a bit more stylish. As usual a terrible gulf exists between what I want and what I can actually have. I suppose I must be showing my disappointment all too clearly because the shop clerk says he is sorry.

The gift of the suitcase tells me without even asking that Mom and Dad expect me to return to the troupe after vacation and not stay home to take care of them. I am so relieved. The longer I remain at home, the more desperate I am to escape. Life at home seems all one drab color...of dried mushrooms or maybe Mother's ecru curtains.

The vacation drags on with nothing to spice up the days. Home is like being trapped in a room while just outside the walls, events more exciting are taking place without me, or so I imagine. On a certain day I will be released from the room...the day my vacation is over... and I can leave.

I long for something interesting to happen...to hear applause again. Denny's biting jokes, George's crabbiness, and Jessica's annoying ways, all seem less threatening now that I am far away from them. They are in a previous act of a play in which the curtain and intermission—the holiday at home—come just before the final act. Now, when I look back at all those scary incidents between George and Jessica, I feel stimulated. I'm curious. How will the remaining act turn out for those characters and for me?

At least on tour we are going to see new towns, western towns this time, and not the same old grocery store that my mother and I visit at least twice a week. How my folks are going to manage without me to drive them places doesn't even weigh on my conscience. Mother will have to ride with a neighbor to do her marketing until spring. Then she is going to take driving lessons. It never enters my mind that it might be nerve racking for an older person like mother to learn something entirely new like driving, or how nervous it will make her to have Dad sitting next to her in the car dictating every turn of the wheel as his cigar smoke circles her head. Ignorance makes me blithely unconcerned.

I get on a bus going west and ride out of town feeling freer and freer as the distance between me and home widens. As I draw closer to St. Joseph, Missouri where the troupe is to gather, the same flutter of anticipation that I felt at the beginning of the tour, returns to me. I picture the desert, the mountains, and unrealistically, an ocean vista. This time, I assure myself, I am going to make an effort to visit museums and meet new people wherever we travel.

SIXTEEN

When I arrived in St. Joseph and checked into the designated hotel where the troupe was to meet, I discovered that Denny and Carl were already there. So were Tom and George who had driven the truck and the car from the storage garage in Des Moines down to St. Joe. Fay showed up soon afterwards but not Jessica.

We all greeted one another effusively as though we were long lost brothers and sisters. Forgotten were the crude words, the character bashing, and the sarcasm. A stranger might have thought we had been separated from each other for months, even years, instead of two and a half weeks. Each one of us, in an attempt to tell our vacation story first, talked more loudly than the other. It was just like "show and tell" back in grade school without the teacher to shut us up. Denny's more resonant voice won out over all the other voices as he told about the great movies he had seen in Des Moines.

From Fay we heard what we had already guessed, Jessica's decision to stay in Chicago. From Carl we learned that a replacement was expected to arrive at any time to fill Jessica's role in the play. Would the new girl be good-looking or wouldn't it matter since she was going to take a boy's part? There was one thing of which we were perfectly sure: she would be short in height because she had to fit into Jessica's velvet costume.

By the following day most of us weren't much concerned about the looks of the new member of the Lost Princess Troupe even if she did show up. We took to our beds with a stomach virus, all, that is, except George. My legs felt so weak that if Bette Davis herself had shown up as a replacement, I still wouldn't have budged from the bed.

One day later when I began to feel well enough to sit up in a chair, George came to visit me. Fay had recovered from the virus first, and she had gone downstairs to ask for boiled milk from the coffee shop. I don't remember whose idea it was to treat our sickness with boiled milk, but it was the only food that sounded appealing to me.

I was still feeling less than perky and intended to creep back into bed even though George was in the room. Before I was able to stand up, George sat down on the arm of my chair. Immediately I felt an uneasiness, besides the one in my stomach. George's brown eyes sparkled with a vitality that tired me, so I focused on his chin instead. It was shadowy with an unshaven beard.

"I want…to talk to you," he started out in his fast speaking, jerky manner of piling up words but stopping abruptly in mid-sentence, as though seeing a red light in the middle of a city block. "You're about the only…one with whom I can be…sociable in this third-class troupe."

"Oh?" That's the only word I felt like saying. In fact, I prayed that George would soon go away and leave me alone until I felt stronger.

"I'm so glad…you returned to the troupe. Jessica's gone…you know. Thank God!" George slippeds his arm from the back of my chair down to add weight to my already sagging shoulders. Then he bent over to peer into my face.

"Careful," I warned. "You'll catch the virus if you get too close." Maybe, I thought hopefully, I could scare him off. I just didn't have enough energy to physically push him away if he decided to get more intimate. Fear, like too much suds in a washing machine, began to churn up bubbles in my stomach. I'm afraid that my tension will cause it to overflow in one direction or another.

"I'm not too concerned," George said. "I already had the virus during vacation." His hand reached up to my neck and fondled my ear. I jerked away but kept a big fake smile on my face to cover up my distaste. I'm not the cruel sort. Why hurt his feelings. Maybe it wouldn't be necessary.

I stalled, "Let's talk about it when I'm feeling better." George isn't my idea of a romantic figure. Even after two and a half months of being around him, I see nothing behind his white teeth, scrawny neck, and nervous mannerisms except narrow-mindedness and a certain astute ability to hang on to his money. He never loaned money to anyone in the troupe even if they were going hungry, and he certainly couldn't act.

"All right...we'll talk...when you feel better."

"Yes, please." I emphasized the 'please'. George touched my forehead lightly with his lips and left the room as quickly as he had come. That kiss switched on a nonstop shaking that I was unable to control. I knew my distaste was a combination of my illness and my repugnance to George's touch.

How will I escape George's attentions tonight, tomorrow, and for the next few months? Repulsing him will turn him sour. I remember vividly how he hit Jessica in the breast and how he had held onto her saliva-soaked scarf long enough to nearly choke her. Now, if I'm not careful, he'll surely turn his vitriol and his narrow-mindedness on me.

I'm still shaking when Fay returns to the room with the boiled milk; right behind her comes Carl and Denny. All my misery must show up on my face, and my obvious inability to stop shaking. As though I have been condemned to a future courtship with George, I blurt out everything that has just taken place including the distasteful kiss. I shiver even harder as though to shake off George's touch.

"You poor thing," Denny commiserates, as though reading lines from a script.

"You do look dreadful," Fay agrees.

"You might as well go back to bed," suggests Carl, "because I'm canceling the rehearsal for this afternoon. Jessica's replacement isn't here yet, so we'll postpone the rehearsal until tonight."

I go back to bed and sleep for a couple of hours. That evening Tom, Carl, and Denny assemble in our hotel room for the rehearsal. In that way I can sit in the chair by the bed and also be near the bathroom.

"The new girl still hasn't arrived, so we'll just read through our lines one time and save the actual rehearsal for tomorrow." Carl says.

"Isn't George supposed to be here?" Tom asks.

"Oh, he's gone. Good riddance." Denny's face works hard to keep his smirk hidden.

"What do you mean?" I ask. I must be missing part of the conversation.

Carl explains, "We can't have someone in the troupe who perpetrates questionable advances on the girls, the kind George has just made on you, Ann."

"Yeah," Denny adds happily, "it's better that he's gone. He doesn't fit in anyway."

I remember how Denny loudly proclaims the exact same thing about Jessica. Once, he even uses the same words about me. "You got him fired just because of what I told you?" I find it hard to believe that Denny and Carl, particularly Carl, resort to such a flimsy excuse as a simple kiss on the forehead to get rid of George. Unless, of course, they hugely exaggerate what actually took place when they talk to Lu-Travis on the phone?

Denny exclaims cheerfully, "Yup…he's gone for good, along with spoiled Jessica."

I glance at Fay when Jessica's name is brought up, but her face remains blank. She and Jessica have been such close chums that I expect her to burst forth in Jessica's defense, but she says absolutely nothing.

"But who's going to take George's place on such short notice?" Tom asks. "We've only got three days until the next performance in Springfield."

"Travis says she's got a substitute who wants the job," Carl answers.

I remain sitting there in the chair, probably with a stupefied expression on my face. Because of my illness, my slower thinking brain is still trying to figure out how they could get George fired with so little evidence. Did they enlarge upon the incident of the kissing? Denny might do something like that, but Carl? If so, he no longer fits the image I had of him as a fair, even-handed person. Could Carl be jealous of George's attentions to me? No, most certainly not. Carl pays no especial attention to me, not since the first few weeks of the tour. In fact he avoids me assiduously, especially after Denny's teasing retorts referring to me as Mrs. Manager.

"Exactly what *did* you tell Lu-Travis about George and me?"

"Oh, we just said he was coming on lewd," Denny explains. "You aren't complaining, are you Annie?"

I know better than to protest too strongly and get Denny riled up against me. Anyway, it's too late to do anything about George now. In one sense, I'm relieved. The rest of the tour will surely go more smoothly without having to shadow box with George.

✶

Though my jelly-like body was content to sit slumped in a chair that evening as each of us read our parts in the play, like a refresher course, my mind flopped about spinelessly without much concentration. I began to wonder about Jessica. Did she leave the troupe of her own volition or had she also been nudged out by some of Denny's exaggerations, his fibbing straight into Travis's ears? Then, because my mind was so unfocused, I missed some of my cues because I was also thinking about Lisa, the much talked about girl from last year's tour.

Couldn't Lisa have been another victim of Denny's blatant lies? Someone from that troupe had certainly tattled on her. Denny most likely had his own personal reasons for wanting to get rid of her. She had stolen more than his limelight. There had been that friend of Denny's in St. Louis that Lisa had supposedly vamped away from him.

After everyone left the room that evening, except Fay, I dragged my body and my dithering mind off to the bathroom to brush my teeth and then fell weakly into bed. Only a thin wave of guilt passed over me because of George being fired on my account, before I lost consciousness in sleep.

SEVENTEEN

*T*he next morning both my body and my mind are more alert, but I still feel a bit like a toddler grabbing at every chair in the room to stay on my feet. My wayward legs are doubtless mirrored as bewilderment on my face. Usually I am anxious to escape any of the hotel rooms we inhabit, but not this one. For all its patchy furnishings, the room is a safe haven, especially so because it has its own bathroom.

Soon after starting the tour, I had begun to grade each hotel we visited either on its horrible disinfectant smell or on its "past glory"... sometimes both. This particular hotel in St. Joe seemed to fit neither category entirely. It had to be graded low on disinfectant smell—it wasn't terribly noticeable—but it also had to be graded low on "past glory." If there ever had been any fine old features to the hotel, they were now obliterated. Here and there a ceiling molding, once elaborately carved, had been hidden under many layers of paint.

Later in the morning as Fay and I descend alone in the elevator, I ask her, "Do you think Jessica has been fired, instead of leaving the troupe of her own volition?"

The toe of Fay's shoe works at the hole in the elevator carpet. "All I know is that she wanted to try living in Chicago."

"So you're really not sure?"

Fay shrugs. She is standing half turned away from me. It's uncomfortable talking to someone who refuses to look directly at me.

"Well," I add, since I didn't get a straight answer out of her, "George has been fired under false accusations, so I thought maybe…."

Fay interrupts in a flat-tone of voice, "I really don't know anything about it."

"Oh, I just thought maybe…"

"George was certainly strange," Fay concedes.

Good, I think. Maybe she's going to open up and actually hold a conversation with me. It makes me feel like a comrade for a brief moment, so I confess to her, "I didn't mean to get George fired."

"Same result," she remarks, and I step forward to get a better look at her face, to see if anything like blame is registered there. Nothing is registered there, just another monotone expression.

Feelings of guilt hovered over me for several days. After all, what had George done to me that was so heinous? Absolutely nothing. How could a chaste kiss on the forehead warrant such a drastic measure as getting someone fired? My tattling on George had been unsporting. Perhaps if I hadn't felt ill—that's how I excuse myself—maybe I would have handled George more wisely.

Right from the beginning of the tour I, coward that I was, should have told George, "I'm not interested in a relationship with you." But I didn't want to hurt his feelings. Poor George. Poor brash Jessica too, though I knew I had often said things about her such as: *she's so shrill,* and *I wish she could be neate*r. All open criticisms.

During lunch with Fay in the coffee shop, Carl and Denny passed by our table and Fay asked, "Has the new girl come yet?"

Carl shook his head, and Denny spoke up in his fake English accent which always made heads turn our way as it certainly did right now. "She'd better get her arse here soon. We need to rehearse."

"Do you have a driver's license?" Carl asked.

"Who me?" I look around to see if he means me or someone else. "Yes, but it's a Michigan driver's license. Doesn't Denny know how to drive?"

"Not me. Never had a need to learn. No one drives in New York City unless they have to."

Carl continues speaking as though Denny hasn't interrupted. "See if you can get a Missouri license today after rehearsal. We may need you to drive the car until we get a replacement for George."

"Sure. I'll try. But can't you drive?" I'm really not that anxious to have the responsibility.

"I'd rather not. My bum leg begins to ache if I keep it in the same position for too long."

I nod in sympathy. "I'll try, but it may take longer than one day to get a license."

I was wrong. The whole process of getting a license in Missouri in nineteen fifty turned out to be fairly simple. There wasn't even a written test to fill out. All I had to do was present my Michigan license and from that the man at the bureau window made out a Missouri license. I pay two-fifty…easy…no driving test either…no questions to answer.

I'm quite aware that one of the rules of the Lu-Travis Theatre Company is that only the guys are supposed to do the driving on tour. I'm not sure why, but probably it's because Lu-Travis doesn't want to pay the women the same wages as she pays the men. At the time, it never occurs to me to demand the extra ten dollars that the men are receiving. I doubt that I'd have gotten it anyway.

✳

Jane Milleson, the replacement for Jessica, arrived the evening before we left for Springfield, and she slept in the same room with Fay and me. Jane was a talker. Long after I had gone to bed and long into the night, I heard her chattering to Fay. "Hey, you two," I finally complained around midnight, "we have to get up early tomorrow, remember?"

We left St. Joseph soon after nine o'clock the next morning with Denny standing in the lobby still chewing on a piece of toast. A few minutes earlier he had waved the toast around in expansive gestures as he aided the truck in backing up to the curb in front of the hotel where our suitcases were piled on the sidewalk.

This morning for the first time, I began driving the Plymouth. I was a bit on the nervous side but enjoyed the privilege of having more sitting space. I would no longer have to be crammed into the back seat along with two other girls. As it turned out, the new girl, Jane, took up half the space of Jessica, who had always managed to incorporate more than her share of the back seat, or Fay, who occasionally folded her legs in Yoga fashion.

On that first day of my taking the wheel, I stuck to the rear of the truck like a pull toy attached by string to the thumb of a tot. I never let the truck out of my sight for an instant. The Plymouth handled just like the Plymouth my folks had at home. In fact, it was the exact same model except for having four doors instead of just two. Still, I never got over feeling tense when I drove. To me it was a heavy responsibility, especially since I knew that it was against Lu-Travis' rules for girls to be driving at all.

Jane, our newest member, spent most of the car trip to Springfield, Missouri, taking in the seams of the costume that Jessica had worn. Jane was nearly the same height as Jessica, but there the resemblance ended. Jane appeared to be a mere stick until one's eyes slid down to her thighs. Like a professional bike rider's thighs, they protruded as wide as her hips. Her face was small and plain, though far from ugly; the plainness allowed audiences to reasonably imagine they were seeing a young boy, the roll for which Jane was hired. Her longish face, straight across eyebrows and hair, cut short, were also believable for the part of a boy. Her elocution was something else. It was pure Brooklynese and all wrong for a young prince in a fairy tale. I saw Denny flinch during the first rehearsal and watched him send a look of complete disgust in Carl's direction.

As I drove along, I heard Jane and Fay prattling with frequent interruptions from Denny as he turned around in his seat to join in on the conversation. Now, I thought, Denny had a brand new set of ears in which to reveal the saga of Lisa and how she stole his boyfriend during the last tour.

I suppose I felt a bit superior. Hadn't I been chosen to drive because I was more reliable than the others? Later the truth sank in:

I was the only one in the troupe who knew how to drive. As it turned out, the replacement for George couldn't drive either. Carl didn't think I was superior in any way. He just had no choice but to ask me to drive or do the onerous chore himself.

What would George's replacement look like, I wondered as I drove along south, around Kansas City and then east? He was supposed to be waiting for us in the Springfield Hotel, the hotel designated on our itinerary. With two new people entering the cast, it was imperative that we rehearse, yet I don't believe we felt the same anxiety over the quality of our performances that we did back at the beginning of the tour. Most of us had repeated our lines so many times that they had become rote and sounded lifeless. There was no one to keep us up to a certain level of quality except perhaps the sponsors in each town, and they didn't have a script.

"Oh the sponsors don't know quality from shit," Denny claimed.

The hotel in Springfield didn't fit into any of the previous categories I had concocted in my head. True, it was low in disinfectant smell, but it had absolutely no "past glory" and never could have even if it remained a hotel until the year two thousand. The lobby was the smallest we had yet encountered and contained just a couple of chairs. The numerous displays of candy, cigarettes, and other odds and ends such as gum and condoms made it look more like a small tobacco shop than a hotel lobby.

When all six of us burst into the hotel lobby with our seven or eight suitcases, we filled the room and literally flushed up from his seat a young man in a long tweed coat. I noticed him immediately because the tweed coat was so heavy looking for such a small person. It appeared to drag him right down to meet the floor as though he were actually standing on his knees. The young man listened as Carl checked everyone in at the registration desk, and then he approached.

"You're part of the Lu-Travis Troupe, aren't you?" he asked Carl. Carl's briefcase must have set him apart from the other guys, giving him the appearance of a leader of some sort.

Denny whispered sotto voce to Fay, "Can't Travis ever hire anyone above runt size? He's going to be great help when it comes to loading flats into the truck."

"Sometimes size doesn't have much to do with it," I said, hinting that Denny didn't work all that hard lifting flats either, in spite of the fact that he was taller and heftier.

"He's got to fit into George's costume," Fay reminded Denny.

"Oh, he'll do that all right with lots left over," Denny retorted with a snort. "Well, it's you girls who will have to alter the costume, not me, thank God."

Carl didn't bother to introduce each one of us to the new member, so the young man in the tweed coat stuck out his hand in a friendly gesture and introduced himself. "Greg Feldman," he said with a grin.

"So terribly pleased to meet you," Denny replied with great insincerity.

"I just got out of the army," said Greg in answer to a question of Carl's, "and I thought this might be a fun experience."

"Oh, it'll be that all right!" Denny rolled his eyes heavenward.

Maybe Greg had just been released from the army, but his wiry, kinky hair had managed to escape long before. It curled tightly on the top of his head. I also noticed a few gray hairs, which seemed incongruous in someone so young. If Greg hadn't been so short—shorter than George and barely taller than Jane—he might have been considered quite good looking. The deep furrows between his eyes were indicative of stress or poor eyesight. Certainly, I decided, the army could have provided the stress. Except for those forehead worry lines, Greg could have been a natural brother to Jane. They both had the same straight across, slash-type eyebrows, medium brown hair, though Jane's was straight, and both had narrow elongated faces.

Our rooms at the hotel were cell size but inexpensive enough to allow each one of us to have his or her own private room. That was a real treat. Of course none of the rooms had bathrooms, just sinks and an allotment of one window per room. The furniture was Danish modern, cheap copies that had been dealt a rough life. I traced the names: Betty, Robert, and Ellen, scratched into the dark wooden arms of the chair in my room. The cloth seat was covered with stains. Stains of what, I wondered? Coffee maybe and alcohol. Blood? Ugh! I hated to touch anything in the room. I turned back the bed covers and was relieved to see that at least the linen, though lifeless from thousands of washings, looked freshly laundered. I'd heard the others in the troupe talking about mites and bed bugs, and I wondered if I'd recognize either one.

The weather was unusual for January, sunny and warm enough for only a light jacket. This hiatus, a glimpse of spring, imbued me with restlessness. I wanted to cling to a day like this and not let it slip through my fingers. Perhaps Fay, Jane, and I could explore the city together or visit a zoo if there was one.

My idea for taking advantage of the great weather came too late. Jane and Fay had slipped off together right after rehearsal, and they hadn't invited me to join them. How easily they had fallen into companionship after knowing each other just one and a half days. I felt keenly disappointed. Why didn't Fay prefer the company of someone she already knew like myself, at least until she became better acquainted with Jane? I realized that in the past I had often remained aloof, but it was partly because of Jessica's boisterous behavior, which embarrassed me. Now that Jessica had gone, I naturally assumed that Fay and I would become closer friends.

Ever since returning from Christmas vacation, I had made a little more effort to be friendly with Fay, but I made slow progress. It was like one of those old country dances where one partner steps forward and the other steps backwards. I guess it was impossible for Fay to see me in the new light of companionship; she could see me only in the old one as a loner. But all this mulling over the past didn't solve my problem of what to do with this beautiful afternoon. I headed for the reception desk to ask about the zoo.

Even as I ask the clerk at the tobacco desk how to get to the zoo, an idea slips into my head that seems inspired. Why not spend my money on a piano lesson instead? I miss being able to play piano music as I did at home during Christmas vacation. In fact, I've brought back with me in my new Christmas suitcase one music book and the dummy cardboard keyboard that will help me memorize one of my favorite pieces, <u>Autumn Leaves.</u>

From the phone book in the hotel lobby, I pick out the names of several piano teachers and then hasten back to the clerk to ask him if any of the addresses are near the hotel. He points out two. From these, I find one teacher willing to give me a lesson this same afternoon. I marvel at my good fortune, and my anticipation builds. I'll get at least a half-hour of actual piano playing, maybe more. It may not be much time, but if I'm lucky I might come across a piano to practice on in some rooming house in the next town or the next; that should be enough to keep my hand and fingers limber. I'm proud of my expediency and never question the sensibility of my decision.

EIGHTEEN

Several blocks from the Springfield Hotel the streets turn into a residential area. The houses are old and small, copies of each other, with only the width of a driveway between. I find the correct address of the piano teacher, mount the porch steps, and press the bell. An older woman opens the door and looks me over thoroughly, not returning my smile.

"Mrs. Wyman?" I receive a nod in return. She is short and square with gray hair and glasses, a combination that always looks benign to me. Finally she speaks up, "Come in." Afterwards, I realize that she must have been suspicious of me, a complete stranger from out of town who makes an impulsive decision to take a piano lesson.

The small living room is crammed with dark furniture. From an initial glance, it's even hard to distinguish the outline of the piano in the dimness. Mrs. Wyman closes the front door and heads straight for the piano where she switches on a flexible-stemmed light. She doesn't ask me where I am from, but I tell her anyway. I chatter on as though she is naturally curious about me. All my past music teachers have been kindly individuals interested in me as a person as well as desiring to promote my love of music. Naturally I expect some of the same interest from Mrs. Wyman.

"Now then," she says, cutting short my ramblings, "That will be three dollars." For a moment I'm stunned. Never in my past have I ever had a music teacher ask to be paid *before* a lesson. If I have been dreamy-eyed with the idea of playing the piano and conversing with someone of kindred interests, it is now over. Suddenly, I am jerked back to reality. My babbling on about where I'm from and where our troupe is going and what kind of music I like best is of no interest to Mrs. Wyman. After receiving her three dollars and tucking it into her pocket, she sits down on the piano bench next to me.

"Can you play something for me?"

I play a piece from my beginning Bach music book and then stumble through something more difficult: the sheet music that I have recently bought on our way through Columbus, Ohio. It's title, *Love is a Fleeting Thing.*

"You play very nicely," she says. "Just keep practicing."

"Thanks, but I know my technique needs improving. Am I holding my hand correctly?" I look at her expecting a pointer or two on the position of my hand or my timing, which I know is poor since I resist counting out loud or sometimes not counting at all.

"Just keep practicing," she repeats and rises from the piano bench.

"Oh, but..." I begin. Mrs. Wyman interrupts.

"Your twenty minutes are up," she says firmly, "and I have another pupil coming. Don't forget your music." She gathers up my music from the piano and hands it to me. Not quite comprehending that the lesson is really and truly over, I sit unmoving on the bench.

Beside the front door, where she is already waiting to let me out, Mrs.Wyman reminds me, "I have another student coming."

I walk nearly a block away from Mrs. Wyman's house when suddenly the disappointment thoroughly sinks in. The music lesson is all for nothing. The woman doesn't even talk to me. Is that what I want even more than the lesson...an adult to talk to...someone to encourage me?

What a simpleton I am, or "arse," as Denny would say. The woman, apparently long past her own enthusiasm for teaching, gives me neither suggestions on improving my technique nor the friendly words of encouragement I crave. I stop on the corner before crossing the street and repeat what the woman said: You play very nicely. I know that isn't the truth, but Mrs. Wyman has collected an unanticipated three dollars this afternoon from a naïve girl, me, and so a fib is a suitable trade in her eyes. Besides, she will never see me again since I tell her quite plainly that our troupe is leaving town the morning after our performance.

Suddenly my anger ignites. Abruptly I turn around and head back in the direction of the piano teacher's house deciding: I'll ring her doorbell and shout in her face, "You're a fraud! You didn't give me even one cent's worth of your time. You're a cheater. I want my money back!"

I stop and stand on a corner fuming. My anger and my mortification are partly my fault. Certainly I am also to blame. Only a stupid person would try to pick out a good music teacher from the phone book in a strange town or take a lesson at all when they aren't sure of a place to practice afterwards. I regard myself with disgust. Thank goodness no one else knows about this fiasco.

A whirlwind of shame flushes up my neck and the words tumble out, a vocal ranting at myself. "You threw three whole dollars away! Dumb, dumb, dumb!" Quickly I look around me. Is there anyone observing me as I rant to myself on a street corner? No, not unless somebody in one of the nearby houses happens to be looking out of a window. Anyway, I tell myself, not out loud this time, I'm not going to let the kids in the troupe know about my stupidity.

On my way to my room, I stop at the hotel-tobacco registration desk to ask, "Are there any letters for me?" Getting a letter from Dorothy or some of my friends from Seaplace, will raise my spirits, balance out the losses of the day. I need something to keep me from feeling depressed. How I miss Dorothy's quiet manner, Peter's humor. They have always made me feel secure, part of a family, and they wouldn't laugh at me if I told them about the music lesson and my lack of worldliness. If only we could be back together again.

The desk clerk shakes his head. "Sorry, Miss. No letters." I smile in spite of my disappointment and keep the shape of that stiff smile until I reach the empty elevator where no one can see how dispirited I feel. Is it anger at myself or frustration or both that bring on the tears? Isn't it also loneliness? Hastily, I wipe the signs of tears away before the elevator door opens at my floor. My-oh-my, I lash out at myself, aren't you just overflowing with "poor little me" thoughts.

I spot not one member of the troupe again until it's time to meet in the lobby for the ride over to the high school where the performance is to take place this evening at seven-thirty.

The first act of the play goes smoothly. It's good to hear the familiar sounds of children in the audience ooooing and aaaahing once again. Their emotions burst out during the play so freely, so unselfconsciously. It makes me realize how much I miss their adulation and applause.

During the second act, there are some long pauses as we wait for Jane to remember her lines. Then Greg, the newest member of the cast, awkwardly drops his fiddle bow and Denny fills in the pause with suitable words...words never conceived by the author of the play.

"Musician, pick up thy bow and play," says King Denny.

"Yes, Sire." Greg bends over to retrieve his bow from the floor and strikes Carl in the butt, which makes him jump forward with a small noise almost like a girl's squeal. Carl then turns abruptly around to see what pokes him and accidentally knocks the bow out of Greg's hand. Once again Greg bends over to retrieve his bow from the stage floor. All this time the phonograph music to which Greg is supposed to mime-play his fiddle, swells and continues without any bowing action. Under cover of the music, Denny says, "That's a royal goose," and Jane openly laughs and I have to bite the insides of my mouth to retain my queenly demeanor as I sit next to Denny on the throne.

"Clumsy!" admonishes King Denny out of the corner of his smiling mouth. Obviously he is trying to break us all up with laughter, but we each regain our proper characters, and the act finishes smoothly, though it is badly flawed.

After the performance Carl tells everyone to study their lines more carefully, and asks Greg to either put glue on his fingers or "tie the violin bow around your damn neck."

"Yeah," agrees Denny, "preferably in the form of a noose."

On our way to Springfield, the day before my disastrous music lesson, Denny had informed all of us that he knew someone in the city who had been a former Lu-Travis performer. "I'm going to get in touch with him if I can." I think I may have caught a glimpse of that fellow the next evening right after Denny slipped quietly through the lobby. That Denny "slipped" through almost unnoticed was not typical, because when he entered most hotel lobbies, he wanted to be noticed and he behaved as though he was going on stage. Not that evening. Right behind him was a man of medium height and slight in build compared to Denny. He wore glasses and looked a whole lot older than Denny, possible thirty years old to Denny's nineteen.

The two men walked through the lobby and into the elevator at such a brisk pace that I wasn't even sure they were together. That the man with glasses might be Denny's friend was purely a guess. I didn't think anymore about it until late that night, nearly midnight, when my telephone rang. A rather hesitant voice said, "This is the hotel desk clerk. Did you see a fellow enter Mr. Bonter's room?

"No," I answered truthfully. Why?"

"Oh, it's not important." The extremely polite voice said, "Thank you," and hung up.

Denny's room was just across the hall from mine, so I waited a few minutes and then quietly opened my door and stepped out into the hall to listen. Sure enough, I could hear more than one voice coming through the open transom at the top of the door. But no light showed through the transom or from under the door.

My interest piqued by the mysterious phone call, I descended in the elevator and asked the desk clerk why he had just phoned my room unless there was something wrong. Maybe, I thought, the man in Denny's room was dangerous, and Denny didn't know it. The desk clerk looked puzzled. "Miss, I didn't phone your room."

"But someone just phoned my room to ask if Mr. Bonter had a guest in his room which happens to be just across the hall from mine.

That person claimed to be the desk clerk, so I assumed something was…"

"Thank you, Miss. I'll do some checking."

I returned to my room thoroughly mystified. If the desk clerk hadn't made the phone call, who had? Who had asked about Denny's guest? Was someone in the Princess troupe trying to check up on Denny? But the voice wasn't familiar and why would anyone care whether he had a guest or not? Belatedly, I decided that it would have been wiser if I had ignored the phone call because notifying the desk clerk might get Denny into trouble.

A few minutes later I heard the elevator door slip open and footsteps in the hall. I could hear everything clearly through the transom above my own door. I heard a sharp rap on Denny's door just across from mine. This time, the voice I heard was the authoritative voice of the hotel clerk.

"Mr. Bonter? Are you in there?"

There was a long pause before Denny answered. His voice came through the door faintly, as though he had just awakened from a deep sleep. "Yes…who is it?"

"I'm the hotel desk clerk. Mr. Bonter, is there someone else in there with you? The hotel doesn't allow two people in a room unless both are registered at the desk."

"No, no one is here…just me," came Denny's sleepy sounding voice from within the room.

He had lied, of course, and I think the desk clerk suspected it too, for he stood outside Denny's door several minutes listening before his footsteps told me that he had headed down the narrow hall towards the elevator.

I figured out why Denny had lied. If the light had been left on, he could have told the clerk that his guest was just getting ready to leave. Since he had been caught with the light off, the clerk might think something aberrant was going on if Denny had openly confessed the presence of a guest. It might even mean…supposing Denny liked men better than women? This wasn't the first time that the thought had flitted into my mind, yet I hadn't bothered to give the idea much attention until right now.

If Denny liked men, why did he sometimes whistle at girls out the car window as we drove along the streets of a town? Did men such as Denny like women even a little bit, or did they actually fear women like me or that girl, Lisa, because we might steal a man friend away from them? There were too many angles to my suspicions regarding Denny and his orientation, all unanswered.

How curious it seemed that a man might prefer another man instead of a woman. Was it really possible? To me the idea seemed in the category of a Ripley sensation or witches, ghosts, and beings from outer space. Surely sex wasn't possible between two men. How could they do it? I was curious to know, but I couldn't risk asking anyone questions so raunchy.

Never had I heard of such a strange phenomenon. To my mind, men liked woman and women liked men and that was that. Growing up in a small community as a child of older parents had kept me under protective wraps. Now here I was, spewed out into the larger world, my mind still bottled and plugged with cotton. I couldn't even imagine a conversation in which my folks tried to explain such an aberration as men liking men. They hadn't actually explained boy-girl sex either. "Ann," my mother had once said, "women and men go to bed together to have children. It wasn't meant to be an act for enjoyment."

My thoughts returned to the mystery man I had talked to on the phone just twenty minutes ago. Someone was certainly jealous of Denny's guest now sleeping in the room across the hall from me; I sincerely doubted that it was Tom or the new fellow, Greg, who had just arrived to take George's place. By the process of elimination, only Carl was left as a suspect.

I recalled certain signs of Carl's protectiveness towards Denny and also Denny's annoyance at Carl for mingling too closely with the girls in the troupe. I well remembered the dirty looks Denny gave Jessica when she had flaunted her dangly earrings at Carl and invited him to dance with her. Denny had also quickly severed the friendliness between Carl and myself right at the beginning of the tour. After calling me "Mrs. Manager" several times, Carl had foregone my assistance with the weekly report to Lu-Travis. I also noticed that Carl and Denny rarely let each other out of sight anymore.

All keyed up over the unusual incident, I stayed awake quite late that night. I kept listening for sounds from across the hall. But I never heard the man in Denny's room leave, if he ever did. When we all congregated in the lobby the next morning, the strange man had simply vanished.

NINETEEN

"Jesus Christ!" Denny swore the next morning as I drove the car out of town on our way to Joplin, Missouri. "Here we go again. Springfield was one place I'd like to have stayed for a while."

Yeah, I thought, recalling the man in Denny's room last night, I'll bet you would.

"The rooms were so small," Jane sighed. "I hope that's not typical of all the places we stay."

"Oh no, Sweetie," rejoined Denny, "not typical at all. Most of the hotel rooms are even smaller and a whole lot dirtier."

It was an easy drive of thirty-five or forty miles to Joplin where we arrived at the Earle Hotel. After the tiny Springfield hotel lobby, this one felt as vast as a ballroom. Our voices echoed loudly in the openness. We each registered separately this time, and I got the room on the second floor at the top of the wide stairs. My room was large with a double bed, chairs, all sticky furniture past its prime plus a sink but no bathroom. I unpacked and a half-hour later met the others in the café off the lobby.

"Well, it's finally happened." Tom said.

"Oh, no!" Carl groaned. "Not your army orders."

"Yup. They were forwarded from home. The delay in forwarding them all the way from Florida doesn't give me any leeway. Sorry, but I've got to leave right today to report to the draft board in Florida."

We all wore the same expression, a weird, "not again" look. Our performances of the Lost Princess had already suffered by having to replace George and Jessica with Jane and Greg who had barely learned their cues.

"We'll miss you," I said, and meant it sincerely. Tom had never been afraid to work. He drove the truck with its broken seat springs, lifted scenery, repaired broken props and in general went quietly about his business with only minimal cussing here and there. It was doubtful that acting would ever be his ultimate career goal. This tour had been just a station on the way, a fill-in of time until he got his orders from the army, and now they had come.

Carl finished his lunch hurriedly and went off to phone the bad news to Travis. We were to give two performances here in Joplin, and the first one was scheduled for the next afternoon at one-thirty. Doubtless it would have to be cancelled.

When we arrived in each new town, Carl had to contact the organization responsible for booking the Lu-Travis Troupe. Sometimes it was a parent-teacher association; often it was a women's club of some sort. In university towns the sponsor was frequently the alumni. In this particular case, Carl phoned a Mrs. Withee of the Joplin Women's Club.

Afterwards, Carl told us what she had said, and it sounded quite hopeful. By late afternoon Mrs. Withee actually had found a temporary replacement for Tom. Her choice was someone connected to the Joplin Civic Theatre.

We saw Tom off at the bus station with much waving and loud cheers, but I had the impression that Tom was half glad to leave this quarrelsome group. At least I didn't perceive any visible signs of regret, even though a term in the army wasn't usually considered something to look forward to. "Maybe you won't see any action," I said. Tom gave me a bear hug in response and then whacked each of the guys on the back.

✳

To everyone's surprise and delight the Joplin performance is booked in a genuine theatre. All those schools with skimpy stages fade from my mind as I stand on stage next to the work light facing this vast auditorium of seats. No more bumping into each other as we cross the stage, no stepping on toes, or in Fay's case dancing on someone else's toes. When I look outward across the orchestra pit and on towards the paneled doors of the lobby, all the mystique of the theatre returns to me. I imagine the heightened sense, the excitement, of being up here on the stage when the curtain slowly rises. In merely stepping off the stage and down into the rows of empty seats, I feel a smallness; once again I metamorphose back into a lesser human being.

The high ceiling of the theatre is covered with faded cherubs and fancy plaster scallops, and as I turn and look back at the proscenium, I observe that it's also elaborately embellished with pilasters and carved Acanthus leaves once covered in a patina of gold. There are small chips of plaster missing everywhere but even that doesn't lessen my awe of the palatial splendor. Backstage are genuine dressing rooms, though only one or two are available to us. The others are crammed with old furniture and unused props.

"Sure could use a cleaning," Greg drawls.

"Well, get a broom," snaps Denny.

"Why me? You get a broom."

"Why are those guys in overalls just standing around?" I ask.

"They're union guys." Carl explains.

"It's filthy! Jane laments. "Our costumes will be ruined."

My queen's costume, the long elaborate dress with fake ermine down the front, has just come back from the dry cleaners, and now it's going to sweep across the stage and the dressing room floor as I make my entrances and exits. There seems to be no one to care what happens to this faded old beauty of a theatre, yet those union stagehands just stand around watching. There are three men to pull one curtain and bring up the house lights.

"Come on, everybody. Pitch in," admonishes Carl. "There's no one else to do the job. If the union guys do the work, someone will have to pay them union wages. Greg, go ask them for a broom, a dustpan, and some clean rags for dusting. You girls clean one dressing room for yourselves, and we'll clean the other one for us."

The afternoon performance goes smoothly with the local actor in Tom's role of the villain. Fortunately he doesn't have many lines to learn. Too bad he isn't free to continue on tour with us, but he isn't. Anyway, he's far too much like a scarecrow, limp and scrawny, for the part of a villain. He can't scare anybody except a crow. Someone must be found to fill Tom's part before we leave Joplin...someone who can travel with us for the remainder of the tour, which is supposed to last into April.

✲

Much to Denny's disgust, our hotel in Joplin was ten or twelve blocks from the main street of town. Denny wanted to be near the movie theatres and restaurants whenever he could. He abhorred walking, though it would have reduced some of his flab.

Again, our hotel, the Earle, was one of a long chain of hotels. The management, either from laxity or budget reasons, had gone easy on the strong disinfectant, yet a trace was still present. The disinfectant smell took second place to the musty trunk odor of unaired rooms and old limp mattresses. The hollowed-out shapes in the mattresses from past sleepers were recorded for posterity, clearly visible under the thin bedspread in my room.

A few elderly men sat around the vast lobby of the Earle during the day reading their newspapers usually in chairs in front of the huge glass windows, then they trundled off across the cold terrazzo floor to the elevator early in the evenings. They weren't derelicts, I was told by the young man at the registration desk, but retired men living out their lives frugally, maybe in hopes of making their money and their lives come to an end at the same time, instead of the money first. They were like furniture on a stage set, removing themselves before the next act at nine o'clock. The exception was Mr. Sutter who hung around the lobby until nearly ten o'clock.

Somehow, I had gained the dubious honor of getting the large room at the top of the first flight of stairs in the hotel. What a flight of stairs! It reminded me of the wide stairs in Scarlet O'Hara's house in the movie, though not quite as steep and not carpeted in red. I felt self-conscious whenever I ventured down those wide steps. I gripped the rail tightly and swung my eyes up at the ceiling high above me at the third floor level, and then suddenly down again to the floor below, letting the whole dimly lighted lobby beneath me turn dizzily until I closed my eyes to stop the motion.

Lu-Travis scheduled us to stay two weeks in Joplin Missouri, our longest in any one town. This gave her an opportunity to find an actor to fill Tom's role in the play and for us to rehearse.

At first everyone in the troupe checked into the Earle, but three days later I noticed Carl and Denny at the hotel desk with their luggage beside them. I wondered what was going on. Next to them stood a lean, good-looking young man slightly taller than Carl.

"You're not leaving us, are you?" I asked.

"Yeah," answered Denny. "We're moving to Larry's house. It's cheaper." Then he remembered that I didn't know Larry. "Larry meet Ann; she's Queenie in the play." The bare necessities of his duty over, Denny walked out behind Carl and Larry who was carrying the bulk of Denny's luggage. Later, I learned from Fay that Larry was the new recruit to take Tom's part in the play. Far too pretty a boy to take the part of a villain, I thought.

After the second performance in Joplin, there was little to do but read magazines and spend time in the coffee shop, a long narrow room that had been stripped of half its metal tables. I could see the dark patches of old adhesive where the linoleum had been wrenched up as the tables were removed. The room's partial emptiness caused the jukebox music to project a lost-in-a-train-station effect. There were seldom more than two or three people in the coffee shop at one time. Often I was there all by myself.

At first the twangy voice of the cowboy singer coming from the jukebox sounded almost laughable to me. But soon his forlorn lament wove its way into my own nebulous longings, and tears threatened to flow. I don't know why, for certainly no one I knew had died on the lonesome prairie nor had I lost a lover. Maybe the tinge of shivery sadness was just loneliness. The velvety voice of Nat King Cole didn't raise my spirits either.

Sometimes Fay and Jane had breakfast in the coffee shop, and then I'd join them even though I'd had my own breakfast much earlier. Later on, during our stay at the Earle Hotel, I lost track of them, except for an occasional glimpse as they passed through the lobby. By then I'd become acquainted with both Charley and Ernie and no longer felt so alone and in need of companionship.

Charley was the hotel clerk, polite and gracious, no doubt from his hotel training, or maybe it was more than that. He was about my age or possibly a little older. He always glanced up to give me a broad, friendly smile whenever I descended the grand staircase from my room. The second morning when I stopped at the curved check-in desk to ask Charley how far it was to the main street of town, he introduced me to Ernie, a tall dark-haired man with the beginnings of a receding hairline. At least thirty-five, I calculated quickly. He's kind-of old, I thought. Too old to interest me.

"Ann meet Ernie. He comes and goes, in and out, so you probably haven't seen him around here before. He drives a semi…and drives the women mad." Charley's eyes twinkled behind his no-rim glasses. Ah, a teaser, I thought.

Ernie laughed easily and added, "Don't believe everything Charley tells you." Then he politely asked me to join him for coffee, and I accepted. It seemed safe enough since the coffee shop was right there under the same hotel roof and just a few yards from the main part of the lobby. Boredom forced me to bend my firm ideas of who was and who wasn't proper company. Generally it would have been unthinkable for me to associate with an unknown man, especially a truck driver. Ignorantly, I put all truck drivers into one narrow category: they were uneducated, they swore a lot, and they had bad manners.

As Ernie and I entered the coffee shop, I caught my heel on the torn linoleum, and he grabbed my arm to keep me from falling. How long had it been since anyone had the good manners to assist me or care whether I fell on my face or not? Just a casual grip on my arm to steady me felt like the fondest attention.

At the table in the coffee shop Ernie expanded on his trucking job. It seemed that he owned his own rig and drove long distances into Arkansas, Oklahoma, and Kansas. He described the precariousness of backing the new cars off the rig when the metal was slick with a thin skin of ice, and the worry of jack-knifing on snowy roads. The subject wasn't of great interest to me, but I listened. Anything seemed better to me than sitting in a restaurant all alone and listening to the sad lyrics of the cowboy singers.

The jukebox was playing a Tennessee Ernie Ford tune about workers who owed their lives to the company store, when Denny and Carl entered the coffee shop. They looked straight at me, and I raised my hand in greeting, but they didn't bother to acknowledge my presence even by a nod. After they were seated, Denny kept glancing over at our table and grinning. Immediately I knew that he and Carl were discussing me, probably making up jokes about my "picking up" a strange man. Ernie asked me who they were, and I explained.

"Pay no attention to them," Ernie said, guessing that I was disturbed. "I've already heard about the so called 'fellows' in your troupe."

What did Ernie mean by that remark, I wondered? Was it that easy for him to spot men who liked men more than women?

*

The second time Ernie and I drift into the coffee shop together, he turns the conversation wholly on me by asking where I'm from...have I been to college...what are my plans when the theatre tour is over?

"What's a beautiful young lady like you doing with this...." He pauses, leaving out the derogatory word. "...crowd you're traveling with? It's only a step above the magazine sales people who usually stay here at the Earle."

I shrug and smile and enjoy the heady feeling of being judged superior to everyone else in the troupe. Seldom of late has anyone focused attention on me. Here is a mature person to talk to, someone who seems genuinely concerned about me and my future. That's all that matters to me at the moment. I begin to relax. Beams of warmth sweep through me. I feel admired and once again sought-after for my company. It's the first time since leaving Dorothy and Peter and the rest of my friends from last summer.

"You seem unlike the rest of the troupe, a bit more refined," Ernie says. That comment is most flattering, and I certainly want to believe that I am a cut above the average; who doesn't?

Ernie continues to toss out compliments. "Most theatre people I've seen, and that's not many, I admit, wear gobs of make-up. You seem more natural. I like the way you've let your hair grow long, and the understated way you use make-up."

I soak up the praise and fall for the next line and the next. It seems to me that I have been ignored so long that my thirst for compliments can't begin to be satiated.

"You're the kind of girl I'd like to settle down with someday. Do you think you could like someone like me enough for that?" he asks me softly.

Whoa, I begin to think, slow up. "I hardly know you at all yet," I stall because I want to avoid hurting his feelings, or is it really because I don't want to discourage him from saying more and more nice things about me. Underneath these wonderful morale-boosting compliments, I instinctively know he is spreading it on thickly to soften me up for his own purposes. Even so, I still enjoy his vigorous pursuit. "You certainly seem like a perceptive individual...hardly the stereotypical truck driver."

Ernie bursts out laughing. "My dear Anne, we truck drivers aren't all crude and rude with blasphemy on our tongues, though I do admit to a few choice words."

Somewhere in the back of my mind a warning voice pricks me. Ernie is pretty smooth. He's more adept at this game than most guys. I squelch that *spoil-sport* voice so that I can bask in Ernie's attention a little longer. He makes me feel so admired, so wanted, like the applause the children give us at the performances. Maybe, I think, I needn't be an actress. Maybe I just need to find someone who thinks I'm special and then get married. Isn't love better than applause?

Anyway, what possible harm can it do to listen to Ernie since I'll soon be moving on to another town and never see him again anyway?

Charley is also good company. Nights are especially dreary at the hotel, and Charley, if he is on duty at the desk has very little to keep him busy after nine in the evening. He usually switches on the radio when the lobby is empty of everyone except old Mr. Sutter. The second evening after our troupe arrives, Charley asks me to dance.

"But you're on duty, aren't you?"

"It's all right. My boss is very understanding. Come-on, you do dance, don't you?"

"A little," I answer. So we dance until the night clerk comes on duty at midnight.

Mr. Sutter stays up later and later. He has nothing to do, so after reading his evening newspaper, seems to enjoy watching Charley and me quietly dancing to the Dorsey music. Charley's companionship is all very open. Charley with his feather light step and his breezy conversation, punctured with corny jokes, draws no great sexual response from me. But that's exactly what makes Charley so comfortable and safe to be around. He is like people imagine the guy next door ought to be. His twist of words and slaying of tired old clichés puts me into a round of giggles that can hardly be more therapeutic. He calls me "Anne of a Thousand Lobby Nights," or sometimes the "Light of the Lu-Travis Brigade." Between the attentions of Charley and Ernie, my ego flies to the top of the flagpole.

One evening, Charley and I are dancing to <u>You Are My Sunshine,</u> a tune coming softly from the radio, which Charley has turned very low so that the sound won't drift up the stairway to the rooms above. At ten o'clock Mr. Sutter says goodnight to us, and we wave a "goodnight" in return. He shuffles off to the elevator.

"There goes unsubtle Sutter," remarks Charley with a smile.

"You mean that he always says what he thinks?"

"Something like that. Oh, he's one of the nicer old guys around here, but he does like to stick his nose into other people's business. Sutter's got nothing better to do. You know, he's been telling everyone about us. That is, everyone who will listen to him."

"What is there to tell? We've done nothing wrong."

"Of course not. But gossip kind-of breeds on itself until something sprouts out of nothing."

An uneasy shiver sneaks up my spine as I consider the trouble Denny might stir up if he hears about the dancing. "Then we'd better stop this lobby dancing," I say and stop dead on the spot.

"And go back to the dull routine I had before you came?" Charley draws me back into the dance. "No sir-eee."

"You must have reports to write up," I suggest.

"Oh, those. They can wait."

"Doesn't the manager object to having me hang around?"

"No, Max doesn't mind." I have stopped dancing again. "Getting tired?" Charley asks.

"No, but could this dancing and Mr. Sutter's gossip hurt your chances of getting into that Junior Hotel Management Program you told me about?"

"Max has already given me a good recommendation for that. By the way, Max and I would like to take you to dinner and bowling some night. Do you bowl?"

"Yes, but I'm not especially good at it." Sports in general leave me passive except for ice skating, roller skating, or biking. "What about Max's wife? Didn't you tell me that Max is married?"

"Sure. His wife has gone to visit her mother in San Antonio, so Max and I have been doing our own cooking all week, and we're thoroughly sick of it. We're ready for a night out. How about it?"

"All right, if it's sometime in the next three days. We leave on Monday."

"I was afraid of that. I'm hoping for a huge snowstorm…one that'll delay you for another thirty years at the very earliest."

"I'll miss your company, too." I say and mean it. "I don't feel particularly compatible with anyone in this tour group."

"I should hope not. They aren't what they seem to be."

I suspect he is referring to Denny and Carl, maybe Larry, too. Once again the incident in the Springfield hotel flashes through my mind.

155

Charley swoops me across the vast lobby past the huge windows, under the stairway, and back in front of the reception desk where we almost twirl into Fay and Jane as they head for the stairs. I wave to them, and Charley and I go on dancing.

TWENTY

The next evening, I had dinner with Charley and Max in a café up on the main street of Joplin. I was disappointed that they didn't take me someplace a bit nicer than the type of restaurant with which I was already too familiar. I had been hoping for something special, white tablecloths maybe, but this was the usual nondescript cafe. Afterwards we went bowling, a sport at which I had never become adept. Max gave me a few pointers on how to hold the ball and where to aim down the alley, but the ball tended to hurt my thumb; my scores remained very low. In the company of his boss, Charley was quieter, letting Max carry the conversation. We were back at the hotel early, because Charley had to relieve the day clerk. I thanked them both profusely. Though I may have been disappointed in their choice of restaurants, I was grateful for their attention and company without which I would have been left to eat all by myself in the hotel coffee shop. Its chewed-up floor did nothing to improve my appetite, nor did the stain, a dog pee color.

Ernie had asked me to go out on a date with him several times, but I had always turned him down. "Maybe sometime," I kept stalling. Finally, after the third invitation, I decided to ask Charley more about Ernie before accepting.

"Oh sure, Ernie's all right. Just don't believe everything he tells you." I didn't confess to Charley that I had already swallowed most of Ernie's flattery.

Eventually I agreed to go out on a date with Ernie. It was to occur on the same evening after he returned from a two-day run to deliver cars into Oklahoma. I rather looked forward to the excitement of a genuine date, but also wished Ernie was less serious and more like the pun-dropping Charley.

Ernie was late returning that evening, and the weather was growing nasty. A fine mist fell before dark and turned immediately into ice. I hovered near the big plate glass window in the lobby watching the frozen mist turn to snow. Charley was at the hotel desk as usual that evening. Finally, he came out from behind the desk to join me.

"If you're looking for Ernie, well, he came in about an hour ago."

"Oh? We were supposed to go somewhere this evening."

"He's probably fallen asleep from exhaustion. He does that after driving his rig for two consecutive days if the weather's been bad."

"I'd better not disturb him then." I waited a while longer, but Ernie didn't show up, so I went up to his room which was just a few doors down the worn hall carpet from mine. I found the inner door open and slices of light leaked through the outer louvered door. I tapped lightly. There was no response. When I put my eyes up close to the louvers, I could see Ernie stretched out across the bed, his feet dangling over the side. He was still wearing his leather jacket. I was in a dilemma. I didn't want to wake him up but on the other hand I didn't want him to think I'd ducked out of the date either. I returned to my room to wait.

Another hour passed, and Ernie still didn't show up for our date. I went back to his room. This time it was completely dark. At first I felt relieved that the date wasn't going to take place, because I suspected Ernie might keep me busy fending off advances. Then from somewhere inside my mind doubt arose. What if Ernie had never intended to keep the date at all? My wits, which had been numbed by flattery and attention from Ernie, began to wake up. Enlightenment spread heat and color from the small hollow at the base of my throat up my neck to my ears, then to my whole face. I had been stood up! After all the extravagant things Ernie had said to me—how pretty I was and how he cared for me—all that palaver and male posturing.

It was laughable. *I* was laughable! I'd fallen for every bit of it because I was so starved to hear nice things about myself.

Pride forced me to pretend nothing was wrong, even into telling Charley, "Ernie has probably forgotten our date." I smiled and pretended not to care.

"Well, that's a relief!" Charley sighed. "That guy is a real charmer, and I didn't think he should be asking you out on a date at all. He just recently became engaged to some girl in Amarillo. He told me the date of the wedding had been set. In fact, I think he's taking off for Amarillo by the end of the week.

"Why didn't you tell me all this before?" I knew I sounded peevish, but the anger was all against myself; how easily I had grabbed the worm. Was Ernie laughing at me? He had so easily baited and caught the fish...me. Had it raised his ego to work me over with smooth talk to the point where he could finally get me to date him, or had it been the "dropping me" after the successful conquest that had given him his "high," and inflated his male ego? I had been manipulated so easily. How ridiculous I appeared to myself. How gullible!

"I didn't want to rat on a nice guy," explained Charley. "Besides, I wanted you to make up your own mind about Ernie. Let's dance." Charley spun me out into the middle of the lobby floor. Before long, he had me giggling at his outlandish jokes all over again. Greg came down from his room and sat around the lobby watching us until Jane and Fay coaxed him off to the coffee shop.

On Sunday afternoon, the day before we were to leave Joplin, the troupe gathered for one more rehearsal. Carl chose my hotel room, as he had done previously, because it was conveniently located at the top of the stairs. It was also larger than most of the other rooms.

"I see you've been enjoying your layover." Denny said to me emphasizing the word *layover.* "Lisa was always picking up guys in hotels too."

I answered with cold dignity, ignoring what he had implied. "Having friends certainly does make time pass by more quickly. You should know." Denny appeared to ignore my last remark.

"Won't you miss your intimate evening dances? Or are you planning to quit the troupe and stay here in Joplin?"

"What gave you that idea?"

"Oh," Denny grinned, "all that cheek to cheek dancing."

"I didn't notice you around here watching." I was curious; how had Denny known?

"Old Mr. Sutter keeps us informed. Greg, too."

I was so innocent of any wrong behavior with Charley that I assumed nobody could read anything questionable into my conduct during my days in Joplin. Still, I felt an uneasiness, like the ominous quiver and shake of leaves before a rain storm.

Carl interrupted my thoughts: "Let's get down to rehearsing and let's be on time tomorrow morning. We leave the hotel at eight o'clock sharp." Carl's statement was followed by loud groans from everyone.

After rehearsal, I laid my suitcase on the bed and packed a few items such as lingerie and clothing that wouldn't wrinkle. I stopped to look around at the sticky dark furniture and hollowed out mattress. I'd grown used to this room. It felt familiar after ten days, as though it were my own. The next hotel room might not be even this nice and the chances of it being this large was almost nil.

I went down to the lobby to pay my room bill and then on into the coffee shop for supper. Someone had put money into the jukebox. I still didn't care much for the nasal twang of the cowboy singers, but the sound touched a sentimental button inside my head tonight. I knew the songs would remind me of this hotel in Joplin for years to come.

*

Around nine o'clock that same evening, I cross the hall from my room and peer down over the railing to the floor below to see if Charley is on the night desk as usual. From the lobby below, Charley looks upwards and gestures for me to hurry down.

"Charley," I remark, as we stand waiting for the next piece of dance music to begin on the radio, "I can't thank you enough for making these ten days a pleasant memory."

"They've been special for me, too. I really hate to see you go. Maybe I'll see you again someday. Will you write to me?"

"Why yes...I'd like that very much." It has never crossed my mind that Charley might be interested in continuing our friendship. All his lighthearted banter has implied only a desire to fill up the dull hours of his nighttime shift. It never occurs to me that he might have a more lasting interest in me. Ernie's little romancing game has inured me from believing in Charley's sincerity.

As the music begins again, Charley holds me closer than usual. I don't mind. This last evening seems a little sad. After tonight I will no longer have Charley and his jovial conversation to bolster my morale. I will have no one. Already I feel a bit depressed and unconsciously snuggle up to Charley.

"Wish I were going with you," Charley says. "This is a dull job, just waiting here until they can find room for me in their Junior Management Program. But you...you'll be meeting new people, seeing new places, and getting acquainted with new desk clerks."

"Hey, now!" I stop dancing. "I don't do this at every hotel on the tour. This is the first time."

"Only kidding. I know you don't. I'm just jealous. You might meet Mr. Right before I can see you again." Charley pulls me closer and lightly kisses my nose. Then with surprising ardor, he kisses my lips hard enough to bruise them against my teeth. I can feel the stirrings in his body, the parts pressing tightly against mine. I feel no sexual awakening in my own...just a nice warm feeling of being very important to this human being. I like him so much that I want to feel something extra. Unconsciously, I must be responding to his ardor. Charley comes out of the embrace looking very pleased about the whole thing. He seems not at all disappointed with my reaction. We pause, stand there, and look at each other for a few seconds. Then Mr. Sutter ambles through the lobby, smiling broadly, as though he has a wonderful secret.

"A little late in the evening for you, isn't it, Mr. Sutter?" Charley looks at his watch and probably wishes the old guy hadn't shown up at all.

"Couldn't sleep." Mr. Sutter grins again. I expect he has caught Charley and me in the middle of our embrace as he crept quietly out of the elevator. Otherwise, why is he wearing that delighted *I have a secret* expression on his face?

Charley and I walk to the foot of the stairs just out of Mr. Sutter's view and range of hearing, or so we hope. "I won't be up in the morning to see you off," Charley says. "Could you give me the address of the hotel where you expect to stay at the end of the week?"

"Of course." I still find it unbelievable that he actually wants to keep in touch. I warn him, "Lu-Travis doesn't usually let us know where we're going more than one week in advance." I climb the stairs to my room to get the itinerary. I'm not really convinced that Charley means to write to me. I fold the itinerary into the shape of an airplane and send it sailing over the banister railing down to Charley. Then I hear him begin to type a copy. A few minutes later he leaves his desk just long enough to bring the itinerary back up to my room.

"You won't forget to send me the next address?" Charley makes it sound terribly important that I not let him down. My laughing, jokester Charley has become so serious.

"I won't forget. I promise." I walk part way down the stairs with Charley, and we stop where Mr. Sutter can't see us from his chair near the windows in the lobby. Then the phone at the registration desk begins to jangle for attention. Charley blows a kiss to me and hurries down to answer the phone. He looks up as I send a casual kiss back to him over the railing. With a wave of my hand and a mouthed "good night and goodbye," I return to my room.

I will miss Charley. He makes me feel important, sought after, if only for this short time. Even the experience with Ernie hasn't been without some merit I suppose, though the disgust I feel for myself and the shame of being taken in so easily, lingers with me for a time. When I think about the incident and my gullibility, I feel like walking with my head down somewhere around my ankles. What if everyone in the hotel knows about Ernie and his campaign to lure me? Have they all been laughing? I think about how I will behave if I accidentally meet Ernie in the upstairs hallway before leaving. But I never do see him again.

Charley is right though. I have other places to see and other people to meet as the troupe travels westerly. At the time, it's hard to appreciate the full importance of leaving a stalwart friend like Charley behind when there is still that invisible thread pulling me onwards. Perhaps the thread represents nothing more than a yearning to *see the other side of the mountain,* or something similar to digging for treasure. Surely the next or the next spade of dirt will bring up the box of gold. Each new town and each school stage is undiscovered territory, a package to be opened. And there will be lots of other people to meet, maybe some as nice as Charley.

TWENTY-ONE

We had traveled to many small towns since the beginning of the theatre tour back in October, but our acceptance as visitors in Muskogee, Oklahoma, seemed a shade off from all the others. The town felt unfriendly.

Muskogee, everyone agreed, gave us the impression that we were foreigners, maybe North Koreans or Russians, whatever nationality was the most unpopular in the United States in 1950. Even the gray sky—the sun didn't shine for three whole days—and the bareness without the softness of winter snow, consorted to give us the ominous feeling of being unwelcome. The coldness of the weather was not the frosted-window cold of Waterloo, Iowa, far from it; rather it was a dampness that turned my fingers quickly white from lack of circulation.

Heads swiveled whenever we entered or exited the hotel lobby. I suppose it was mere curiosity that made folks, who seldom had strangers visiting their town, watch us. Outside of a salesman or two, most of the men we saw in the lobby were dressed in overalls, boots, and wide brimmed hats. I never saw any women in the lobby at all except for Jane and Fay. After all, what husband would punish his wife by deliberately taking her to one of the hotels in which we had to reside?

The lobby-watching men made no attempt to disguise their curiosity about us. Since it was all so open, it was probably completely innocent; however to me it felt as though they were waiting for us to do something wild or lawless in their town. Perhaps they thought, as

Denny suggested at least twice, that we were another group of those disreputable magazine sales people. Whatever the cause, their scrutiny made me uncomfortable. I didn't feel my usual freedom to wander down the street alone. Not that I believed any actual physical harm would come to me, but I felt so self conscious over being watched that I couldn't enjoy going off by myself.

There were only two movie houses in Muskogee, and one of those was closed, so that left only one movie choice for all of us. Denny had seen the movie currently playing when he and Tom had stayed in Des Moines over the Christmas vacation, but he decided to go along with us anyway rather than be left at the hotel by himself. Being more of a social creature than most, he probably needed other people around him as a sounding board to his own existence. How else would he believe himself alive unless actually reflected by other people.

We all trooped into the movie theatre together, seven of us, and Carl asked the manager for free entrance. I doubt if the manager had ever heard of complimentary passes, a tradition of the acting profession in other parts of the country, but after a moment of contemplation in which his face spoke strongly of 'what am I getting myself into,' he shook his head. "No," he said flatly, "but I'll let you in for half price." Reluctantly, we agreed to his terms. I hoped the movie would be worth the price.

His concession was not given graciously and not accompanied by the slightest upturn of his lips. Our motley group was not welcome. I had to admit that we all looked more vagabond than usual. I had worn the funeral-looking black lamb jacket over slacks because the damp air seeped through me like water through a vegetable strainer. The other two girls wore jeans and long winter coats and scarves over their heads. Greg wore his usual, the dowdy old tweed coat which seemed to drag down his stubby figure even further. Denny's coat had lost some of its buttons, and his unbuckled galoshes shuffle-shuffle-slurped as he walked into the theatre lobby. Carl alone looked presentable. If we had worn farmer's attire, doubtless no one would have looked at us twice.

Five of us sat together in seats somewhere around the middle of the orchestra section. Denny and Larry went to the balcony where popcorn was allowed. I felt several pieces of popcorn drop on my head from above during the first ten minutes of the movie. So much for the popcorn rule.

✻

About a fourth of the way into the film, <u>Love on the Riviera,</u> which turns out to be pretty saccharine, Greg, who is sitting next to me, begins to clutch his head with both hands and moan.

"What's wrong?" I whisper, but he doesn't answer. . .just moans a bit louder. Then I can see his head move from side to side with his eyes shut like a medium in a trance. His moans grow louder and people nearby begin reacting to the interruption of the movie. "Shhhh!" I hear from a seat in front of us, and "Quiet!" comes over and over again from different locations.

At first, I think Greg is play-acting to liven up a dull movie, the way Denny sometimes pretends this or that to draw attention to himself, but when Greg begins to clinch his teeth and yell out loud as though in deep pain, we all five get out of our seats and pull him up the aisle between us. As we reach the top of the aisle in the darkened movie theatre, we are met by the manager.

"You're disturbing the rest of the paying audience." He holds the door open to the lobby and herds us through. In the subdued light I see his disapproving scowl. "What's wrong?" he demands.

"We don't know what's wrong," I indicate Greg. "He just moans and holds his head as though it hurts terribly. Even now Greg is holding his head in both hands and weaving it back and forth and moaning, but not quite as loudly as before.

"I'll call a doctor." The manager hurries into his little office. It's so narrow that Fay, Jane and I hover in the doorway unable to squeeze inside. "I'll call a doctor," the manager repeats as he reaches for the telephone. That's when Greg finally manages a bleary, "No. Please. I'll be all right in a minute. Don't bother to call a doctor."

Why not call a doctor, I wonder, unless Greg is faking. He still seems too trance-like to speak clearly, though his groaning has ceased, abruptly. Again the manager offers to call a doctor, but Greg waves a hand at him, a clear signal meaning, no.

"Is he on drugs?" the manager whispers to Carl.

"Not that we know about." Carl sounds as baffled as the rest of us. Greg has overheard and shakes his head. He does seem to be rapidly getting better.

"I'll take him back to the hotel," Carl offers. "The rest of you can return to the movie if you like."

"Yes." The manager agrees with alacrity. "That's a good idea." Again he looks suspiciously at Greg. Evidently the idea of Greg as a drug addict is now firmly ensconced in his head along with his innate wariness of theatre people in general.

"Are you able to tell us what's wrong now?" I ask the hunched-over form of Greg. He shakes his head at me. "I'll tell you all about it after we get back to the hotel."

"I'll refund your money," The manager looks extremely relieved to be rid of Greg and hopefully the rest of us as well. He doubtless thinks the sooner these queers are out of his movie theatre the better for the ordinary good folks of Muskogee.

Carl goes up to the balcony to tell Denny and Larry that he is leaving. By this time the rest of us have missed so much of the movie that we also decide to go back to the hotel with Greg and Carl. Besides, we are curious to find out exactly what is the matter with Greg. The manager also refunds our money.

"Let's get moving," urges Greg as we leave the theatre lobby. Suddenly, his voice sounds much stronger. During the two blocks back to the hotel, Greg refuses to answer our questions, just lowers his head and chin into his oversize collar, turtle fashion. So the rest of us do the same against the cold and dampness. We hustle back to the warmth of the hotel lobby through the blackness of night passing unlighted store windows. Somewhere in the empty street behind us I can hear the footsteps of Carl and Larry and the swish-click of Denny's unbuckled boots.

We gather just inside the hotel doors. I rub my white fingers to get the circulation moving again. Fay and Jane stomp their cold feet to warm up. We are all stalling and waiting for Greg to open up and volunteer a reason for his weird behavior.

"Well, tell. We're waiting." Carl presses Greg for an explanation when none seems forthcoming voluntarily. By now Greg is quite calm with no visible signs of severe pain. No one, I think, can be as sick as he seemed to be back in the movie theatre and then just minutes later appear to be perfectly normal. All of us can see that Greg is smiling. We, however, are not. We stand circling Greg like medieval interrogators bent on the truth before execution.

"Hey, look," Greg waves a hand airily, "I got you a refund on a lousy movie, didn't I?" Greg is almost jovial as he takes the credit for getting our money back.

Carl is angry. "You mean you hauled us out of that movie on a fake headache?"

"Oh, no…no. I really had a migraine."

We all stare at Greg not knowing what to believe. Denny is the exception. He begins to laugh. "Well, that's one performance I've never tried." Evidently he considers the episode a remarkable acting spree and probably wishes he'd been the one to pull it off.

"I really do have an old wound that causes my head to nearly split open," explains Greg. But now we are not so convinced. It sounds like a line from an ancient movie and Denny thinks so too.

"Sounds like a plot I've heard before…something from an old Peter Frobish movie," Denny says. "A silent movie, actually. Except in that movie the feeling, or rather the lack-of, was in the guy's private parts."

"I hear Larry suck warm air through his cold nose, "Too bad this one wasn't silent, too."

Greg, looking around from face to face, must be seeing nothing but stony disbelief. He will have a tough time convincing even one of us that there is anything to his head clutching and groaning.

"They actually put a metal plate in my head…right here." Greg points to the spot on his skull. Larry, standing a head taller than Greg, tries to tap the spot, but Greg ducks aside. "And it gets to hurting so much that I end up screaming sometimes." He looks towards Carl to see if he has convinced at least one of us. Carl's face reveals nothing. He seems as unsure of the truth as the rest of us.

"You won't tell Lu-Travis, will you?" Greg looks around at all of us for reassurance.

"What if it happens again, during a performance for instance?"

"Oh, it won't," Greg assures Carl. "Besides, I keep my pain pills nearby most of the time. Tonight I forgot them."

"Ha! I'd like to see those so called 'pain pills'," Denny smirks.

We are all torn between sympathizing with Greg and kicking the jerk. We have absolutely no way of checking out his story one way or another unless we can actually see the prescription pills he speaks about. As we move further into the lobby to pick up our room keys, I overhear Larry tell Denny, "Sometime during the tour he's sure to slip up...then we'll discover the truth."

"Yeah," agrees Denny. "At least the movie refund put enough money in my pocket for a meal that I wouldn't otherwise have, plus he gave us an evening of high entertainment.

Whatever Greg's problem, wound or grandstanding, he never has another seizure quite like the one that took place during the movie in Muskogee. I wonder what the theatre manager means by "drugs"? I have never heard of anyone getting—what was his expression—hooked on drugs? Aspirin is the extent of my knowledge; and oh yes, I recall an opium den in a movie I had once seen.

The seizure incident is written up in the next evening's newspaper. It's just a small item which states: A male member of the Lu-Travis Troupe which presented The Lost Princess for grades two through six at the high school, became ill from unknown causes at the local movie theatre. He recovered fully and was able to perform the following afternoon.

We didn't want to chance being turned away from the local movie house on the second night in Muskogee. Anyway, the movie isn't that good. Everyone, including Fay and Jane, decide to visit one of the numerous local bars, so I trail along with the others mostly out of curiosity. I have never been that I recall inside a place where liquor is served.

We push our way slowly through the disarray of tables and thick tobacco smoke to find a vacant table. At first, I place my hand across my nose to keep out the smoke and stink of beer until I realize how futile my efforts are.

Behind me, as we slowly work our way to where Larry has spotted an empty table, is a man practicing his burps. "Bet you can't do that, Little Lady," he says, tapping me on the shoulder. I glance at Fay and wrinkle up my nose. "Let's leave," I urge.

"We just got here."

"Too much for your delicate senses?" Denny gives me his well-honed combination of a laugh and a sneer.

No one, besides me, seems to mind the unclean tables, wet from someone else's spills and burps that end in regurgitations, or the terrible noise of everyone talking at once. Folks shove and squeeze past our table. What a disgusting place. It's not at all like the bars I've imagined with their glitter of bottles, onyx counters, and waitresses dressed in fashionably revealing dresses. Actually there is one bar maid here, but she's dressed in a prim dirndl skirt and a blouse buttoned up tightly. She's probably a tired forty-year-old. My first bar experience is entirely disappointing, neither rowdy enough to fulfill my idea of a cowboy movie saloon, nor slick enough to admire as New York glamour. "Crummy," I say out loud but no one hears me above the din of the jukebox.

TWENTY-TWO

*A*fter leaving Muskogee we touched down to perform in Coffeeville, Kansas, Bartlesville, Oklahoma, and Arkansas City where our truck was impounded for parking in the wrong downtown space. Imagine our consternation in discovering that the authorities of this tiny town where the streets were mostly empty of cars on a weekday, bothered to haul away our dirty old truck. The delay in getting the truck back was minor, but the stain on the Princess Troupe's reputation was not. Carl had to report this infringement of the law to Lu-Travis; he returned from the phone looking glum and holding his left ear. Lu-Travis had shouted at him through the telephone. Our carelessness had cost her ten dollars.

There was no snow in Amarillo, Texas, but there were patches of old ice on the roads, and I had to drive cautiously. Much to my surprise, the hotel in Amarillo had provided two sheets of writing paper and an envelope in the desk drawer next to the bible. This was most unusual. Most hotels had been too frugal, though the Earle Hotel in Joplin had provided one postcard for its guests. Inspired by this unexpected convenience of finding free writing paper, I wrote a letter to Lu-Travis explaining how unfair I thought it was that the girls were not allowed to switch around in the car and occasionally sit in the front seat. This plea for treating the girls with more equality seemed quite reasonable to me. Why Fay or Jessica or I hadn't complained before during the first half of the tour, I blamed on a passiveness that I was now eager to rectify.

I wrote the letter, licked and sealed the envelope with satisfaction. Inwardly I praised myself for facing up to a chore that seemed as engaging as washing out underclothes night after night. I felt benevolent. After all, I already sat in the front seat of the car where I was more comfortable because I drove the car. I had written the letter for Fay and Jane…not for myself. The girls, I smugly convinced myself, would thank me. Nevertheless I decided not to mention the letter that I'd just written unless it actually accomplished something. I would wait for Lu-Travis's answer.

On the following day, February 20th, we headed west and south on route 40 out of Amarillo, then south on 70 to route 54. Soon the warmer climate caused us to shed our winter coats and jackets, and we flung them into the trunk of the car. The new scenery outside the car windows kept us all alert and calling out to each other with, "Did you see that?" Or sometimes, "What's that reddish-brown thing sticking up way over there on the horizon?"

"It's called a butte, dummy," Denny laughed. "I remember seeing stranger stuff than this on the last tour."

I could foretell that we were about to be told another story concerning Denny's last tour, naturally with himself as the hero and Lisa in her role as a witch spelled Denny's way with a "B."

✻

Just as I predict, Denny once again mentions Lisa's name, but this time, I interrupt, "Tell us, Denny. I'm so curious. Who in the troupe tattled on that girl Lisa and got her fired?"

"Who asked you to butt into my story," Denny snaps at me and shifts his bulk around so that he faces Greg and the girls in the back seat leaving me out of the conversation. Then he continues with his tale, that I only half listen to since I need to keep my mind on the road.

At first it seems to me that we have come upon this summer in winter just in time to give us an infusion of new interest. We arrive on the outskirts of Las Cruces, New Mexico, late in the afternoon and stop in a dry, rutted parking lot beside a diner, its two-tone silver and blue stripe burned away by the scorching sun. The metal appears hot to the touch even this late in the day. As I step from the car, I notice the change in the air…not just warmer, for the temperature has been rising all day long as we drive south. The air here, barely moving, touches softly on my arms and carries a sweetness that is suspect. It's heavy with something, maybe over-ripe melons? No, something much more spoiled, more likely an overturned garbage pail near by. But the strangeness isn't only in the smells; it's also in the voices, in the too passive attitude of the waitress who seems to drag lethargically from behind the counter to our booth. It's as though she can barely manage to keep from sagging like the melting, misshapen clock in Dali's painting.

"You'll just love the hotel here in Las Cruces," Denny informs us as we sit eating our eggs doused in peppery tomato sauce. "It's the same one we stayed in last year."

"What's it like?" Jane asks.

"Well, it's cheap. That's the only good thing about it."

"We sure won't mind that," Larry smiles, and we all nod our heads in agreement.

"Oh, you'll mind all right. The place is shitty, and the bathrooms are down the hall."

"Aren't they always?"

"Not like this. These bathrooms are down a hallway that's open to the whole outdoors."

"You mean anybody passing out on the street can see us head for the John?" Jane gives Denny a disbelieving leer.

"Let's not stay there," I hasten to interrupt.

"Greg, Larry, and I are broke. We have no choice." Denny assumes that this fact alone determines the matter. It does, as usual. We girls never have enough "votes" in the matter of where we stay or eat. Nor do we this time.

After we check-in at the hotel, I discover that Denny is absolutely right. The bathroom really is outdoors at the end of a balcony. Does one scurry down the open balcony in a bathrobe in full view of folks driving past? Not that I even have such an article of clothing.

Unlike a regular hotel, this one has no lobby to visit and no coffee shop, just a little cubby of an office. There aren't even any stores nearby. In the soft dusk, I stand out on the balcony of the second floor looking down at a gas station, a few cement block single story houses, and a truck crammed with people speeding down a dirt road. The truck is followed by a long tail of dust that settles across the balcony where I stand watching. I wipe my hand along the railing. No one has ever cleaned it or the rooms either.

Each time I venture out of my room, I expect to see someone from the troupe, but I never do. Perhaps their rooms are on the opposite side of this strange hotel. Everything here feels alien: the hotel, the voices speaking rapidly in Spanish, and most of all…the smells. Under the soft sweet air is that other mysterious odor, something cloying, something allowed to go rotten.

I feel dropped here in this foreign land by mistake…never to find my way back into familiar territory. US. 70, the road we arrive on, is somewhere lost in the dust. Maybe I have slipped off the map where no one will ever look for me if I should suddenly go missing.

If I could hear a familiar voice, Fay's or Carl's, all my fearful imaginings might evaporate. But there isn't even a phone in my room, and now that it's getting dark, I hesitate to go down to the little office on the other side of this building to find out their room numbers. I feel the same reluctance to creep down the open balcony to the bathroom, though it's becoming more and more necessary. I stall as long as I can.

Out on the balcony it is now completely dark except for the yellow bars of light seeping from under the louvered doors of the other rooms. Here, as at the Earle hotel, there are two doors on each room; one door is solid, the other louvered to let air pass through. There are no lights on the balcony itself. Behind these doors people babble in a foreign language. My suspicious mind warns me that there are things going on that I might not care to know about. I grab a towel, quickly lock my own room door with the key, and almost run past those slats of light coming from other doors. Inside the bathroom I quickly hook the door after me. There is no conventional lock.

The light bulb in the bathroom is a forty-watt one, bug splattered and dim, but not so dim that I'm unable to see the filthy bathtub and the strange creatures with many legs crawling around on the floor. I will never, ever, consider taking a bath in this place. As I wash my face in the sink, I listen for the footsteps of some unknown person who might be waiting out on the balcony to attack me. The sooner I get back behind the locked door of my room, the safer I'll feel.

Cautiously, I open the bathroom door a crack so that I can quickly slam it shut again if necessary. Just then the headlights of a bouncing car flash across the balcony. Seeing that the balcony is totally empty, I dash to my room, unlock, then bolt the door from the inside. Lastly, I drag a chair over to wedge under the doorknob.

When I finally turn out my room light, I cover my ears against the sounds of squabbling coming from the room next to mine. How abandoned I feel in this place; it seems so much more remote from home. Memories wash over me: my clean room at home, the wood stove at the cottage, the bacon smell at breakfast. I try to stifle the odd sensation rising in my stomach...homesickness.

The high school stage in Las Cruces is a mere twenty by fifteen feet, the smallest on which we have yet to perform. In order to fit the scenery to the space available, we leave out half of the canvas flats. That is simple enough and we've done similar things before. The hard part is adjusting our actions in the play to the smaller space without a rehearsal.

Fay performs her little dance near the end of the play and succeeds in making her steps fit the reduced space by simply staying in one spot. When the music swells at the end of her dance, Fay makes her usual twirl to culminate in a curtsy to her father, the king. But instead of a smooth curtsey, she stubs her toe on a metal plate set in the stage floor and plops heavily with a resounding thud onto the wooden platform at King Denny's feet. From months' of habit, Denny speaks his usual line without thinking. "Little Princess, you dance so gracefully."

The audience laughs and laughs.

"Thank you, Sire," says Fay, the princess, between grimaces of pain and tears. "You are too kind."

Fay's big toe on her left foot swells up so much that she's unable to wear anything on her foot except her soft dance slipper for the whole following week.

After the performance that afternoon in Las Cruces, we strike the set—-a new record in speed—load the truck, and head straight from the school parking lot to Van Horn, Texas, where our pay envelopes are supposed to be waiting for us. It's Friday and all of us are either short on cash or completely broke. In fact, most of us, including myself, can't afford to have an evening meal until we reach Van Horn and first pick up our pay envelopes.

I drive through El Paso, and then it seems miles to Van Horn on Route 80, though it's actually under a hundred miles. There in Van Horn, my mother's weekly letter is waiting and also a letter from Charley. I put off reading Mother's letter. There is always a tingle of fear running down my spine before opening hers. Will this be the dreaded letter, the one asking me to come home and help take care of my dad and drive her to the grocery store twice a week?

Before going up to my room, I sit down in the lobby and read Charlie's letter. I can't help but chuckle out loud at his cornball jokes and the mixed-up words and phrases he invents after hitting the wrong keys on the old typewriter at the Earle Hotel. I can visualize him sitting late at night in the empty lobby in Joplin, pounding out, two-finger style, this letter to help pass his dull night shift at the registration desk.

Charley speaks about old Mr. Sutter, who sends his best regards to me. Charley also gives me news of other people who have come and gone from the hotel. Ernie, the semi-truck driver, has finally gotten married and gone off to Alaska where drivers of heavy equipment are being paid enormous salaries. Charley tells me how much he misses me and our lobby dancing. He ends his letter with "Love."

As I pause in my reading, I become aware of Denny looking over my shoulder and realize that he is reading the address on Charlie's envelope, which rests on the sofa arm beside me.

"Who's Charley dancing with these nights?" Denny asks.

I don't bother to answer, but Denny continues with his light banter, "How can the men in the Hotel Earle possibly get along without you?"

"What are you trying to imply?" I ask pointedly.

"Well, I mean, who will they find to fill in for you, a woman of experience?" Denny's broad grin, so innocent looking under his snub nose, widens to show his splendid white teeth.

Without answering Denny, I fold Charlie's letter and open the one from home. Out of my peripheral vision, I see Denny saunter away towards the elevator with Carl.

I skim quickly through Mother's letter and realize after two paragraphs that I have been holding my breath, anticipating the worst. She hasn't asked me to come home. What a relief! Then I read her letter more carefully. Mother's letters, unlike Charlie's, which always give a pleasant lift to my spirits, are prosaic and include such things as which day she has gone grocery shopping with her neighbor, or the weather. Mundane or not, I depend upon her letters. They are a support of a different kind from Charlie's. I'm grateful for them simply because they are regular...every single week without fail. I know for sure, no matter how lonesome I become or how mean others behave towards me, that back home there is a family.

TWENTY-THREE

*F*rom Van Horn where we had no performance, we worked our way across the four hundred miles of mostly open country to San Antonio with an overnight stop in Fort Stockton. The scenery through the car window was flat, though south of us we saw a line of blue-gray mountains in the distance that turned a delicate peach and lavender at dusk. There was sagebrush, sand and more sand, and oil wells.

Fort Stockton, where we stay the following night, seemed to exist mainly because of the oil wells. I remember it as a gathering of low, flat-roofed hovels out in the middle of nowhere. We passed dirt side streets, empty except for a few children playing ball. That's the entirety of what we saw, emptiness everywhere on our way to the hotel. But the Hotel Stockton itself was vibrating with life. Where did all those people come from, I wondered? Then I realized that every single person was male. The bar was so full that the men stood shoulder to shoulder. We soon learned after checking in at the registration desk, that the bar was the only place in town that was open in the evenings to buy a meal.

Directly behind the bar on the wall was a stuffed rabbit head with horns attached. With a serious face, the bartender pointed to the poor stuffed rabbit. "That's how everything grows down here in Texas...big, very big, usually with horns."

It was certainly larger than the rabbits I'd seen in Michigan, but horns? Anyway, none of us felt like contradicting such a tale openly in front of all those men in sweat-stained work clothes milling about.

There was a gap of silence as some of the men stopped munching and drinking to listen for our reactions.

"Oh really?" I said, hoping to convey the idea that I knew the rabbit tale was just a big joke. Fay and Jane didn't openly dispute the rabbit-horn story either.

I believe we enjoyed all the attention we were getting by being the only women in the bar among so many men, but an inner voice warned me that it wasn't a safe spotlight to be under, no matter how enjoyable at that particular moment. I sensed a tension in that body-packed bar and felt relieved when our sandwiches were ready and we could take them upstairs to our room.

After being confined to the car for many long hours, we were all in need of diversion, yet there was no place to go after dark, no sidewalks to walk on, no stores to peruse, nowhere to go except downstairs to the bar or the lobby. We girls guessed that both places should be avoided, especially as the evening wore on and the sounds from below our room grew louder, making it clear that some men were well into a state of alcoholic euphoria.

Fay began to put her hair up on fat curlers while Jane and I took turns using the sink to wash out our underpants. We were aware that the guys in our troupe were still in the bar downstairs because their room was right next to ours, and we hadn't heard them return. Actually, both rooms were connected in such a way that one could make a circle from our room on through their room and then to the hall and back again through another hall door to our room.

✳

About nine o'clock that evening there is a knock on the door. "Let me in, girls." We recognize Denny's melodic voice so we open the door. In steps Denny pulling a tall young man by the arm.

"This is Tommy, I forget his other name. He says he's awfully rich...oil wells and all that sort of thing." Before we can stop him, a boyish looking fellow steps further into our room. "Here's your chance, girls! This is Jane and Fay. Fay plays the princess in the play. That's *queeny* over there." Denny points towards me. "She's experienced," he adds slyly.

"What is it I'm supposed to be experienced at?" I ask jokingly, and then I catch on to Denny's crude meaning.

"Oh," Denny says, turning to Tommy, "you know what I'm hinting at."

"Hmmm, sure," Tommy nods. This is followed by a slow meaningful wink. "Hello, girls." The young man looks quite eager to consume us with his friendly brown eyes.

"Take him away, Denny," Jane says. "We want to get ready for bed."

"But she's the one you want to concentrate on." Denny points again at me and ignores Jane's demand. The young man looks hopefully at me. "She's got men friends in every hotel." Denny laughs and ducks out the door before I can protest.

"I'm afraid Denny has fed you a…" But I don't get a chance to finish my stern lecture for Tommy has already advanced across the room and thrust his arm around me.

"Come-on," he says, "Let's get acquainted, Queeny. Now don't pull away…cause I wouldn't hurt a…I just want to marry someone."

Tommy is definitely tipsy. There's no use trying to set him straight, I decide. I'll just outsmart him. I duck out the door that goes into the boys' room hoping Tommy will follow, and then I can dump him there.

"Carl looks up in disgust as I pass through. "Not in my room."

Not in his room, what? I wonder, as I move rapidly on into the hall and back into the girls' room where I quickly lock the hall door. But I'm too late. Before I can turn around, Tommy returns through the other door, the one from Carl's room, and begins a long verbal dissertation on how much he loves me.

"He really is under the influence," Jane laughs.

Being a little drunk makes it easier to excuse Tommy for his playful behavior. Anyway, as I slip in a convenient circle from room to room again, the other girls follow. Fay and Jane throw pillows at Tommy in order to get rid of him so that we can lock both of our doors at the same time and have privacy. There's lots of giggling, running, and pillow throwing until some of our pent-up energy is spent. Finally, complaints begin to reach the management, probably from nearby rooms of oil workers who have to rise before dawn the next day. Tommy is corralled by someone and taken downstairs.

After we settle down for the night, Denny's insulting implications begin to roll over and over in my mind gathering into a ball of hurt feelings. I try to understand why he should make such crude remarks about me to the young Tommy...to anyone. Why the innuendoes and oblique cracks about my 'experience'? Is he merely teasing in order to get a rise out of me, or does he really believe I did sleep with Charley and Ernie at the Earle Hotel? What if the others in the troupe think the same thing? In the dark, I feel the warmth of embarrassment flooding over me.

Surely the others in the troupe wouldn't judge me an "easy mark" just for making friends in Joplin. None of my behavior in Joplin compares with the vivid tales Denny tells us about Lisa. Maybe it isn't what I've done so much as what Denny hopes I did. A bad reputation foments excitement and drama. Denny loves such things. My, how well he would have fitted into the colorful French Court of Louis the Fifteenth with its labyrinth of intrigue.

Even before the last two performances, I perceive a difference in the way Denny is treating me, though he never treats any of the girls with much respect. It's not an aboveboard hostility, just an undercurrent of snide remarks, mostly innuendoes here and there in the conversation, yet nothing as embarrassing as the insinuations of this evening in front of Fay and Jane. I try to recall when I first begin to notice the change in Denny's attitude towards me. Is it right after Joplin or even before that? Perhaps it goes back as far as Springfield.

Springfield! I recall with chagrin, the city where I stupidly toss away money on a useless music lesson and also the same city where Denny's hotel room is located directly across from mine.

I never do find out who makes the whispered phone call to my room that last night asking about Denny's guest. Only that it is someone who pretends to be the desk clerk. I suppose it's just possible that Denny learns of my blundering that night and now blames me for the hotel clerk coming up to his room to rout out the unregistered male guest he is harboring. Maybe that's why Denny has begun making cutting remarks about me...remarks that smack of retaliation.

Oh, how I want to fall asleep, but my mind keeps taking devious twists and turns, always poking and probing. I recall how Denny and Carl have lied to Lu-Travis to get rid of George, and maybe Jessica, too. What about the vivid stories Denny tells about the girl, Lisa, from last year? Was she really disruptive, or did Denny lie as a means of forcing her out of the troupe? Is it possible that I'm about to be the victim of another smear campaign by Denny? Stop, I command myself! I know how mulling things over at nighttime when the mind is most vulnerable, tends to enlarge and exaggerate the smallest problem.

Downstairs in the bar, the cowboy singer on the jukebox is once again lamenting over a loved one left behind and the long trail home.

TWENTY-FOUR

Looking up at a lovely blue, cloudless sky the next morning, I dismiss the idea that Denny is treating me with more than his usual needling manner, putting it down to nothing more than his way of entertaining himself. I wipe off my concerns much as I dust off the desert sand on the windshield of the car. Besides, I assure myself, there is absolutely nothing about my reputation for Denny to besmirch... nothing to tattle to Lu-Travis about. I've done nothing wrong.

It's far easier to assume that Denny is an overly emotional actor and pretend not to notice any difference in the way he treats me lately. Fleetingly though, it does occur to me how much wiser it would have been to refrain from dancing so openly with Charley in the lobby of the Earle Hotel in Joplin. But it's only a passing thought. My behavior has always been perfectly innocent, and I can't believe that it might appear otherwise to anyone else.

In Junction, Texas, Carl surprises me by announcing, "I'll drive today." He doesn't explain, but he is never overly talkative to me. Perhaps the warmer climate helps to ameliorate the stiffness in his leg. I think he looks healthier too. A trace of color replaces the mime-like chalkiness of his face. Yet, his protruding cheekbones still appear sharp enough to pierce the surface of his stretched skin.

Three-fourths of the tour was now over, and nothing catastrophic had occurred, that is, no car accidents and few arguments now that George and Jessica were gone. I felt that the remainder of the tour would be smooth, perhaps even dull. The warmer Texas weather brought about an easiness, a relaxed attitude, fomenting complacency on my part.

We arrived in San Antonio, Texas, on a Tuesday afternoon with the next day an "open" one with no performance and no traveling. After being confined to the car for so many hours during the long trek across the widest part of Texas, we were looking forward to a day of freedom.

Once again, the hotel designated on the travel itinerary proved to be too expensive, but we stopped there anyway to pick up our mail before going on to find a cheaper hotel. Carl and I were the only ones in the car who received mail that day. Lucky us, I thought, and felt sympathy towards Jane and Fay who hadn't received any letters for several days. Greg and Larry, sitting in the parked truck nearby, were also reading their mail. Denny handed over my letter and slid his backside, covered in stiff new jeans, into his place beside Carl who had been driving. As Carl opened his letter in the front seat, I, sitting in the back with Fay and Jane, opened mine. It was from Lu-Travis in answer to the one I had written to her and mailed way back in Amarillo, Texas. That was the letter in which I had complained about the guys hogging the front seat of the car.

Lu-Travis's answer was a very sympathetic one, and the thought passed through my mind that perhaps I had misjudged her character. She told me how she appreciated my speaking up about the unfair seating arrangements in the car. I folded the letter and stuffed it back into the envelope. At that moment I felt a rise of satisfaction within myself for having at last faced up to the issue of the seating; I had done my bit against women's discrimination. I recalled how from sheer lethargy I had put off writing that letter for months and months until finally I had literally pushed myself into action. Well done, I told myself.

Looking towards the front seat, I noticed that Carl had also finished reading his letter. Silently he passed the letter on to Denny. Suddenly Denny flung both of his arms into the air, twisted his bulk around in the seat, and bellowed at me: "My God! What did you have to do that for?"

"Do what?" Jane and Fay asked in unison.

"What did I do?" I'm stunned by Denny's sudden burst of temper.

"Turn out to be a fuckin tattle!" Denny produced a snort and followed it with a devastating leer.

Now I guessed. Carl's letter must be from Lu-Travis reprimanding him and the other guys in the troupe over the unfair seating.

"I simply told Lu-Travis the truth." I tried to keep my voice level and rational sounding, or maybe I was really trying to emotionally calm myself. This wasn't at all the reaction I had expected from reading Travis's letter.

Without even turning his gaunt head around to face me, Carl's usually passive voice carried a load of scorn, "If you didn't like the way things were done, why didn't you just leave the troupe?"

This was the first time Carl had ever spoken to me so angrily. Naturally his harsh words had a deeper effect on me than Denny's bombastic swearing, something everyone was used to, including me. I felt a sudden coldness creep over me, an alienation. Carl's words cut much deeper into my feelings.

"Yeah," Denny splurted. "Why don't you just go home right now!"

Again Carl tossed words over his shoulder as though he didn't want to face someone so dishonorable. "You could use your sick father as an excuse for quitting."

I was astounded that the seemingly level-headed Carl, the one person who seemed less prone to emotional ups and downs, had so quickly turned against me. It muddied my thinking. Words to defend myself simply fluttered out of my mind. Why had everyone, especially Carl, reacted this way?

Denny tossed the letter over his shoulder into the back seat, apparently not caring where it landed, and I picked it up from the floor to read before passing it on to the other two girls. It contained a sharp reprimand against the men in the troupe for their lack of thoughtfulness in treating the girls with equality. Of course, Lu-Travis herself had already treated us with far less equality by paying us lower wages than she paid the men. Her excuse was that the girls weren't physically setting up the scenery or striking it at the end of each show or doing the driving either. But I didn't make that connection, not at the time. I didn't question the fairness of men being paid more than women.

I tried to explain to Jane and Fay. "I wrote the letter because of the unfairness...not just for myself, for you as well."

"We can speak up for ourselves," Fay claimed coldly.

"I don't even want to ride in the front seat," Jane retorted with a laugh. "Who cares."

Jessica would have cared, I thought. Far too belatedly, I began to admire Jessica's scrappiness.

"See," sneered Denny, "how you made trouble for nothing?"

Indeed, it did seem to be for nothing. Carl drove the car more often during the warmer weather, allowing either Denny or Greg to sit next to him. Lu-Travis had placed me in an unfair position. Why, I asked myself, couldn't she have reprimanded the guys without revealing my name?

Carl started the car and we drove in silence to find another hotel where the rates were cheaper. The girls didn't ask me if I wanted to share a room with them. No one in the car spoke to me again that day, not even about the letter.

✻

Later, after we all check into the San Antonio Hotel, I phone Fay and Jane's room to ask about their plans. "We haven't made any yet," Fay answers. I can hear caution in her voice, but I prefer to think it's all in my imagination.

"Well," I pretend to ignore the change in her voice. "give me a call when you decide. I think there's a museum we could visit, and there's the Alamo of course." A long hesitation occurs while Fay consults with Jane. I hear a murmur of voices before Fay comes back on the phone.

"Museums don't interest us. We don't know what we're going to do." Before I can make further suggestions, she abruptly hangs up.

It's quite obvious that Fay and Jane are giving me the shoulder, the cold one, and naturally my pride doesn't permit me to impose myself on them if they don't want me. I assume that Denny has been persuading them to shun me because of the letter to Lu-Travis. I rationalize that Jane and Fay will forget the whole incident after today, and everything will return to normal...well, normal for this odd group of people.

I spend the remainder of the afternoon, the evening, and the whole next day quite alone. This situation is not so unusual, for I have often chosen to go off by myself in the past. Somehow, this is different. Now Jane and Fay are managing to make themselves unavailable on purpose.

On the previous day, before the arrival of the damaging letter, I overhear Carl tell Denny that Lu-Travis wants him to take the car to a garage for an oil change when we reached San Antonio, so it was no surprise to find none of the guys, except Greg, hanging around the hotel lobby. The three, Carl, Denny, and Larry always stick together. As for Greg...well, there is no desire on my part to seek him out after his weird behavior back in Muskogee, Oklahoma. Occasionally, he also tagged along with the guys in the troupe, shorter than all the others, but attempting to appear tough with his sleeves rolled high on his arms and a pack of cigarettes twisted tightly in the left one.

Even though we have been driving south-east all the time to reach San Antonio, the cutting little March breeze that blows through the streets feels like it first crosses a snowy mountain or perhaps the source of chill is really from the dark slippery river that winds back and forth dissecting the streets. In spite of the sharp breeze, this is not the climate for a wintry lamb jacket either, and my spring coat is locked in the costume wardrobe inside the truck. So I wear neither. As I walk through the streets, I shiver and try to stop in as many stores as possible to gather warmth. Sometimes I'm lucky enough to find a bench in a sunny protected spot where I can sit and use up some of the excess time on my hands.

I think about visiting the Alamo by myself, but wonder how much it might cost. What if it isn't free? What if I run into someone from the troupe? Since they don't want to be with me today, I decide, perversely, that I don't want to be with them either. Anyway, a day away from all of them will be a relief.

I wander around the city looking in shop windows and wishing I could have something new to wear, something more suitable for the warmer southern climate. Late in the afternoon, I spot a "sale" sign on a small shop window. Inside is a bin of mixed items. Amid the bras, slips, and unmatched earrings, I pull out a wrap-style blue crepe blouse. I try it on and it fits. Outside again, I walk around the block to think further about buying the blouse. It will cost me twice the price of a meal, though it has been marked down from six dollars to three. A second turn around the block and I succumb; I buy the blouse.

My purchase makes me feel as though my long day alone is a success, but my elation is short-lived. As I follow the river a bit further, something about the long shadows of buildings and the reflections in the dark river make me feel melancholy. That "not invited to the party" feeling overtakes me. My upbeat feelings over the new blouse evaporate along with any warmth left from the setting sun. Now I seem to be one of the few people walking along the cement banks of the river, which appears cold enough to wear a skim of ice. Most of the stores are closing and everyone except me has someplace to go. They have a home to fold them in like a warm blanket, but I have only a bleak hotel room and its gummy furniture to return to.

I head back to the hotel. Perhaps Fay and Jane will also be back. By now, I assure myself, they will have gotten over their pique about the letter from Lu-Travis. We can all go off to a free movie after dinner. In anticipation I walk faster, eager to reach the hotel with its blinking over-the-door sign.

As soon as I arrive, I hurry straight to the third floor and knock on number thirty-six. I pull my blouse halfway out of the shopping bag in readiness to display. There is no answer to my first knock or my second one either. I chuck the blouse back into the bag feeling a disappointment that I can't show it off. Perhaps Fay and Jane haven't returned yet.

Back in the lobby once again, I sit down on one of the two facing sofas hoping to catch Fay and Jane as they return from wherever they have been most of the day. In one direction is the street door and in the other the elevators. I wait a half hour, but the girls still don't appear. Every time I glance around, I catch the older man at the registration desk eyeing me. Does he think I'm sitting here to pick up a man? He makes me feel too self-conscious. Finally I give up waiting and go on into the coffee shop where I order an omelet and coffee for my supper.

Later, I check several times, but the girls never seem to be in their room. I even phone Carl's room, using the excuse that I need to know what time we plan to leave for Corpus Christi the next morning. But there's no answer there either.

It's quite obvious, I tell myself, that the whole troupe has gone somewhere together and purposely left me out. It's meant to be a punishment for the "tattling" as Denny calls it. The best thing for me to do, I decide, is to brave it out and not let-on that it matters in the least whether they invite me to go along with them or not. But, I think, it's a shame to waste an evening in a city where there are lots of movies to attend. Again, I feel disgust at my own weakness, for being too shy to ask for the professional courtesy that the others will surely get at a movie theater. Though it's still just seven o'clock, I take a last look around the lobby and go back up to my room for the night.

TWENTY-FIVE

The following morning I spot Larry, Greg, Denny, and Carl in a large circular booth in the coffee shop where they are eating breakfast. The table is loaded with food: a plate of sausage, home fries, eggs, coffee, and even juice. Juice is something I can never afford. I hope my eyes don't give me away and reveal my hunger, but I don't need to worry. No one even bothers to look up or speak to me. I placate myself with the thought that churlish behavior at breakfast time is nothing unusual.

"What time do we leave for Christi? I ask. Still no one even says hello. Even Carl keeps his eyes sealed on his plate.

Finally, after I stand there waiting for a few minutes, Carl does answer without looking at me. "Nine o'clock."

I wait a second or two more at the booth expecting they might ask me to join them as they've done in the past. There's plenty of room on the padded bench if Denny slides his big fat bottom over and stops taking up half the space, but no one invites me. Obviously, I am still being punished for the letter to Lu-Travis.

"Have you seen Fay or Jane?" I stall a bit.

Carl shakes his head but doesn't speak.

I begin to feel embarrassed since everyone ignores me. Well, I think to myself, I can't stand here forever. "See you later," I add cheerfully, though I didn't feel that way at all. As I walk away to sit at the counter, I hear Denny make a crack, one he certainly intends me to hear. "All too soon."

"I'll have coffee and one of those corn muffins, toasted," I tell the girl behind the counter. That's all I can afford after buying the blouse yesterday. The blouse is worth a bit of hunger, I keep telling myself without much conviction.

As I sit at the counter slowly munching my toasted corn muffin to make it last as long as possible, I wonder how the guys can afford to spend so much money on food. Is it possible that just ten dollars more per week in salary can actually make that big a difference?

A half hour later than the designated time, actually nine-thirty, Fay and Jane arrive in the lobby with their suitcases, so we don't get started out of town until nearly ten o'clock. But this delay is not unusual. Someone is always late and forces the rest of us to sit around in the lobby while the truck and car sit out in front of the hotel in a yellow loading zone.

"Darlings, where *have* you been? Denny calls across the lobby as Fay and Jane step out of the elevator with their suitcases. Neither girl bothers to answer.

"Let's get this show on the road," laughs Greg, repeating the trite old phrase loud enough for everyone in the small lobby to hear.

Larry opens the rear truck doors and stands inside to stow away our suitcases as we lift them up to him. "Is that all?" Larry asks.

As he is about to close the big doors, I inquire, "Do you know who has the travel iron? I'm going to need it in Christi."

"I've got it," Jane says. "But I need it."

"And I'm next in line to use it," Fay adds.

"And I'm third." Denny chimes in.

"That's really funny," I smile at Denny. "You've never ironed anything before that I know about. Anyway," I continue trying to put a good face on their attempt to monopolize the flatiron, "I just want to make sure the iron isn't getting locked in the truck." The whole idea of keeping the flatiron away from me as part of my general punishment is so childish. I cover up a laugh and turn to Carl who stands waiting beside the car. "Are you driving this morning or am I?"

Denny answers snidely before Carl can open his mouth, "Would he be standing beside the car door otherwise?" Then Denny plops himself into the front seat, and I squeeze into the back with Fay and Jane. Greg shrugs good-naturedly. "Guess that leaves me to ride in the truck with Larry."

As we leave San Antonio, Denny turns around in the front seat to ask, "Have you girls brought your swim suits with you? It's going to be warm enough to go swimming in Christi."

Both girls shake their heads and I do also.

"Not you," snaps Denny, gesturing towards me. "I'm talking to Fay and Jane."

He must be kidding, I think and begin to laugh again. Denny can't possibly be serious in trying to exclude me from the general conversation in the car. But evidently he believes he can.

"Oh well," continues Denny trying to address himself more directly to Fay and Jane, "you can go skinny dipping after dark. We hit Christi on the tour last year and Lisa scandalized the hotel management by swimming in her undies."

It clouds up long before we reach Christi, which is about a hundred and fifty miles away. By the time we arrive a slow drizzle is coming down, giving the famous place rotogravure colors. The ocean is a dull slate color on which there are zigs and zags of chalky foam scribbling to shore.

We settle into cottages across the road at least a block away from the beach and the large luxury hotels. The boys are in one small cottage and we girls share another. Since we are forced to share space again, I believe we'll just naturally fall back into our previous relationship, the one prior to the damaging letter from Lu-Travis.

The rain continues off and on, making the parking lot in front of the cottages one big mud puddle. The rooms have been doused with a sweet, sickening spray to fight off the mildew. There are only four wire hangers in the open closet, so I use one to hang up a skirt and the new blouse. I leave the other three hangers for Fay and Jane. The dampness makes everything wrinkle even more, but to iron my skirt means asking to use the flatiron and that might stir up more trouble. It isn't worth the risk.

Attempting to relieve the strain and get our relationships back to normal, I ask, "What did you two do back in San Antonio?" There is no answer from either one of them, so I continue talking in a friendly manner as though they have answered. "I did some shopping...found this blouse on sale in one store." I lift up the hanger to show the blouse. Again no one speaks, but I catch Jane sneaking a quick glance in my direction. Curiosity is too much for her. The rest of the time I seem to be invisible. The girls are certainly carrying their vendetta a bit far, or could it really be Denny who has instigated the silent treatment? In time, I assure myself, everything will get back to normal.

"Looks like the rain is letting up. Guess I'll take a walk along the beach," I announce. "Anyone want to come?" Fay and Jane shake their heads. At least their headshakes are a response, a small thaw of sorts.

I circumvent the huge puddle that spreads in front of our cottage unit, cross the road, and cut between two large ornate hotels to the wide sandy beach. In a half-mile I meet only one or two people along the entire shore. I'm disappointed even though I know that this is the off-season for tourists. In my imagination, I had visualized myself sitting on the warm sand, going barefoot through the edge of the water, and maybe even stopping to chat if anyone asks me where I'm from. Today, unlike yesterday, I have a growing hunger to talk to someone, and I'm not fussy about who that someone might be, as long as they look normal.

It begins to drizzle again so I cut my walk short and hurry back to the grim little cottage with its sickening mildew spray. Anyway, if I'm not back before dinnertime, Denny and Carl will have the perfect excuse to drive off to a restaurant without me, and I already know there are absolutely no places to eat within walking distance except the big expensive hotels across the road along the shore.

Even before we get to the restaurant, I can tell that I'm in for a most unpleasant time. We sit around a large round table in a spaghetti-type café. Right from the start I am frozen out of the conversation. Once, I begin to tell about my walk along the beach, but Denny loudly interrupts me before I have three words out of my mouth. It's as though I'm not even there, perhaps no more present than the wooden leg on one of the tables. I wish I were a ghost or preferably a poltergeist. At least I'd have the fun of making the spaghetti sauce fly across the table and splat in someone's lap or reach my spirit fingers under the table to pinch Denny's fat bottom hard enough to make him squeal like a pig. At that idea I nearly burst into laugher. If anyone bothers to look at me, they'll wonder why I suddenly appear so happy when I should look miserable because of their shunning. But tonight they are all up against my sense of humor. Besides, I refuse to believe that any of them can keep up the silent treatment much longer.

We have no performance scheduled in Corpus Christi and therefore absolutely no reason to suffer the damp units a second night. In the morning we pick up our pay envelopes, pay our bills, and move on to sunny Brownsville, Texas.

After lunch when it's my turn to drive the car, Carl trades seats with Greg and rides in the truck with Larry. That's when I first hear Denny and the girls talking about going across the border into Mexico.

"I'm going to buy a new leather purse. Leather's cheap over there," Jane says.

"Yeah," agrees Denny, turning to face the back seat, "me too."

"I hope you don't mean that." I hear Greg laugh.

"Well, a billfold then. But lots of guys in New York carry purses."

"Not that I've seen," Jane scoffs.

"That's because you come from a foreign country," is Denny snide retort.

"Where did you get that silly idea? I'm from Brooklyn!"

"Exactly...a foreign country." Everyone laughs including Jane.

"When do you plan to go across the border into Mexico," I ask and immediately wish I hadn't. No one answers. Out of my peripheral vision I can see Denny shaking his dark head at the girls, a signal for them to keep quiet. I didn't bother to pursue the question. It will be smarter, I decide, to question the girls privately without Denny being nearby to coach them into silence.

✴

For three days now, I have been constantly reassuring myself: They'll soon get over their anger at me for the letter I wrote to Lu-Travis. After all, what have I done that is so heinous? I haven't robbed a bank, kicked anyone's grandmother, or wrecked the car. It doesn't surprise me that Denny holds a grudge, for I vividly recall the mean way he treated George and sometimes Jessica, but surely Carl is more mature than to continue to blame me for a circumstance actually brought about by the guys in the troupe. He and the girls will slowly come around to treating me as they have done in the past...even if Denny doesn't. Just be patient, I soothe myself, and continue to behave as though nothing unusual is happening.

Brownsville turns out to be bright with the sunshine that Corpus Christi lacks, and the hotel Cameron is one of the most cheerful small hotels we have yet to visit on the tour. Each room has a ceiling fan and the louvered extra door for ventilation. The most remarkable thing about my room is the cottage-white woodwork. Even the stock hotel furniture assumes a higher quality when surrounded by white walls and a dazzling white bedspread instead of the standard beige one. Compared to all the other dark, scabby-walled rooms we have occupied, this hotel is a delight to the eye. I will almost feel content to sit and read in this sunny room, and that's exactly what I do the remainder of Friday except for going downstairs for supper. I look for the others in the hotel coffee shop, but they aren't there so I eat alone.

On Saturday morning I take the elevator to the fourth floor where the ten o'clock rehearsal is to be held in the hotel conference room. Nearly a week has passed since our last performance back in Las Cruces, New Mexico, so we need to refresh our memories. Lines have a way of getting switched about so that the next speaker doesn't recognize his or her own cue. One flubbed line seems to lead to the next and even the next one until forgetfulness infects the play like a virus.

After rehearsal, I see Greg walk off hand in hand with Jane. They look almost like youthful twins from the rear in their matching blue jeans and jerseys. Fay follows closely after them, but I catch up with her just inside the door. I notice her head is covered by a scarf under which the fat metal rollers peek out at the top and sides.

"Fay?" I call. She looks cornered and glances quickly back at Denny to see if he notices her predicament. "When do you and the others plan to go across the border into Mexico?"

She shrugs, "I don't know exactly when."

She does know, I think, because she has trouble looking me squarely in the eyes. But I can't very well call her a liar. "Will you give my room a buzz when you know for sure?" Fay nods, and then tries to squeeze past me.

"I'm in room twenty-two." I persist, but keep my voice calm and steady, for I want her to get the impression that everything is as normal between us as before, and that my going with them is a natural conclusion. "So, give me a call," I repeat cheerfully, and walk off briskly, stepping ahead of her through the doorway.

✶

As soon as I notice that the hall in front of me is empty, my smile slips off as easily as if spread over salad oil. Putting up a good front is important, but under that mask I feel exposed...naked on a cold, raw day. There is no escape from their mean treatment unless I quit the troupe. Now, for the first time, I give some serious thought to the idea of going home. The very word "home" with its soft "mmmm" sound is so comforting, and I let it resound soothingly in my head for a few minutes. Then I decide that going home will be the same as admitting, "You've won, and I can't go on with the tour if you won't speak to me." No, my pride can't bear the idea of letting them believe

I'm running home just because I can't take a mere three days of their silent treatment.

I wait in my room for half an hour hoping Fay will still call me on the phone. The phone doesn't ring. Then I decide that I might better be waiting in the lobby where Fay and the others have no choice but to walk right past me when they leave for Mexico. Immediately, I descend in the elevator and sit on a sofa in the lobby for twenty minutes or so. Not a single person from the troupe passes through the lobby. Finally I get up and go to one of the lobby phones and call Fay's room. The phone rings and rings but no one answers.

At the registration desk, I question the clerk, "Did you see any of the others in our troupe leave the hotel?"

"Yes, about an hour ago. They must have been going to a performance."

I shake my head. "The performance is tomorrow evening. I think they may have been going across the border into Mexico."

"Oh yes, perhaps so," the desk clerk cheerfully agrees. "They did ask several questions about getting there, and they also called a taxi."

All six of them have gone without me. Another punishment. Here I am so close to a foreign country and have missed my chance to visit it. And naturally that's exactly what Denny and the others want. . .to make me feel thoroughly hurt and abandoned. They are probably all laughing over their success in slipping away from me. What better way of getting even with me for what they call "tattling." Tears begin to form in my eyes. I quickly turn away from the desk clerk. "Thank you," I murmur and hurry to the elevator as my shoulders begin to shake with sobs.

Back in my room and safe from other peoples' eyes, I fall across the bed and cry. What a relief to give vent to my hurt feelings. Three days of holding them in check seems like living through months of misery, months of pretending not to care if the others dislike me or not. But I really do care. What if Denny and the others don't relent and get over their grudge against me? What if it goes on and on? Maybe I should consider going home.

TWENTY-SIX

*M*y tears flow on and on, venting all my frustration and loneliness into one bottomless pit. "They have no right... no right to treat me like this!" I sob. "It's my one chance to visit Mexico." As soon as this idea takes hold in my mind, my hurts begin to metastasize into anger. Anger is far better than a styptic stick on a bloody cut to quell the tears.

I sit up on the edge of the bed and pat dry my wet face. If Denny and the others are successful in keeping me from going to Mexico, they will assume that they have won an easy victory. It means their get-even plans have worked. The more I think about it, the more adamant I become to thwart their success. Maybe I can find a way to go across the border alone. Alone! The idea makes me quiver.

Again and again I splash cold water across my puffy eyes, trying to shrink the swelling down to a normal size. I have heard that tea bags might reduce the swollen look, but I don't have any. Some people can cry gracefully and end up still looking pretty. Not me. My nose always runs non-stop and turns hot pink at the very tip.

As soon as I think people will not guess that I've been crying-my-eyes-out, I return to the lobby to ask the desk clerk if there's a way to go across the border into Mexico by myself.

"Oh, it's very simple. Just go two blocks down the road in that direction, and you'll see a bus stop sign. Take the number twenty-six bus."

"Will I have to change buses at the border?"

"No, the number twenty-six takes you all the way. The bus will be less crowded tomorrow, Sunday, but there will be fewer shops open."

I am grateful for his help and return to my room once more to think things over. Between the lobby and my room, some of my cold determination oozes away. My confidence needs propping up. No amount of anger seems powerful enough to out-weigh my timidity at the idea of going into a foreign country by myself. Haven't I read newspaper clippings about young ladies being abducted across the border in foreign countries? And there are those movies of women kidnapped into white slavery. I waste time agonizing over whether to go immediately or wait until tomorrow. But fear is the stronger, determining factor. I'm unable to snuff it out. I begin to shiver even though it must be at least eighty outdoors. I roll up in the white bedspread to get warm and stay there the rest of the afternoon.

Finally, on Sunday morning I steel myself to go across the border. The idea that I might be cheated out of seeing a bit of Mexico because of the sheer meanness of the others in the troupe temporarily overrides my fears.

It is nearly ten o'clock when the Matamoros bus arrives on the corner where I stand waiting. Three people watch me from the bus as I climb aboard: a woman, Mexican I assume, a man whose face is shadowed by a battered straw hat, and the driver. For the sake of safety, I take a seat right behind the driver. I'm the only American on the bus. Easy prey, I tell myself. I sit up as tall as I can and stiffly hold that pose hoping to portray cool assurance. At the same time, fear is taking my stomach for a roller-coaster ride.

At the border the bus pulls to one side and stops. What's going to happen now, I wonder? Will we all have to get off the bus and be searched? A man in a beige uniform wanders casually out to the bus, and the driver shoves some papers through his side window. Then we are waved onwards by the uniformed man. How simple. I'm relieved that we aren't told to get off the bus and that we weren't interrogated, but I still feel uneasy.

As we pass into an area threaded and crisscrossed with railroad tracks and low abandoned looking factory buildings, I pray that the bus will speed up and not stop. This glut of derelict buildings looks like the perfect place for someone to climb aboard and abduct me with a gun. The driver does stop at least three times, one for each railroad crossing. Each time the bus stops, the driver opens the bus door, and each time that happens I hold my breath and focus all my attention on that door praying that no one will climb on board. Slowly we weave over the tracks and several more blocks before reaching a shopping district where a few people mill about. I have arrived safely. Now, I tell myself, I must get back again to the United States without mishap.

When I descend from the bus and the man whose face is shadowed by the straw hat doesn't follow me, I feel great relief. Before leaving the bus, I ask the driver how soon the bus will return. Then I try to identify the street corner in some way so that I can easily find it again since I see no signs. All the dumpy stores and all the corners look exactly alike to me. What if I get lost? I decide to venture only one block in each direction and no further, always keeping in sight where I have just stepped down from the bus.

Except for a few sidewalk stalls, most of the stores are closed. After all, I remind myself, it is Sunday. From a vender I buy a cheap broach and matching earrings edged in silver. At least the silver looks genuine. The green stones are supposed to be jade, but I know they really aren't. That doesn't lessen my pride. I'm terribly proud of myself. In fact I'm exhilarated. Somehow I have quelled my turbulent stomach long enough to visit a foreign country and now have a purchase to prove that I've actually been to one.

As I ride the bus back to the American side of the border, I find myself smiling cheerfully. What a brave, adventurous person I am! My pride in the pitiable achievement easily matches the success of a mountain climber. Only after gaining the safety of my room back in the hotel, do I realize that my nervous tension has caused a severe migraine.

Before and after the performance that same evening, everyone jabbered on and on about their wonderful Saturday trip across the border into Mexico, and they raved about the restaurant where they had eaten genuine Mexican food. I suspected that Denny exaggerated their experiences a bit in order to impress me, another attempt to make me feel left out. When an opening in the conversation occurred as we returned to our hotel in the car, I showed Jane the brooch and earrings I had bought in Mexico. It was gratifying to intercept the look of surprise passing between Fay, Jane, and Denny.

"Sure, sure," Denny tossed the words over his shoulder, "you can buy stuff like that brooch right here in Brownsville." Those were the first direct words he had spoken to me or rather *at* me for several days.

"How did you get there by yourself?" Jane asked as she rolled up a stick of gum and jamming it into her mouth.

"There's a bus that goes directly across the border." I guessed that none of them believed that I had really gone into Mexico.

"The desk clerk didn't tell us about any buses," Fay said doubtfully. She made it sound as if I were lying.

"Well," I answered with conviction, "there is one, number twenty-six."

Then, before Jane and Fay could get a signal from Denny to hush up, I asked Jane, "I suppose your taxi had to stop at the border?"

"Yes, and on the way back too. We even had to get out of the taxi and show what we bought. How about you?"

"No. There were only three of us on the bus going over and the driver just shoved some papers through the window to a guy in uniform to sign. Did you buy anything?"

Fay held up her hand to show me a ring, but she didn't speak. That seemed to be the extent of our reciprocal conversation. Denny had long ago turned his back to us, making a pretense of disinterest though I knew he was listening to every single word. So much for your attempt to punish me, I thought, for I was sure that it was Denny's idea to shut me out. He and the others had given me a bad time, but they didn't know just how bad or how forsaken I felt. They didn't know how I had sobbed all over the white bedspread back in the hotel room. As far as they knew, they had failed to make me miserable.

I felt so good about that shopping trip into Mexico for another reason as well: I had overcome my fear, at least temporarily, of going to a strange place all by myself. I didn't have the spunk of someone like Lisa; hers must have been in-born courage. I knew my courage was just a passing thing forced on me by circumstances and bolstered by my anger. Still, my little triumph carried me through that day and even into part of the next. Then it became clear that Denny and the others weren't through punishing me for the tattle-tale letter. . .not yet.

TWENTY-SEVEN

*A*t first, after the arrival of the letter from Lu-Travis, reprimanding the men in the troupe, my attitude towards them is an optimistic one, quite hopeful. I assume everyone will soon get over their peevishness towards me. Then, after Brownsville and their grudge continues, I become excluded both from their dinner arrangements as well as the movies they attend. I try to hide the fact that I'm in any way affected by their shunning. I reason with myself: Their kiddy behavior, weird clothing, and gum cracking often embarrass me when I am part of their group, so why do I feel the loss of their companionship? Now I can use my free time for more worthwhile things.

I decide that in the next town we visit I will find a library and browse through the stacks. Of course, I soon realize that no town or city locates their library anywhere near bus stations, breweries, bottling plants or the third rate hotels in which we stay, the exception being the small towns back East. Another thing I vow to do on the coming Sunday is attend church as I once did. Yes, I tell myself, I will begin going to church again unless we have to travel on that morning. But that turns out to be the exact case. Sunday is a travel day. I also discover that the churches are invariably in the nicer parts of town and miles away from the places where we stay overnight.

Sometimes I forget that the girls are no longer speaking to me. On our way North from Brownsville, I call out without thinking, "Look! You can see the ocean from this high hill."

Jane also forgets momentarily and responds, "...and there's a freighter way out on the horizon. How tiny it looks." Fay turns to look out the car window, but she says nothing. Then Denny twists around from the front seat and waves his hand like a wand, a signal for Jane to shut up. Silence follows.

Carl drives half of the two hundred and thirty miles to Victoria, Texas, and I drive the remainder of the trip. Victoria is just a stopover; we have no performance there. Our late start, because of Fay and Jane's slowness the previous morning, puts us so far behind schedule that we fail to reach Nacogdoches even by suppertime. Instead, we stop for our meal at a roadside diner. Five of the troupe squeeze into a booth meant for four, leaving Greg and me to sit at the counter nearby.

At least with Greg beside me, I don't have to sit completely alone. I face the counter eating my supper and half listening to the conversation at my back. Greg keeps turning and twisting playfully on his stool, partly to join in the conversation taking place behind him and partly for the fun of showing off. He eats a bite or two of food and then twirls around to talk to the others behind us, never saying anything to me.

Out of the corner of my left eye I can see Greg give another joyful twirl to his stool. He even says, "Wheee," like a happy child. Then I see the seat wobble. Greg must feel the insecurity of the trembling disk beneath him, for suddenly he rises to his feet and grabs at the seat. Too late! Having come completely unscrewed from its tubular base, the seat drops to the floor with a heavy clung-clunk. I see Greg standing there beside the stool looking utterly foolish. Everyone splits with laughter, including me. Still laughing, we watch Greg attempt unsuccessfully to screw the seat back onto its base.

Denny loudly adds every pun he can think up involving the word "screw" and quickly grabs all the attention away from Greg.

Long after the others have stopped laughing, my laughter goes on like water bursting down a sluice. Not even a sea wall can stop the force of my released emotions. I swallow and press my lips together. Still, tears go on flowing down my cheeks. Thank goodness my back is turned so the others are unable to see how I've lost control. I dab at the tears and slowly regain my composure. I mustn't let anyone know how emotionally unsettled I have become. That will be giving Denny and the others an advantage that I intend to deny them.

As we finish eating, Carl and Denny decide that we should not only complete the drive of fifty miles to Nacogdoches but also continue right on through to Carthage, Texas, an additional fifty-five miles. Carl doesn't bother to ask me whether I'm too tired to drive that much further or not.

✳

At first, I drove along the highway amid a blaze of headlights from the on-coming traffic. As the evening grew later, the traffic dwindled to sparseness. Beside me in the front seat, Denny had leaned back his head either to rest or to sleep and I no longer heard voices from the back seat of the car. Everyone was silent or sleeping.

I couldn't see the landscape that rushed towards me in the dark but there seemed little deviation in the straightness of the road or the flatness of the land. Occasionally I would peer off into the blackness beside the car just to stir my mind from the monotony of the road; it was a moonless night so the landscape, remaining unknown, swam by in profile only. Suddenly from the edge of the road a strange creature moved into my headlights. Its slow, mechanical-like walk just gave me enough time to brake the car in an abrupt, jolting manner.

"What in hell!" someone shouted. The weird little animal was so shockingly different from anything I had ever seen before that for an instant I wondered if I'd fallen asleep and arrived in a fantasy land of abnormal creatures. When I looked again, the animal or illusion had slunk off into the shadows.

"The creature wore armor!" I exclaimed, and added, "sorry, but it loomed up so suddenly."

"Next time just go ahead and hit it," Greg joked from the back seat of the car. Everyone was now fully awake.

"Hah," Denny said, "wouldn't Lu-Travis love that. Oozing blood all over her car."

"Maybe it was an armadillo," suggested Jane.

"Yeah, I think they have those in Mexico. Maybe here too," Greg added.

"Some driver you are," grumbled Denny, still irritated but quite ready, I noticed to lean his head back again to sleep.

The abrupt stop had tossed the maps all over the floor and also a milkshake container from the dashboard. Still keeping my eyes focused on the road, I groped with my fingers for the maps but was unable to reach the milkshake container. "Denny, could you please pick up that leftover milkshake? It's going to drip all over the floor and make a mess."

"It's not mine," grumbled Denny, not lifting his head. I could hear the container rolling around on the floor by his feet for the remainder of the trip to Carthage.

After coming close to slaughtering a poor helpless animal, I slowed back down to forty miles per hour. Anyway, the truck was still a considerable distance behind us instead of in front of us, and there was no reason for the car to arrive in Carthage too far ahead of the truck. If we did, it would mean waiting for our suitcases to arrive.

Soon after the braking incident, I realized that my foot holding down the accelerator pedal was getting numb. I wanted to take my foot off and stretch my leg, but the change in speed might waken Denny or disturb the others. No thanks, I thought. I've been shouted at enough for one night. Slowly and as gently as I could, I eased my left foot onto the gas pedal and removed the tingly right foot. There was a slight deviation in the car's speed as I switched back again sometime later.

Mile after mile of nothing but black outlines swept past the car window making the distance seem twice as long and the driving so much more monotonous without scenery to keep me entertained. The one hundred and five miles to Carthage seemed like three hundred.

Of course, there was a plus side to my tedious night drive. Instead of staying overnight in Nacogdoches as the itinerary advised and rising early the following morning to continue to Carthage, we would already be in Carthage and could sleep late the next morning.

❋

I open my suitcase and hang up my skirts in the closet at the Hotel Kelly in Carthage that night after our long drive and then return to the lobby to look for a magazine to read in bed. I notice Greg sitting in a chair as though waiting for one of the guys to join him. "Hi," he greets me in a friendly fashion. I nod instead of answering. Then, as I'm about to walk past him, he holds out his hand as though to stop me.

"Where's our next performance supposed to be?"

"Huntsville, Texas. Didn't you get a copy of the performances, towns and hotels for next week?" I ask.

"No, Can you sit down for a minute?"

Can I believe what I'm hearing? Sit down? After all the snubbing, someone is actually asking for my company? I drop down on the sofa immediately, not wanting to miss this rare opportunity to talk sociably with someone for the first time since San Antonio, nearly a week ago.

"Can I make a copy from your itinerary?" Greg asks politely.

"Sure. I'll go and get it."

"Oh, don't bother. I'm on my way upstairs anyway. I'll just stop by your room and copy it."

I agree and go on looking for a free magazine, then climb the stairs to my room on the second floor. Greg must be following behind me closely, for soon afterwards there is a knock on my door.

"Come in," I call.

"Don't you keep your door locked?" Greg asks in a concerned voice.

"Usually, yes, but you were coming soon so why bother?" Greg gives me a short lecture on keeping my door locked, and I think how nice it is to have someone worry about me. "Here's the itinerary," I hand the list to Greg. "Don't forget to give it back to me."

"Why don't I just copy it right here?" Greg gestures towards the desk.

"Oh, sure, if you want to." My plans are to take my bath and read in bed, but I willingly give up the idea. It will be nice to have someone to talk to for a change. Maybe after all, I think, this guy is different from the others in the troupe. Maybe he's more thoughtful and more gentlemanly. Is it possible that I have misjudged him? Because everyone else snubs me, I am ready to forget and forgive a great deal in my lonely situation.

I note how Greg's hair has grown longer and curlier in just the few weeks he has been with the troupe. Why haven't I taken notice before of the gentleness of his voice? I try to pinpoint the slight regional accent. Certainly it isn't southern and definitely not from Brooklyn. Because Greg occupies the only chair in the room, I sit down on the edge of the bed. "Where are you from, I mean originally?"

"Ohio, but I spent a few years in New York before going into the army." Then in return, he politely inquires, "Where are you from?"

"Michigan," I tell him, hoping he will ask more questions and we can keep up the friendly conversation a little bit longer.

"Finished. That's all I need to copy," he says, handing the itinerary back to me. "I suppose you'd like to go to bed."

"There's no hurry. Would you mind telling me what really happened in the army? How you got that metal plate in your head?"

"It's something I'd like to forget," his voice is a mixture of sadness and little boy need for attention. "I just want to forget it," he repeats. Plaintively, he adds, "Actually, my head is bothering me again tonight." Greg stands up and looks directly into my eyes.

I notice for the first time that his eyes aren't brown as I have previously thought, but gray with flecks of brown. At the moment they appear so sincere, surely as sincere as my own hazel eyes when I look at myself in the mirror.

"The kids in this troupe aren't too friendly," he says sitting down on the bed beside me, "especially the guys."

So that's the problem, I decide. He's feeling left out because he's not one of Denny's favorites. Then, before I can decide whether Greg is just putting on a performance for my benefit or not, he gently lays his head down in my lap and looks up at me wistfully, as though yearning to be understood.

I'm caught so by surprise to find his head in my lap that I do nothing. Even my thoughts are momentarily frozen. I don't move.

"Between you and me," Greg continues, looking very wise and knowing, "I think we're the only normal ones in the troupe."

"You and Jane seem to get along pretty well."

"Oh, Jane." I note a shrug in the tone of his voice. Then he adds, "Let's you and me be a twosome for the rest of the tour."

"Sure, why not," I agree lightly, not interpreting his meaning any more literally than "being friends."

"Oh God," he groans, and begins to clutch his head in the exact same way he did back in the movie theatre in Muskogee. "Sometimes I think my head is ready to burst. Could you rub right here?" Greg points to his forehead. So I gently rub and hope that I'm not being *led down the garden path.* That was a favorite saying of my father's.

"That's so soothing," Greg sighs. "Can I stay here with you for a little longer?" He supplements his little boy sweetness by adding, "I won't be a bother."

I must look dubious in spite of my sympathetic forehead massaging, for he adds, "No one will know. I can keep a secret."

"A secret about what?"

"That you've got a man in your room."

"What's so terrible about that? We aren't doing anything wrong and this isn't the nineteen hundreds."

Greg groans again as though in agony. A few minutes later he opens them again. His eyes really do look bleary or maybe just sleepy; it's hard to tell which.

Greg speaks to me as though he can barely force his words out through his steely pain, "I'd really like to stay here with you for a while if you'll let me until this headache gets better. The pain makes me dizzy. You can go on doing whatever you were going to do...you know, get ready for bed or whatever."

I don't know quite how to handle this situation. What should I do? Should I boot him out or wait a bit until his pain lets up. Does he really have a headache? I raise his head off my lap and gently lower it to the chenille bedspread. He moans and lies there quietly with his eyes closed.

What if he goes to sleep, I ask myself? What then? I take my pajamas and towel to the bathroom down the hall to undress. After a quick bath I return to my room and find Greg still lying there on the bed. Right away I notice something different about the scene. Something's been altered: Greg's shoes are on the floor beside the bed and he is no longer resting on top of the bedspread, but snugly under the bedspread, as though ensconced for the night.

After brushing my teeth at the sink in the room and creaming my face, I call out softly, "Greg? Are you awake?" There is no response. Now what, I ask myself? I decide to sit up and read for a while until Greg leaves, except that the only good reading lamp is above the bed. So, I sit uncomfortably at the desk wondering what to do about Greg when I hear a tap on the door.

"Who's there?" I call softly through the door, hoping Greg will not take this particular moment to wake up, though I do want him to get up and leave my room.

"It's Carl. Can you open the door?"

Strange, I think. Carl seldom comes to my hotel door. It's far more usual for him to phone any changes in the troupe's schedule. Right now I'm not too keen on letting him into my room, though there really is nothing of which to be ashamed. But I know if Carl sees Greg lying under the covers in my bed, it will be misunderstood. My dancing with Charley at the hotel in Joplin had been twisted into something immoral, so wouldn't finding Greg in my bed be considered twice as bad? Thinking how easily this situation could be misinterpreted, I quickly turn off the overhead light, so Greg won't be seen in the dark, and open my door just a crack.

"Oh," Carl exclaims, noticing that I'm in my pajamas and ready for bed. He steps back further into the hallway. "I didn't mean to get you out of bed."

"That's all right. I was just now going to bed."

"I've left a call at the desk for eight o'clock. We take off at nine."

"Fine with me," I agree. "See you in the morning."

"Have you seen Greg? He doesn't answer when I knock on his door."

I am about to answer with "no, I don't know where he is," when I hear movement on the bed and the bedside light snaps on. Then Greg calls out in a bright, wide-awake voice, quite unlike his former weak, sick-little-me tone, "Here I am."

Carl gives me a disgusted look and backs further away from the door. "Give him the message about leaving at nine o'clock." I watch him limp rapidly down the hall to his own room.

"Oh, how unfair!" I haven't meant to say it out loud. But it is unfair that Greg just happens at this precise moment to turn on the light so that Carl can clearly see him in my bed under the covers. Besides that, Carl can see that I am undressed. Why-oh-why have I been so stupidly careless!

Evidently Greg's headache has miraculously disappeared, for he bounces off the bed with vigor, picks up his shoes, and runs his fingers through his kinky hair.

I want to throttle him. "Why did you turn the light on just then?"

Greg shrugs and smiles. "Why not?" As he goes out the door, he waves his hand at me, and I hear him humming softly as he proceeds a few doors down the hall where he stops to knock on Denny's door. I watch him slip inside the room and immediately hear both of them begin to laugh.

What kind of exaggerated tale is Greg weaving in Denny's ear? Or has the incident been a planned one between them? Perhaps Greg has placed himself in the lobby as a decoy on purpose...the purpose being another "get even" stunt for my tattling about the car seating.

I am far more distressed at my own gullibility—my lack of caution—than angry at Greg. This isn't the first time I've been naïve. It now dawns on me just how imprudently I behaved back in Joplin, though Charley and Ernie were not out to deliberately get me into trouble. Being friends with them had been all very innocent but oh-so-foolish.

Tonight's occurrence is just as innocent, yet Denny will grab at the incident voraciously, plunge it into a tray of developer, and out will come a picture of me as a woman craving sex. Another Lisa.

I wonder if Denny will go so far as to report this trumped-up incident to Lu-Travis as he and Carl have certainly done against George? Still, Denny's own morals might not bear too much scrutiny, especially after what went on in the Springfield Hotel. As before, I visualize Denny walking secretively through the lobby of the hotel that evening. Closely behind him follows the older man wearing glasses. This knowledge about Denny makes me feel more secure for a time. Surely he dare not report me to Travis if his own actions aren't above suspicion.

Sleep eludes me. My anger at Denny and Greg—at myself too—keeps me awake. All my life I have this belief that a sort of magic protection takes care of the innocent and now that fairy tale mentality has taken a hit. Look what's been happening tonight! How can I have been so gullible?

TWENTY-EIGHT

*A*fter a sleepless night and the early wake-up call, I jammed my
clothes into the suitcase, three or four items at a time, only
half aware of folding anything. I couldn't concentrate. My mind was
entirely occupied with the incident last evening, the one in which Carl
found Greg in my bed under the covers. Too late, I had grasped the
fact that Greg, by playing upon my sympathy, had orchestrated last
night's performance. He had set the stage, pulled the curtain, and
even timed Carl's entrance; doubtless with Denny's help and blessing.

Why then, I asked myself, don't I go straight to Carl and explain?
Because he wouldn't believe me, I told myself. How could I talk Carl out
of believing what he saw with his own eyes? He might even slam the
door in my face. Is it possible that he could be part of the plan to get
me fired? Ever since the letter from Lu-Travis chastising the fellows
for not sharing the front seat, I felt Carl and the others patiently
waiting, crouched like animals ready to pounce on anything that
could be twisted to my disadvantage, an easy excuse to force me out
of the troupe. Now they definitely have that something—or am I
becoming paranoid?

I snapped the suitcase shut; it was time to go downstairs and
face the others in the lobby. I couldn't think up any reason to delay.
I picked up my suitcase and purse, closed the door, and stood there
in the hall for a minute. I needed time to adjust the expression on
my face from dread to a good natured fake smile that I'd wear like
heavy makeup all day long until I entered another hotel room, a safe
zone. Then, I'd shed it instantly. No cold cream necessary. I vowed

that Denny and the others weren't going to have the satisfaction of catching me with a beaten-down expression on my face. They wouldn't be allowed to see how humiliated and embarrassed I felt.

As I entered the lobby, I saw Carl sitting in a lounge chair smoking and staring off vacantly. When he inhaled on his cigarette the cadaver-like appearance of his cheeks became more pronounced.

"Anyone else here yet?" I asked in a brisk manner, maybe a bit more brisk than was normal. Carl didn't look directly at me but jerked his head in the general direction of the coffee shop. Larry, his shirt neatly tucked in at his thin waist, came ambling out of the coffee shop followed by Denny and Greg. None of them greeted me with a "good morning" as they once had done so long ago, or it seemed long ago. Greg glanced at me quickly then turned aside. I watched his mouth split into a gigantic grin. He stretched up to reach Denny's ear and whispered something. I could almost hear him say: see what a clever thing I've done for you? Thanks to me you've got some dirt on the broad.

✳

Our next performance is an evening one in Huntsville, Texas, about one hundred and sixty miles south and west of Carthage. There is to be a reception after the performance, allowing the children to see us, the actors and actresses, up close. It's a nice idea, but very few children actually come. Perhaps the parents think the youngest children, the five and six-year-olds, should be home in bed after nine o'clock, or maybe the performance is too mediocre to generate enough interest in meeting us. I recall how faint the applause sounds to me at the end of the show.

We all stand around in costume with forced smiles on our tired faces, not knowing what exactly is expected of us. The cookies and colored punch look so frugal, quite lost on the long library table that is set up in the schoolroom behind the stage.

"Is that real fur?" a little girl asks me as she hesitantly reaches out a tiny finger to touch the fake ermine down the front of my costume.

"No," I answer. "It's just fluffy cotton with black markings to make it look like real fur to the audience." Have I disillusioned the child, I wonder? Though our performances are specifically for children, no one has given us a single clue on how to communicate with them face to face.

Denny, as the king, is very popular with the children as he smiles broadly at them. At the same time he growls little asides to Carl out of the corner of his mouth. "No one told us we'd have to deal with these little twerps."

"Just keep smiling and shut up," Carl warns.

"How are we going to get the scenery struck if this goes on much longer?" Larry complains.

As it turns out, the kids are mostly interested in Denny, the King, Fay, the Princess, and myself, as the Queen, which leaves the others free to change out of their costumes and begin to strike the set while the reception continues.

It's after eleven o'clock when we all pile into the truck and car to exit the school parking lot. Most of us don't have enough money for a hotel in Huntsville so, in spite of the late hour, we have no choice but to drive the one hundred and forty-seven miles to Port Arthur where our payroll will be waiting for us.

This time, I really dread facing the long night of driving. If I drive forty-five miles per hour, we will probably reach Port Arthur around three in the morning. I'm so very tired from acting a double role all day; pretending that nothing is wrong between me and the others in the troupe is one part, and the roll of the queen is another. It's a strain. A little relief comes to me when I think all the others in the car are asleep or pretending to be asleep.

As I drive the first leg of the journey, the National Forest etches itself in a dark jagged outline against the lighter sky. After midnight and after passing through Woodville, we head south towards Beaumont on route sixty-nine. It's then that I first notice wisps of fog. Soon, every dip in the road contains fog. No problem so far, I think, as I quickly adjust to another and another cloud of wet fog.

Then the fog begins to appear in the perfectly flat sections of road as well as in the valleys. That's when it begins to play peculiar tricks on my balance. Sometimes when I peer though the windshield, the fog starts at the exact level of my eyes and billows upwards. Below eye level, the view is unimpeded and I can see the middle line in the road. The swirls of ghostly fog soar and writhe eerily. Just as I get relatively used to steering with the fog at that level, it swoops downwards touching the hood of the car but still blanking out the road, forcing me to slow to a crawl.

There is no warning, no way to forecast ahead of time when the fog will make its antic rise or fall. When it changes over and over again, my inner sense of balance goes askew, and I feel myself swept upwards from the road—soft as the rise of a feather—into slow moving clouds. I float just above the ground with the car wheels still turning.

"Where is the road?" I haven't meant to speak out loud. But where is it? It has sunk, and leaves me gently floating somewhere above the earth in the white layers.

"Can you see?" Greg's voice whispers from somewhere over my shoulder. It's a relief to hear an earthly voice, to know for sure that the nightmarish scene in front of the windshield is not just my fancy. "Most of the time," I answer, not wanting anyone in the car to feel alarm.

A few miles further on I spot some tall highway lights up ahead. They cast a pink carnival-like aura over the fog. Oh, good, I think, lights! That's got to be a sign of human activity. But upon reaching the area, there are no human beings at all, no cars either…just a place where main highways converge…a world of pink. It's easy for my imagination to read the pink as a portent of some catastrophic occurrence that will eliminate me and all mankind.

"My God, look at the time. It's almost four o'clock." Denny rouses himself from sleep. "Aren't we in Port Arthur yet?"

A few darkened stores begin to appear, and occasionally a lone car passes us. Apparently there is little life at four in the morning, except in the form of an occasional lighted filling station.

By the time we find our hotel, daylight has broken. I am more exhausted than I ever remember being in my whole life. Finally, I can relax my grip on the wheel and very soon I can take a warm bath and sleep, sleep, sleep.

Leaning against the counter in the hotel and waiting my turn to register, I feel my eyes shut and make no attempt to force them open. Carl is next in line to sign in. He partially turns towards me while continuing to fill out his registration card. "You follow Larry to the filling station where he'll leave the truck for an oil change, and then bring him back to the hotel."

"What?" I have only half comprehended what Carl is asking me to do. "Why so ear...."

Carl interrupts me in a do-it-or-get-out tone of voice. "You can either go now and sleep late, or I'll do it now, and *you* can get up at ten o'clock to give Larry a ride back to pick up the truck."

"But Carl—I try to make logic out of his order—we stay in Port Arthur two whole days. Why can't the truck be taken for the oil change later in the morning?"

"Because I said so."

"All right," I succumb, hoping I can stay awake that long. With envy I watch Carl, Denny, Greg, and the girls enter the elevator on their way to bed. I scribble my name on the registration form and accidentally drop the key on the floor. Wearily, I pick it up and head back to the car. The clock behind the registration desk tells me that it is now five in the morning.

I follow the truck to the filling station located several miles from the hotel. Evidently the same station had been used on former tours and was considered reliable by Lu-Travis, or maybe just cheaper. At the station we wait, Larry in the truck and me in the car, until the mechanics come on duty at six. Then I drive Larry back to the hotel.

"Did the fog bother you?" I ask Larry. He nods his answer.

"Do you know why the truck has to be picked up at ten? Surely it isn't needed until Sunday morning, that's two days from now."

"We three guys are taking off for New Orleans this afternoon, and we won't get back in time to move the truck away from the filling station. Besides, we aren't supposed to leave it parked there at all. It might get broken into."

"Oh. I'd like to see New Orleans too, but I don't have enough money. Are you going by bus?"

"Ummm...I'm too tired to talk." Larry leans his head back against the seat and closes his eyes. That may be partly an excuse to keep from talking to me, but I believe Larry really is tired, just as I am. He has also driven through the long night in and out of fog. At least he has spoken to me instead of freezing me out completely, probably because Denny isn't around to remind him to shut-up. I drive the remainder of the way back to the hotel in silence.

It's afternoon when I finally wake up. I feel refreshed though I've slept only six hours. My attitude is full of hope. Since Larry has spoken to me, perhaps the rest of the cast may slowly thaw out and treat me like a member of the troupe again. Also, I have some vague notion, foolish I soon admit, that those riding in the car owe me some kind of tribute for getting them safely through the fog. Because I drive carefully and prevent accidents, they ought to feel grateful towards me.

As I leave the hotel coffee shop, Fay and Jane are just entering. They too, have just awakened and are coming for their breakfast though it's now nearly three in the afternoon. I remember thinking how propitious our meeting is because Denny isn't with them to remind them to give me the silent treatment. "Got any plans for today," I ask?

"Just rest, I guess," Fay answers and gets a sharp elbow in her side from Jane as a reminder to snub me. Without another word, they walk on into the coffee shop. At least Fay has given me an answer. I decide to take it as a favorable sign. Naturally I'm looking desperately for such signs, cracks in the wall of their silence. Pretending that my relationship to everyone in the troupe is quite normal puts a huge strain on me. Still, I'm determined to keep on behaving as though nothing is amiss. If I persevere just a bit longer, I may be able to wear them down.

TWENTY-NINE

*O*ur travel destination on Monday was El Dorado, Arkansas, a drive of three-hundred and twelve miles. It was a much longer drive than noted on the itinerary because naturally Lu-Travis didn't know that the guys weren't returning from New Orleans until late Sunday night. In fact, she didn't know they were even planning to visit New Orleans.

I had been ready and waiting in the lobby for over a half hour. As each one of the group sluggishly gathered in the lobby, I smiled as though I absolutely loved the world, their churlishness, and their silence. All of this fake camaraderie was marvelous training for the stage, at least that's what I kept trying to convince myself. I made sure my back was straight and my chin held erect, but inside I felt a slow crumbling, maybe like a wet clay statue without its inside armature.

Denny and Carl were each holding a paper cup of coffee as they came into the lobby. Larry and Greg arrived next and stood nearby. Finally the girls, Fay and Jane, came out of the coffee shop and headed for the elevator to collect their luggage.

"Get a move on it, girls," Denny called.

"No sense opening the back of the truck till they come down again, I guess," said Larry. Carl looked at his watch and said nothing.

"Are you driving this morning or do you want me to drive," I asked, feeling quite certain that I'd get an answer from Carl to a direct question.

"I'll drive the first half," Carl said, not bothering to make eye contact. I was getting used to his eyes sliding past my head and onto a nearby wall.

We all waited. Still, Fay and Jane seemed in no hurry to get themselves down to the lobby. Why couldn't the guys see how much more prompt and professional I was than the other two girls? After a few minutes passed, Carl said, "Let's get this stuff loaded. Maybe the girls will appear by then."

From El Dorado, Arkansas, we moved on to Pine Bluff where we gave an afternoon performance. By Wednesday we were on our way to Greenwood, Mississippi. And there in that miserable little hotel we remained two nights.

For some time now, it had been established that Jane and Fay would share a double room and divide the cost beteen them while I had to spend one seventy-five to two dollars just for a single room. I had no choice. The more I spent on my room, the less I had to eat. My whole salary was only thirty-five dollars, so I often left the coffee shops hungry.

In Greenwood, my room was on the same floor as the lobby and just a few doors down the hall from the reception desk and also the bar. The Spanish courtyard entrance to the bar overflowed with the comings and goings of men; some even stood in the lattice archway with drinks in their hands and cigarettes dangling from their fingers. Had I been unable to find my way to the lobby from my room, I could have found it quite simply by following the smoke and alcohol trail down the hall.

Whenever I visited the coffee shop I had to parade past the opening to the bar and the men standing there. I dreaded that and kept my eyes averted. "Come and have a drink with me, pretty lady," one man called out to me.

After having my supper alone in the coffee shop, I hustled back to my room feeling several sets of eyes follow me down the hall. Quickly, I slipped inside and locked the door. I spent the whole first evening trapped in my room, unfairly, it seemed to me, forced to listen to the loud juke box until the bar was shut down around midnight.

The following evening after we had returned from our afternoon's performance, I stayed in the coffee shop longer than usual, hoping to exchange a few friendly words with the waitress. My coffee cup had already been refilled twice and soon I would have no more excuses to linger.

At the beginning of the Princess tour, I had often deliberately discouraged the friendly attempts of a waitress to draw me into conversation. Some were far too inquisitive, plain nosey. Now everything was reversed. It was I who started the conversations. Any tiny morsel of attention from a waitress aroused my gratitude…my smile. There were two kinds of hunger: stomach hunger and hunger for companionship. Anyone, or nearly anyone, would do to talk to. Just talking out loud was a testament to my existence, proof that I was alive. When people ignored me—as the kids in the troupe had been for weeks—I felt like a nonentity, as though I weren't even here in body.

"Thank you," I said, as the waitress filled my coffee cup for the third time. "You certainly are busy tonight. Are you always this…"

"Waitress!" someone called, and she hurried down the counter to fill someone else's cup. I drank my last sip of coffee and hustled through the lobby, scurrying like a little animal back to its nine by ten-foot hole.

✻

The jukebox music from the bar was swinging into full evening volume, one hillbilly tune after another. Once in a while an old classic was played, which was as unusual as seeing a Monet painting hung between fence art. I lay down on the mattress, no limper than most. I wanted someone to talk to…to advise me." Should I leave the troupe or not?

For the remainder of that evening in Greenwood, I decide to divert my attention from the claustrophobic little room by repacking my box, which holds whatever couldn't be crammed in my suitcase.

Right after the school performance, I had asked Larry for the box as he stowed the flats away.

"What box?" He shrugged. "I don't know where your box is." He takes out a small pocket comb and slicks back his hair.

"It's that square one tied with string. My name is on the top in large black letters."

"Oh, that one." With his cowboy boots he kicked it roughly towards the tailgate of the truck.

"Thanks," I had muttered.

Now I remind myself, if I do decide to leave the troupe, I'll have to wait three days for my paycheck to buy a bus ticket; just three more days to holdout before heading home. What a relief it will be! I let out a long drawn out sob. Just planning about my escape partially relieves me of the deep hurt I feel.

My mind continues to think up retaliatory remarks to things Carl and Denny might say or do tomorrow when I tell them that I'm leaving. Maybe I should dump all their suitcases into the street. Totally childish, I admit, but the absurd image gives me a giggle. It relieves pressure.

Instantly, I tell myself, *I have a better idea of what to do! I won't even tell them I'm leaving. I'll walk out on the bunch of them. Let them wiggle as though caught in a trap and try to explain to Travis exactly what has been happening.* I wipe at my eyes as though to see more clearly the predicament in which they'll soon find themselves and their attempt to explain the inexplicable to Lu-Travis.

That night when I rouse myself between restless dreams, my mind continues to repeat over and over the clever things I'll say to Denny and Greg or Carl and Denny. I'll lash out at everyone in the troupe with my words of disdain. They'll be sorry when I finish with them. Wearily, my thoughts go tumbling around and around all night long. I feel so terribly humiliated. So alone. Did that girl, Lisa, feel like this too? No, of course not. She was tougher and more resilient than I. But then, what do I really know about her or what had happened on that last tour...only what I've been told by Denny...and he lies about a lot of things.

All of them will lie to protect themselves, but I can write a letter telling Travis what's really been happening, the whole truth. There might be an entire week of performances to cancel while someone is bused out to Knoxville...that's where our next paychecks will be waiting...and trained in the part of the queen. My other role, the servant girl part has very few lines and will be easy for a substitute actress to learn.

Just three days to wait; three more days to hold out before heading home. What a relief! I let out a long drawn-out sob. Just secretly planning my escape gives me new vigor. Almost immediately I feel upright again, and taller. That's exactly what the jukebox in the bar is whining about. Something about *standing tall on the mountain and being free again.* What a corny coincidence. I chuckle and gulp and cry some more.

THIRTY

*F*eeling weak, I carefully sit up in bed the next morning. Maybe I really am sick? The debate and wrangling that's been going on inside my head the whole night long, leaves me sapped of energy. *You're not sick,* I tell myself, at least not that kind of sick. You have to get up and face everything. That's when I remember the decision I made the night before to leave the Princess Troupe. A marvelous free-floating sensation slides over me. For a brief moment I hover there in serene relief...before dropping hard into reality. I will have to weather several days of ill treatment before I can make my escape.

I splash cold water on my face and hope my red, swollen eyes will not draw attention. Quite early I hurry to the hotel coffee shop in order to avoid the others; I need time to adjust to last night's decision...time to build up a wall of immunity. Otherwise, tears will waterfall down my face in front of everyone. They mustn't have the satisfaction of seeing how well they have succeeded in undermining my self-confidence.

I tell myself, *this will be a chance to perform my most difficult acting role.* With a calmness I do not feel, I enter the coffee shop. Why does Denny want to make life so miserable for me that I'll be induced to quit the troupe? Isn't that his plan?

Surely there must be more to Denny's vendetta than revenge for the letter I have written about the car seating way back in Amarillo, Texas. I didn't mention his name specifically or anyone else's name in that letter. Is there another reason that makes him dislike me so much?

Even the Springfield incident—discovering the male guest in Denny's room--doesn't seem that sufficiently important to me. Perhaps though, Denny thinks otherwise. Is it possible that he fears that I'll write a second letter to Lu-Travis and this time mention the incident of his harboring a male guest in his room all night?

*

My decision to wait until payday before leaving the troupe is made from sheer necessity. I simply do not have enough money for the bus fare home. So the challenge for me is to get through the next few days without breaking down, without letting others see how battered I feel. I vow to myself not to let on. I will cover up and keep on pretending that they haven't wounded me, or they'll close in for the kill. Isn't that what animals do to other injured animals?

Later, when it's time to meet the others in the lobby, I pretend to enter briskly, though in truth I have to talk each leg into moving forward like an invalid learning to walk again. My smile is frozen, prone to the stiffness of a Parkinson disease victim. When I see Greg and Denny exchanging whispers followed by Greg's nervous cackle, I know the subject is probably me. I manage to keep my feelings on leash and partly hidden behind a newspaper that someone has left lying on the sofa. The headlines about Korea are nothing but blurred ink in front of my eyes.

"Where are the girls?" I hear Carl ask as he comes out of the coffee shop with his paper cup of coffee.

"I'm here," I answer brightly, knowing he doesn't mean me at all. He ignores my answer.

We wait fifteen minutes longer for Jane and Fay. How I wish they would hurry. I feel so vulnerable sitting here, the target of one huge consolidated beam of ill will. Obviously, I am meant to see the sneaked glances and hear the whispered innuendos. The longer I sit here, the more likely that tension will detonate me and out will come a blast of angry recriminations towards everyone. But isn't that exactly what they hope for?

I yearn to let loose with a volley of insults and abuse; blister each one of them with invectives! The inside of my head sizzles with the urge, barely held back, to scream at everyone. As the tension grows, I grip the newspaper harder to the point of crumbling one edge.

"Fay, baby!" I hear Denny call. Fay and Jane have at last shown up in the lobby with their suitcases. Immediately, I rise and hasten to bring the car around from the parking lot to the front of the hotel. It's a temporary release. As I walk to the car, I begin breathing normally again; I think, let them talk about their *tricks and get it over with* while I'm out of hearing.

From the mangy Greenwood Hotel, we travel two-hundred and fifty-two miles to Birmingham, Alabama, where we are to stay just one night. Amid the rush hour traffic of Birmingham, I have difficulty keeping the truck in sight, yet I have to follow it because no one gives me the address or the hotel name where we are to stay.

I switch from lane to lane to catch up with the truck, not knowing ahead of time whether it might make a right or a left hand turn and disappear altogether. All the signaling with my arm out the window keeps me busy. The truck is now a block ahead of me with a long line of cars and a city bus in between. Up ahead I see a policeman stop the truck, probably for driving on a main thoroughfare where trucks aren't allowed, and I am finally able to catch up and double park.

Cars behind me complain loudly with their horns, and a few drivers shout at me out their windows as they pass. I hope their noise escapes the policeman's attention. At last the policeman lets the truck proceed and I follow. Already, I hate the city. Dirt lodges in my left eye from the open car window, and I see paper shifting and swirling along the curb whenever a car rushes past.

The hotel has only two rooms available: one for the boys and one for the girls. A cot has been added to each room. At the registration desk I notice the exchange of looks between Fay and Jane. Maybe they are embarrassed by having to share a room with me, but knowing that they don't want me, makes me feel more uncomfortable about the arrangement than they possibly can. Fortunately, the room is large and has its own bathroom. Fay and Jane immediately drop their purses and coats down on the twin beds like animals marking their territories. They leave the cot to me. I'm certainly not going to make an issue of the beds since there are more important problems between us without fighting over who gets the most comfortable bed. Still, it might be nice to be given a choice, however insincere.

Now the sticky question arises: what to do about dinner? I can no longer tag along with the girls now that relationships have deteriorated too deeply between us. There is no sense in forcing them to accept me as a companion and then be ignored. That would just be further humiliation to my already wobbly ego and far more embarrassing for me.

I am so tired from lack of sleep the night before that I nearly dozed off while waiting for Fay and Jane to use the bathroom and get ready for dinner. My seeming to be asleep is the solution to my problem and theirs. I simply continue to pretend to be asleep so that Fay and Jane will not be forced to accept me, or I forced to accept them, as dinner companions.

As I lay there on the cot waiting for Fay and Jane to comb their hair and gather their purses, I make a calculation in my head. By dividing the cost of the room between three people I will have an extra fifty cents to spend on dinner or tomorrow's breakfast. Thinking about food makes me realize how empty my stomach feels, and I mentally try to hurry up the girls so I can go out and eat. I half wish they might ask me to tag along with them, just so I can have the pleasure of turning them down. But naturally they fail to ask me.

✳

When I am quite sure the girls have left, I get up off the cot and change my clothes. I leave the key at the desk in the lobby since Fay and Jane might return before I do, then I walk out onto the street to take a look. It's obvious that there are at least six or seven movie theatres and plenty of restaurants within walking distance of the hotel. Now all I have to do is pick a restaurant where I'm not likely to run into the rest of the troupe.

I walk leisurely along the street avoiding the restaurants that look too high priced, though there aren't very many of those in this part of Birmingham. If a restaurant has a menu posted on the outside window, I stop to check on the prices. In general, Italian food isn't too expensive, so before long I settle on a "spaghetti joint" and step inside. I look around carefully to make sure none of the troupe members are inside.

After eating my fill of pasta, I walk past several movie theatres trying to decide which movie to see. Mostly though, I'm stalling... trying to muster up enough courage to ask for professional courtesy. It's still a half hour before most of the movies are to begin, but I need all that time to build up my courage to the point of facing a theatre manager alone, something I've never done before. I realize there is nothing shameful about asking for professional courtesy, or at least that's what Denny claims. "It's common practice," he often professes. To me it feels like asking for charity. My pride balks at asking for anything free, yet I'm unable to afford the price of a movie. Nor do I want to spend the entire evening alone in the hotel room.

It's still early when I decide upon the movie I want to see: <u>That Bright Year.</u> As yet there are no other people standing in the line at the ticket window. Good, I think. If nobody is watching me, I will feel less embarrassed if the manager turns me down.

Just inside the outer lobby a young man is using the carpet sweeper on the orange carpet crossed by bands of blue and yellow. Even the jolt of the awful carpet can't distract my mind from the dread of speaking to the manager. The young man points out the manager behind the popcorn machine.

"Excuse me." I try to override the pop-popping noises, wishing I could hide myself inside the fluffy, white stuff. There is no return smile on his face, so I anticipate the bluntness of his refusal and begin to turn away. The young man sweeping the carpet looks up and nods as though urging me on. "I'm from the Lu-Travis Children's Theatre Troupe staying at the Hotel Hillman."

The manager says nothing...shows not a flicker of interest. I find it difficult to continue. "Urrr...I wonder...if you will extend..." My nervousness flies the correct nomenclature, 'professional courtesy' right out of my head, and I have to end up uttering the dreadful words..."let me in the movie free?"

I turn half away from him, preparing to make a quick retreat after the expected blow of his disdainful, "no," which I'm sure I see in his eyes. If only he would smile or ask me a question, anything to ease my embarrassment. I wait and think: never, never again will I lower myself to ask for free favors.

"Why yes," he says, still not smiling. "Enjoy the movie." He turns abruptly and begins to walk away. I am stunned. Finally I manage to blurt out to his retreating back, "Thank you...thanks very much."

I am so relieved and grateful that I haven't been humiliated by his turning me down that tears of release gather in my eyes. I reprimand myself; so silly of me to get so emotional over a little kindness.

"Let the young lady inside," I hear the manager tell the fellow sweeping the carpet.

Inside the still empty theatre, I pick out a seat and wait for other people to arrive, the lights to lower, and the local advertisements to begin. Maybe I will stay to see the movie twice if it's a really good one. That way I needn't get back to the hotel room before Jane and Fay. I didn't want it to appear to them as though I had never left the room the entire evening simply because I lacked a companion. There's that "pride" thing again.

It's a good movie, family fare with poignant moments and humorous ones too. I am constantly laughing or holding back the tears. During a powerfully moving section near the end, Larry and his little brother are plagued by two larger boys who chase, trip, and verbally abuse them on the way home from school. They have been accosted by the same bully and his friend many times before. We can see the terrible fear in Larry's eyes. But the bigger of his tormentors makes a mistake. He shouts taunting remarks about the father of Larry. We can see Larry's mind turn from fear to blazing fury. He runs towards the larger boy, and by the suddenness of his attack knocks him clear off his feet. Still raging, Larry sits on his enemy and pounds his face. Some folks in the audience cheer out loud at this very "just" turn of events. Some of us cheer just as much inside our heads. The comeuppance is so gratifyingly sweet. If only one could get even as easily in life as in the movies. One can't, I'm learning.

In the denouement of the movie, the younger brother picks up Larry's broken glasses and runs home to get help. Their mother arrives and gently pulls her son off the bully. She seems to understand what has been going on inside her son, and the frustration that has been building up by the months of taunting. At last the terror is over. Larry and his brother can be free of the menace. Now the movie audience is quiet.

Tears have been running down my face, and I have to force back the lumps of emotion swelling upwards in my throat. I put my hand over my mouth to muffle my noises. I know why I have been so easily moved by Larry's troubles in the movie and why I want to break down and cry with relief when the boy finally gets even with his tormentors after months of living in misery. I put my hand over my mouth to stifle my own gulps.

Just as Larry bashes wildly at the older boy's face, I am lashing out at Denny and those in the troupe who are making my life miserable. They are abandoning me to hours and days of silence...to evenings spent in solitary, alone in ugly hotel rooms.

Before the lights in the theatre are brought up fully, I hurry out into the lobby, cross the orange carpet with my head averted from the ticket taker, and hasten down the street. The shadows cast by the buildings give me some privacy or so I think. There, facing a closed store window, I struggle to regain my composure. My emotional outbreak very likely leaves my face red and blotchy, an unusual nighttime sunburn.

Now, as I walk along the sidewalk and away from the flow of people exiting from other movie theatres, I deliberately slow down to give myself time to harness my emotions. I don't want my wet face to be interpreted by strangers, not by anyone, especially not by Jane or Fay or the others in case they are all sitting in the hotel lobby.

As it turns out, neither Fay nor Jane have returned yet, so there's time to further compose myself and take a leisurely bath. When they do arrive about eleven, I again pretend to be sound asleep.

☆

On March seventeenth, we drive from Birmingham to Knoxville, Tennessee, another hundred and sixty-six miles or close to that, and on our way we pass through Chattanooga, snug in its surrounding hills.

At the Park Hotel in Knoxville our pay envelopes are waiting, and for me there are two letters, two powerful morale lifters. One letter is from my mother and the other from Charley. Oh Charley, I think, thank you, thank you for writing. Dear Charley doesn't think I'm a tattler or a loose woman; he will never treat me as though I have a contagious disease.

Already, I tell Charley in my letters about the way everyone in the troupe is treating me, though I still do not say one word of it to my mother and father. But now that payday is here, it's decision-making time: Should I leave the troupe or stay? If I decide to leave, then I must phone my parents and tell them that I'm coming home. Naturally, they will ask me why. How can I explain the reasons without breaking down and maybe even sobbing on the phone? Then my mother, so full of common sense, could say, "Why Ann, it's so near the end of the tour..." implying that I should be brave and wait. How will I counteract her perfectly logical attitude?

Charley's letter is full of his usual flattery, exaggerated of course, but his compliments are my lifeline right now. They keep me steady when I want to stomp my foot and flail out at everyone in the troupe. For a few brief hours his letter is so successful at pumping confidence back into me that I think seriously of continuing with the tour. After all, there are just six or seven more weeks to go, and I really do want to stick it out. I want to prove that I can. Pretensions again, I suppose, defiance too. The money and consequently the means of my escape, are here, right here in my hand.

Charlie's delightful letter, so full of affection and zany jokes, makes the decision to go or to stay much tougher. My spirit soars. At this moment I can go on forever letting abuse roll off, leaving nothing but a mere scratch. I so want to prove that I can hold out. Why give Denny the satisfaction of thinking he can shove me or anyone else out of The Lost Princess whenever he chooses, the big fat prissy! That's how I think of him. I don't even know the technical term for guys like Denny who prefer men to women.

I recall the whispered voices coming through the open transom above the door of Denny's room in the Springfield hotel. Perhaps Denny thinks I overheard more of what was going on in his private life than I actually did. That would certainly explain his meanness towards me and the recent "set-up" of allowing Carl to purposely discover Greg under the bedspread in my room. Will Denny go so far as telling Lu-Travis out and out lies about me? He's certainly done that before to others, probably to George and maybe even that girl, Lisa, of whom I've heard so much. Yes, of course! Now that I think it through, the incident in Springfield seems a far more logical reason for Denny's persecution of me than my letter to Lu-Travis over the unfair car seating.

My dilemma: Should I leave the troupe or not? Why not wait at least one more week—just one more—until the next payday. I wouldn't be much further away from home by next Saturday, just a trifle further east but also quite a bit further north.

Yes, I finally come to a decision. I will delay my leaving for one more week. Next payday I'll leave for sure.

After that decision, I open my mother's letter but with less enthusiasm than I felt in opening Charlie's. Denny is still across the lobby at the check-in desk along with Fay and some of the others. Just as Carl heads for the elevator, I look up from my letter and call out, "What time do you want to leave for Harrogate tomorrow morning?" Carl mutters something over his shoulder which I can't hear, so I ask Fay who sits nearby.

"Fay? Did you hear what Carl said?" Fay shrugs and gets up to follow Jane towards the elevator. I feel certain that I won't see any member of the troupe for the rest of the day, and I'm right. At the moment I almost don't care if they snub me or not; the letters have given me a temporary high. Even the afternoon rain fails to squelch my feeling of well-being.

Nighttime though, is different. By then the cheery influence of Charlie's letter begins to wear off. The lonesome feeling, like chilly dampness finding cracks around the window, seeps into me and takes over again. Saturday nights often leave me with an empty, depressed sensation, even in the best of times. Saturday, that's when everyone else in the world, or so I imagine, goes out with their friends for an evening of jolly good fun.

✳

The rain begins in the early afternoon and continues into the evening. I wonder if Carl will let the others use the car to get to a movie. Hasn't he succumbed to Denny's pressure several times before? I picture all six of them cramming themselves into the car, laughing and joking. Some of the degrading jokes will certainly be about me.

With nothing better to do, I descend in the elevator to the lobby to ask the desk clerk what time the coffee shop opens in the morning. It's just an excuse to start a conversation, but since my room has no telephone, it's at least a legitimate excuse. It occurs to me that this desk clerk might be as sociable as Charley. The man is indeed pleasant enough but continues to shuffle busily through some index cards as he answers my questions. I thank him for the information and turn away. What am I going to do to fill up the next four hours until bedtime?

As a treat to myself, I go back into the coffee shop for the second time and waste another nickel on coffee. I just want someone to talk to. The waitress generously keeps my cup filled, but between customers, whenever she has a spare moment from her duties, she is drawn like a magnet to a young man sitting at the other end of the counter from me. Even she has someone to share her thoughts with on a rainy Saturday night. Slowly, I sip my coffee, knowing that all the free refills have more than used up my nickel's value.

Before returning to my room I amble to the front window of the lobby where a few older men are sitting and staring out at the rain, which is coming down in torrents. It's difficult to tell where the sidewalk and the street separate. Together they are one wide river. Alarmed—a flood seems imminent to me—I hurry back to the desk clerk to report my news. "It looks like a flood out there!" I gesture towards the street.

The clerk seems quite unconcerned. "We do get lots of rain this time of year. Better rain than ice."

While I have the clerk's attention I quickly think up something else to ask. "How far are the movie theatres from here?"

"About two miles. Even if it weren't raining I'd suggest you take a taxi, Miss. This isn't the best part of town, you know."

"Yes, I guessed that. Thank you for the information." The taxi of course is quite out of the question. I can't afford both the taxi fare and the movie. And I certainly am never going to beg for a free movie again...not ever.

"Damn those kids; they're so mean," I say out loud as I rise in the empty elevator to the third floor. I am positive that the troupe is using the car to get them to a movie or a cheery restaurant while I am stuck here in this gloomy hotel.

Another evening is about to drag by. The wonderful euphoria brought about by Charlie's letter has now evaporated. One depressing thought follows another as I lie there on the bed. All my problems swell up to twice their normal size like beans left to soak overnight.

Finally, I cajoled myself into getting up from the bed to wash out some underpants and hang them up to dry. After that I make a quick trip back to the lobby to leave an eight o'clock wake-up call, since I still don't know when Carl intends to have us leave the next morning. With no phone available in the room, wake-up calls came through an intercom in the wall above the bed. Soon I go to bed but not to sleep.

I lay there regretting that I haven't taken the bus and run for home, even though I know what a masterstroke that will be for Denny. It would mean that he has successfully forced me out of the troupe. I can visualize Denny rolling his eyes and passing his chubby hand through his dark hair, taking all the credit for my ouster. Then he will toss off his caustic remarks with a humble grin on his face. "We got rid of that old maid bitch," he'll say. Everyone will laugh at his dramatic antics. "Now maybe we can get a real trouper," he might add.

Well, I am a real trouper! I drive the car, do my performing, and I'm always on time for rehearsals and ahead of time for travel calls in the mornings. The more I think about it, the more stubborn I become. I want to prove to Denny and to everyone else that I will not be drummed out so easily. No! Denny admires the toughness of Lisa? I'll show him toughness!

I'm not going to leave at all. I'm not going to give any of them the satisfaction. They'll have to shake me off like a dog worrying at a bone. I'm going to hang on to the very end.

THIRTY-ONE

*D*enny was clasping his scrapbook in one hand and his over-stuffed black suitcase in the other as I followed him through the lobby of the Park Hotel in Knoxville. Through the glass doors to the street I could see Larry waiting beside the truck to load up our suitcases. Half way to the outside door something fluttered to the carpet in front of me. Immediately I assumed that it was a loose clipping from Denny's scrapbook. I started to call out to him, but my curiosity prompted me to stop and pick up the newspaper clipping first. It was a picture of a girl, and the caption under the picture mentioned a Lu-Travis children's performance. At last, here was an actual photo of Lisa, the much maligned girl, from last year's troupe.

I looked at the picture carefully. Lisa was tall compared to the runts in the Princess Troupe. She quite obviously wore a black wig and makeup for her role as the witch in Hansel and Gretel. The makeup was not dramatic enough to scare the children and give them nightmares, yet it changed the youthful face of Lisa into the facsimile of a haggard old woman with a long nose. What a disappointment. I was no closer to knowing what Lisa herself looked like than before, just as I still didn't know who had tattled on her, though I had my strong suspicions. The blurb next to the photo stated that Lisa was nineteen years old and originally from Columbus, Ohio. I wondered what had eventually happened to her? When I caught up with Denny at the rear of the truck, I thrust the clipping at him. "You dropped this." Just as I expected, he grabbed it from my hand without a "thank you."

On Monday we drove from Harrogate on to Big Stone Gap, a town over the border into West Virginia. The rain soaked us at the hotel door as we left Harrogate, and rain continued off and on most of the day. The scenery was beautiful even as seen through the slanted rain. I couldn't give it my full attention because the road had switchbacks and hairpin curves. I longed to stop the car and let my eyes feast on the scenes. Even that would have been too brief. I wanted to let the moisture touch my bare arms and catch a whiff of tang left from the recently melted snow somewhere higher up on the mountain. I could spend hours watching the stream make its suicidal plunge down to the valley. But of course I couldn't stop. We had a schedule to keep.

I continued to talk inside my head about the loveliness of the mountain scenery. From there my thoughts wandered onward to the subject of the tour, its end, and my return to a completely different sort of life. By now I had talked myself into staying to the very end of the tour. I didn't know what my future would be like, not exactly, but I certainly didn't want it to be like this, one of inferior hotels and narrow-minded companions.

Even home life, if I had to live for a time with my parents, had taken on a huge upgrade in my mind. It sounded pretty wonderful right now. Home was a place where one could eat breakfast in a bathrobe instead of dressing to descend in an elevator to a coffee shop. Home was clean rooms with no hotel disinfectant smell, and it meant sitting down on a toilet seat without first checking for splashes. But most important of all: home was knowing that Mom and Dad spoke to me straight without the dishonesty of "darling," or "sweetie" or other false terms of address. How conveniently my mind blotted out the monotony of the weekly grocery shopping trips and the dinner conversation that discussed nothing more stimulating than the high price of meat. Still, right now, dull conversation was better than being punished by the silent treatment.

My parents had, of course, dealt out some punishments, not the silent treatment, but some as lonely though for a much shorter time period. Those occurred long ago when I had sassed my mother or argued on and on to the point of shouting. She'd take me by the arm, her arms surprisingly muscular, march me to my room where she would leave me and close the door. After a period of angry tears, I'd sit and wait, not daring to come out of my room. Mother never came to tell me I could. I'd wait and wait. And that, I suppose, was the punishment itself. After what seemed like hours, though of course it wasn't, I'd slowly and quietly turn the knob on my door and tiptoe out to sit on the top step of the stairs. Below in the kitchen I might hear Mother starting lunch or dinner—depending upon the time of day—so I'd go down and ask if it was time to set the table. That was my job. She might say "yes" or "soon" and not mention a word about going back to my room. That's how I knew my punishment was over.

Folks in Big Stone Gap seemed inclined to be suspicious of outsiders like us. Perhaps it was because they were more isolated from other people by their thick forests and their mountains. We were there only long enough to perform on that single afternoon, but it was an unforgettable performance, one that none of us would be likely to forget.

Fortunately the children, except perhaps those in the very front rows, couldn't see the chipped paint on the canvas flats that had been constantly jostled through narrow school doorways and scraped across the tailgate of the truck. Sometimes damage also occurred to the flats when the truck hit deep ruts in a country dirt road or when Larry stacked the flats carelessly. Also stored in the truck was the wooden throne, which had been painted to appear velvety soft and studded with precious jewels of rubies and emeralds. Up close, there were no jewels at all and no velvet cushions, just the rock bottom hardness of a park bench. This double throne had always been under great stress from the weight of Denny's rotund form with the addition of one hundred and nine pounds, my weight.

That afternoon during the performance in Big Stone Gap, we began the royal court scene near the end of the play expecting nothing more dramatic than a flubbed line of dialogue, or maybe two at the most. In the middle of Fay's last dance there was a small creaking sound, much like someone sitting on a wobbly kitchen chair. It was immediately followed by a thunder-loud crack of splinting wood from somewhere beneath the throne. Denny and I exchanged an astounded "my God what's happening" kind of look as we felt the boards beneath us quake and suddenly give way. Quickly we moved, not too gracefully, off the throne seat itself to the platform below, a separate unit upon which the throne rested.

When Fay finished her little dance with a twirl and turned to face the king and queen, we weren't up there above her on the throne where we were supposed to be. The throne was empty. Fay looked astounded and probably imagined that she had twirled to the point of dizziness. There was a long ungainly pause until Fay refocused on the platform several feet below the throne where we sat with our knees up to our chins, a most undignified royal couple. What Fay also saw was Denny holding his stomach to keep back his laughter or to keep from throwing up. Fay choked on her next line and the next. I could almost visualize the words she was supposed to speak flying out in all directions from her wispy brain cells.

By now each one of us, Greg, Carl, Larry, Jane and even myself, was making weird grimacing faces in an attempt not to laugh. I wondered if the children in the audience thought we had all come down with stomachaches at the same time. If we were all so sick, would the curtain be pulled down and the play end before it was really over?

I was also laughing, only I was laughing for an entirely different reason. A marvelous cartoon popped into my head of Denny falling all the way through the seat of the throne to end up disappearing inside the big boxy unit and then the unroyal appearance as he struggled out, deflated by the ignominy of it all. What an uproariously funny picture! So wholly just and fair. Here in my mind was revenge for his weeks of ill treatment of me. I ached to let loose with a volley of unqueenly guffaws. Carl and Greg, standing on the other side of the throne, were doing something twisted with their lips, probably biting the linings of their mouths until they bled in order to control their laughter.

The line in the play following Fay's forgotten cue was mine, and I managed to squeeze it out with difficulty, though I did get it spoken. There must have been a happy smile on my face, which belied my very words. "To think that cruel man beat you and your little brother. How wicked!"

Denny was still choked up with laughter and missed his next line, so I spoke it for him since it mattered very little which character voiced the words. All of us tried desperately to control ourselves and slip back into character, otherwise the stage curtain would have to be lowered and the play prematurely ended.

Luckily, the broken throne incident occurred near the end of the third act. Somehow we managed to scrape through the remainder of the flawed scene. But as soon as the curtain dropped, we broke into spasms of uproarious laughter. Greg literally rolled on the stage floor as Denny related with much exaggeration and raising and lowering of his dark eyebrows, what it felt like to have a throne disintegrate right beneath his buttocks.

✻

During this hilarious incident, I feel like part of the troupe once again, accepted, a close companion to all these giggling and laughing kids. It's almost as though the letter incident or whatever it was that caused my alienation, had never happened. It seems as though we are all united again. I feel so relieved.

Finally we do calm down, and each one of us begins to tell his or her version of the funny event. "When we felt our seat literally moving," I begin, "Denny gives me the weirdest look, as though he's been sitting on eggs about to..."

Denny interrupts me and swivels around to face Fay, his back to me. "...so I decide to get off damn fast."

"Poor Fay," I continue unfazed by Denny's interruption, "the look on your face when you stop twirling and look up at the empty...."

Fay isn't listening, "...throne. You have such a stunned expression on your face." I watch Denny put his arm around Fay and shift her so that both their backs are facing me. I find myself finishing my account to Greg and Jane. "I was laughing so hard..."

Denny's voice booms right through my softer one, "...so I don't know how I managed to get my next line out, but..."

"You didn't," I interrupt dryly even though I have to speak to his back and also Fay's. "I'm the one who spoke your next line and the next one too. You were still choking up with laughter."

Greg and Jane don't wait to hear more from me either. They move away, talking and laughing between themselves, leaving me with Carl and Larry. I watch Carl and Larry turn the throne seat upside down to see where it can be reinforced before the next performance. I start to tell Carl where I think the splintering noise had come from, but he gives me a blank look and limps off the stage to change his costume.

I give up trying to tell my side of the incident. It loses its power to make me laugh. Everyone either interrupts me or talks loudly to shut out my voice, as though I do not exist. Anyway, no one is left standing nearby, not even Larry. He goes off to fetch the hammer and nails. I'm left in the middle of the stage alone. I recompose the hurt expression on my face and follow the others into the wings. In my sweeping queenly costume, it's much easier to act dignified... to hold my chin high and pretend that absolutely nothing is wrong. That's what I hope everyone will believe if anyone is monitoring my reaction to their snubbing. Oh, how I want to run across that stage, run and disappear forever so that I will never have to face any of them again.

In the teachers' rest room I take off my costume and my makeup. The room is institutional white with gray terrazzo floor. It's stark, ascetic...cold. For a few minutes I stand there shivering before the mirrors, thinking of the warm camaraderie I enjoy during the first few minutes after the curtain falls at the end of the third act. There, for a brief moment, I actually believe that everything is going to be all right between me and the others in the troupe.

But it isn't all right. I feel further out in the cold than before. Trying to regain my place in their closed circle and suffering the rebuff hurts far more than if I had not tried at all. I'm like a puppy wiggling and begging to get inside a warm house. Why am I so ready to expose myself to fresh hurts? I should go home.

By the time Jane and Fay enter the restroom to change out of their costumes, I have removed, along with the make-up, all traces of my disappointment and my tears. Fay and Jane are still chattering gaily to each other about the throne incident, but this time I am wiser. I make no attempt to join in their conversation. I simply go on pretending that I am a queen or a princess who mustn't stoop to converse with her vassals. I fake a smile of complete bliss, gather up my costume, and sail out.

THIRTY-TWO

We stayed three days in Lynchburg, Virginia, and one night in Charlottesville. It was the end of March of 1950 as we headed north and back towards Missiac where we had first begun the tour so many months ago.

Most mornings now, I found Carl already in the driver's seat of the car. I guessed why. He didn't want Lu-Travis to know that he had allowed me, a girl, to drive knowing it was against company rules. I didn't plan to tell Lu-Travis about the thousands of miles I'd driven unless she quizzed me on the subject, but Carl didn't know that.

Outside of being squashed in the back seat, I really didn't mind losing my driving status. In fact, driving in the traffic of the larger eastern seacoast cities was hectic and something I'd seldom been exposed to except for that time we drove though Birmingham, Alabama. If Carl wanted to test his nerves, let him. These mornings he looked more tired than ever before. Was Denny keeping him awake? Carl's blue-shadowed eye sockets were as prominent as his emaciated cheeks. His health might have invoked sympathy from me if the circumstances had been different.

By the first week in April, we were headed for a small town called Paoli in southeastern Pennsylvania. Our itinerary suggested that we stop overnight in West Chester, a town just a few miles south of Paoli on the same route. We entered West Chester late in the afternoon and admired what we saw: street lamps shaped like early American lanterns and buildings freshly painted, predominately white. The town had more character in its architecture, more picturesqueness about it, than most of the towns we had passed through during the entire five months, with the exception of the quaint little white New England villages at the very beginning of our tour.

We spotted the hotel listed on our itinerary as we drove into town. Carl stopped the car around the corner from the hotel.

"A doorman!" Jane exclaimed. "I haven't seen a doorman since leaving New York.

"There was one at the St. Louis hotel, but you wouldn't know about that. It was back when Jess-the-gypsy had your part in the play," Denny informed her.

The African American man held the door open for us. "Thank you," I said. What a gracious feeling it gave me. No one at any of the other hotels had ever held a door open for me except Charlie. Inside the lobby we saw comfortable couches, each covered in a green bamboo print instead of the dark brown frieze upholstery meant to disguise stains.

I overheard Denny whisper to Jane, "It'll cost plenty to stay here."

"Look over there." Jane's short legs toddled over to look at the colorful budgies flying around in a ceiling to floor cage along with two tiny monkeys. Denny and I followed. How unusual, I thought, and also noticed the hyacinth bulbs blooming on a table near the window.

"I'm going to ask anyway," I said, and walked over to the desk with Jane following. I was thankful that she wasn't cracking a wad of gum at the moment. I didn't want us to look unmannerly or cheap to the well-dressed woman behind the desk.

"We have just one room available for tonight. I am sorry." The pleasant woman even smiled. We weren't used to smiles. Most hotel desk clerks assumed a cool, disinterested face, as though they were doing us a favor by letting us stay in their hotel.

"How much do you charge, " I asked.

"Three dollars for this particular room.

"Oh." I couldn't help but let my disappointment show. Three dollars was far more than I was used to paying. I tried to figure out in my head just how many days until payday and whether I could possibly scrape by until then if I rented the room. To stall for time I asked, "Does the room have a bath?" Maybe that was the reason for the high price.

"No, but the bath is right across the hallway and no other person uses it. Very convenient."

"Hurry it up, girls," Denny nagged from somewhere behind me. I could feel the color rising in my face. Why did Denny have to behave like a boar in front of this refined lady? I felt so embarrassed. I half turned around and saw Denny and Jane disappearing through the door. There is no time left for me to make a decision about the room.

"Thank you," I said hurriedly. "I'll think about it."

Back in the car, I heard Denny telling everyone about the monkeys and the doorman. "Too rich for my blood," he joked.

"There was only one room available anyway," Jane told the others.

"Let's try that rooming house we passed on the way into town," Carl suggested. So we drove back to the rooming house, which was large and white and not at all bad looking on the outside. This time I didn't go with Denny and Jane. When they returned to the car, they were beaming with the news that we could have two rooms for seven dollars for all seven of us.

"Well now, that's a great bargain. What do you say?" Denny looked around at everyone as though he expected applause. Everyone agreed that it was an excellent price. "Yeah," said Greg, "but you girls will have only three in a room whereas we guys have to chuck four bodies into one room."

"So? You've done it before," Jane challenged.

"What's the verdict?" Carl voice sounded irritated by everyone's lack of decision. "Should we take these rooms or look somewhere else?"

All the time the others were mulling over the attributes of the rooming house bargain, I was thinking about the gracious hotel lobby we had just seen. Its spring colors were refreshing; the flowers, the birds chirping, and the pleasant woman behind the registration desk opened up an entirely different world. Staying there would be like taking a vacation. But it was more expensive, more than any place I had ever stayed. Three dollars was a lot of money to spend knowing that payday was still two days away. But neither did I want to be trapped in a room with Fay and Jane again knowing that I would have to go through the humiliation of being ignored. At dinnertime I would have to ask them, or more likely beg them to take me with them to a restaurant since the rooming house was several miles from the downtown area. No, no. I couldn't go through another whole night and day of being made to feel unwanted.

"I'm going back to stay in that other hotel."

"What? Denny asked sharply, not realizing that he had addressed me directly.

Everyone peered at me in disgust. With a shiver of dread I repeated, "I'm going to take that room at the hotel if it's still available."

"There goes your big bargain," Greg guffawed, and Denny added, turning in his seat, "You would manage to spoil things."

"The censure came across plainly in Carl's voice. "We were there just a few minutes ago. Why didn't you decide then? Now we have to drive all the way back again."

"And lose these rooms," Jane added.

I didn't think any of them really wanted me to explain, but I tried anyway. "Denny and Jane hurried me off before I could make up my mind. Besides, I wasn't sure whether I could afford three dollars."

Denny swore. "Oh, sure. It's our fault. Jesus!"

"Maybe this rooming house will give you an even better rate with fewer people staying," I suggested.

"We'll get rid of this extra baggage first and then come back here or find another place," Carl said.

By "extra baggage" he meant me, of course.

"Let's leave the truck here." Larry squeezed into the front seat and Greg got in the back and took Fay on his lap. We drove back to the hotel. Again, Carl stopped the car just around the corner from the hotel. For that I was thankful. I didn't want the doorman to see any more of our motley group than necessary. Carl left the car motor running, and got out to open the car trunk. He hauled out my suitcase, and, before I could grab it, slammed it down right there in the street where it toppled over. Then, not speaking a word, he hobbled back to the driver's seat, shifted gears, and sped away. I was stunned at being dumped so unceremoniously, but quickly rescued my suitcase by moving it from the street to the sidewalk. Carl hadn't even waited for me to find out if the room was still available.

"Say hello to your relatives, the monkeys," Greg yelled out the window as the car swung around the corner. I waved a cheery goodbye, pretending that Greg's sarcasm was just a joke. For a brief moment the same old feelings of oppression hit me and I felt the beginning of a cramp in my stomach.

THIRTY-THREE

I stop to shift my suitcase to the other hand and give my shoulders a tremendous shake as though to slough off the burden I've been carrying around—the strain of pretending that everything is "all right," so that Denny and the others will never catch-on to how much they are hurting me.

As I begin to struggle through the hotel door with my suitcase, the doorman comes across the lobby at a run and grabs it from me.

"Thank you," I smile, then look down at my coat. "I'm afraid I rubbed against your new paint." Now I notice that there are plenty of "fresh paint" signs to warn me, but I have been so stunned by the abrupt dumping of me and my suitcase in the street that I'm blind to everything else including the paint signs.

"Yes, Miss. Three or four folks done the same thing, but I've got some turp that'll fix everything." He hastens away to get his can of turpentine while I inquire whether the room is still available. Where will I go if the room is already rented? But it isn't, and I sigh with relief.

A paint spot on my spring coat might ordinarily make me fuss. I am very fastidious about my appearance most of the time, but at this particular moment it seems inconsequential. I'm not going to let a trivial paint stain take away from my great escape into this nicer hotel. There is no doubt in my mind that I have inadvertently stepped—or fate has slipped me—into an entirely different mode of life from the one I have been enduring for over five months. I have gone through a mirror from drabness to sunny splendor.

I sign the registration card handed to me but when the woman at the desk doesn't ask for my three dollars, I hesitate until she notices my uncertainty.

"You can pay when you check out tomorrow," she says, and I nod trying to cover up my surprise. Most of the cheap hotels we have been staying in demand their money in advance unless the troupe remains there for over a whole week as occurred in Joplin, Missouri.

"I think you will like the room," the woman says, continuing to treat me as though I'm an honored guest. "The owner of this hotel often stays there; it has her own personal furnishings."

The porter-doorman returns with his can of turpentine and a stained rag, which he dabs at the streak of paint on my coat. It really isn't much of a spot, but I fear that he is smearing more paint onto my coat with his rag than he's taking off. Even that fails to upset me. Next, he takes me and my suitcase in the elevator to the first floor above the lobby. I could easily have walked up the staircase from the lobby because my room turns out to be the first one at the top of the elegantly curved stairs. The porter unlocks the door and politely hands me the key. Then I realize that I'm expected to give him some kind of tip so I fish in my change purse and come up with twenty-five cents. It's all I can spare. Actually it's far more than I can afford considering the expense of the room.

"Thank you, Miss. The "necessary" room is just across the hall." He gestures in the direction of the unmarked door, and I thank him.

As I turn to watch him go back to the lobby by way of the stairs, I catch my reflection in a long oval mirror set in an ornate gold frame hanging in the wide hallway at the top of the stairs. Is that wrinkled-coated figure in the mirror really me? I frown in disgust at the image. It has been a long time since I've seen myself in a full-length mirror. What a disappointment. I wave my hand at my reflection as if to make my image disappear. Why, I ask myself, does one always look so completely diminished in a mirror compared to the fine image one keeps alive inside one's mind?

I push the door of the room further open and surprise overcomes me. Can this be the right room? It's furnishings are like a bedroom in someone's cherished home. Here is no shabby hotel type furniture. The cushioned rocker with a tall reading lamp beside it catches my eye first. I throw my coat down on the bed and head for the rocker even before unpacking my bag. There I sit gently rocking. Across the room I see an antique desk with Queen Ann legs. The two longish windows are hung with crisp white Priscilla curtains edged in eyelet ruffles. A blessed serenity flows over me as I rock.

Even the old dresser has a polished, cared-for appearance. And the little table beside the bed holds several magazines and a rose patterned china lamp with a white shade, cloth, instead of the usual cheap paper turning yellow. There's another chair in the room as well, an upholstered one with a high back to keep out the drafts. I have to try it just like Goldilocks, so I leave the soothing rocker and grab the yellow print comforter neatly folded at the bottom of the bed and wrap myself up snuggly and cuddle down into the winged chair. Why would anyone ever want to leave this pretty room, this haven? I jump up again and shift back to the rocking chair where I sit and rock for a long time.

As I rock, I marvel at my good fortune in arriving at this particular hotel where by mere chance I have slipped into a softer, seemingly more caring state of existence. Oh, I'm quite ready to believe that some benevolent spirit is watching over me and making up to me for the misery of the past few months.

The gentle movement of the rocking chair helps me to sort out my feelings. Denny and the others have verbally isolated me by shutting a door, not for just hours of punishment but for days. They are succeeding in making me feel as though I am flawed, inferior, and not worthy of being spoken to. My self-esteem is being chipped away as surely as rain makes pits, drop by drop, in a limestone statue. The sly remarks and innuendoes behind my back are as convincing as if a jury has yelled, "Guilty!" I have almost grown to believe that I really am guilty of something or other and that my crime is visible to everyone, not just to those in the troupe.

Tonight I am safe from the stigma placed on me. I have escaped into the comforting atmosphere of this room. A gift of time has been bestowed upon me…time to literally pick myself up. I wonder if it's possible to grow a brand new skin of confidence, of toughness, and do it in a single night.

After pressing my blue skirt on the bed with the travel iron, I put on my one good white blouse and am ready to go down to dinner. I stop in front of the oval mirror at the top of the stairs and note some improvement from the previous glimpse of myself, though the image still falls short of the very glamorous one I long for. In order to luxuriate in the soft carpeting, I walk very slowly down the curved stairway to the lobby below.

As I face the registration desk, I notice that there is an opening to a dining room on the right as well as one on the left.

"Which one do you recommend?" I ask the woman, a different one, who now stands behind the desk.

"Both are good, but you might like the one over there better." She points towards her right where the sound of organ music flows through the doorway. "There's more going on in there."

"Thank you," I smile. Maybe this is my third or even my fourth genuine smile since entering this hotel today. I feel like smiling again and again, and tossing out happy little nods to everyone.

There are plenty of empty tables since it is still quite early, barely five-thirty. The hostess seats me at a table near the door and not far from the small stage where the organ is being played. For once I hope the service will be extremely slow. Then I'll be able to sit here for a long time and soak-in the atmosphere of candlelight and the pristine white tablecloths and the music.

I'm a bit worried about the prices. Tablecloths and candlelight invariably mean higher prices. Throughout the tour, I constantly fear that I will come up short of funds when presented with the check. Tonight I order the cheapest thing I can find on the menu, which happens to be meatloaf, mashed potatoes and a vegetable. I have already eaten tons of meatloaf and mountains of mashed potatoes in the last five months as we crisscross the country. My dessert will have to be a cup of coffee. I can afford nothing more.

The organ music is soothing. So is the quiet step of the waitress. There are no loud sounds of dishes being stacked or shouted orders to the kitchen. All too soon my empty dishes are cleared away and a fresh cup of coffee poured, making my departure from this sanctuary imminent.

"I wonder if you would mind sharing your table with one other person since you're nearly ready to leave anyway?" It was the hostess bending over my shoulder.

Oh bother, I think. Nothing like spoiling my last few minutes by having to share the table. Naturally, I nod my agreement, and the hostess seats a man across from me. I steal a quick glance at him as he scans the menu. Perhaps in his early forties, I decide. His dark hair is combed straight back. I note his gray suit and rather subdued necktie. When he has finished ordering his meal, he looks straight across at me.

"I hope you didn't mind," he said.

"Oh no," I lie.

He smiles. "It's either share a table with you or with that grumpy looking older man across the room. I thought you looked more interesting."

I peek over my shoulder but am unable see anyone of that description...not even one older man. Then I catch on. He is giving me a line. I smile and shake my head as though to say "shame on you."

"Now don't rush off on my account. I hate to eat alone. Drink your coffee slowly."

I feel like chuckling out loud. He is obviously gregarious and practiced at buttering-up women. If ever there had been printed instructions on how to pick-up girls, his next question would surely be included.

"You look familiar. Are you from around here?"

"No. I'm with a theatre troupe. We tour around the country and present plays to children in schools."

"An actress. Now that's really interesting. Where are the others in your troupe?"

"They're staying somewhere else. There was just one room available at this hotel." Then I add, unnecessarily, "We're staying in town just one night."

"Well then, let's make the most of it. How about having a cocktail with me? It's my treat. Waitress? Could we order a...?" He looks at me questioningly.

"A glass of red wine," I answer. It's all I have ever tasted before that beer back in Oklahoma. Does this guy think he can get me drunk and then take advantage of me? It's quite typical of me to imagine sordid drama out of a few casual remarks. After the waitress leaves I ask bluntly, "Are you a salesman?"

"I see you have me typed," he answers with such a sparkle in his eyes that his charm is impossible to ignore. He is so easy to like. "Just because I wear a suit and a tie, doesn't necessarily make me a salesman."

"But are you?" I persist, but try to put a little more candor in the tone of my voice.

"You might call me that," he answers but adds no further information on the subject. "My name is Allen, and yours?"

"Ann." I guess that last names are to be withheld but give no thought as to the "why" of it. I notice that he eats his meal in the same amount of time it takes me to sip my wine. Am I being too slow or is he eating rapidly so that we can both leave the restaurant at the same time?

"You're too attractive to be out on your own," he says with that same come-hither glint in his dark eyes.

What a smoothie...so obviously practiced in the art of picking up women. Also, I think he knows that I know this. Still, it is such a fun game and especially for me since I am in particular need of attention, sincere or not makes little difference. Here, for the first time in over a month, I'm sitting across from a well-dressed, cleanly shaven man who is flattering me, not an unkempt boy in jeans. Naturally, I'm ripe for attention, made vulnerable by weeks of the silent treatment. A hungry person is likely to eat anything and everything without thinking whether it's good for them or not. My reaction to the man's flattery is to literally glow and sparkle with aliveness. I bask in the sunny warmth of his applause. How could he interpret my effervescence in any other way than as an attempt to lead him on?

"Which floor is your room on?" he asks right after we have finished another cup of coffee and no longer have an excuse to take up the table in the restaurant at its busiest time.

"The second floor," I answer as we both reach the lobby.

"I'll see you to your door."

"If you like," Since I know that my room is smack at the top of the stairs in full view of the lobby below, I have no fear over letting him come to my door. If I need help, my call will easily be heard in the lobby below. We climb the curved stairs together, he in more of a hurry than I.

"My room is right here." I stop at the top of the stairs.

"Right here?" He looks puzzled.

I can see his disappointment and that maybe his hopes might not come to fruition after all. My room is far too public.

"Why not ask me in so we can talk for a little while longer."

"No, that's not such a good idea." But I do wish I could think of a way to prolong his company. His flattery is like having bouquets thrown on the stage to be gathered up by a leading actress. How nice it might be to bask in his attention just a little longer.

"I'd like to get to know you better."

His eyes are so sincere. There seems to be no kind way to avoid that cold word, *no.* Thank you so much for the pleasant dinner conversation and the wine."

"I'll only stay a few minutes," he coaxes.

"I'm sorry, but no."

"You're sure?" His soft voice implies that I will be missing something of great value.

"If you really want to talk, we can go back to the lobby for a while," I suggest. But I know it isn't conversation that draws him to me. He isn't a Charley craving companionship, but neither is he a trickster like Greg.

"I guess I'll wish you, good night then," he says reluctantly but maintains his good humor even after his failure to succeed with me. I like him for that. He isn't angry. If he were, it might spoil my one night of feeling sought after.

"Good night, and thank you again for making my dinner so pleasant." I mean it sincerely.

"Thank you for doing the same for me," he politely returns the compliment.

I watch him go back down the stairs to the lobby and out of my sight. Will he immediately look for some other woman and set his charm to work on her? Even that thought doesn't douse my good spirits. I still feel the aftermath of his attention; it's surely working as part of my healing.

I wash out some lingerie in the marble basin across the hall from my room. Though it's the usual chore, nothing seems routine tonight. Things I've done a hundred times before have a first-time approach. I mend and snip threads and iron; my interest in looking neat has a sudden revival. My wafer-thin self-confidence and negative image of myself are quickly rising like fizz on a shaken soda. Refreshed by Allen's words, I resist allowing myself to dwell even a second on the fact that his poured-on flattery is strictly aimed at bedding me down, though underneath I know that it is the truth.

The gracious room now draws all my full attention. I marvel at the good reading lamps, comfortable chairs, and magazines to browse through. I am anxious to climb into the high bed and pull the yellow comforter right up to my chin and just lie there wallowing in the peace and comfort that will flow over me.

This room, the hotel, and the meeting with Allen seem like gifts, purposely ordained to restore my self-image and to build a resistance against any further depression I might fall into. If good things like this can happen to me, then I needn't feel so mistreated and forsaken. Right now I am strong again, strong enough to weather the remaining few weeks of the tour and whatever Denny and his cronies dish out.

It seems as though I might even hold out to the end of the tour which will be all the way back to Missiac, the place where we first begin. If I can do it, I'll feel like a success.

Special blessings have been given me. It's my belief that such things always come to the rescue of the innocent. They do in Broadway musicals and movies. Why not for me, too? No drug lulls me more effectively than that notion, that idea.

THIRTY-FOUR

Since our afternoon's performance was to be in Paoli, a town barely six miles from West Chester, I felt sure the others in the troupe wouldn't arrive to pick me up until about eleven, if then. This week I didn't possess a copy of the itinerary, nor did I know if the performance was scheduled for two o'clock or two-thirty. Anyway, I was all packed by ten o'clock and carried my suitcase down the stairs to the lobby. I placed it just in front of the check-in desk where it could be spotted easily. Then I paid my room bill but retained the key so that I could return to the room to write a letter. I meant to enjoy the comfort and hominess of the room right up to the twelve o'clock check out time or until the others stopped by to pick me up. They hadn't bothered to inform me of the hotel or the rooming house where they were staying or even given me a phone number where I could get in touch with them. They had just driven off. Truthfully, I had no way of knowing when they might come to pick me up.

The sun shone through the white Priscilla curtains; the April day promised to be warm and lovely. The complete change in atmosphere from the usual cheap hotels where I could literally smell the layers of past lives piled up, one on top of another, had been reversed. Now, all the heaviness and depression had fled. I felt revitalized, made of tougher, stronger stuff, brick or stone instead of canvas. Now I hoped that I would be able to ignore Denny's insinuations and withstand the silent treatment for the few remaining weeks of the tour. I smiled inwardly when I thought about the previous evening and acknowledged that my confidence was partly due to the attentions Allen had given me.

At eleven-fifteen I checked again with the woman at the registration desk in the lobby and found that no one had come to ask for me. I thought very little about it because late starts were not at all unusual. Perhaps then, I'd still have time for an errand. I remembered that we needed new cacti needles for the phonograph that played the music for Fay's dances during the performance.

I found a music store just two blocks from the hotel and bought the needles with my own money, assuming that Carl would reimburse me from the company funds. On my way back to the hotel I stopped in front of an interesting lunchroom. The Quaker—that's what it was called—looked squeaky clean and plain except for the flowered china at each place setting. Should I take a chance on the kids arriving even later at the hotel and stop for coffee? My minimal breakfast had been several hours ago and this place looked so inviting. No, I cautioned myself, you'd better hurry back to the hotel.

Once again I approached the desk clerk and inquired, "Has anyone called or asked for me?" The woman, a different one from earlier, shook her head. "No, were you expecting someone?"

I explained to her about the troupe and our afternoon performance. Still, she shook her head. Back in my room, I finished writing my letter at the antique desk and then slowly descended the curved stairway for the last time. It was now twelve o'clock, check-out time. As I reached the bottom step, I saw Carl, Fay, and Denny sitting in the lobby and heard Denny say, "She can't be far; her coat is here."

"Well, then where in hell is she?" Carl sounded irritated.

"I'm right here." I answered and smiled cheerfully. No one responded. Carl, Denny and Fay all rose together as though attached at the feet like paper dolls and without uttering another word to me, headed for the street door. Their behavior embarrassed me because I could see the woman at the desk watching and listening and probably wondering why they were so rude to me. I felt the black theatre scrim being lowered again. The heaviness of my former world returned. I placed the hotel key on the desk.

"Are you off to another town?" The lady clerk smiled sociably.
"Yes. Good bye. I enjoyed my stay very much."

✳

Yesterday it was so easy for me to return cheerfulness for cheerfulness...
now I must pretend again. The gift, my respite from the troupe, is
quickly playing out. I slip back into my wrinkled gray coat and pick
up my suitcase. I dare not take the time to stop and look at the bright
birds flying around in their cage, but I can hear their soft warbling. I
will remember everything. Even the gay yellow crocus by the window
are pasted forever in my mind.

Carl has left the car trunk open, so I place my suitcase inside and
lower the cover. No one speaks as I seat myself in the back next to
Jane and Fay. Carl is driving and Denny sits beside him with a map
in his hand. His chin is shadowy again, unshaven, and his eyes are
particularly red this morning...this noon, I correct myself. He and
Carl must have overslept or not slept at all.

"Here's route eleven." Carl points to the sign beside the road.
"Now which way do we go from this corner? Well? You're the one
with the map, old boy. Tell me."

"It goes straight ahead." Denny's finger follows the red line on
the map. "No, it also goes to the right."

"I'll try turning right."

"A few minutes later we returned to the same four corners. "Now
what?" asks Carl. He sounds weary and disgusted.

Denny looks at the map again. "Try going straight ahead this
time."

"That can't possibly be the route. It's the wrong direction. I'll
try going right again. Somewhere, we must have missed a turn sign."
Carl finally spots our route sign to Paoli on the outskirts of West
Chester.

"Hope we have time for coffee before the show," mutters Fay to
Jane.

"Didn't you have breakfast?" I ask politely, not expecting an answer.

"No." Jane answers sharply, and that's when I should have stopped questioning her. Since she has answered me the first time, I reason that perhaps she's grown tired of the enforced silent treatment and will now be more sociable. I sympathize with her lack of a breakfast. "That's too bad; why not?"

"She asks, 'why not'," Fay says loudly, loud enough for Denny to hear her in the front seat.

"We used up all our breakfast time just waiting for you," snaps Denny.

"But I was there all the time...just waiting for..."

Carl interrupts peevishly, "You weren't there at eleven when I first stopped there."

"But I was." I protest. "I was up in my room writing a letter. I even asked the desk clerk if anyone had come for me."

"The desk clerk said you had checked out."

"Well, I paid my bill before eleven and brought my suitcase down to the lobby so that I would be all set to go, but I kept the key to the room. Didn't you see my suitcase?

"*You* should have been sitting in the lobby waiting, not just the suitcase. Those are the company rules."

"Isn't it also the company rules that you should be on time? You and Denny and the girls certainly don't adhere to the rules a lot of times." Why do they always blame me.

Carl half turns around in his seat as he keeps a hand on the steering wheel. His emaciated face no longer inspires pity in me. Bone and skin are nearly reversed but I see only an ugly skeleton.

"Just shut your mouth," Carl says between his teeth.

"Why should I just sit there in the lobby and wait for you for a whole hour?" I persist.

"Oh, shut up, you whore," Denny says in the same tone he would have used to condemn bad spaghetti. But no one has ever called me a dirty name like that to my face. That word "whore" strikes a button in my head that automatically spews out retaliation like red-hot lava. "How dare you call me a whore!" I shout.

"Are you calling us liars?" yells Carl from the front seat.

"You bet I am...and you're something far worse than that!" I fling out. The specific word, homo, evades me in my anger. But Carl and Denny know exactly what I mean. Immediately, the car begins to swerve over the centerline. Then it careens back to the shoulder of the road where it jolts to a stop.

"Get out," Carl screams at me in a voice several octaves above his normal one, which isn't very deep anyway. Then, in a hissing voice he repeats, "Get out of this car!"

"Why?" I am completely flummoxed by his reaction. Aren't I the injured party? They have called me a whore. "Why should I?" I ask no one in general as I watch Carl limp around the other side of the car to the back door and yank it open.

"Get out!" he screams again and gives my arm a surprise yank that jerks me half out of the car. He has always seemed so weak and puny before.

"Don't you ever call me a liar, you whore," he says and gives my arm a violent twist.

"Yeah," adds Denny who has gotten out of the front seat and stands beside Carl so that it must appear to the slow moving traffic passing by on the road as though two men are about to beat up on a girl.

"You've slept with every man in every hotel since we started the tour. Lu-Travis even got a letter from the hotel manager in Joplin telling her all about you."

"I don't believe you," I snap. I knew that Mike—it had been Mike and Charley who had taken me out to dinner one night in Joplin— would never write a letter like that. "That's simply not true...you, you," I spit the words out at Denny, "you were probably the one who wrote that letter. Is that how you got rid of Lisa too...by telling lies? What did she do to you...steal your boy friend?"

"Two of a kind. You're both whores!"

Carl steps towards me menacingly, and Denny grapples my arms behind me to keep me stationary while Carl hits me across the mouth. I can taste the blood, but my lips don't hurt much. My frothing anger short-circuits any present feelings of pain. I kick out and Denny swings me away, attempting to protect Carl, but too late. I see Carl holding his leg. I have aimed well. Some humane part of me hopes it isn't his bad leg. All this time, Fay and Jane just sit in the car. . .saying nothing. . .doing nothing.

Some cars creep past us slowly and then almost stop, curious to know what's going on with two men and a kicking girl. When Denny notices this, he tries to push me back towards the door of the car. "Get back in the car," he orders, as though nothing unusual has just taken place. Maybe to him nothing unusual is happening. He is so used to theatrical scenes. They are his glucose, his sustenance.

"Get in!" Denny's voice is more demanding this time as he tries to shove me into the car. "We're attracting attention."

"Shall I call the police?" A woman calls from a car that has come to a complete stop in the opposite lane heading towards town.

"Yes," I yell, "and hurry!"

"Come on, shut up, and get back in the car." This time Denny's voice, though rough, is clearly asking me to cooperate. We have attracted too much attention even for him.

"So this is the kind of trouper you are," Denny tries to shame me into getting back inside the car. "After the next performance you can leave and good riddance. We don't need bitches like you on this tour." Again, Denny tries to grab at me.

"Let go of me!" He does, because I am hitting at him, but he keeps on the other side of me so that I can't turn around and run. As I reach into the car for my purse, I feel another shove from behind. I grab the car frame for stability and kick backwards at Denny. He dodges out of range.

"Get out of my way!" I swing my purse at his face, and he ducks further back. By now I am so upset that my brain records the scene like a faulty movie camera; some moments are sharp and clear, others are all fuzzed at the edges or completely blank. During one of the focused moments, I see Greg come trotting down the side of the road from where the truck has stopped. "Need some help?" he calls out and I think: thank goodness, someone is going to take my side, so I am even less on guard and more vulnerable when Greg, instead of helping me, tries to grab at my arms. "I'll hold her for you," he says to Denny.

Suddenly Carl barks, "It's one o'clock! We have just one hour before curtain. If the police come and hold us up, we'll miss the performance." To me, he commands, "Get back in the car."

"No." I say, my voice comes out grating and hoarse from shouting.

"Then get out of here!" Carl opens the trunk of the car and throws my suitcase out onto the road.

Through a blur I see and hear the car screech away down the road. I keep telling myself that I positively must not cry even though I know I'm already sobbing. Just a few feet ahead, yet so indistinct that it appears very far off, is a car with a man standing beside it. The man seem to be waiting. Then I see him beckon. Is he called out to me? An ocean-like roar pounds in my head blotting out sounds. Is the man asking if I want a ride? I start in his direction but see a second faint figure beckoning as well. Now I'm truly confused. Is it the man by the car or the man by the white gate who is mouthing words at me? If only I could hear over the roar in my head.

For the first time I realize that there are houses along the road. Still, the roaring in my head confuses me; it smothers the normal sounds of car motors and voices. Why does everything appear surreal? The scene reels onwards, unstoppable, giving it an airy, floating tilt. It makes me feel a bit nauseated, yet I seem to have nothing to do with what is happening...something or someone else is moving things all around. I'm not in control. At the edge of the scene, two mouths of two different people open and close. There is animation but no voices. Who has turned off the sound? Or have I become deaf and dumb... must I resort to reading lips?

"Miss...Miss, over here. Come over here!"

The roaring fades; my head clears. Now voices begin to penetrate. At last, meaning is traveling all the way from their mouths to my brain. I look in the direction of the house. There is an elderly man standing at the gate waving. Though I'm not really conscious of doing any reasoning at all, my mind automatically chooses the older man by the gate as the safer one to trust instead of the man in the street standing beside a car. Someone is calling me to come. Somebody wants me—that is the important thing—someone wants me. I walk towards the elderly man and the gate. I hurry across the street without looking for traffic—without seeing—right through the gate, which the man holds open, and right on up the steps to the front door.

"Come in, Miss. I can't bear to see a woman hit. I saw that man hit you. Are you hurt? Come-in," he repeats. "Let me take the suitcase for you."

THIRTY-FIVE

Just inside the door a woman waits, far younger than the man. Further on into the room another woman stands, maybe the older man's wife. My patch-quilt vision prints only part of what it sees so that information seeps slowly into my brain like defective wiring, off and on, off and on again, giving me snatches of information, not letting other bits through at all. The younger woman takes my coat away; she is plain and kindly looking. The house is small, the stairs narrow and steep. I am crying and gulping as though gasping for air.

The younger woman says, "You can rest here for awhile."

The elderly man keeps repeating, "I saw him hit you; I was coming to help. Can't bear to see a man hit a woman."

The older woman says, "I hope they weren't relatives of yours."

I'm unable to speak so I just shake my head.

"Did they hit you anywhere else?" she asks. Again, I shake my head.

"I'll get a wet cloth for your bleeding lip." She fades out into the edges of the scene somewhere. Most of the comings and goings of the people in the room aren't registering. Figures are there, and then they aren't, as if I have a high fever.

Some of the conversation must be passing me by without my recording it at all for the next thing I become aware of is the younger woman's hand holding my elbow as we climb the tiny staircase. She says, "I haven't done my housework yet so you'll have to pardon the unmade bed."

The bedroom has a slanted ceiling, and there is a window in a dormer. The smallness of the room makes it seem cozy and safe. While she makes up the bed, I sit in a rocking chair at the foot of the bed. I rock and cry and rock and cry as if to rock away everything that's been happening.

"There." She says, giving the bedspread a final smoothing. "Why don't you take off your shoes and lay down for a rest. Here's something to hold against your swollen lip." She takes the cloth—for now the gray haired lady is there again—and hands it to me. I lie down on the bed and hold the cloth, which is wrapped around an ice cube, to my lips. They feel bulbous, but I no longer taste blood...just the salt from a flood of tears. I feel no concern for the hurt lip. It's so trivial. The real rawness and the bloodiness are inside me, somewhere in there, maybe in my chest or my stomach. The crying, which bubbles up like the natural spring near our cottage at home, just flows on and on, endlessly.

"I can't seem to stop." I apologize.

The younger woman's voice is soothing, "It will stop when your thoughts get better."

Silently she tiptoes back into the room every now and then to see if I'm all right. Once, I raise myself half way up to tell her something, as though it's important for me to explain: "I tried not to have it end like this; we were almost to the end of the tour."

"You just lay back down and rest awhile longer. You'll soon feel better." She removes my shoes, which I have forgotten to take off. I curl up with my head snug against my knees and my arms safely between, similar to the way my fists curl over my thumbs. The fresh hanky lays beside me on the bed, ready when I need it. I begin to dwell on the kindness of the folks in this house, and that shifts my attention away from my own misery long enough for me to gain control over my crying.

I slowly uncurl and lower myself from the high bed and creep to the dormer window. Right there, across the road, is the place where I have been abandoned...publicly yanked out of the car, assaulted, and left standing in the street all by myself...right out there in the road. I feel miserably sorry for myself and the tip of my tongue tastes salt again from tears reactivated. Then I hear someone coming up the stairs, and I renew my efforts to control my crying.

It's the younger woman who appears. "Chief of Police Bagely is here to see you. Wouldn't you like to tell him what happened?"

"I don't know if I can, not without crying."

"He's very understanding."

"Anyway," I add mournfully, forcing back more tears, "what can he do?" It isn't really a question; it's a declaration of hopelessness.

She hands me another clean hanky. "He's real nice...maybe he can help you."

When I start down the stairs, I hear the older man telling someone, "They just threw her suitcase out onto the street and sped away!"

My hand on the stair railing begins to shake. I reconsider, if I have to repeat the whole incident over again, I'll end up sobbing. I begin to back up.

"My father is giving him most of your story. You won't need to say very much." The young woman gives me a gentle nudge as a sign to move on down the stairs. As I come out of the enclosed stairway, Chief Bagely is copying down my name from the tag attached to my suitcase.

"Here she is," the older woman smiles. "That lip doesn't look too bad after all."

"The ice helped. Thank you," I respond rigidly. I am so afraid her kind voice will kick in my sorry-for-self emotions and send them flowing to the surface again. I firm up my lips hoping to stop the heaving in my chest and seal in the endless weeping.

"This is Chief Bagely," the older man introduces us. Chief Bagely has gray hair and he isn't in uniform. I record these facts but not much else. I hold my hands tightly interlocked around the damp hanky, and sit down on the sofa. The chief also sits down on the sofa leaving some distance between us.

"Now," he begins in an authoritative voice, then softens it to a more conversational tone as though he realizes interviewing a distressed woman needs a different touch. He has probably been warned that I will get all upset again. "Mr. Paulson has told me what happened, but I need to ask you a few questions, and then maybe we can help you."

I nod. The Chief asks the name of the theatre troupe and the name of the fellow who hit me on the mouth. He doesn't ask me what conversation took place to precipitate the fight, but I told him that Carl, the manager, was angry because he thought I wasn't at the hotel waiting for them to pick me up. "That's how it started, I explain."

I shirk from telling him that I have been called a whore. That's too shameful a thing to talk about. And deep down inside me is the fear that he might believe it even if it isn't so. People get set ideas about theatre folks. They quite expect their morals to be looser, their makeup thicker, and their behavior more affected. Besides, I can't very well prove that I'm not what Denny has called me. What if Chief Bagely talks to the hostess there at the restaurant in the hotel? Hadn't I accepted a drink from a strange man, and allowed him to walk me up the stairs to my hotel room door? That wouldn't look well to most people. Who would honestly believe that I hadn't invited the man into my room?

When the Chief finishes questioning me, he says, "It's my duty to inform you that you can charge this man, ur...Carl, with assault."

"Oh, could you?" I feel a resurgence of my faith in the "eye for an eye" theory of justice. I can feel my face brightening. The idea of getting even is so enormously gratifying. "They have a performance at two o'clock in Paoli," I tell the Chief, trying to keep the eagerness out of my voice.

"I can have one of my men pick them up at the end of the performance."

"If you do that, will I have to stay here in town and appear in court?" In my inner vision is a movie scene of a courtroom packed with people.

"That's right. Mr. Paulson saw the young man," the Chief pauses to look at his notes, "hit you and promises to be a witness. But take your time to think about it first before deciding."

"Thank you, Mr. Paulson...thank you for taking me in. What would I have done if you..." I swallow, forcing the escaping gulp of emotion down deeper and capping it with the lid of a forced smile.

Mr. Paulson's wife brings in coffee for the Chief and offers a cup to me. I shake my head. I need to think or rather to sort things out. If Carl and Denny are brought back to town, will they tell the court that I am a whore? Will Greg tell the tale of how he had been discovered lying under the covers in my bed? What exaggerated story will they all weave over the innocent dancing that Charley and I had done in the hotel lobby back in Joplin? Who will believe me against six others? How can I possibly take the humiliation of their accusations in front of all those people in court? Getting back at Carl and Denny will be hopeless without entangling myself. In the end it will be me, not Denny, Carl or Greg, who will be accused.

"It wouldn't do any good," I sigh, then realize that the Chief doesn't understand the hopeless words I have inadvertently muttered. "No, let them go."

He nods. I can see by his face that he approves of my decision. Probably he doesn't relish forcing a car full of misfits to return to West Chester and have the case fill up his time. After all, a cut lip isn't a serious crime.

"Do you have enough money to get home?" he asks.

"No. We weren't to get paid until Saturday."

Then maybe we can help you in that way; better still, you might try phoning this Lu-Travis person and ask her to pay your way home. It certainly is her responsibility."

"Yes, that's a good idea," I say, and faintly add, "Maybe I'll do that." But it is the last thing I want to do. The Chief doesn't know Lu-Travis' irascibility.

"All right. Now when you decide to leave, Mr. Paulson can give me a phone call, and I'll come and give you a ride into town to the bus station."

"Oh, I can give her a ride into town," Mr. Paulson says, as he and Chief Bagely walk to the front door.

"You can make that phone call right now," suggests the younger woman. She has a name, but I seem to forget it. Very little sticks in my mind. I think, this must be the fluttery way people feel after a funeral...numb and wrung out from crying and vague because their minds are merely skimming across the surface of what's happening, not wanting to delve into the past, not yet. Or, like me, able to think or act normally.

The young woman urges, "If you phone now, you'll get your money and can catch a bus before the day is over."

I nod but still sit there not moving. Why did I agree to phone Lu-Travis? I know her nasty disposition. How I hate to make the telephone call. "It's long distance," I say, erroneously thinking that it makes a good excuse.

"Go ahead, anyway. You can ask if they'll accept the charges. Here, let me get the number for you. Just give me the name of the town in New York State and the spelling of the woman's name."

There seems to be no way out; I'll have to talk to the ogress. I hear the woman tell the operator to ask if Lu-Travis will accept a collect call from a member of the Lost Princess cast. The woman turns to me, "They're calling Mrs. Travis to the phone right now," she says, and hands me the receiver.

"Mrs. Travis? This is Ann Gulbrith calling." My voice must sound faint and shaky. That's the way I feel. "I'm calling from West Chester, Pennsylvania." Immediately she cuts in.

"What are you doing there? You're supposed to be in Paoli for the two o'clock performance!"

"We had a fight, and they all left town without me." Courage begins to fail me and my voice wavers, "I nee-need my pay envelope to buy a bus ticket for home."

She screams into the phone, "You get yourself to that performance or you'll get no pay!" She slams the receiver down. My hands begin to shake badly. The encounter is exactly as I predict, exactly as I fear. I am so thankful to have it over.

"She won't do it. I'll have to call my mother."

"All right, but first let's find out how much the bus fare is going to cost so you can ask your mother for the correct amount. And she does exactly that. She calls the local bus station for the information. I am so grateful to her. My own brain must be paralyzed, for it takes me several minutes just to remember my own phone number in my own hometown.

"Why Ann, is something wrong?" My mother's voice sounds so wonderful to me, but it also sounds fearful. Rightly so. She knows immediately that something has gone wrong since our family never uses long distance phoning for anything except emergencies. "Are you all right?"

"Yes." My voice feathers out, snagging on tears again. "I'm all right."

"You sound strange. Where are you?"

The smallest bit of kindness in her voice overwhelms me with the urge to cry. I press my lips together, hoping to seal in the awful heaving in my chest. All my next words come out garbled. "Mom, we had a fight and I want to come ho—mme..." I lose control on the word "home," so the young woman takes the receiver from my hand and speaks to my mother.

"Yes, yes, she really is quite all right...just a minor cut on the lip. She wants to go home, and we've already checked on the bus fare. It's twenty-two dollars. There's a bus out of here at seven-ten this evening, and it arrives in your town about ten in the morning the next day. There is a pause in the conversation, and then I hear the young woman say, "That's correct: West Chester, Pennsylvania. Yes, I'll tell her. Goodbye."

"Will she send the money?" I don't know why I ask such a silly question for of course I know my mother will.

"As soon as she can get downtown to the bank and the Western Union."

Poor Mom, I think, there is no way for her to get downtown to the bank except by bus. I always seem to cause her trouble. "Did she say anything else?"

"No, except to ask if you were hurt."

I guess what I want to hear her say is: "Tell Ann we love her and to hurry home." But in spite of this lack, I didn't feel unwanted at home. I simply accept the fact that I am. Yet how I wish Mother would say those magic words just once.

Twenty minutes later, Mr. Paulson is ready to drive me back into town. It's now about two-thirty in the afternoon. He and his family have been so kind to me, but I suspect that they, especially the younger woman, are glad to have me off their hands to resume their own quiet lives. Perhaps I have already infringed upon the older couple's afternoon naptime.

I have regained enough presence of mind to get the Paulson's address written down so that I can write and thank them properly when I reach home. Also, I feel an obligation to launder the three handkerchiefs that I sniffle and cry upon. I want to mail them back in a clean, ironed and folded condition. It is the only way I can thank them for intervening on my behalf... for saving me.

THIRTY-SIX

*M*r. Paulson carries my suitcase into the Western Union Office for me. Away from the house, he seems so frail, yet the dear old man had been willing, if Carl and the others continued to hit me, to come right out into the road to save me.

"Are you sure you'll be all right?" he asks?

I didn't want to be a burden to him any further, so I said, "Don't worry. I'll be just fine from now on," though I'm not at all sure I will be. "I'll never forget what you've done for me." I want to hug him but instead shake hands. "Goodbye." Mr. Paulson leaves, but he looks back at me once and waves.

The clerk in the Western Union Office says there is nothing for me. I'm disappointed that the money from my mother hasn't come yet. What will I do with myself for the next few hours while I wait?

This part of town doesn't look at all familiar. What has happened to the old fashioned street lamps that I saw in the other section of West Chester? These sick green bulbs, turned on early because of the dark sky, are high above the street. The whole scene—shops with mismatched facades, some a bit shabby—make me feel gloomy and forlorn.

My stay in the lovely hotel of the night before—was it really just last night—feels like something that has occurred months ago in another world, not in just another part of town. Maybe it has never happened at all.

The Western Union clerk advises me not to expect the money for another three or four hours. Since I can't spend all that time sipping coffee in a restaurant, I check into a hotel around the corner. The rent is cheap, one dollar and fifty cents. The desk clerk eyes me suspiciously, but I didn't figure out why until later. The brown bedspread is very like all the other bedspreads, with a couple of exceptions, in all the other hotels throughout the tour.

I lay down on the bed for a while hoping that I might be able to sleep. I feel so terribly exhausted yet at the same time agitated, as though on a coffee high. I can't relax and sleep because there is no escape from the dreadful scene along the road that keeps repeating itself. Even the sounds: the splat of Carl's hand on my mouth, the chunk, firm and final, of the car trunk. I find my chest beginning to heave all over again, as though I have just been in a frightful accident. If only I could escape from going over and over the details by isolating myself in a decompression chamber of some sort until the trauma of being abandoned beside the road stops reeling over and over in my brain.

Finding no escape in sleep, I get up and wash my face in the sink. I repeat this several times, checking my swollen eyes and attempting to eliminate the persecuted, mouth drawn downwards, expression on my face as I look into the mirror above. But the old "someone's hurt me" face slides right back into place again, as though from a lifetime of tragedy. I feel worn and old, and I look at least thirty which is a well-advanced age to me. My swollen, swampy eyes are not going to get back to normal by the time I have to show my face again at the Western Union Office.

The vain part of me cares how I appear to others, but the hurt part of me cares only to scrub out the scene along the road. It's no use trying to rest, so I walk around and around the room. Movement seemed to help to calm my agitation, so I leave my suitcase there in the room and take a good long walk down one street and up another. I keep my head down trying to hide my swollen eyes. Suddenly I stop. Will people think I'm one of those "women" because I have checked into a cheap hotel in the middle of the afternoon and am now walking up and down, back and forth in the street? I know very little about a prostitute's behavior except that in the movies such a person usually picks up their clients from the street. The horrible name Carl had flung at me comes back. "You whore!" Abruptly, I stop in the middle of the block and hurry back to my hotel room, not to show my face again until absolutely necessary.

Around five o'clock, I return to the Western Union Office and the money is there. What a relief! Escaping town has not been a certainty up until now. The sooner I leave, the sooner my poor mixed-up brain—so obsessed with the scene by the side of the road—will stop repeating it over and over again like a stage drama, a tragic one.

At the bus station, I lift my suitcase into one of those coin boxes and go to the lunch counter for an early supper. After eating a hot sandwich of meat and gravy on soggy white bread, I still have an hour to get through until bus time, but I find a Good Housekeeping magazine thrown in the trash container and sit with it open on my knees in front of me, puffy eyes lowered to the print.

In reading the magazine, I try to fool my mind into attaching itself to a character in a story, but never get further than a line or two before my thinking lunges straight back again to the scene by the side of the road. Each and every time my mind goes there, it brings back all the repeat responses; the scariness, the heaving in my chest as though I might not be able to draw a complete lungful of air. I feel so clubbed-down with hurts.

"It isn't my fault," Carl, Denny and the others, will be in some hotel tonight laughing about the day's events and congratulating themselves on how they finally succeeded in booting me out of the troupe. *It isn't fair. . .it isn't fair.*

Sitting there in the bus station with my eyes staring at the magazine and the floor, all I see are legs coming and going and sometimes running to catch a bus. When someone sits down next to me, I turn a page or two even though I'm not absorbing a single word. Tonight I need this magazine as an excuse to keep fellow travelers from trying to communicate with me. I don't want to talk to anybody.

At seven-ten, just before the Harrisburg bus is announced, I hurry to the luggage coin box to retrieve my suitcase. This is that moment, just before turning the key, when I fear it will get stuck in the lock and I'll miss my bus. But the key turns readily and I hoist my suitcase down and go off to the gate.

The bus fills up rapidly and someone sits down beside me. As the bus pulls away from the station, I close my eyes immediately to preclude any idea of conversation from the person sitting next to me. My headache is sharper now, and I'm less clear headed. Between West Chester and Harrisburg I hear the bus door wheeze open and shut a number of times to let folks off and on, and, I suppose, to stop at railroad crossings.

We are late arriving in Harrisburg, and my bus connection to Pittsburgh is just pulling away from the gate and might have left without me, but the driver from my bus hails it with a series of rapid toots. Then the driver kindly helps me shift my suitcase to the Pittsburgh bus. That bus is also full, and I have no choice but to sit beside a woman who asks me, even before my bottom makes physical contact with the seat, "Where are you heading, Deary?" I want to answer, "Mars," but that will surely prolong the conversation so I give her a straight answer, and quickly close my eyes.

The inside of the bus is kept dark except for the small lights along the floor of the aisle. I am so grateful for the darkness, otherwise, someone might read on my face exactly how the whole day is clearly hammered out in repoussé. Surely my humiliation is obvious, written right there on my face.

The next bus, which I transfer to in Pittsburgh, is less crowded, so at last I am able to have two seats to myself. I cry a little in the dark as I recall how much I had wanted to finish the tour of <u>The Lost Princess.</u> I'm a failure. I have so wanted to prove to myself—and especially to everyone in the troupe—that I could endure in spite of their silent treatment.

When I write to Charley he will understand why I'm going home, but what about Josh and Silvia, my friends who recommended me to Lu-Travis in the first place? Eventually, they will hear about my failure.

Carl and Denny will claim to Lu-Travis that I simply "ran off" leaving everyone in the lurch. It isn't true of course, yet the truth does nothing to obviate my feelings of shame or a need to slink away. I've let Silvia and Josh, my benefactors down.

When I first leave home nearly a year ago, I have no intimation that hate and vindictiveness are out here waiting. No one in my past, that I'm aware of, has ever disliked me, but neither have I ever traveled and lived with any of those people for weeks and weeks, each of us learning the worst foibles of the others.

I'm still shaking, quite literally, from the trauma that has occurred earlier today. Why have things gone so askew? I still can't understand. Is it really just a case of my writing that letter about the unfair seating in the car? Or was it a far, far deeper fear that I might tattle about Carl, Larry, and Denny's preferences for men over women? Is their attempt to establish my promiscuity, so unfounded, simply a way to cover up their own lifestyles?

My pride aches to mete out revenge. But just suppose I do write a letter to Lu-Travis giving her the facts of my abandonment along the road? I wonder which will take precedence in Lu-Travis' mind: her religious abhorrence of men sleeping with men or her wily regard for making money? I think the only important thing to her is to have the "show go on" and the money keep flowing in. I doubt that I'll ever have the pleasure of seeing Denny and Carl fired.

My headache is beginning to affect my stomach. This bus, like the first one out of West Chester, begins to make lots of stops. I believe we fail to miss even one of the four corners shown on the map. At every little town the bus motor is left idling, letting fumes filter into the bus through the open door. Sometime after midnight, my headache causes nausea and my stomach feels like it's going to heave up. At the small town of Marion, I get out of the bus and stand in the fresh air.

Marion is announced as a ten-minute stop, so I tell the driver that I'm feeling sick and might have to rush inside the terminal to the restroom. I don't want him to drive away without me. It's embarrassing to interrupt him as he stands talking to another driver, but he responds with a nod. I'm not even sure that he fully understands me.

The contents of my stomach are going to come welling-up into my mouth at any minute, but the thought of it happening on the bus throws me into a panic. In the restroom I lean over the stool but nothing happens. My sick misery goes on and on...almost, but not quite, on the verge of reaching a climax. I keep repeating to myself: I'm not going to get sick...I'm not going to.... Reluctantly, I wander back to my seat in the bus and curl up under my coat. Right at this moment nothing exists in my thoughts—not the failure of the tour and not the meanness or the hurt—just my fight against throwing up all over the seat of the bus. It fills my mind to the brim and crowds out every other thought.

I must have dozed, for when I awake, I see the bus driver walking up the aisle counting his passengers. When he comes to my seat, he stops. "Feeling better?"

"Yes, I think so," I answer, not realizing that it's really true, but wishing to sound cheerful. Isn't it nice of him to show concern, I tell myself, and I go on thinking along those same exact lines. He isn't the only kindly person I've met today. There have been others: the bus driver who helped me catch the Harrisburg bus as it was pulling away from the gate, and Mr. Paulson who had taken me right into his home without knowing a single thing about me, either good or bad. And what about Chief Bagely and the two women in Mr. Paulson's house? The world isn't completely filled with Dennys and Carls, Gregs and others.

I doze, and later when I sit completely upright—a test to see if I am whole again—I find that the nausea has left me completely, even the headache is diminished. Only the sensation of supporting a heavy cement helmet on my forehead remains. In place of the sickness and the hurt is a kind of numbness, as though an amnesia wall has slipped between me and the morning's incident, which now seems several days in the past. Did this healing occur while I slept? I embrace this wall of numbness...this forgetfulness. I am not going to delve under or climb over this wall that has been built while I slept. At least not right now.

Maybe I can try to sort out everything that has happened today sometime in the future when it hurts less. Right now, the relief I feel from nausea is enough. It's the most important thing in the world. I'm not going to throw up all over the seat, my clothes or the floor. All else seems trivial compared to this simple mastery over my stomach.

In a few more hours I will be home. At the beginning of the tour I had wanted to stay away from home; not be obligated to return there to help take care of my ailing father. Even now I am in no hustle to get there, for the idea of "home" is a mixed one of protection from the harsher outside world, and also interminable dullness...a looking forward to and a dreading. It's simply an exchange of one reality for another.

Do I want reality at all? As if anyone has a choice! Reality as depicted in the movies is so much smoother, so much more exciting, a wonderful place to escape into. I close my eyes again and snuggle back down under my coat as the bus and road noises mingle. All I want this minute is to fully appreciate the relief I have won over my sick stomach; it's a triumph that seems like a true miracle.

It's only my dad who ever calls me "princess", and—like the princess in the play—I have been lost, though not quite in the same way. At last, the princess in the play finds her rightful place in the kingdom and why shouldn't I too? Such nonsensical thoughts! I'm not really and truly a princess of course, but surely, like her, I will find a place to fit-in and where I can like and be liked by others. Thinking of Charley, I actually manage a half smile in the growing light from outside the bus window.

I have learned a lot this year; certainly I am no longer untouched by events or totally unseasoned as before. Things have happened to hurt me. When the bandage of "home" has done its healing job, perhaps I'll leave again. Either I'll go back to college, or maybe Dorothy will want me to come back to the Seaplace Theatre next summer. Something will turn up. This tour is like an entresol and home will be the same. Both are the "between floors" of living. The main floors are still to come.

AUTHOR'S NOTE

*A*lthough Ann's story is written up in novel form, it is a true story that I, the author, remember. I never did learn the truth about Lisa, the girl often mentioned by Denny from a former tour, so her character in the story remains conjecture.

Back in 1950, after returning home, I made copious notes of my travels and experiences, though of course they were colored by my hurt feelings at the time.

Names of people in the cast have been changed, as well as the title of the play that was being presented.